Shades of Teale

*To Peter + Gail
Best wishes :)
Sue Crossman.*

Susan Crossman

Manor House

Library and Archives Canada Cataloguing in Publication

Crossman, Susan
    Shades of teale : a novel / Susan Crossman.

ISBN 978-1-897453-16-2

    I. Title.

PS8605.R685S53 2011   C813'.6   C2011-907694-2

Copyright 2011-08-30 by Susan Crossman
Published November 28, 2011
Manor House Publishing Inc.
(905) 648-2193 www.manor-house.biz

First Edition. 288 pages. All rights reserved.
Cover design: Michael Davie/Donovan Davie

Manor House extends special thanks to artist Anna Sponer for use of her outstanding work *Broken Heart* and invites readers to view more of her exceptional art at: www.AnnaSponer.com The artist may also be contacted at: anna@annasponer.com

Printed in Canada.

We acknowledge the financial support of the Government of Canada through the Canada Book Fund for our publishing activities.

Shades of Teale is purely a work of fiction. All content is owed in its entirety to the imagination of the author. Any and all characters and situations are solely the creation of the author. Any perceived resemblance to real people/events in the pages of this book is purely unintentional.

For Steve Quigley

Acknowledgements:

Special thanks go to many people — my children, who fill my world with magic; my family, who no doubt tired of hearing I was writing a book but cheered me on anyway; dear friends Leslie MacDougall and Jeremy Manser, in whose serene English home I parked while editing my final draft; editors, Mary Williams and Robert Lecker, who helped with hyperbole, among other issues; Brian Henry, who prodded me along in my evolution as a creative writer; Mike Davie at Manor House Publishing, who gave me a chance, and most of all, Steve Quigley, who never stopped believing in me.

Author's Note: A Disturbing Journey

I began writing this novel out of a sense of dismay over the many stories I've read in the newspaper or heard on the news about another woman found lifeless in her own home. With her partner arrested and imprisoned, the woman's family – parents, siblings, children and friends – are left with the anguish of re-building lives shattered by the violent end of their loved one's life.

Abuse, death and shattered lives – a disturbing pattern that is more commonplace than we imagine. On researching this topic I came upon recent statistics from the Canadian Women's Foundation that paint a bleak picture: Every six days on average a woman in Canada is murdered by her intimate partner – nearly 70 such deaths a year.

On any given day in Canada, more than 3,000 women (and 2,500 children) are living in emergency shelters due to domestic violence incidents, which annually account for over 40,000 arrests and $4.2 billion in social/health/judicial services and lost productivity costs.

As someone who has never been in an abusive relationship, I was intrigued by the dynamic of abuse. What would make a woman choose to involve herself with a man who appears to despise her?

I began to ask such questions while working for a women's shelter where I met some amazing women who shared their stories with me. I also read everything I could find on the topic. And I listened. Friends also spoke in strict confidence about difficult circumstances they'd survived. Ladies, I'll protect you and your identities forever.

This has been a sad but enlightening journey. But out of all of those fascinating and heart-breaking pieces of tragedy I was able to weave together the purely fictional story of Teale's escape from abuse to freedom. Her abuser, David, is no man I've ever met, although I've seen glimpses of him in the stories other women have told me.

It is my hope that this fictional story leads to a deeper understanding of a very real problem that causes untold pain to women every day.

Susan Crossman, November 8, 2011

1

It's a lousy day for a walk on a beach but I've dragged my carcass out into the gray morning anyway, hopeful that a little exercise will lift my mood and generate the energy I need to tackle the issue of the Rest Of My Life. I'm not exactly fond of exercise, but I am fond of beaches and the one I'm trudging along today would be a fine one if it weren't for the cold rain the wind keeps slapping my way.

My feet are wet.

Somehow, though, I need to forget about all that and figure out what to do next, now that the fairy tale marriage I started with so much delight has foundered and sunk on the uncharted shoal of Reality. Whatever was I thinking? It helps to have a friend or two dancing in my corner and the one who owns the house I've borrowed is quite a dreamy guy. Realistically, he's probably bad news too, but he does own a house on a beach.

When I was young I loved to run on warm sand made shadowy in the setting sun and frighten the seagulls that collected near the water's edge. They would scatter into the pastel sky and circle above the darkening, rippled surface of the water and I'd turn and race back along the shoreline in search of other birds to antagonize. The game made me feel powerful but I eventually became tired of stalking prey I could never capture. And I realized that I didn't like seagulls much.

What's to like?

Seagulls are impatient, nervy, relentless and greedy. They scavenge the beach for the soggy remnants of picnic lunches and junk food crumbs, their cold, steely eyes darting in all directions and their beaks poised to snatch any gritty morsel they find appealing.

Their squawks are jarring, like the screech of ill-fitting metal doors; they fight. Do we really need seagulls in this world?

David — my husband, not my friend — loved seagulls and maybe I should have known the match was doomed from the start. It was a long haul and the dissolution of what began as a colourful adventure has left me tired, drained and depleted, stranded on the edge of a rainy brown beach with only bitter memories, broken dreams and a couple of empty beer cans for comfort.

Molson Canadian.

David hated Canadian, preferring Heineken or Grolsch and the cachet of sophistication they imparted to elegant men like him. Foreign beers were exotic, sophisticated, expensive and subtle. Canadian was domestic, common, and cheap — I loved the stuff but David's nose never failed to tip upwards, nostrils flaring slightly, whenever I ordered one. There is a right way to do things and a wrong way, apparently. Even when all you want is a cold beer. Sometimes I wanted two.

Today, I have shown amazing restraint and tucked only two cold red-and-white cans into the pocket of my bright-yellow raincoat. I'm a long way from home and it's still early morning but I don't care about the right way to do things anymore. I'm going to do things my way now, and that might mean a beer before lunch on a public beach from time to time. Who cares?

My mother thinks I'm falling apart and she calls from time to time to remind me that a little lipstick is a great way to brighten a gal's mood. But right now my socks are creeping down my legs like sluggish children on a broken slide and my hair keeps whipping across my field of vision like the manic tails of falling kites. I need a decent cut and a dab of colour at the roots, too, heck maybe I need a new life, but for now I'm walking on a beach trying to figure out how I ended up here and where on Earth I'm going next.

God I'm tired.

Divorce is a nasty game preceded as it often is by years of relentless bickering, sarcastic put-downs and the broken hopes of two people trying to pretend that everything is perfectly fine, thanks, we'd love to come for dinner Friday night —what can we bring? It's like a war in many ways, with the opening salvo fired by the one brave enough to say "I want a divorce." The guns blaze back and forth for years as the contestants fight it out. Lawyers and accountants, child psychologists and best friends, the world and everybody in it, or so it seems, charge onto the field to pick a favorite and tell the pretty part of the truth that makes their champion look best on paper. Affidavits and financial statements, dirty tricks and bitter accusations —ammunition and propaganda, it all combines to create a vicious weapon that is then wielded with as much skill and cunning as either side can muster. Both parties want the battle to end, and both want to win it —whatever winning means when there are crying children involved. So I am tired beyond measure, disappointed beyond belief, and angry, always angry. How DARE he…anything?

I heard some woman screaming at my car radio the other day and was awfully surprised to discover that she was me. She – I – had stopped by the time I got to work, but my throat felt sore all day and the pain chastened me. David would have made pithy yet scathing comments had he known and another damaging note about me would have been added to the custody file. He must never know.

I like that word, "chastened," though.

It does not hint at the bleak sense of defeat I worry will someday suck me home, back into my mother's circle of anxious questioning and sharp disapproval. I might become forever stranded, then, a grown woman caught in her mother's loving grasp, lost and remembered, held and admired. But for now I'm pleased to think that a story that begins with a chastening can end with a beginning. In fact, the idea offers me a tiny flake of hope.

Was I was alone in my delusion?

For years on end, I expected the magic of life, the mystery and the delight, to appear before me in a blinding flash of magic. I waited hopefully for the happily-ever-after excitement I was sure existed and when it came – oh! I would savour every moment.

I am a regular woman, after all – though I drift and struggle to find meaning in the ongoing avalanche of life. I work hard, pay the bills, ignore dirty floors and create clever dishes out of noodles and meat that have been in the fridge since…Friday? I book the doctor, pray for peace and return library books I never have time to read. Life can be so hard, so impossible, so confusing, so clear-cut, so easy, so busy.

And so what?

There's a big dog running down the beach towards me now – a Lab perhaps? — and another day I might find him irresistible. I would probably run towards him and rake my cold fingers through his long golden fur. Maybe I would baby talk him into dropping the water-soaked branch he's carrying so proudly and then I might throw the branch back into the surging waves for him to rescue again. We could play together, maybe for hours, just him and me, a woman and a dog, having a normal walk on a beach. I don't feel normal today though.

The dog is in an awful hurry and his ears flap rhythmically with the prancing movements of his body. He's a beautiful dog and someone must love him very much. I wish I had a dog – I might call him Trooper — but what's the point? Why surge like an ocean wave towards a hopeful shore only to sink below the darkening sand, discouraged and unconsoled? Why plan, why hope, why dream of anything at all when the greatest dream, the one that ends with the words "happily ever after" has turned out to be a criminal fraud? As a child I believed in fairy tales and I grew up believing that the man I married would be someone I could be mostly happy with most of the time.

We would twirl through life together and he would carry me gently into our future, sweet future, love in the clouds. I was so terribly naive.

Trooper is at my side now, wagging his tail and asking for my attention. His owner is nowhere in sight and I wonder whether I would ever let my dog run free like this if I lived on a beach – not every stranger can be trusted. He drops the stick and wags some more, with his tongue hanging out and what I could swear is a smile on his lips. The dog's hopeful nature is an intrusion on my moodiness. I don't want to play. I want to think. He's a puppy by the looks of him, although growing towards maturity. He's bouncy and energetic, full of an infectious joy that overspills the boundaries of his body and dances delightedly in the very air above.

"Trooper, sit," I say. Obediently, the dog parks his rear end on the wet sand beside me and looks expectantly at my face. I don't want to throw the stick but he looks so appealing, so unmarked by fear or hostility.

I looked through my high school yearbook last night – my therapist's idea – and I was struck by a similar look of painful freshness on the faces snapped in place by the now-forgotten photographer whose name we never knew. There we were, all tender and downy-soft like a large litter of puppies, prancing and bouncing through high school hallways, sniffing expectantly for the grains of nourishment they call education, unaware of the slaughterhouse of adult life. We were bursting with hope.

Like so many other dreamers, I still hope to do wonderful things, some day. That may never come to be but I still think that maybe, just *maybe*, if I dream long enough and hope hard enough and do all the right things at all the right times, some of those dreamy ideas will become just a little bit real.

But life is not about maybes. It's about the space that exists between the goals you set and the goals you reach. That space is turbulent at the best of times and utterly demoralizing at the very worst. It can be thorny and unpredictable, brilliant and gratifying. In a marriage that descends into misery, it is a heart-breaking and fearful space where goals and dreams are mocked with condescending laughter, and fairy tales go up in flames.

As I stand with my beer can and my sense of betrayal, watching birds standing stupidly on the rain-swept beach, resisting the urge to throw that heavy wet stick, I wonder what others do when they discover there is no fairy tale, no happily ever after? Bury the thought and carry on, because fairy tales are for children? Create their own furtive fairy tale life and live it — secretly — in their hearts, alone? Or scratch and scrabble for something they *could* call a charming life? Pretty tablecloths and a fenced backyard? Or maybe friends for dinner Saturday night. Board games with the kids on a Sunday afternoon, season tickets to somewhere. What fun it all is. Does it pass for a charming life now? Does it manage to hide a broken heart and an ugly, angry soul, scarred and bleeding, screaming for the love you thought they had promised would be yours all yours *all yours* until the end of time?

Who out there has never felt a secret loathing for the one they live with so deep and cutting that they dare not admit its existence because it would spoil every sweet illusion of normalcy they've worked so hard to create? Of course it must be put away, that thought, buried deep down inside that bottomless well they don't even know is their eternal soul. Because it's not a *nice* thought, and not comforting at all. If you let it creep out into the light of day it will eventually drive you insane unless you do something about it, which would require you to make a painful change. And who wants to do *that*? When I finally stopped to look at the devastation my marriage had brought to my life I was astounded: how ever had I walked into such a mess without benefit of blindfold? Who *did* that to me? Obviously not me. Dammit — *I* had wanted a happy ending. *I* had wanted roses and dancing and happily-ever-after children playing at my mothering knees. *I* had wanted romance and love and music playing in my heart as I awoke beside the man I loved. And of course, the story would carry on this way until I died, one long parade of delightful events and happy moments. Certainly there would be disagreements but we would solve them calmly and maturely and…DROP DEAD YOU MISERABLE BASTARD.

That woman who might be me is screaming again, and the pain in my throat is echoing her misery.

"Where is my happy ending?"

Chastened, am I? The fury in my head is dark, vicious and predatory. It carves at every thought I have ever had, stabbing and slicing the broken mirror of my life and reaching for my veins to empty my angry body of its life blood, its purpose, its order. I am hate. I am disgust. I am an ear-splitting scream of refusal, shrieking and tortured. I cannot, dare not, stop the explosion of anxiety that bleeds out my ears in a deafening rumble of anguished pain. It lives inside me and will not go away, will not ease, will not fade.

And inside the madness of me is the theatre where I play the home video of a life gone wrong. There is the silent woman sitting at a table, fingering the delicate white petals of daisies in a cut-glass vase. The smell of Sunday dinner fills the air and the late afternoon sun slants through the window spotlighting a million particles of dust floating in the canyon of the white kitchen. From another room come moody strains of Tchaikovsky's majestic *Romeo and Juliet* overture and there is a man — a handsome man with an angry voice and a fist raised in anger, a curtain of fear crashes to the floor and the camera cuts to a bedroom where loneliness and pain paper the walls in the false and ugly colours of a lifeless marriage. Fists clenched in horror, sobs dare not shake her body and what do I do now? He loves me, hates me, protects and admires me, forgives and despises me and where did I lose track of the real truth? The phone rings, the man's voice is cheerful and hearty now, oblivious to the echoing words of fury unleashed not three seconds or half a decade ago. He smiles broadly and winks at his face in the front hall mirror and another tiny little piece of her soul dies an untimely death.

Stop now, I want to get out! But I am out and still the show plays on. The threatening voices, the chill frost of evening, hide the knives, the worries, the dreams, the hopes. And watch the dancing feet made heavy by fear — money, health, children, work, time. The bitterness of two people locked in love's deathly dance rejoices in more tears, searing loneliness, outrageous humiliations, exalts in the blackness of the future. Nothing is fun, nothing is fair. I will explode and then it will all be over. Can it ever be over? Where did I go? Who am I now? It's all nightmare and no daydream anymore, and the worst part is, I created it all and like I said before *it wasn't supposed to be like this.*

My story is not unique – so many others thought everything was possible, once upon a time. Every time I hear a young woman chattering about her upcoming wedding I see the woman I once was and I want to stop her, to convince her that she's wrong, we were wrong, they were WRONG. ALL WRONG.

She is so full of faith, so certain of a happy future that I am stunned into breathless anticipation of her story's end. Part of me sneers at her ignorance and part of me pities her.

I say nothing, naturally. There were so many beautiful brides last summer — too many to lecture, too many to save. They were white ones, mostly, and they fluttered around the public parks on sunny afternoons with bright red and pink smiles opening like flowers to reveal the pearly white of their stainless smiling futures. There is no-one happier than a bride on her wedding day. I was too.

"Stand there Mother."

"I'm so relieved no-one tripped."

"Dinner will be wonderful."

"Wasn't it funny when he dropped the ring!"

"Smile for the camera everyone."

"This is the first day of forever, and I will love you until the day I die. Thank God we don't have to make any more plans."

"Steady me a minute, Sweetheart, would you please, while I check my shoe."

What a beautiful event! What happy people! What lovely presents! What perfect pictures! We'll remember, forever, how happy we were today, the most important day of all days. We'll remember, forever... until, perhaps, we wish we could forget.

2

Yes, I was married once.

Like a seagull soaring joyfully on the high wild wind of a coming storm, I gathered my faith, leapt into the matrimonial sky and flew. I loved the idea of marriage, the possibilities that resided in the promise of Forever and sweet words of commitment flooded my heart as I faced the prospect of a lifetime with David.

Years of racing down the beach in search of the man who would bravely meet my approach had finally yielded The One. We would fly together now, high into the evening sky, linked in marriage and the certainty that fairy tales do come true.

I'm wishing I had another beer, and maybe a few more tears to waste on self-pity because I still don't know why David seemed so perfect to me at the time. He wasn't the first twinkly-eyed guy to look my way – I had met plenty of nice men in my life. Why hadn't I settled for one of them instead?

Ah. I think, now, with the wisdom of hindsight, that it might have been pride or panic urging me on, or possibly the fact that I absolutely *knew* my perfect partner was out there waiting for me and I had decided to find him or die trying.

I certainly wasn't interested in re-creating for myself the barren no-man's-land my parents called a marriage. My mother pursued the impossible dream of the spotless family in a spotless-house while my father worked late or played golf. It was obvious their partnership wasn't focused on coaxing each other up into the paragons of virtue we all want to be but did they secretly tear each other down, one smirking word at a time into little islands of lonely humanity, adrift in the universe like ashes from a cold, dead fire? I never knew. Their marriage was secretive and therefore suspect.

"So, are we going to hear wedding bells next year?" my mother had asked brightly one Christmas as she hovered over her ironing board.

"Marry Jerry? Doubt it," I said – convincingly, I hoped, but annoyed even so at the tiny lump forming in the back of my throat.

A long silence followed, during which I could almost hear my mother's disappointment lurching through her heart. She and Jerry liked each other. They were both tidy, sensible people with tidy, sensible lives. I didn't want to be sensible at age 23 – the prospect of steaming my husband's shirts to perfection while wondering what to make for Sunday dinner was akin to life imprisonment with no chance of parole. The small part of me that felt comforted by the smell of hot, dampened cotton was totally eclipsed by the part of me that wanted to wander the world in search of…what? Food I didn't recognize or names I could not pronounce? Diesel fumes belched out by strange-looking trucks roaming the cobblestoned streets of a foreign city? I wanted some adventure. I thought.

"Oh," she said, a meaningful prelude to another long silence. It was a mother's silence, the calculating pause in conversation that simulated an army commander's assessment of enemy strengths, tactical wisdom and balance of aggression. Her silence was a brooding sign of analytical intelligence as she settled on the tactic most likely to further the great goal of marching her daughter onto the battlefield of holy matrimony.

An unmarried daughter represents a failure to a mother, a poor reflection of mother's only measurable work, the successful ability to help sustain the human race, to see her own mother's eyes shining out from her granddaughter's face. And, too, she is a subtle reminder that Mother is herself not free to choose again, choose better, and taste anew the hope of a fresh future warmed by love.

Some issues are better left unexamined.

"That's surprising, Teale," my mother replied. There was a business-like arch to her pronunciation, as though the words themselves represented the raising of the battle flag, the start of an ardent campaign.

"He's such a nice young man — sensible and kind, and so *reliable*. Remember how he drove you to Toronto for that job interview? He really seems to care about you." I knew she'd really wanted to say "love," – "'He really seems to *love* you.'" But "love" for my mother was an embarrassing word that somehow stripped its user of the protection afforded by moderation. My mother did not like messy things, and she had a special dislike of emotional outbursts and neediness. She didn't want to humiliate herself by making serious incursions into my emotional world, but she needed to know if there was a wedding in her future.

It had been kind of Jerry to drive me to Toronto for my job interview. The memory made my skin crawl. I knew he had wanted to keep me close, folded tightly into the circle of his strong arms, perhaps a smile frozen sweetly on a pair of slightly parted lips that waited for him, and him alone. He wanted Saturday nights spent sitting together watching videos in his parents' basement and mid-week lunch dates passed comfortably in cheerful diners that smelled of coffee and fried onions. But Jerry was practical at heart, and kind.

Jerry knew at some deep, earnest level of his heart, that the way to hold onto me was to help me achieve my dream of becoming a famous reporter, a reporter who made her name writing gritty stories about broken dreams and cracked lives that spilled over onto the mean streets of an uncaring world. He staunchly decided that he would prove his support by escorting me to my interview at the *Toronto Star,* miles down the highway and light years away from his understanding. His caring hurt.

Driving slowly and cautiously toward the city, he chatted sweetly about my future.

We were already 15 minutes late when Jerry carefully parked the car seven blocks from the *Star* building; I was nearly in tears when he insisted on accompanying me all the way to the interview. To ensure my safety, he was going to ride the elevator to the 34th floor with me. It was the gentlemanly thing to do. He was sad and broody by the time we arrived in the reception area.

He grabbed my hand and gently kissed it; then, gripped by an overwhelming sense of loss he drew me into his arms and kissed me passionately. He had great lips. But no sense of timing. I was furious with him and I felt bound and gagged by his love for me. I was mortified but I got the job anyway.

After I moved to Toronto our relationship limped along. There were successive disagreements about weekend plans and my growing need for some "space." Jerry was waiting for me to raise the signal that would launch our charge to the altar, a signal I could not give and still be honest.

"Don't you want to get married and have a family?" This was an accusation, not a question.

"Sure I do, Mom."

"Then what are you waiting for?"

What *was* I waiting for?

Why not marry Jerry? He had a gentle voice and a firm handshake. He stowed his perfectly matched socks in the top left-hand drawer of his dresser. He believed in reading good books and getting a good night's sleep. He read *"The Investment Review"* for fun and drank hot cocoa instead of alcohol. He was generous, gentle, thoughtful and intelligent. He was handsome, too, in a clean-shaven kind of way. And very tall. I like that in a man. Jerry was a real catch, no doubt about it, and there was a little spark between us that made everything a little mmmmm *interesting*. What I actually wanted, though, was a man who had his eyes on a distant mountaintop, a man who would spend his life trying to defy gravity, not chain himself to the Earth. I wanted fireworks, fun, and fascination.

"Fly with me, my love," his heart might sing to mine as we planed through the fairy tale.

Somehow I missed the fact that "crash" follows "plane" like "sting" follows "bee".

"I need to think about it some more," I said reasonably. "Marriage is a big step. Besides, I'm not sure he's The One."

My mother shook her head, sighed and grabbed another cotton sheet from an enormous pile of rumpled whites. We both stared out at the early evening sky. It was wistfully beautiful, a velvet cloak of deep blue with a brilliant red scar streaking across the western rim.

The back ravine gaped below it and the night was very still. The scene is burned forever into my memory. I was 23 years old, bold and beautiful. How could my mother possibly understand what it was like to want it all? She ironed *sheets* for heaven's sake!

Her man was somewhere else now, at least in his heart, and she was fading away like a rose plucked from her wedding bouquet and left to crumble between the pages of a never-read book.

What faint spark of affection had ever led my parents to believe they could bond for life? How could she have compromised herself so profoundly — this nice, calm woman with the small container of tiny tranquilizers hidden away in the bottom of her jewellery box? Mama's little helpers. Who was she hiding them from? Who could blame her for giving up? Who could forgive her?

And what was it about my mother that scared me so much about myself?

3

My mother was an average kind of a gal, I think, when she was young. Not especially ambitious or driven when measured by today's standards, she had become a secretary in the sales office of a company that sold, of all things, soap products, the kind of job a woman was expected to conscientiously attend to until marriage rescued her from the need to earn a living. Her hair smelled of herbal shampoo and she left behind the unmistakable scent of a spring garden when she passed through a room. It was a soothing smell —as soothing as her calm presence could be in the midst of the chaos of Christmas dinner or the panic of a school concert. I wanted to be soothing and calm too, but I preferred the cocky undertones of perfumes with names like Tangerine Spice or Ginger Lime Tango, and I was more likely to throw people off balance than soothe them towards a lump-free gravy or a perfect performance.

My mother once told me that she couldn't be a nurse or a teacher, among the very few occupations open to young women of her day, because she hated both the sight of blood and the sound of whining children. She, too, had wanted a little adventure, and a job in a large corporation seemed to be just daring enough to give her a thrill the neighbours wouldn't question. As we grew older my brother Joey and me were slightly unnerved by the fact that our mother had chosen a career with the idea of avoiding contact with children and it was just possible we might not turn out normal after all; at 14, however, I figured we were just like everybody else, and probably even a little better, given that my mother had her hair done every week and my father got a new car every two years. A *company* car.

Back when she was 21 years old and spending her days pounding away at her state-of-the-art Remington typewriter, my mother had been charmingly stubborn about maintaining high expectations of male behaviour, and she was very, very pretty.

According to family legend, my father, the company's leading sales rep, pursued the woman destined to become my mother with flowers, poems and invitations for coffee, lunches, dinners and dances until she wore him down to the point of proposal. Everybody laughs at that story and of course most families have one just like it. It would be rude not to laugh. But I think the truth is that my father was struck by an uncharacteristic sense of respect for a woman who knew her own mind and could hold on to her virtue in the face of the three-alarm fire that was my father in his days of debonair bachelorhood. At one point he must have been the man of her dreams, perhaps no surprise, since he favored a strong aftershave redolent of musk and lemons and clove, something spicy and exotic that a lady might find enticing and powerful.

And so they married.

My mother was very polite, clean and tidy, and about as easy to ruffle as a brick wall. She took everything in stride, it always seemed to me, and she never had a bad word to say about anybody. Having accepted the prevailing wisdom that her real job was to mother her children, that's exactly what she did until Joey and I were old enough to leave home. After that the anguish of motherhood was something she kept to herself as best she could, and she rarely intruded into our personal journeys.

My father was an imposing man. He had a gray face like a granite cliff, stood six feet tall, and appeared about as warm and pliant as Mount Everest. He was not a daddy who would get down on his hands and knees and play, although I have some lovely memories of him reading books to Joey and me in the old green armchair that came into the house when my grandparents moved into their apartment. The three of us would sit together before bed, snug as sardines within the ring of my father's arms, restful, happy and likely a little fidgety, knowing Joey. We kids would be freshly bathed and smelling of Ivory soap and our damp hair would be plastered to our skulls like bathing caps. Four little stick-legs would jut off the seat cushion like shapely baguettes and every now and then my Dad would lean his face down toward us and inhale a deep breath of our dewy youth, the Ivory soap mingling with the innocent smell of Johnson's No More Tears baby shampoo. It was an uncomfortable paradise, given the size of the chair and the size of us, but we reveled in it until bedtime loomed and Mom came to spoil everything.

My father was not given much to laughing and, even as he got older, he was competitive and ambitious and not particularly flexible about the rules he'd set. But occasionally he'd be overwhelmed by a soft-heartedness that told us he loved us, truly.

Sometimes those moments would surf into our lives in the wake of tearful outbursts, like the time I wanted a new pair of bell-bottoms to wear to the eighth-grade dance. Both my parents had rejected the idea on the theory that bell-bottoms were just a fad with an unpredictable "best before" date and the money was better spent on something more lasting, like knee socks. They were probably right, but I found it outrageous that my parents consistently refused every request I made. Couldn't they let me feel *human* once in a while? Even Dorota Polanski had bell-bottoms, and she was about as fashionable as a moldy potato. I was the only kid in the world who couldn't wear jeans to school, and now I wanted nothing more exotic than one lousy pair of non-denim pants to wear to one lousy little dance, and they were saying no. Again. They obviously didn't love me at all. I would just have to leave home and find a loving couple to look after me. People who really wanted a 13-year-old girl. People who actually understood the importance of bell-bottoms.

I dissolved into tears right there on the front porch for all the neighbours to see, even that horrible boy Judd Wilson, who had put worms in my hair when I was five. My father put his arm around me and brushed the hair out of my eyes and said "Teale, Teale...there, there, little girl. It's not the end of the world."

"I am *not* a little girl and it *is* the end of the world! You just don't ever care what I want or what I need and no one is going to look at me or dance with me or talk to me cuz I look like a *freak* all the time!" My sobs were loud, now, my tears were blinding me, my nose was starting to run — it was going to be a *great* cry.

"You hate me, both of you! You say you love me, but you're wrong, and I never get what I want, and I HATE MY NAME!"

Daddy held me while I vented my sorrow; he patted my head and gently led me inside and away from the neighbours who were drifting to their front windows to see what was going on over at the Covey's. Joey, sprawled on the living room couch watching *Gunsmoke* reruns on TV, looked at me, raised his eyebrows, sneered slightly and snorted out the words, "What's her problem *this* time?" reminding me that I also hated my brother. I hated my life. I hated my family. I hated my clothes. And no one cared. How could anyone survive this misery?

Two days later, Daddy came home from work carrying a bag from Eaton's department store. He handed it to me and inside I was shocked to find a pair of pale-blue hip-hugging bell-bottoms and a thick, navy-blue suede belt with an enormous buckle. UNBELIEVABLE! My mother threw him a glance that said, "And how much did *those* cost?" but she remained silent. My arms flew around my father's neck, and I cried out, "Wow! THANK YOU DADDY!!!" He was suddenly a hero in my eyes.

I came to realize tears had an instant effect on my father, and I don't think he minded that I knew. I tried hard not to take advantage of his weakness because it seemed like the only one he had.

My father always paid his bills on time, incurred no debt that we ever knew of, planned for retirement, and took my mother to Florida every year for two weeks — no more, no less. Dad disliked spicy food and believed that unless the moon had fallen, his dinner (one meat, two vegetables and a starch) should be on the table by six o'clock every night so he could eat and go back to work. He liked room-temperature water with his evening meal and a cup of clear, weak tea directly afterwards. He never complained out loud but his polite approach to my mother seemed to hint at dissatisfaction with something beyond the veil dividing the generations; he exercised a pacific control over his kingdom and behaved with decorum.

My parents spoke little, smiled rarely, and laughed less often with each other as the years rolled relentlessly forward. They looked after each other in a neutral kind of way, as though confirming the marital transaction that had been worked out at the altar: you will cook and clean; I will pay the bills. You will weed the garden; I will take out the garbage. You will shop for groceries; I will sweep the garage. You will iron the sheets; I will drink just a little too much on Saturdays. Theirs was the ultimate business arrangement, as all enduring marriages are.

As my father settled into an executive job he was required to travel more often and whenever the word "Winnipeg" was mentioned a huddled shudder would pass through the walls of our house. It was a tidy two-storey red-brick home with white shutters and cream-coloured sheers separating life on the main floor of our home from life in the real world. With Winnipeg again threatening to intrude on life in eastern Canada my mother's lips would compress into two pale, thin lines, a divided highway of opinion, and she would clean the house with great intensity. The smell of lemon-fresh Pledge furniture polish and Fantastic cleaning spray would hang heavy in the air and for weeks before and after my father's absence she would barely utter a word. In the evenings my mother would shut herself in her room and lie on the bed fully clothed with all the lights on. I wonder now what she was trying to prove or salve but no-one said anything and our family life moved ahead, one distressed hour at a time.

That was the house I grew up in, and I know it better than anywhere. That's the driveway where Joey and I used coloured chalk to draw beautiful under-sea worlds brimming with monsters and sea-maidens and that's the garden where I once buried half my lunch so my mother wouldn't know I hadn't eaten it. (Tuna salad, puh-leeeeeze!)

That's the front yard where we would build snowmen to wave at the ones three doors down that my best friend, Cheryl, had made with her father. The snowmen waved at each other every winter for years, until Cheryl and I moved on into new lives and now the front yards on our street look sad and empty in winter. Sometimes we would dig snow forts out of the huge snow banks created by the plows that cleared the street and clamber over mountains of snow, our noses tingling with cold and our breath crystallizing on the soggy scarves we'd looped, poorly, around our necks. Cheryl and I liked digging caves in the snow banks and we loved pretending we were defending our castle from gangs of marauding invaders that always included siblings and various other enemies. Passing cars were enemy tanks we had to hammer with our artillery: "Fire at will, soldiers!" we'd cry. After our long battles in the gripping snow we would retire to our indoor tea cave and pretend to be great ladies who could fight like the devil but also entertain honoured guests with graceful elegance. We usually created our imaginary tea treats from balls of icy snow but if we were especially well-organized one of us might sneak some ginger snaps from the cookie jar on top of the refrigerator, leaving an annoyed mother to mop up furtive puddles of melted snow. Ah, the adventure of it all.

Funny how our parents let us scale those great big banks of snow, only to tumble down them toward the street, let us slide around in snowsuits made slippery with wet and wind chill – without concern for our safety. I guess maybe they checked on us secretly from behind the living room drapes...but could they ever have saved us from an out-of-control car? Times have changed.

In summer, there wasn't much to do except set up a lemonade stand and wait for a kind old person to stop by, but after the initial thrill of wondering how to spend our loot wore off the project tended to run out of steam. Very few people seemed to drink lemonade, even in those days, but I suspect it was a good way for our moms to keep us out of the house and out of their hair as they chatted on the phone or did whatever it was mothers did in those idyllic days before freezer pizza and chicken nuggets burst into grocery stores. I remember my mother sitting down with a glass of ginger ale every afternoon and watching *The Edge of Night* and there was always ironing to catch up on. The house would fill with the scorching fresh smell of steam-pressed clothes as my mother sprinkled the cottons with water, rolled them up and let them sit for a few minutes so they could "relax." She seemed to like ironing, and attended to the job as if the act of smoothing wrinkles out of a shirt or a pillowcase could somehow make the whole world a better place. Maybe it did, in a way, for her. I remember her vacuuming, cooking, doing laundry, dying her hair, and sitting with her head in a wreath made of pink foam curlers while she perused the *TV Guide*. (We had it delivered!)

My mother was the undisputed keeper of our house. She quietly did her duty, went out to play bridge once a week and learned important things like flower arranging, macramé and growing old without wrinkles. She swept the kitchen floor twice a day and washed the floors weekly. She worked stubborn stains out of the collars of my father's shirts and hunted down weekly specials at the supermarket. She dutifully clipped coupons for the products she used on a regular basis.

There were no microwaves in those days, no central vac systems, no computers, no Internet banking. My mother had a dryer, although she preferred to hang the washing outside on the clothesline because it made everything smell fresher. I don't remember ever going to a park with her, but by God that housework was done. It was my mother's point of pride, it's what she did, was supposed to do, always did, no matter what.

Perhaps it was all that housework that earned her ownership of the house. Perhaps going down on her hands and knees with a bucket of soapy water and a sponge was a form of payment, and every swipe along the baseboards bought her another inch; every window she washed increased her stake by a few more cents. All I know is that the house was hers, exclusively. She knew every nick, every dent, every nail of this house, my house. Mine, too.

There is nothing about the physical aspect of the house that I don't know although, unlike my mother, I have always recoiled at the thought of having to clean it. For example, I know you have to pull the door out just a little to get the key to turn in the front door lock, and I know that the spare key hides in the third flower basket to the right of the barbecue in the backyard. See that big nick in the concrete of the front porch? That's where Joey threw the hammer when the birdhouse he was building wouldn't fit together just right. That drainpipe at the end of the porch? That's where I hid the butt of the first —and last —cigarette Cheryl and I smoked, when we were 14 years old. In the basement of that house there is a hook on the wall to the left of the furnace where we always hung our skates; there still might be a few wisps of blonde doll hair floating around the fruit cellar from when I cut off the lovely corn-silk tresses of one of my Barbies because she was supposed to be the "uncool" one of the crowd. (There always has to be one the others can be mean to.)

In my bedroom, there's a loose floorboard under which I'd hide notes I didn't want my mother to find when she cleaned. They were notes that said things like "I hate my mother," and "I love Jason Phillips," and "Screw everything," and "22-46-8," which was the combination of my bike lock until my bike got stolen. I guess it wasn't a very good lock. I knew which stairs to avoid when coming home late from a date (numbers three, four, six, and nine), and I knew I couldn't climb up the drainpipe just outside my window because it wasn't fastened securely enough to hold my weight. Pity.

In that house, I gradually came to realize a complex and intricate truth: my life was my own, and every single thing I did mattered. While I lived in that house, I remained an innocent —a virgin, a dreaming damsel waiting for her prince to come. Asleep in my bed at night, I stayed pure and untarnished by blame or fear or disillusionment. There were no stains on my past, no clouds on my horizon. That house held me safely while I slept.

And although the house was my safe haven, it was also a house of mystery. There were things I never quite understood, like how the radiantly happy bride and the broadly grinning groom in the framed photo on the mantelpiece had become the silent and solemn entities who tiptoed around the house full of politeness and empty of passion. They had married young, of course. They had probably once thought that the love they felt for each other would help them weather any storm, and I suppose it did. But if that's love... I never saw my mother laugh uncontrollably, never saw her cry. Did she trade joy for security? A life of excitement for a roof over her head? The pursuit of growth for the mirage of security?

Her life seemed small and cheerless to me. I was sure I would never fit into one like that.

4

But time goes by and sometimes the things we struggle against are not the things that threaten us most. As far as I could tell at the time, Jerry was the kind of guy who would guarantee I had my feet planted firmly on the path marked "Shortcut to Your Mother's Future," so it would take an army of mercenaries or some kind of supernatural intervention for him to slide a wedding ring onto my finger. Sweet as he was.

I wanted more and I took a pass, convinced that the love I was looking for was out there, somewhere, waiting to deliver me into utter happiness.

It seemed reasonable at the time.

Movie heroines may have to endure all kinds of trials and tribulations, but they get their heart's desire in the end and along the way they learn that love can be many things —spontaneous or gradual, illicit or open, explicit or vague, erotic, low-key, generous, selfish — in short, love might be a slippery fish that's hard to define but in the movie world it always arrives, eventually, to rescue us from our lonely, quirky existence. Doesn't art mirror reality?

We pull towards this love business relentlessly, I think, to assure ourselves that we are normal after all, but the problem is that when we turn one love down we run the risk of never ever loving – or being loved — again. And when you get right down to it, I think finding the love we seek is about as easy as defining the taste of rain.

Jerry's love might have turned out to be pretty enduring but then again, so is life with no parole and I thought I would die of boredom first. In hindsight, that might not have been so bad after all because when you get out into the real world you find that love is a dangerous idea. It lies, cheats, changes and destroys. It runs and hides from rational thought and attacks with impunity the very things you care about most. It is a weapon masquerading as a refuge, a four-letter white flag that gets pulled out to signal a surrender that is actually your own. That sweet gooey stuff we chase isn't actually real, of course, it is simply something the movies made up. Real love just hurts.

"You have to work at it," people say with a knowing nod of the head, as though I am dismissing a sacred trust with too little effort. They are naïve. How can "work" guarantee us the kind of sustenance that makes everything else worthwhile —how can it deliver a magic potion that blends a dash of adventure with a dose of security, a drop of perfection, with a splash of naughty excitement? My father worked at his office. My mother worked at home. Did they "work" on their marriage? And where did it get them? The same place as every other person on the planet: simply into their future.

Love didn't do anything for either of them – or millions more besides — and the ease with which the word itself gets used to control a willing heart scares me half to death. It darn near killed me, in fact and I am one of the lucky ones.

I would like to say that I was coerced into marriage, and I'm embarrassed to admit that I embraced it completely. I may have been blissfully unaware of the danger that lay lurking on the other side of the marital threshold, but that's no excuse. I was a happy fluttering moth drawn to the flame of David Allan Masterson. I was blindly in love and when this tall, lean man lay beside me on my 27th birthday —one of the few he ever remembered —and said romantically, almost shyly:

"Happy birthday, Teale,"

I was thrilled that he'd remembered. When he placed his index finger under my chin and tilted my face up toward his so he could look straight into my eyes, I was nearly reduced to tears. Such sweetness!

"I was going to get you a diamond pendant, but I thought it would seem pretty dull next to that million-dollar smile of yours," he whispered, gently stroking my lower lip with his thumb. Now *this* was living!

"Oh, David," I blushed. Then I laughed from sheer pleasure at the thought that he'd considered such a generous gift. Had he really been thinking about it? I half-hoped it were true, half-hoped he would, in fact, buy me diamonds one day, and then I immediately felt ashamed of my own greed.

"Teale..." he said, tracing the line of my eyebrows with his index finger and brushing the hair from my face. He looked into my eyes again, and I could have lain there forever suspended in his loving gaze.

"Would you make my life perfect by agreeing to be my wife?"

Oh David, how could *you* have chosen *me*? And how could I have settled for *him*?

He had impeccable qualifications for marriage: a PhD in business with an interest in Third World economic strategies (Wow —a businessman with a conscience!); he had a law degree, which he'd completed in French; he was a spectacular athlete (five marathons and two Iron Man competitions to his credit); he was a linguist, a champion of the common man and a leader in the field of gender equality. He was also well-traveled, well-spoken, and well-read. Sociable, good-natured, hard working, ambitious. Sexually undemanding, good with children, a family man. And the magic!

How did this perfect example of humanity manage to reach the ripe old age of 28 unencumbered by a spouse? I believed him when he said he was saving himself for that special someone —*because that's just what I had done, too!* Thank God I had waited! I was elated and realized I had set my heart on this very moment way back on our first date when, cheerfully naked and happily ensconced in David's bed, I felt the first stirrings of hominess settle in upon me. And to think it had led to a marriage proposal!

We had met at a fundraiser for the sailing club I belonged to. I was a junior sailor, just finding out about sheets and rigging and spinnakers and booms. Learning to sail had been a lifelong ambition, and I was finally working to make it a reality. David was an important figure at the club — an avid competitive sailor and a member of the board. Although I had heard his name and knew about his accomplishments, I didn't recognize his face when he was introduced to me that night.

"How charming to meet you, Ms. Covey," he said, taking my outstretched hand and holding it a few moments too long. He looked deep into my eyes, smiled, and winked. I was won.

"Charmed as well, Mr. Masterson," I replied coyly. We seemed to share a secret.

David was just under six feet tall. His dark hair was unfashionably long and he combed it over his forehead in a fetching fashion that was boyish and manly somehow at the same time. His arms were a trifle long for his dark-blue pinstriped suit jacket. The cuffs of his white shirt were mostly very white and his shoes were slightly scuffed, but his dark-red tie was unstained, and his teeth, as revealed by that winning smile, were very white and very straight.

His dark-brown eyes pierced me and probed my soul like a Lunar Lander digging up soil samples for future research. I had a fleeting sensation of what a small animal must feel when caught in the headlights of an oncoming vehicle. It seemed that he could intuit things about me that I didn't know myself.

"Want to join me and the boys for a beer or something in the Director's Lounge?" he asked casually, looking down and humbly shuffling his feet. A little shiver ran down my back. Of course I did!

The lounge was indeed full of boys of every size, shape, and age, all hovering over trays of cocktail snacks — grilled shrimp, crab salad on tiny toast rounds, oysters, smelly cheese —all offered by a team of plain young women wearing sensible shoes. The room was stuffy and smelled of warm food and aftershave. Wine flowed, hands motioned, men smiled. Beer splashed exuberantly inside frosty mugs as ideas billowed, careers blossomed and deals began to take shape. The buzz of conversation electrified me.

"We've invited all the club's sponsors here tonight for an open bar," David explained. "Everybody loves getting a little positive attention and some free booze. Sorry it's such a staid bunch. I'd appreciate it if you could lighten things up with a little bright conversation and a few flashes of those pearly whites." He delivered the compliment in such an offhand way it seemed credible. To me at least. He leaned over to speak directly into my ear.

"You've certainly dressed up *my* evening, that's for sure."

"Not at all," I responded, for lack of anything witty to say. Something didn't feel quite right – it was too much perfection happening just a tad too quickly. Was I dreaming? This was the kind of man who should be spending the evening with women who had names like Caroline or Dee.

Why was he interested in me? One minute I had been on my way back from the washroom to rejoin my friends Sarah Johnson and Dinah Westcott in a crowded reception room to nibble on cubes of processed cheddar and three kinds of crackers; the next, I was self-consciously tussling with bacon-wrapped water chestnuts that had been subdued by a little black caviar. My drink ticket lay crumpled in my pocket as I happily anticipated my second glass of free champagne. Sarah and Dinah had no idea where I was. Would they be worried?

Under normal circumstances, I would have been feeling uncomfortable in a crowd like this one and guilty about ditching my pals. But I had been swept away by a very handsome, debonair man who genuinely seemed to like me. How could I have resisted him? He hadn't insisted that I do what he wanted; he'd just humbly assumed that I'd comply. I felt beautiful and important that night, animated and enchanting. Never mind that my PR career was stagnating in my inbox, there were unpaid bills piling up on the dresser, and the rent always seemed to be way past due. I had a

Shades of Teal

retirement fund, I had a pension, I had some savings. And suddenly I had David Masterson to quite possibly fall in love with. He almost even looked like a real prince.

We talked, David and I, for the next hour or so, becoming warmer and warmer toward each other. The seconds ticked by and the champagne blossomed inside me. It turned out that David was a devotee of Victorian literature and read from his collection of first editions every night before bed. He had an extensive assortment of books by Dickens, and a smattering of other authors, and he would rarely pass an antiquarian bookshop without giving in to the impulse to run inside and buy something.

David also had an enormous collection of classical music recordings. He loved Beethoven and Bach above all else but succumbed frequently to the charms of Tchaikovsky and Strauss. Just like me. David went on to explain that he had spent the previous spring in Europe sourcing the work of lesser-known students of Rembrandt and Rubens, and he was going to have to make room on his walls for the new paintings he was planning to buy when he got his next bonus check.

We didn't actually get around to discussing my reading tastes (Thank goodness! I've been known to devour an entire Harlequin romance in a single evening...) or my musical preferences, which is just as well, because when I don't feel classical I throw on some Barry Manilow or a little Abba. Art wise, I was proud of my framed posters of Monet's water lilies and the Beatles' *Abbey Road* album cover, but I really didn't have enough money to put toward anything that couldn't be worn or eaten, so my walls were a little bare. But David Masterson didn't need to know that. Yet.

And so my silence protected me from his poor opinion. After our cozy tête-à-tête, we moved through the room, met a few pleasantly inebriated gentlemen, and made our way to the ballroom for dinner. David said he regretted that he was required to sit at the head table with the other directors but it had been delightful chatting with me and I floated happily along to wherever this evening would take me. The meal was fine and my dreams that night were sweeter than hometown sunshine. I was a fairy princess who had met her prince. My mousy-brown hair didn't matter, that small blemish on my chin hadn't inflated into an angry boil, and my brand-new outfit (complete with matching shoes and purse) had been perfect for the one moment in my life I needed perfection.

I don't care what the Birkenstock Brigade says, I think we women need to feel beautiful from time to time and I find it outrageous to hear that somehow shaving our legs supports an oppressive male vision of femininity. In those rare moments when the planets align and we're kissed by Venus, we women are empowered to make the world a better, kinder, more hopeful place. In believing herself to be beautiful for a moment, an ordinary woman can act from a courage she doesn't otherwise enjoy. I think.

Following the dinner, I desperately wanted David to call. And eight long days later, he actually did. I had begun to give up hope so I was surprised to find that I had impressed him as much as he had impressed me; extraordinary men didn't normally pay me that much attention and I was quivering with nervous energy when I got off the phone with him. He'd asked me out to dinner, and I was to meet him at his apartment first.

I organized myself onto a bus, a subway, and a streetcar to make the 90-minute trek from my home in the city's northern reaches to his quaint place in a trendy west-end enclave.

I walked the last four blocks to his apartment, and he met me at the door of his apartment with a big smile and a joke about bad haircuts. (Was my hair a mess? I was overcome with worry that I didn't look suitably irresistible.) Naturally, it never occurred to me to wonder why he hadn't chosen a restaurant near my apartment. And wasn't the prince supposed to fetch me on a white horse — or, at least, some other form of transportation?

Old fashioned thinking or the wisdom of hindsight?

But the meal itself was heavenly and lingering. We had walked the three blocks to Chez Gustave, a charming little French bistro with white tablecloths and very few diners.

An extraordinary dinner began with a couple of martinis and oysters on the half-shell and it was followed by a dish of garlicky frog's legs, a boneless chicken breast in a heavenly white-wine reduction, hand-made fettuccine topped with shavings of Roquefort cheese, mushrooms, and scallops (how unusual!), and a bottle of Australian cabernet sauvignon. The wine did not quite complement the meal, but it was very nice, and after the second glass it seemed just fine.

We ended the feast with snifters of cognac and a cunning little crème brulée and walked arm-in-arm through a light rain to David's apartment for coffee we were too impassioned to brew. Instead we holed up in the dark messy cave of David's bedroom and did the usual things lovers do for a solid twenty minutes.

I could not honestly admire his decorating sense, and I made a late-night, post-coital mental note to teach this young man a thing or two about colour schemes. The bedroom curtains were brown and the carpeting was gray shag. There were dirty socks scattered on the floor, a pile of underwear in a corner. Aside from the bed, the only furniture in the room was an old dresser and a cheap little desk. There were no bookshelves in the bedroom, or, come to think of it, anywhere else in the apartment, and I idly wondered where he kept his stellar collection of Victorian fiction.

"Where are all your books? I asked him sleepily. He gave me a little hug.

"I'll show you tomorrow," he said. There were no pictures on the walls, no radio, no stereo system — and hadn't he told me he loved music?

"Play me some music then, too, 'kay?" I said. He nuzzled my neck and gave me a raspberry. I giggled.

"Anything you ask, Princess," he said.

This was a home strangely devoid of personality — or, perhaps, full of it. It did not smell nice. Jerry would have been horrified. My mother would have been horrified. So many people would have been horrified. Everyone except me. Plenty of time, I thought, to get the domestic end of things in order. I giggled again and snuggled down into David's back, prepared to join him in sleep.

"Um, Teale, do you mind?" he asked.

"Hmmm?"

"I hate to feel crowded at night – can you scooch over to the other side?" His voice was soft and I felt embarrassed at my insensitivity.

So my beloved had a couple of little idiosyncrasies that I would have to deal with carefully. It seemed that bedtime etiquette was terribly important to him, and it wouldn't do to score low marks first time out.

"No problem, Davey." I gave him a loving little peck on the shoulder — a shoulder that was now clad in flannel pyjamas — and slid over to face the wall to give him plenty of room. He would see what a wonderful mate I could be. He would see that I was the woman of his dreams. A ragged crack in the plaster traced a border between floor and ceiling and I idly wondered if there were others there I could not see.

"I have to leave early tomorrow morning," he whispered at my back. A splatter of cold fall rain hit the small sash window as I drifted off to sleep beside this amazing sweet man wrapped in an orange and avocado-green bedspread. I wished I'd found him sooner.

5

When I awoke the next morning after a restless night in an unfamiliar bed David had already left.

A small brass key sat on the kitchen table along with a point-form note directing me to make myself some coffee and drop the key in the milk box in the hallway on my way out. David had signed the note with a smiley face, and I grinned. I felt liberated and cheerful, swept up in the promise of a new happiness that was flooding into my life.

There was no cream in David's fridge — no problem, I could pick some up later — and no soap in the shower, although the few drops of shampoo left in the bottle seemed to do a reasonable job on my hair. Rubbing myself dry, my euphoria allowed me to ignore the sour, unwashed smell the gray towel released and I set about composing my own cute little thank-you note, which I taped to the coffee maker before letting myself out. Funny how much of life revolves around coffee, isn't it? It warms us up, calms us down, gives us a lift or an excuse to chat. How many romances have started over a cup of coffee? How many have ended that way? David couldn't miss my note, and I couldn't wait for him to call.

Those were the days before deadly sexually transmitted diseases were unleashed on the world, before the divorce rate hit 42 percent. Women were equal, officially, and the birth control pill could give us choices our gender never had before. Or did it? If you take away the consequences, how can a girl say no? There's no down side to a little roll in the hay, no alternative, sometimes, to giving in to seduction, that powerful, sweet sinking into another's body that makes you feel like you're floating on his soul. Really, the question becomes, why *not* have an interesting sexual experience with someone, almost anyone, since it carries no consequences? And it is such a superb, wickedly wonderful slide, as, eyes glittering, we allow ourselves to ignore reason and embrace the exploration of pleasure. Magnificent, isn't it, to play — first with words, then the soft pads of your fingertips, touch your hair, touch, and titillate, fondle a glass instead of your lover, tempt, tease, promise, deny and finally, the denouement, deliver... How blindingly complete the act of seduction can make us feel, and how destructive it can be. The mistake I made was to confuse it with the idea of forever.

If I'd just dropped David's key in the milk box and walked, emotionally, away, all would have been well. We'd had some fun and excitement, some comfort and warmth, and if the story had ended there, well, I guess there would be no story to tell. Perhaps I would have looked back nostalgically on the romance of it and recalled how we had pleasured each other on a rainy fall night. Perhaps I would even have wondered what had become of that charming, handsome man I had slept with. It would have been a happy story —or, at the very least, a bittersweet tale of a woman, now older and wiser, who is still searching for love, still a believer.

But I couldn't let it rest, perhaps because he didn't call. Two weeks passed. How many women are intrigued by the man who doesn't call, despite having given every indication that he will? The subtle disdain that un-made call communicates is irksome, and so hurtful. It reminds us that if we want love in our lives, we have to wrestle it in through the door ourselves. As unobtrusively as possible, of course: chase him until he catches you.

Did I say love? I suppose that's the pretty word we use to add lustre to its evil twin, lust. For "love" cannot possibly mean that insatiable longing for another's hot and heavy body leaning over us, into us, thrusting, charging, releasing home — and it's over. Yes, lust it is when you can't wait for that call, when you yearn for the sound of his voice, the scent of his cologne, the touch of his hand as it brushes, accidentally of course, against your thigh. Lust is easily hurt and hurting. It comes out of nowhere, roiling up like thunder clouds in a clear sky. You panic at the thought that he isn't here right now. So where is he? Who is he with? Lust pulls your eyes toward him when you meet. It pulls your body toward his when you're alone together. It draws you away from your friends, your family, your career, and, ultimately, your life. Lust is pure magnetic instinct; it drives you to couple. Eyes glisten, hearts throb, mouths water, skin prickles, and it feels like soul. Pathetic how we hunt for lust, rejoicing when it sinks its claws into us. "I'm in love," we crow. "He loves me," we chirp. "My life is complete." We are in lust until we are firmly gripped, committed, married, imprisoned in our decision to mate. And then we have to make it work.

Is love between a man and a woman even possible? Or is it a concept used to sell wedding gowns and anniversary cards? Do we use the notion of love simply to make ourselves feel less afraid of what we brought upon ourselves when we made the colossal mistake of uttering that time-honoured phrase "I do"? We call it love, but the bond that joins two adults is no more stable than the sand upon which I sit, blowing sand that is now a pile, now a hole, here a castle, there a cold vessel for stagnant water. It's been around forever, but it never changes. It never becomes anything more glorious than granulated rock. Cold, cruel rock.

***

Her name was Darien. Gorgeous, blonde Darien with the friendly girl-next-door smile and the great back end. Or so the man I picked from the line-up of love told me. "Wow, what a butt, too," he said when she moved in next door to us and started needing a lot of his help. I smiled, thinking that was just like David to make a smart comment about a woman's anatomy. He didn't mean it, of course, because he was a champion of gender equality and affirmative action. Women were much more than a commodity to him.

"David, that's terrible!" I laughed. It was just an innocent comment, delivered with a grin, a wink and a toss of his black hair.

"What?" came the reply. "She's stacked, Teale, but she's probably nowhere near as smart as you are. What are you worried about?"

We weren't married yet, although we were living together in a nice little rented house near David's old apartment.

We were planning a glorious wedding that was mere months away. The church and hall were booked, the flowers had been ordered, and the first fitting for my once-in-a-lifetime bridal gown had just been scheduled. The invitations were going out soon, and I was transcendently happy, as brides tend to be...

I liked her. Darien was very sweet and very good-natured. Quiet but nice, nothing more, nothing less. We went shopping together once or twice — just a couple of companionable outings to a row of quaint shops in our neighbourhood.

There was little evidence of the wild panting that she and David engaged in every Tuesday night while I was out at my English class. I had decided I wanted a Master's degree in English and had begun a class in Romantic Poetry that would be the first step along the way. David had been supportive in a neutral kind of way.

"Why do you need to know about that stuff?" he'd asked with a snort. "I give you all the romance a gal could need!" But he didn't stop me.

A pair of unfamiliar panties appeared one day under the armchair in the living room and I once found a tube of Vaseline that I'd never seen before under our bed. I even found Darien's name scrawled on a scrap of paper along with the address of an airport-strip hotel. One night, I came home early from class and saw her leaving by the side door.

There were other signs, too, but for many months I wilfully ignored them. David always had a perfectly plausible explanation and insisted that I was losing my mind. He loved me, me, ME, not anyone else, forever and ever amen.

How could I doubt him? When I finally, tentatively, presented him with my suspicions, my heart pounding in my angry chest, my future hanging in the balance, he was outraged.

"Have you no faith in what we're building here?" he demanded, stunned. "I knock myself out trying to show you how much I love you. I am totally committed to us. I'm even going to marry you, for God's sake. Teale — how can you poison our future with your petty jealousy?"

I was an *insanely* jealous woman, he said. My suspicions were shockingly dishonourable. His poor parents would be horrified by my lack of trust in their son. They would wonder why he was even marrying me!

"And poor Darien!" he said. "Why would you try to ruin that sweet young woman's reputation? I can't believe you! Are you out of your mind? Maybe you're as off-balance as your mother. Maybe I'm the one who should be doubting *your* commitment!"

His anger floored me. It filled my heart with doubts about my doubts.

"But David, it doesn't add up."

"Only for you, Teale," he said. "I'm not sure I want to be married to someone who doesn't even trust me. What would I want with Darien? She's just a neighbour who happens to look good and dress well. Maybe you're jealous of her. Is that what this is all about? You want to be as pretty as Darien? Cripes, Teale, she can barely spell her own name she's so dull! Why would I even want to spend time with her?"

He was right, of course. He would never cheat on me. How could I suspect him of such a terrible thing? What was wrong with me? I was embarrassed by my suspicions and wished fervently that I had never said a word. How insecure can a gal be?

It was over after a few months, I think. And I married him anyway, idiot that I am.

Because, you see, I was just like countless others out there. I didn't think such a thing could ever happen to me. I didn't believe my man would wrong me. I believed the words and ignored the actions.

And it didn't make any sense at all that David would cheat on me. It was illogical. I was loving and kind, I cooked and cleaned and worked and played. We were completely compatible, or so I thought. If he ever wanted sex – which was rare — I never turned him down in bed. I didn't think I ever gave him a reason to cheat on me, and David was a man of honour.

When I was growing up, no one ever discussed infidelity. It must have been happening under our very noses, but it was never acknowledged. Especially in our house. To be sure, there was the haunted look in my mother's eyes whenever "Winnipeg" was mentioned. In the fantasy world that was my teenhood, a man never did that to a woman.

In the fantasy world that was my pre-marital joy, the thought was too awful to be true. *My* man loved *me*. We would soar together...

6

Soar. Snore. Score. Shore. Just words.

The weather sucks and the beach is nameless. If I'd been lucky enough to have been born a million years ago I'd be dead and gone already and not sitting here, fresh out of beer and faith in the future.

It's not that I'm bitter, exactly, although some days I am. More than that, I am deflated by the soggy fizzle of the pretty starter life I once enjoyed. How can something that began with such promise blossom into such despair? I was hopeful, confident, and clever once. The changes in my attitude must have taken place by tiny degrees, because I didn't notice them until after they were already infused into the contents of the two-litre jar that is my brain.

But maybe I'm not alone. Maybe God's pretty discouraged about the fizzling of his big dreams for humanity, too.

Some say humankind emerged from the murk of a massive chemical soup that had boiled and churned for centuries until we crawled out of it, choking and heaving, onto savannas bristling with danger. It could easily have all started here, on the scrap of beach I defend against these stupid gulls. Maybe I should be more careful. One more beer and I might be wondering if the gulls on this beach are descendants of the giant meat-eating dino-birds that patrolled the skies looking for dino-rodents like me to chomp.

"Look! There's a dino-rodent throwing stones at us — let's eat her!" they might squawk.

Go ahead, boys . . . Just sitting on nice wet sand here and wondering where I came from *originally*. Just communing with my instinctive self and thinking maybe David was right after all — maybe I'm crazy.

"Piss *off*," I shriek, but the tiny dino-gulls ignore me. Maybe that's because Teale does not use words like that. These are not her words. She is a nice girl who does everything right. She is a sweet girl who communicates reasonably with people and *compromises*. She would never say "Go away" to a bird, let alone "Piss off" —oh dear me, no. Teale is a calm, cool, collected girl. Everybody has always said so. She never gets ruffled, never raises an eyebrow. So calm was Teale, so nice, in spite of the Ginger Lime Tangy cologne she used to favour.

But she wasn't really me. Perhaps she used to be —I don't know. Maybe she was hiding from something buried deep inside her, or maybe she was just plain stupid. I've never known her to sit alone on a beach in lousy weather and cry, though. We hurt down to our very core, me and Teale.

They are too close, these idiot birds, swooping just barely above my head, teasing me and Trooper, blinking oddly and clearly mocking a deluded woman who has sand in her eyes and lake spit in her hair. The sun is finally burning its way through the clouds, vaporizing them, almost, in a relentless quest for dominion of the skies, the sand, the drudge-gray lake. It has been there, that sun, powerful and life-giving, since the dawn of time – and it has steadily watched while we miserable humans struggled our way up the food chain, scrapping over a patch of sand or a rag of meat. Subservient, we've always been, to greater powers like the sun. Is that what He intended?

"Put the bone down, She." A friendly statement. A harmless command from the He-monkey to the She-monkey, back in the morning of man, before we were so civilized and equal. She has taken food that does not, technically, belong to her, although she raised and butchered the animal that provided it and neatly stacked, stored, and protected the precious slabs of meat that resulted from her labour. She is hungry after all that work. He is disappointed, surprised she so boldly took what wasn't hers. He raises his eyebrows, two black pointer sticks in the ragged classroom of his face, ready when needed to slam angrily on the desk of the unruly student.

"Oh!" He is surprised but thinks perhaps she needs further instruction. She never seems to do anything right. He feels cursed by her stupidity.

"We decided you couldn't have that, remember? Maybe you just forgot. There's a good She —now give it over. Just drop it into my hand. Goodness, you're a forgetful little thing. That's it. Be reasonable. I just don't understand what's gotten into you. You used to know how to please me. Do it *now*, please."

Palm up, He waggles his fingers in her direction —the universal sign for "hand it over."

She looks at him uncertainly, dizzy with hunger. He is bigger and stronger —the protector of his clan, the conqueror of new territory, the only hope for the future of this fledgling species. And He is always so good to her, in his own way — a little misunderstood, perhaps, but good to her all the same. They had indeed agreed that He needed this bone. If He failed in his work, they were all doomed. The new life stirring within her would have no future if He could not rage against their enemies. One meal a week was plenty for her. He needed, well ... whatever He took was what he needed. She knew that, too.

He was standing in front of her now. Looming . . .

"I am so sorry, He. But I'm hungry . . ." She hangs her head in the shame and fatigue of living.

"Now, now, She, we are both reasonable. You took meat yesterday and actually you didn't really need it, did you? We both know you don't do anything but play around in the dirt with the children. You don't need this bone. I wish I didn't need it either, Sun knows I wish hard, but I am condemned to spend my days fighting for my clan, searching for food, killing the wild animals that threaten us. Do you have any idea how hard it is to be clan leader? If it weren't for you, I wouldn't have to work so hard. I wouldn't have to maintain such an elaborate nest. I could run free, as I deserve, mate with whomever I wished, feel the joy of living. I long for that and I deserve it. You don't want me to leave, do you? How would you feed those hungry brats you like to collect? I could leave, you know." He smiles a grim smile. His eyes are hard.

"But you are *my* burden, She." He sighs.

She feels terrible that she is a burden. She is sure she hasn't always been this difficult to look after. She'll have to try harder to be less trouble. She is afraid He will leave them to starve. How would She ever manage without He? Panic grabs her heart and starts to squeeze.

He shuffles over to where She perches and holds out his hand. She owes her whole life to this male. She gives him the bone, defeated, the pride she once felt in being mated to Clan Leader replaced by the knowledge that she's no good to him now. Their union had started as an adventure but has now sputtered down into mere existence. Where once, He had looked at her with sunshine in his heart and warmth in his eyes, he now barely tolerated her. How had She let this happen?

She sits on her log on this very beach and cries the secret dry tears that one day will crystallize into the sand I now throw at these hideous seagulls. I can protect her memory from the predatory birds of this world. They look like enemies, and I know how to keep them away. But I can't save her from He-monkey's reasonable manner, his charm, his twisted thinking, his threats, his smiles, the power he holds over her. Did he not *choose* to mate with her? If she were such a burden, then why didn't he just leave her instead of eternally threatening so to do? And for heaven's sake, why did she mate with him? Why did she stay until death indeed parted them?

I've asked myself the very same question and the answer runs like blood through She-monkey's veins, through my own. I once throbbed for challenge and lusted for brilliance. I could have had Jerry, with his neatly arranged socks and fondness for local history, but I wanted something brighter, something bolder. I wanted to push the outer bubble of my life step by incautious step towards the unknown brilliance of a fire yet untamed.

"Tame the fire in the untamed man," She-monkey's spirit whispered, "and you will feel the fire in your own heart grow." Hers was hardly the example I should have followed, but I didn't know that at the time.

I didn't know the fire was me.

Some people believe that life must be tough to feel real; life must be impossible, almost lost, to have value. Some believe that love, too, should involve struggle, and they thrive on winning the heart and hand of the one who must be *won*. Captivating an elusive and unavailable lover and binding that person to us is a way to prove our power. We spend hours plotting to get what we want from our elusive partner, hours more hiding the hurt:

"He'll notice me if I change my hairstyle."

"He'll pay attention if I lose some weight."

"He'll marry me if I keep forgiving him."

"He'll come to mother's tomorrow if we have sex tonight."

"He'll treat me right if I teach him how."

He'll treat me right if I teach him how.

There it is, that's the one, the one lonely little lie that sticks to the inside of my brain like a fly to a strip of mustard yellow flypaper, twisting slightly in the breeze of images that glides through my mind, smelling old and looking dirty, specked with the death of life, worn right out and used right up.

Depletion.

And there beside the first is another fly-on-flypaper thought, a memory of David, six months after our first date together, giddy in a roadhouse restaurant, drinking beer and.

"Hey, Teale, want some seafood?"

"No thanks, David I'm not fond of . . . *David, that's disgusting.*" His mouth is open. He holds a plate beneath it. A wad of chewed-up bacon double cheeseburger is balanced on his bottom lip. The "see-food" joke was repeated with increasing frequency throughout the eight long years we were together. I tried to discourage him from doing it, and when that didn't work I coaxed, teased, lectured, shamed, argued, berated, yelled, and finally cried. One day, I knew, he would love me enough to stop, but it was up to me to teach him how.

"Where's your sense of humour?" he'd crow. Making me squirm was David's way of teasing me. It was a loving act.

"What's the matter with you, Teale? It's not a big deal," he would huff when I threatened to leave the restaurant. You're being *very* disagreeable tonight." As though I were only moderately disagreeable every other night.

You have to understand, David was no jerk. He was a good person. He ran every year in the Race for the Cure, diligently raising money for cancer research. If a friend was having a hard time, David would take the poor guy out for a few beers or a hockey game —his treat. As a kid, he had sung in his church choir, and he regretted that he no longer had time to attend church, as it interfered with his golf schedule. In fact, he once told me, he had come *this close* to entering the ministry, but his father had dissuaded him and he had ended up in business school. He championed numerous causes at work and always had a joke or funny story to share. He was a hard worker, he was fond of literature, he loved classical music, and he was kind to puppies and small children. His good qualities so far outweighed his very minor faults that I was inclined to overlook the occasional lapse of judgement. And wasn't forgiveness an important part of a relationship? Weren't loving people supposed to compromise?

David had great judgement. That's why he was so successful. He was brutally honest, and you could usually be sure that he was telling most of the truth, most of the time. If he said I had no sense of humour, then I would have to take him seriously. What reason could he have to lie about something like that?

Shades of Teal

Who was I, after all, to give him etiquette lessons? While David was out solving international trade disputes, I was writing press releases and convincing news reporters that my employer, the Ministry of Justice, had everything well in hand. While David was lunching with the movers and shakers of the business world, I was eating a limp ham sandwich out of a brown paper bag and wondering why the Ministry had printed forms for complaints about training allocations for employees. While David was organizing academic conferences on important ethical issues, I was manoeuvring to get a seat on the bus. So what if he had a compulsion to tell the "see-food" joke? He was just playing —he meant no harm. That awful phrase "Boys will be boys" rang in my head and I knew it would only be a big deal if I turned it into one. It's not the kind of issue that should rupture a committed relationship, unless you are a very petty person. And I certainly wasn't petty, was I? Plus I loved the guy.

And so he continued, and I endured month upon month of sitting down every night in front of a man who, at any moment, might open his mouth to reveal a loathsome mouthful of masticated food. I began getting up from the table in angry protest, only to be greeted with a repeat performance when I returned. There was no respite from the "see-food" joke. David was such a card. I wanted desperately to find the whole thing funny. Maybe if I tried hard enough I could teach myself how.

It didn't work and I began to suspect that I didn't have a sense of humour after all. Nine months after our wedding, there he was, playful yet again and feeling on top of the world, slyly sticking his hand up my skirt and pinching my undies, trying gleefully to pull them down.

"David, *stop it* —people can see."

He laughed.

"Aw c'mon, Teale, where's your sense of humour? You should see your face!" He chuckled again.

I didn't want to see my face. I tried to squirm away from him but he was bigger, faster, stronger, determined. And *he* had a sense of humour. Everybody said so.

The pull-the-panties-down joke became an irresistible favourite. David simply could not stop himself. I know I should have done more to help him break this terrible habit, but what else could I have done? I asked, reasoned, discussed, described, demanded, yelled, threatened, smacked, pulled, pushed, pleaded, begged, cried, slammed doors, and finally gave in to jaded, discouraged hysteria.

"See, Teale – you're laughing too. It's funny, isn't it?" he said.

Memories of my struggle to teach David the lessons that should have been instilled in him decades earlier play like a bad foreign film in the screening room of my memory. I watch these chilling scenes in an eternal loop, cringing at how powerless I feel now and how desperate I was then. Here's the one I like the least: eight months pregnant, Teale waddles as fast as she can along on a slippery city street, trying in vain to escape David with his grabby little hand, a hand that is now on her thigh, now on her buttocks, the familiar tug of panties and panty-hose scraping down the backs of her legs as she wriggles, squirms, slips, screams and cries, "No, David —the baby!"

"Shhhh, Teale, people might hear."

I have to teach him, teach him, teach him . . .

The movie continues. . Act 3, scene 5: Teale scampers up the staircase at home, milk oozing from her breasts, baby crying, radio blaring. "Stop it, David!" Hysteria, laughter, don't, don't, don't, stop, please, stop . . . a sticky tear of frustration squeezes from the corner of her left eye. Teale, poor Teale. He refuses to learn —what will you do? It's just a joke, Teale, where's your sense of humour? Boys will be boys. No big deal. No harm done.

No harm done. He loves me. He adores me. He would never want to hurt me, not ever in a million years. He married me, for heaven's sake!

7

And what a wedding we had!

Glamorous, glorious. Timothy Eaton United Church was dazzling — long white tapers and enormous white bows, solemn and serious organ music, lovely and elegant guests, and six beautiful bridesmaids, pink and pretty, nervous as cats and eager for the reception party after the show. Have you seen that movie, too? There they are, all six stepping one by one down the long aisle of the romantically lit church, hands tightly clutching bouquets of pale-pink roses, gown hems delicately sweeping the dark-red carpet. All eyes drink in their performance. Had one rehearsal been enough?

Four o'clock sharp on the third Saturday in June — David had had to pull a few strings to book that date and time! Aah but the young women shone with beauty, preparing assembled family and friends for the bride's appearance. The young women pray that they are projecting gracefulness, and they will themselves not to trip. Six ushers wait, stately, by the altar. The groom awaits his bride. The minister (now, what was his name?) stands calmly in attendance. The organ music reverberates in air scented with freesia and beeswax, the scent of a wedding in the air. Suddenly the bride appears at the back of the church gripping her nervous father's arm. Her face is veiled and her stance is regal — she's a life-sized Barbie doll in satin and chiffon, her gown smooth and shiny as icing, covering the woman inside with the sweet opaque glaze of her wedding day. Little seed pearls sprinkle over her and never was there a more beautiful bride. Teale is twenty-eight now, and she's never been lovelier. This is the best, the brightest, the most beautiful day of her life. She's almost crying with the joy of the moment and she is the centre of attention. Down the aisle she moves, one quivering step at a time, pristine white shoes glistening against the blood red of the matrimonial carpet. She is steady, sure, certain of the choice she is about to confirm.

"Dearly beloved," the minister begins. "We are gathered together in God's holy sight to join this man and this woman in holy matrimony . . ."

The congregation sits at attention —a colourful landscape of blue hats, navy suits, red striped dresses, green shawls, yellow purses, a garden of supporters all listening, watching, backs and backsides pressed into cool, hard polished pews. They are enthralled by the event that is playing out before them —this is a wedding, a ritual of commitment, a joining of hearts in the presence of God, in the presence of His holy community.

The promise made today is a very public decision to care. Forever.

The service lasts only a few minutes, but in some way it feels like a lifetime. The register is signed, the tears are dried, the nerves are calmed and the rings flash in a bar of light slanting through stained glass. They are now man and wife. They have promised to love, honour, and cherish, for richer or for poorer, in sickness and in health, as long as they both shall live —and oh, David. I loved you so much that day of days. My beloved, my husband, my knight in shining armour, so handsome, so dashing, so charming the way you cleared your throat and waited, as though surprised, before responding with a solemn and serious "I do." A Kodak moment, and I still have the video to prove that it really happened just the way I remembered it. I still have photos of a clutch of black and pink attendants clustered around a smiling bride and groom. "The couple will honeymoon in Europe with friends," read the caption beneath the photo that appeared in the newspaper. I still have that, too. We were going to be travelling with Jake and Claire. The Hudson's. Friends of David's.

"Teale, I hope you don't mind, but I've invited Jake and Claire to come with us on our honeymoon." The wedding had been only weeks away and David had looked deep into my eyes and waited, hopeful and sincere, for my answer, but he continued before I could speak.

"Their own honeymoon was a lousy camping trip, and things aren't going so great for them right now. I think they could use a little holiday to bring the magic back into their marriage. You don't mind do you?"

The wedding was speeding toward us and I was overwhelmed with things to do. But wasn't he thoughtful! Balanced on the threshold of a momentous life event, he was generously thinking of his friends instead of immersing himself in his own selfish concerns.

"Of course they can come, David," Teale exclaimed, surprised but not upset. She didn't get upset in those days. This was the calm, agreeable Teale I once knew. She never even raised an eyebrow. If this was something David wanted, then he should have it. And in the back of her mind was the shameful memory of how she had wrongly accused him of having an affair with Darien. She had to make up for that somehow, and maybe by welcoming his friends to join them on their honeymoon she could show him what a great wife she was going to be.

Jake and Claire were fun, easygoing, and cheerful people. Jake was one of David's oldest buddies. I had first met the Hudson's about a year earlier, at a barbecue. They were "Jake-and-Claire," the kind of couple one tended to think of as a singular noun that required no adjectives. They held hands, laughed while looking into each other's eyes, and leaned on each other in that chummy, "You're my best friend" kind of way. There was no space between them, no commas separating the listing of who they were, together or apart, and I wondered if their marriage was how the intention of forever looked. They even looked alike: both had curly brown hair of about the same length, gold-rimmed glasses, dark-brown eyes, and wide, friendly smiles that invited you into their happy little world.

Except they weren't always happy.

Jake was a real estate lawyer at a large downtown Toronto firm, and he was reputed to be a real shark. This was an odd description to apply to a short, stocky, balding man who had entertained us on many occasions with self-deprecating stories of his childhood. He was a real sweetheart —kind, soft-spoken, and quick with a joke. A shark? I just didn't see it.

Claire, on the other hand, despite her warm manner, did have an edge to her. She taught grade seven at a downtown middle school, so it took me by surprise the first time I heard her swear at Jake. I soon came to realize that she did this whenever he let her down — and this, sadly, seemed to happen regularly.

"You jerk, where did you put my iron last time you used it?"

"For pity sake, Jake, how many times do I have to tell you to put the toilet seat down when you're finished in there?"

"You idiot, you put the corn flakes in the soup cupboard! Can't you do anything right?"

All of this made me uncomfortable, but Claire would deliver her put-downs with a tight-lipped little smile, and Jake didn't seem to take much notice other than to offer some mollifying comment and a promise never to do it again. Maybe this was just the way their marriage worked. Or didn't work. In any case, they always reverted to their tender-hearted mode after Claire's little storms and, really, who knew what a jerk he could be in private?

So maybe the Hudson's did need a holiday to rekindle their romance. If that was so, then, by Jove, I would be glad to help. After all, David's friends were my friends now, weren't they? Claire and I didn't seem to have much in common, but she was nice to me, and I figured I could spend two weeks in her company. Besides, David and I would be lost in our own little romantic reverie most of the time. The four of us almost always had fun together —so, a holiday with friends in Corsica! Why not? Fun was a decision you made, not an accident that happened to you. Right?

David had made his request so sweetly. He knew how excited I was about the wedding, how I longed to spend luxurious hours with him and only him . . . if he had asked Jake and Claire along on our honeymoon, it must be awfully important to him. Of course I wouldn't let him down.

It wasn't until years later that the flag went down at the three-yard line of my mind and I realized that David couldn't have been craving time alone with me anywhere near as much as I wanted time alone with him. A man intent on enjoying his woman's full attention does not dilute the experience with more people; he fends others off, pushes them away, sends them running so he can have his woman all to himself.

Had he ever really loved me?

Jake and Claire were at our wedding —just two of the 250 cheerful guests milling around the ballroom of the Harbour Castle Hilton. Wine flowed, ice sculptures glinted, a classical quartet quietly strummed greatest hits from 18th century Germany or Italy, or somewhere long ago and far away. Dinner was exquisite: a glorious salad of fresh mint, mango, cantaloupe, and cognac on mixed greens, followed by a shimmering five-onion and ginger cream soup (to die for!); next, a simple pasta dish of shrimp and scallops poached in white wine and served on a bed of angel hair pasta and finally the main course was a tender prosciutto-wrapped filet mignon in a sherry reduction accompanied by mushrooms, tiny white onions, a few spears of asparagus, some rounds of zucchini, and irresistible little spheres of oven-roasted potatoes, browned to perfection.

It was going to take my father decades to pay for this event and it was worth every penny!

After the meal, right on schedule, there were speeches, a series of toasts, and the ritual cutting of the cake. Happy couples danced, midnight arrived, and finally the bride and groom strolled off to the privacy of their honeymoon suite. David stripped off his tux, pulled on his pyjamas, yawned, and crawled into bed.

Enter Teale from the bathroom, dressed in her new, and exquisitely seductive negligee —see-through cream lace enhanced with chiffon; matching peignoir coat, silk and satin, just like her wedding dress, only less so, darling little pearl buttons undone just to *there*. Her dark hair frames her timid face, her breasts sway slightly, her soft shoulders invite a caress. Listen —swish, swish, swish —her silk whispers as she slides into bed beside her husband, strokes his face, sighs his name, gently, lovingly. She's a newlywed.

"David."

"What?"

"Can I get you a glass of champagne? I just opened the bottle."

"No."

"How about a little cuddle?"

"Teale, we have to be up early to say goodbye to everybody from out of town *and* catch our flight. C'mon now —it's nearly one o'clock in the morning, and I need to go to sleep."

"I love you David."

"Yeah, me too."

"Great day, huh?"

"Hmmm."

And that was our wedding night. No searing flames of physical passion, no triumphant satisfaction, no tender kisses, no response. Teale got up and poured herself a glass of champagne, moved to the window, and drank while gazing out at the big friendly city. The lights were mesmerizing. On that soft June night, through the glass shield of the window, she watched airplanes pass overhead and cars stream by on the avenues and expressways below. Finally she witnessed the gentle glow of her first married-life morning, a pale pink blush streaking across the eastern sky.

A beautiful morning.

A beautiful wedding.

A beautiful husband snoring gently in the king-sized bed across the room. He'd had such a long day. He'd worked so hard. He needed this holiday so badly. So this was married life. She crawled in beside him, kissed his cheek, and slept.

8

If ever David and I got along well, it was when we travelled. Eyes open wide, we would examine, enjoy and discuss all the wonderful things we encountered in the great glorious world. There was no right or wrong in this discovery —no pain, no push to try harder. Two weeks relaxing in Corsica with a couple of friends was sheer bliss. What better way to indulge in our newly-married mirage of the joy of being together? We wandered the streets of the sweet little village of Evisa, and the town of Calvi (birthplace, it is said, of Christopher Columbus) and we marvelled at the sculpted but wild beauty of the Scandola Nature Reserve. Sometimes we just lay on a beach and relaxed in the sun.

Corsica is an interesting place and very, very beautiful. Everywhere you look there is a breath-taking vista or a charming scene. Although it's closer to Italy, it is technically part of France and although we did see some thirsty fields and weather-beaten farmers, the country seemed mostly as heavenly place for people to take a holiday. The landscape was beautiful and our rented car would chug laboriously up the steep incline on one side of the island's main mountain and barely cling to the road as it sailed down the other. We ate mushrooms and seafood, drank wine by the gallon, and consumed enormous quantities of cheese.

We drove through a country balanced between the ancient and the searingly new, a country full of fresh sea air and endless skies above. We sat in quaint little bars and listened as passionate fingers coaxed music from the strings of guitars, the memories of tragic love echoing from the walls, bouncing off hearts that were themselves overfull and yearning. These moments resonated inside us, in that small place inside where we keep our understanding of a wider humanity. It was beautiful and a little embarrassing to wear someone else's pain. This is actually a larger world.

A world of want.

At night, David and I did little more than sleep.

"I'm too tired, Teale."

"It's been an awfully long day."

"Stop crowding me."

I felt a little jilted —a little disappointed, perhaps, that there was such a lack of physical affection between us on our honeymoon. Sure, it's great to stroll through a museum holding hands, or sit hunched over a map together, laughing at how terribly lost we are, but I had hoped to enjoy a little cozy, animal rutting with the man who was now my Mister. I had actually thought that David was saving his vital energies for the honeymoon, that in Corsica our occasional lovemaking would blossom into more regular contact, that we could stay up all night exploring some happy unseen places. I was aching to strip down to my instinctive self for a few hours with my brand-new husband, but we were always too busy or too tired to make the effort. Every time I touched David in a less- than family-entertainment manner, he bristled.

"Teale, that's hardly appropriate right now, we're in a restaurant!" he might say. Or, "Teale, that's just not the kind of behaviour I expect from my wife. You are supposed to set an example for others, not try to drag them into ditches."

"I'd like to drag you into a ditch, David," I leered.

"Teale, let's just enjoy our holiday. Don't ruin it."

"David, this is not a *holiday*, it's our *honeymoon*."

He glared at me and paused a moment before speaking. "Well, at least one of us married for intelligent company. I find a lot more to value in you than just your body. It would be nice if you valued my intelligence as well."

I couldn't help it, I wanted to make love. And now I felt like a cheap hooker at a church tea party. This was my husband. I wanted to feel his hands warm and insistent on me, exploring every inch of my skin. I wanted to stay up all night basking in the pleasure of conjugal bliss. Sure, he was smart and interesting, funny and entertaining. But he was a damned good-looking guy; I wanted to enjoy everything about him. Was that wrong?

David and I were learning about each other, and the lessons came slowly and painfully. Maybe most marriages are like that — months of high-stress decision making and planning, followed by a euphoric and exhausting wedding day, followed by a honeymoon clouded by unmet expectations . . . no wonder David was tired!

"I see you're wearing that top," he said the morning of our second last day in Corsica.

"You betcha! It's a great T, don't you think?" I twirled and did a seductive little dance for him, hips swaying and hands moving erotically to an imaginary tango. My new "La Corse Of Course!" T-shirt was a souvenir — all blue and red and white. I loved it!

"Well, Teale, it's very *touristy*." He was right, but,

"David, we're tourists."

"Yeah, but you don't have to advertise it like that. Maybe you should change into something else."

"Change? I don't think so — it goes so well with my shorts."

"Aren't you embarrassed to be seen like that, Teale? Gee, I sure would be. If you really want to look decent, you should change."

I felt silly and cheeky.

"Nope, *my* tee." I grinned at him.

Teale, I have to be seen with you all day and you'll make me look like an idiot if you parade around in that stupid thing. If you really cared about my feelings, you would *go and change the top*."

"Well, you don't have to make a federal case of it, David."

"You're the one making a federal case, Teale. I've been extremely patient with your immature need to buy cheap, stupid, tourist-trash souvenirs, but I'm really getting sick of it. I can't believe you feel the need to embarrass me like this all the time. I thought you were a person of reasonably good taste, but obviously I was wrong. Wear what you want, but if you don't take off that ridiculous shirt, you can't come sightseeing with me today." He was shouting at me now, index finger pointed aggressively at my chest.

Whoa. Talk about a reality check.

Was he for real? I loved him, but did that mean I had to change my clothes in order to keep him happy? Who was he to threaten to leave me in the hotel? Did this mean he was actually the boss? I hadn't even suspected there *was* a boss in this relationship. Immature and stupid. I *embarrassed* him, for God's sake. My mind spun like a broken merry-go-round.

I was off-balance, confused. I stared at him. I felt dizzy. Virtuously, David turned around and marched out of our room, quietly closing the door behind him. He made it a point to never slam a door, as though winning a fight depended on maintaining control at all times. But I slammed doors all the time when I was mad. It was an adjectival statement describing the word "angry."

After he left I stared at the gently closed door for a long time, thinking about what had just happened. David had never talked to me like that before. Was this how he really felt, or was he worried about something else? Work, perhaps? If I changed my shirt, would it mean that I had lost? And what, exactly, would I be losing? Maybe there was nothing to lose by changing.

After all, I wanted him to be happy, and marriage was all about compromise, was it not? Really, it was a small thing to have to do to please my man, even though it made no sense at all to me. He had spent so much money to make this honeymoon fun for me —so what if he had a thing about tourist kitsch?

I went onto the terrace and looked out over a profusion of beautiful flowers and greenery to the magnificent blue of the Mediterranean Sea. Sunshine sparkled on the surging expanse of water and varnished everything with the brilliance of eternal summer. I leaned forward against the balcony wall and inhaled deeply. The flowers smelled heavenly, and my body relaxed. I felt completely at home with the isolation of the island. How lucky I was to be here! How happy I was to be married to a wonderful husband!

How stupid it was to fight over a silly little shirt! I went into the bedroom, took a drab, cocoa-coloured, short-sleeved blouse from my suitcase, and pulled off the souvenir T-shirt. Buttoning the blouse, I decided this was a little thing to do to please David. I wanted to make him happy, mostly.

Unfortunately, the entire day was marred by our bickering.

"Hey, David —don't you think it's my turn to drive?"

"No."

"Oh. Why not?"

"You're not a very good driver."

"*Pardon me?* What do you mean, I'm not a very good driver? I'm a *great* driver!"

"No you aren't. You rev the gas."

"I don't rev the gas."

"Yes you do."

"Well I can't possibly do it any more than you do!"

"Yeah, right . . . and anyway, you don't brake properly."

"What are you talking about? I brake just fine!"

"Look — you just can't drive."

"Who made you king of the car keys?"

"God did."

"Stop this car I'm getting out."

"Yeah, yeah, tell it to the Marines."

Fuming, I sat in the back seat with Claire while the men drove and traded sports trivia questions. I had let him win again. Reluctantly, this time.

Not much could be seen from the back seat of our tiny car. I was hot and cranky. My knees had been tucked up under my chin for hours. I didn't want to honeymoon anymore. I wanted to go home.

That night, I sat on the balcony overlooking the hotel garden long after David had fallen asleep. There were little tree bugs singing along with the crickets, and the night was soft and gentle, a far cry from the colour and commentary of our hectic day of sightseeing. The sky was quiet, the air was clean and I didn't want to move for fear of losing the exquisitely beautiful feeling that was washing over me — the sense of being me, Teale, alone in a foreign country where no one knew my name, no one cared what I wore or how I looked or what I said.

Here I had a chance to be someone entirely new, yet entirely me. Here I could just sit and watch and feel the calmness of a summer's night envelope me. Shhhh — so quiet, so calm. I could almost touch the night, wrap it snugly around me and snuggle down into its peace, alone and at rest. How nice to be alone. How easy it is. Shhhh Teale.

9

Our honeymoon was over and the silent disappointments had all been tossed out the car window on our way to the airport for our flight home. We landed in Toronto with a suitcase full of trinkets in spite of David's disgust, and our hearts were full of the excitement of returning to our beautiful new home —a modest red-brick house on Fairlawn Road. We were happily married and looking forward to planning our life together. There were dozens of thank-you cards to write —woman's work, David said, and I laughed. I didn't mind, because if I left it to him it wouldn't get done. There were presents to arrange on shelves and settle in cupboards, new towels to wash and admire (plush and plumpy – how nice!), decorating to consider (sage green or butterscotch for the living room walls?) and the crazy rush of work.

Although my job was not as illustrious as David's, it was still a good job. Realistically, what more could a former newspaper reporter hope for than to find work in a government media relations department? I wrote material for my provincial government, researched for it, creatively skirted the truth for it, and generally fended off the slings and arrows of outrageous journalists. But, after two years of intense work in the communications department of the Ministry of Justice, I was ready for a change.

My new home beckoned. I wanted to get busy with a paintbrush. But once the commotion brought on by the wedding and the honeymoon had died down, we re-entered the whirl of activity we'd inhabited when we were dating. Life as a member of David's circle —outside of working hours —was an endless round of parties, receptions, plays, symphonies, and dinners. There were also bills to be paid and transportation issues to be resolved; our commuting options were bus, subway, and one beat-up old car. David's car. He needed a new one.

Although marriage gave David a renewed sense of purpose in life, it also intensified his compulsion to tease me. The lock trick was a brilliant invention, and it pushed me beyond the limits of my ebbing sense of humour.

Our two-storey home had hardwood floors, leaded crystal doorknobs, and eight-inch baseboards; the kitchen had seen no upgrades for decades and although I dreamed every day of new appliances, it was still my dream home. It was perfect, and, needless to say, we couldn't afford to live there. David had a spacious main-floor addition built off the back of the house to serve as his den; I had a closet off the furnace room set aside as storage for my boxes of books. As David so rightly pointed out, I never had to bring work home, so I didn't need a room of my own. There was space in the dining room for a decent-sized table, and beyond the kitchen was a sweet little glassed-in family room.

David installed his TV set in the family room, and although he told me I could watch it whenever I wished, he always complained if it wasn't set on the channel he liked when he got home from work. I'm not sure exactly how that happened as I rarely had time to sit and watch television, but occasionally I did, and I sometimes failed to remember to reset the channel. I took his good-natured grousing in stride and suggested it was quite easy to find the channel he wanted. As time went on and the years pulled us forward and the grousing became angry and loud, I took to checking the TV each night before he came home to spare myself his searing put-downs and the endless complaining of a self-righteous man with Truth on his side. While I hated the fact that there was a bulging knot in my stomach whenever David came home from work, I didn't want to make trouble. It was so much easier to fix a problem before things got loud.

The house needed a lot of work and it would take us years to get it all just right, but as a starter home, it was beautifully loaded with potential. Many of our neighbours had already undertaken extensive renovations, and David loved the thought of making a killing one day on the resale. The neighbourhood was a comfortable one and although we were not quite on the edge of the ritzy part of town we were respectably situated and therefore part of the target list for the element of society whose main line of work was breaking into other people's homes and stealing them blind. Cheerful though the house might be from dawn to dusk, the threat of a break-in made me edgy at night. I sometimes thought longingly of my old apartment, with its security entrance and nosy neighbours. I felt surprisingly unsafe in my house of dreams and as I archly pointed out to David when the deadbolt on the back door was tampered with one night, we were lush fruit on a heavy vine, ready and ripe for the plucking.

He sneered.

"You're always afraid of something, Teale. You've got a big strong man around to protect you now. You have to learn to relax."

This was a tall order.

David came up with a great way of curing what he considered my ludicrous obsession with security. One night, we were in bed, drowsy and comfortable, about to drift into sleep, when I realized I hadn't checked the doors.

"David, did you lock the doors?" I quietly asked, the pull of sleep stretching my waking moments farther than I wished.

"Maybe I did, and maybe I didn't," he slyly whispered.

"David, don't play games tonight. I'm too tired."

"Well, I guess you'll just have to trust me on the door score."

Have you seen the video? He rolls over and passes an enormous amount of gas. Teale pulls herself out of bed, trudges down the hall to the stairs, and slowly descends. At the front door she starts the checking procedure David should have initiated, and maybe did complete, but she needs to be sure. Front door: locked. Back doors: locked. Side door: locked. Windows: all locked. Good. Score one for safety. Another night is ready to tuck away on the great scorecard of Eternity and up Teale creeps. She slides back into bed, her beautiful bed, aah, sleep will drift in soon. She crawls between the sheets and David pops out of bed and heads quickly down to the front door, his feet making soft swishing sounds against the carpeting. Teale can hear the sound of the deadbolt sliding back and forth, fast and loud . . . *click click click clickikikikik* . . . she can't count the grinding clicks. He rattles the chain and abruptly races up the stairs and hurls himself into bed, chuckling still, overjoyed at his power, like a thirteen-year-old prankster.

"David, please don't do this to me —you know I hate to guess about safety."

"Aw, Teale, you're too neurotic about it —we're probably safe."

"I don't want probably safe, David, I want definitely safe. The Jackson's were broken into not three weeks ago because they forgot to lock their door."

"I guess you'll have to go check for yourself, then," he sighs, pleased with his little game of cat and mouse. Teale trots down the stairs yet again; and again three minutes later, and five minutes after that until David tires for another night and lets her win or until she exhausts herself and gives up. Always a winner; always a loser. She argues and pleads with him to no avail.

God, I'm glad I'm not her anymore.

But she was happy, I guess, most of the time. She loved waking up beside her husband and brewing him coffee while he showered. She loved watching him rummage in his messy sock drawer for something black or navy blue, loved talking about their next holiday while he wrapped his tie around his fifteen-and-a-half-inch neck. Before the babies started to arrive, she loved getting on the bus with him or riding with him in the car to work. She loved the travelling, the parties, the theatre, the social life. She loved cooking extravagant meals for ten people and cleaning her oh-so-beautiful house. This was the life she had been raised to want. Everyone enjoyed an evening at the Masterson's. They were the perfect couple —so charming, so nice to each other, so obviously in love. This was marriage. This was life. This was what you got when you grew up and got married. Every heart should be so lucky.

10

The truth of the matter is, lucky hearts can be cold hearts, too, chilled by the glacial breath of a lover's frosty words and iced with a dainty gloss of sarcasm. Some say a marriage promise must be kept until death and they might be right. I did die. A slow death, one that occurred by imperceptible degrees, like temperature falling on the glass tube of a thermometer one lingering black tick after another until the reading of life was gone. It was a surprising death, since I still walked the Earth, spoke in sentences and took out the garbage, but it was a death all the same, marked by absolute fatigue and a distinct disinterest in anything remotely connected to — well, me.

I always figured women like that weren't trying very hard, that they were the kind of ladies that had been complaining of headaches since birth, ladies who had become experts in the gentle art of complaining. Limp-wristed, weak-willed, lily-livered and any other cliché you can imagine, they were just lacking in will, determination, fortitude and goals.

I used to think they needed to try harder to make the magic work, to recast the spell that had fallen over their men and themselves as they lurched along on the adventure of their love. Now I think that even if they were a little bit like me, they probably did try.

God knows I tried. I loved the man, the institution, the house I lived in, my sheets, towels, dishes, plants. I fought to save them all.

Well, maybe I didn't fight; David and I never disagreed and fights were what small people did when they couldn't solve their petty problems rationally. I felt very mature clamping onto this opinion, and I guess I was so busy proving how broad-minded I was that I agreed with just about everything my husband suggested. I wanted his happiness more than my own. Isn't that what love does?

"No, David —of course we don't have to stay home if you don't want to. I love going out!" Well, I *did*!

"Yes, David —of course we can have your department over for dinner Saturday night." I loved entertaining!

"Well, David, if you want blue in the living room instead of green, it's fine with me." (It's just paint —what difference does the colour make?)

Don't misunderstand. There were gentle times between my man and me, too, happy times of harmony and contentment. My favourites were those rare Saturday nights when we had no plans and we would sit quietly on the old sofa we had rescued from my parents' garbage pile and watch terrible foreign films on David's brand-new TV. We would eat corn chips and enjoy the subtitles, but best of all we would snuggle under the old black-and-gray blanket my father had decided no longer belonged in the trunk of his car. We would park there together for hours, leaning against each other like a couple of forgotten two-by-fours in the darkest corner of the lumberyard.

Sometimes, on a cheerful Sunday afternoon, we would go for a walk in Allan Gardens. We would admire the spring blossoms or fall colours and David would breathe deeply of the fresh cool air that blew on our faces as we strolled. Sometimes we would absentmindedly link arms or hold hands, with David's large black-leather glove gently retaining my small blue mitten. He would smile at me and I would smile back.

David hated to see me cry, and he wasn't very helpful when I did, although I think he tried to make me feel better when he wasn't the cause of the distress. After one of our very rare disagreements, if he felt an unpleasant prickling of guilt rubbing at the back door of his conscience, he might trot home with a fistful of flowers for me. If the guilt were actually knocking on his brainstem, and he remembered saying some vaguely nasty things that should probably have stayed unsaid, the flowers might be something other than daisies. I have never liked daisies, but David loved them, and I think daisies were his way of saying, "Hang in there, kid." Personally, I would have preferred a flower that said something a little more poetic. For example, a clutch of purple and gold pansies would tell me how sweet he thought I was. Pink and white tulips would have hinted at the fact that he thought I possessed a quality of ethereal beauty. Wild roses — red ones with seven leaves and a thousand thorns —would have said he found me a tremendously untameable woman, mysterious and headstrong but complicated and wildly gorgeous. Daffodils would say that I was cheerful and warm and close to his heart. Orchids, violets, petunias, lilies-of-the-valley, gladiolas, primroses, buttercups . . . the list could go on and on for chapters, but the common (yet uncommon) denominator, would be the implication of beauty, dignity, fragility, strength, the gentle reminder of how much a man loves a woman, how he admires, treasures, respects and loves her, wants her to look at something beautiful tomorrow, when he's not even in the room, and think about him, and smile. Daisies just aren't that kind of flower. For one thing, they are about the most plain and ordinary weed growing in your average vacant lot. They live right there at the corner of Elmhurst and Main Streets and people walk by and toss cigarette butts and old chewing gum in their direction without even noticing that they are there. The daisies nod dumbly in every passing breeze as if to say, "Thank you for almost noticing me." They live there in that scraggly forgotten lot with last year's candy-bar wrappers, and an old gray running shoe, doggy doo-doo and a broken umbrella, shards of brown glass left over from one more beer for the road, a soggy blue mitten, an old leather glove. Daisies grow up through the detritus of other people's lives. Hang in there, indeed.

Daisies have long scraggly stems that usually have brown spots on them and they have very few leaves, Leaves are nice, a critical part of the unspoken phrase "I love you" that giving flowers is supposed to say. Daisy leaves are rare, as though the flower was worried about spending too much effort producing something that didn't have a really great return on investment. The flower itself is composed of numerous pointy white petals, as though it's meant to give stabs of pain, not joyful, unexpected ripples of pleasure. Compare that with, say, a rose. A rose petal is all curvy and foldy and hidden in beside all its neighbours, tucked up close with mysterious hidden passages and warm dewy secrets all waiting to be discovered. But a daisy offers nothing more than plain white pointy petals with a bug-eaten yellow centre. And no smell at all. If a flower isn't going to give off a beautiful, frangible scent that is the envy of all Creation, then don't you think it ought to at least look good?

However, daisies were, I suppose, better than nothing. David always sent his secretary, Anita, a dozen red roses on her birthday "Got to keep her motivated, you know," he'd say. The roses were very expensive, but, as he pointed out, he could deduct them as a business expense. Daisies were David's way of saying something that didn't involve too much emotion, dependence, admission of guilt, or gush. And roses?

David was not one to apologize verbally after a fight, unless he had cuffed me or shoved my shoulder just a little too hard as he broiled out of the room in a huff, and this happened so rarely it's hardly worth mentioning. I think he probably felt quite sorry on those occasions. But in general he felt justifiably committed to defending his point of view from anyone, anywhere, anyhow. He expected his woman to be tough enough to take what he dished out and sure, if she wanted to dish it right back, she was welcome to try. There was a puritanical self-righteousness to David's determination to remain unswayed by anyone else's opinion or interests, and this I did not share. I never worried about being swayed because swaying was the way I passed my life. You sway a little one way and sooner or later you'll be swaying back in the opposite direction, no harm done. If you really wanted something in life, you just had to sway towards it and sooner or later you'd sway your way up to it. Of course, you might sway into the path of an oncoming disaster or sway into a disgusting patch of something sticky that was tough to sway out of…but that was just part of the normal risk of life. In any event, all that swaying did not imply a lack of opinions, it just meant they were not always show-stoppers.

David wasn't like that. His opinions were very strong and endlessly important. David did not sway. He spear-chucked. He would set his sights on something he wanted and then throw the biggest darned spear he could find. If the first spear didn't bring down his prey, he would run headlong after it and sling another one. If that still didn't work, he'd bring out axes and daggers and even a rusty old shovel, if need be, until he got exactly what he wanted. What he wanted might be dead by that point. And the process was not a pretty one. But it made David happy and that was what counted to David.

So, you see, between his spear-chucking and my swaying, it was very hard —no, impossible —for me to deny him anything. Why cause a big ruckus over something that wasn't all that important to begin with? David almost always kept his voice reasonable and when I was alive I didn't have a bottom line, really, so a calm voice and a persuasive spear or two were all it took for him to get what he was after. Sometimes it took more spears or bigger spears and once a really *big* rusty shovel...but obviously those were times when I didn't sway very well and he won anyway. He always won. David was so much smarter than me. He was so much better educated —he had attended the very best schools. He was so cultured. He was stronger. Better looking. He had much nicer taste in clothes. While I could hold my own in most company, I hadn't ventured very far beyond my very small corner of this very large world. The Coveys did not hobnob with movers and shakers like the Masterson's.

David's father had been a president of the Toronto Stock Exchange and a Liberal minister of finance for the Ontario government. He was a wealthy man whose business interests ran the gamut from grain elevators in Saskatchewan to a small fishery in Nova Scotia. Jock was polite to me, but I often felt that enduring a family dinner with David's girlfriend or, eventually, his wife, was among his least favourite ways of passing an evening.

"Don't you do anything *else?*" he had asked me at our first meeting, as though working in communications and sailing, reading, and knitting were so pointless that the idea of spending one's day at such pursuits strained the limits of credibility. I believe he thought I was stupid. I tried to think of a "something else" that would impress this imposing man and decisively raise my desirability as a daughter-in-law in his eyes. It had never occurred to me before that my life was narrow. It was a surprising thought.

"Well, of course," I said, reaching back to my distant adolescence for a snuggle dolly of hope for my future. "Well, of course, I collect stamps."

Jock looked at me in shocked confusion, or maybe it was disgust. Perhaps both. I felt even stupider.

"Stamps," he replied.

"Stamps," I said.

"I didn't know you collected stamps," said David.

"Oh, yes. I have quite an extensive collection," I lied. I couldn't breathe.

"Would anyone like more coffee?" asked David's mother, Mimi, ever the gracious hostess. She smiled. There was no hint of arrogance in her voice. I felt enormously grateful to her.

While David's father's face often betrayed a range of emotion that would impress the most cynical Hollywood director, his mother's rarely displayed a look of anything other than serenity and sympathetic neutrality. She mounted an annual cultural symposium to raise money for the Toronto Symphony Orchestra and was involved in countless music-related projects. She was also one of Toronto's ladies who lunched. She lunched with artists and politicians, friends and musicians. She lunched with administrators of cultural institutions, and she lunched with her children, upon occasion. Although I was never invited to join her, I didn't really envy those who were. (What if I were expected to pay??!!) Mimi, who had been a highly regarded violinist in her youth, was pleasant company, I suppose, but the things she spoke about could never in a million years be of pressing concern to me. Her speaking voice even now was imbued with a lovely melodious lilt that was delightful to listen to but which always distracted my attention away from the content of what she had to say. While I felt merely stupid in Jock's company, I felt downright invisible when I was with Mimi.

David's entire family was larger than life. He had a sister who was a tax lawyer at a big Toronto legal firm, and his brother was an artist living in northern British Columbia. I had been raised in a good home with a hard-working father and a decent stay-at-home mother, and I was fundamentally a pretty ordinary person. My parents had seen to it that I received a good education, and I had worked hard to succeed in life. My parents were not what you would call gregarious, but they were nice people, both of them, and although they might not tell you much about themselves, they could wheedle a secret out of a CIA operative with their gentle, non-invasive interrogations. Mine was not a showy, show-off kind of a family. My father was a company man, and my mother wouldn't know a treble clef from a G-string. My little brother, Joey, had been a real cut-up at school —that is, in the early years – before he became a high-school dropout – and he had eventually parlayed that great brain of his into a college diploma that claimed he was a first-rate auto mechanic. My parents were as relieved as they were proud, as there had been a time when they worried he might end up in debt, in jail, a gang or a pine box. Even my normally restrained mother had cheered aloud at his vocational college graduation ceremony.

Looking back, I sometimes think that David married me out of spite —choosing me was his way of taunting his snobbish parents. Now his parents and I were stuck with each other, and I would just have to deal with their condescending indifference.

I don't know if Jock and Mimi had consciously taught their son to insist on getting his own way at any cost. And I don't know if my parents had consciously taught me to avoid conflict at any cost. But it was not a happy combination of inclinations, since the collision of the two styles meant the Spear-chucker would inevitably vanquish the Swayer. Every time.

I was certainly no good at spear-chucking, even when the issue at hand was important to me.

"How can a smart woman like you do so many dumb things, Teale?"

"What do you mean, David?"

"These dishes are new."

"Yeah. I bought them yesterday at Wal-Mart. They're seconds, and they were really cheap. I love a good deal!"

"I don't want to eat off these dishes, Teale. I want the old ones back."

"But David, the ones we had were the dishes your father had at university – they were old and chipped and none of them matched, for crap's sake. We can't keep serving people meals off those old things – it was time for a change."

"Don't use that language around me, Teale. It's revolting. Those dishes were fine. You're always throwing money away on stupid things. Who decided we needed new dishes, anyway? No one asked for *my* opinion on new dishes. And would I have picked ones with blue on them? Not bloody likely. Who the hell said you could buy new dishes? I bet they cost a fortune!"

"Well gee, David, I paid for them, not you and like I said, I got them for a great price, and they were the cheapest ones they had."

"What does 'great price' mean? I suppose they're seconds as well? Why are you always getting me frickin' second-hand things? I work hard enough that I should have the best, but oh no, little wifey needs to rush out and spend all my money on the things *she* wants. Do I ever get to buy the things I need to have? Oh, no, but grabby little Teale does. I'm outta here." He stormed out of the house.

After a year or two of strange outbursts over silly things like dishes, tea towels, toothpaste, and new shoes, I finally learned how this needed to work: marital harmony would depend on walking the fine line between doing what he wanted and feeling gutted. Do what you think he wants, second-guess his every mood, and you'll stay inside the safety zone. Stay inside the safety zone and you pretty much give up on thinking for yourself but that was okay because it meant I could breathe. Breathing is good. I don't know at what exact point I made that decision to aim for safety, but I did, and the temperature inside my heart gradually came to mirror the temperature inside my home.

Shades of Teal

David liked a cold house. Thirteen degrees centigrade, "And that's the max," he announced, "because we don't need heat. Let's keep the heat off at night, too, so we can sleep with the window open." David liked fresh air. I liked being warm.

I did the calculation, having been raised in an era when metric was foreign, European, even exotic. David was very proud of having made the intellectual leap to centigrade with ease. It showed he was a forward-thinking kind of a guy. I will probably go to my grave converting centigrade to Fahrenheit; applying the "double it and add 32" formula, I realized that David's prescribed maximum was a chill 58 degrees. Not perishing, perhaps, but too cold for relaxation. Certainly too cold for comfort.

"But David, I can't function at 13 degrees. Look, why don't we agree on 18 around the clock?" Sixty-eight degrees. Now *that* was living it up.

"Nope."

"C'mon David, *please*!!!"

"Nope."

"David that's just not reasonable."

"Oh, *I'm* not being reasonable. God, Teale, if I left it up to you, we'd have a damned beach party in here every night. You don't need that much heat —do you have any idea how expensive it is? You know, you really need to do something about the way you throw money around. You're very extravagant. My parents wondered if you were marrying me for my money, and I told them at the time that there was no way you would do such a thing but . . ."

"But David, I get so cold."

"Put on another sweater, then."

"I'm already wearing three, and . . ."

"NO! Jeez, Teale, if it weren't for me, we'd be totally bankrupt. I bust my butt every day at a job that's ten times more stressful every minute than yours is in your worst week —just to keep you in pantyhose —and you go throwing my good money away because you've got the stamina of a two-year-old. Do you think heat's free, or something?"

He looked disgusted and wounded at the same time.

No, I knew quite well heat wasn't free.

I also knew his suits did not need to cost thousands of dollars each, that the cases of wine he bought did not need to be privately imported from a particular little vineyard in France, that the evenings out he enjoyed with his friends didn't have to involve $400 charges on our credit cards, that he didn't actually need season's tickets to the games of every sports team in the city, that he didn't have to upgrade his stereo system every year, that . . . it didn't matter. He made more money than I did, he covered most of the expenses, and perhaps I *was* spending a little extravagantly. There had been that cute little sweater I had bought at the craft market the previous summer and I *did* have five pairs of shoes, which wasn't, strictly speaking, necessary —although I loved shoes in those days so very, very much. It wasn't, after all, my money I was spending, it was *our* money, although it came out of my bank account, and David made sure I was never lacking for anything I actually needed.

So, I did what I did best. I compromised. When he was home, the temperature stayed at 13 chill degrees, but as soon as he left, I would crank up the thermostat and sit in front of the open oven door with my hands cupped around a steaming mug of coffee. A hot oven was an efficient way to defrost myself, and as its 375 delicious degrees wafted out to greet my stiff morning fingers, I would dream of a southern vacation, a villa in Greece, a warm sandy beach, and a little control over the furnace. I would turn the temperature back down before leaving for work in case David got home first at the end of the day. I wanted to ensure that I was never caught stealing heat from my husband. David always checked the thermostat as soon as he got home from work to reassure himself that I hadn't tampered with the setting but he never said a word. Always cold, were Teale and I. Always cold.

11

Somehow, I still believed in the Magic, the one that had been promised to me all those years earlier, the one that said "Happily Ever After," so-help-me-God, Amen. But the effects of such propaganda can be devastating. I had bought into the myth: I knew that "marriage means compromise," and "no-one is perfect," and "there are bound to be rough patches." I had made a promise, and I would stick to it —no matter what.

When I crawled into bed at night, I believed my marriage was going exactly the way a marriage was meant to go and if I would only focus on the bright side, everything would be fine in the end.

If we were spending the evening at home, I would cook up a wonderful meal as soon as I got in the door. It might be curried shrimp and rice with a cunning little Thai salad on the side. Or perhaps braised lamb chops with homemade mint sauce, fluffy clouds of garlic mashed potatoes, and green beans dressed with slivered almonds, bacon, and cilantro. On a slow night, I might throw together some oven-fried spiced chicken with pesto noodles and steamed vegetables.

David liked a nice meal after a long day at work, but he was not fond of cooking himself. In fact, on the nights I worked late, if he ever got home before me, it would have been unthinkable for him to start dinner, although he might run out and fetch himself some takeout to spare me the trouble of cooking for him when I got home later. He was so thoughtful.

"I'm just no good in the kitchen, Teale," he would bray, pitifully. "No-one ever taught me how to cook. And you're so good at it — it would be a waste of time for me to even try."

Although I would have liked a night off at home every now and then, it would have been silly for me to complain. After all, we went out to eat so often that I certainly didn't need a break from cooking.

So we would sit and have a chummy meal together, during which David would talk about some of the deals he was working on and some of the people he was working with. I hung on his every word, of course, and didn't add much of my own news to the conversation. After all, my job was not nearly as fascinating as his.

As soon as he pushed his plate away, I would wash the dishes, do some laundry and maybe a little vacuuming, and start yawning ferociously. It would be eleven o'clock before I knew it, and I'd be longing for bed. We usually climbed the stairs together, changed into our pyjamas, and crawled into bed, tired and ready to sleep. I would peck my beloved on the cheek, roll over, sigh with contentment, and feel so very lucky to be so happily married. There would be no passionate writhing under the covers. David didn't favour that sort of activity much; in fact, he considered sexual congress slightly depraved and sexual urges best ignored until they disappeared. It was nice not to be pestered all the time for sex. Love didn't have to be wild — t could be comfortable and secure.

And so I'd lie in bed waiting for sleep to overtake me as my husband turned his long, handsome form away from me and settled his head into his soft pillow. It would take a while before I could relax as I never knew when David might leap out of bed to go tease me with the locks but eventually the sweet sound of his snores would fill the bedroom. Everything was wonderful.

But the cloak of night can create great illusion and when the sky is black and hearts are still and listening, wondering, hoping for soft words of sweet seduction, we sometimes feel our losses.

Sometimes a whisper of memory from a high school dance would drift into my mind as I slipped into sleep, and I would begin to dream, and with my dreams would come visions of darkness on a long-ago Friday night, cigarette smoke curling through the frosty air, feet crunching along an icy sidewalk. Jumping from our parents' cars, we'd scurry in twos and threes toward a portal of light that masqueraded by day as the front doors of our big red-brick school. We were not cold in those days — never cold, always warm with the wonder of the night, the wonder of being 15 or 16 or 17 and out to finally write the great adventure that should be our lives in bold, bright letters. Adventure lurked beyond the big glass doors of Parkside High, and it was troubled and thrilling and promising all at once. What mysteries and adventures waited for us within the canyon formed by the walls of our high school gym?

I remembered that gym. Dark as night it was, too, unlit and stuffy and smelling still of the all-pistons-firing running and jumping of teenage bodies, hard and eager and ardent in their strength as they leapt and twisted, strained and triumphed during grade 11 gym not six hours ago. Even above the noise of decades I can still hear the echoes of clean white shoes squeaking on the smooth tile floor as the basketball team raced down the court, practising for the big game Thursday against Mohawk Secondary School – "these are our mortal enemies, guys, let's all go cheer the boys on" — the echoes of those swift feet and excited voices, shrill and loud and young still fill the gym, that large cavernous gym, on Friday night, but the shoes aren't white now and no school gym uniforms grace the suddenly awkward bodies of the young people clutched inside the school now.

The boys stand with their backs pressed against the concrete-block wall on one side of the gym, while the girls slouch along the other, fidgeting and chatting with each other, flicking their hair and looking nonchalantly – they hope — at the boys. The genders face off across a no-man's land of anxiety. Which boy will be the first to cross the minefield of the dance floor? Which one will be brave enough or dumb enough or quick enough to be the first to ask a girl to dance? Which girl will be asked first? Oh, the anguish of it all! "What if I don't get picked?" "What if she says no?" Delicious anxiety is in the air we breathe on a Friday night in the Parkside gym.

The DJ is there, on a black plywood stage at the far end of the gym, sitting hunched behind a tiny pool of light that shines down on his not-quite-state-of-the-art control panel. He is dressed in black T-shirt and jeans, his long dark ponytail hanging neatly down his back. This man, this 21-year-old high school dropout, is the essence of teen cool and it is rumoured that Jody and his live-in girlfriend are planning to move to Texas as soon as they get the money together. Wow! Texas — land of wide-open spaces and longhorn cattle. A sky as vast as the seven seas. All of the men there, and even some women, own a gun. In Texas, nobody tells anybody what to do. Dreams come true in a place like that, and a man can become rich almost overnight.

But for now Jody, spends every Friday night in the high school gyms of London, Ontario, spinning tunes and tall tales, dreaming of his big break and knowing it'll all be different when he and Marla pack everything into his '62 Chevy and head south to freedom. For now he is an adult tall to these overgrown children, he is the high school priest of the dark night, master of fantasy, magician of music, man of all men. They glance over to where he sits in shadow behind the tiny prick of light that spills like starshine onto his equipment, they look up to him because he knows how to bring the night alive, to bring this crowd, any crowd, to a bold and brooding Friday night fever. There is no music missing from this man's stack of albums — look, there they all sit on the table beside him, hundreds of big, flat squares waiting for his careful command.

He'll do it again tonight, we know — he'll set the mood for a night that could be unlike all others that have ever come before. From eight o'clock to nine, he'll play a standard set of unremarkable tunes, odds and ends of things he likes to hear from time to time, none of them dance tunes per se, but all of them popular in a random, forgettable way.

Jody the DJ satisfies his own tastes while waiting for critical mass in the high school gym 'cuz there's no point wasting the good stuff on the nerds who spend the whole night standing there looking like homeless puppies waiting for a treat. Jody the DJ knows that outside the walls of this one room the world is on fire. Teenagers of every age, size, shape and description are visiting the bathrooms and scarfing Pepsis from the pop machine outside the cafeteria. They are heading out the back door for a stolen smoke in the bitter night air. They're checking out the booze and drugs appearing from the trunks of cars in the parking lot and more than anything else, they're scanning the turf to see who's where, who's hot, who's wired, and who's dangerous. Dancing is of secondary interest to most of the kids gathered here tonight. These kids are here for the scene. But Jody knows that, eventually, they'll come for the music.

Yes, only the nerds, the goody-two-shoes, brown-nosing "nice" kids enter the gym before nine o'clock and they're too scared to dance. Even if the music were any good, but it isn't, so the socially insecure and scared-to-death among us keep the walls standing straight and tall while everyone else looks for action. At 9:10, when the wholesome crowd in the gym is about to give up and go home, Jody the drop-out DJ slowly starts to ramp it up. Music is his life, his passion, his livelihood, and he dreams of one day making it big like Casey Kasem with his wildly popular American Top 40. Jody figures he plays a crowd like Jimmy Page plays guitar and when the moment is right — just right — he looks along the stiff lines of the shy and the flighty, along the vast yawning crater of an empty gym floor and nods knowingly to the phantom god of high school dances.

It's time. He carefully selects a record from the stack beside him, slips it from its sleeve, and checks the label. Yeah, this is it all right. Jody blows ever so lightly across the face of the album, checks the label again and sets 33 rpms of black magic down ever so carefully on a turntable that cost him an unholy fortune to buy. With a deft hand and a knowing glance at the floor, he guides the needle over one, two, three tracks and deftly sets it down. "Let the show begin," he's thinking, and from the massive black speakers idly sighing at the end of the gym emerge the dainty opening strains of Beethoven's Fifth Symphony.

Ahh — Beethoven's Fifth! A sigh of relief ripples down the ragged lines of opposing humanity milling in Park Side High's main gym: finally something we can dance to! Electric Light Orchestra's rendition of "Roll Over Beethoven" is everybody's kind of tune. We're all too hip to bother with the Chuck Berry version – the guy might've written the song but he's yesterday's news now. This is the good stuff. It belongs to us. And, oh man, it's now or never — seven brave boys scurry across the enormous gaping cavity in the middle of the floor and pick off a girl — but not just any girl — and away they go. Ten bars into the song, twelve couples are moving, shaking, and sweating, and by the time the tune ends, a quarter of the people in the gym have paired off and are trying not to smile. Not bad, but not good enough for Jody the DJ, who is here tonight to bring the whole world to his feet. Hard on the heels of "Roll over Beethoven" comes the next track on the album —"E-e-e-vil Woman" — the guy who wrote that one, that Jeff Lynne guy, man he was a genius, he *knew* this stuff, man, he *knew* how it felt to be played by a girl. Which might have been true or not but right now half the couples fall away, returning to their corners like prize fighters after a hard round in the ring, to chatter and giggle with the girls who *didn't* get asked to dance or to stand self-consciously with the other guys and pretend it wasn't really exciting to dance with Simone Harcourt, size 36D. Yeah, right.

The music is loud and getting louder, and soon comes T. Rex, purring and howling and moaning through a hard-core version of Marc Bolan's pulsing, throbbing, hunger of a song *Bang a Gong* that we knew as simply "Get it On". . .

Well you're dirty and sweet
Clad in black
Don't look back
And I love you
You're dirty and sweet, oh yea.
Get it on
Bang a gong
Get it on.

Pretty heavy stuff for the little grade nine kids, but what a great tune. Classic.

Back in the girls' bathroom Dinah Wilson has just vomited in the third stall, the hard luck of her first half-bottle of vodka, and none of the other girls know what to do about it. She should have stayed outside if she felt like barfing, stupid idiot. She's probably still a virgin, too. Duh. Who's going to clean it up? And where are we going to stash Dinah so the principal doesn't find out? Damn. The chaperone teachers and the uniformed cop are checking for signs of drugs and booze, but somehow Dinah has made it past them to the safety of the can, and now she's the problem of four 15 year-olds who would really rather be outside sneaking a smoke or inside rubbing thighs with the football team. At least Dinah didn't get any puke in her hair.

Inside the thumping walls of the gym, the mood turns a little soft and sleazy as Jody the DJ spins the very dangerous strains of Led Zeppelin's first track of the night. "Dazed and Confused" is none too danceable, but those with no shame ooze and groove to its sultry bluesy badness. Wasn't that one written by that guy Jake Holmes? Nah that's gotta be Jimmy Page's piece. Page wrote that one? Well, maybe. Robert Plant did the lyrics, right? Nah that was Jake Holmes's work. Does this matter right now?

The principal and assorted chaperones feel completely uncomfortable. Should they make the DJ turn it off? Should they turn the lights back on? While they stand and debate the issue, Robert Plant groans orgasmically to words penned by the one and only Jake Holmes, and Jody closes his eyes and longs for a cigarette:

Been dazed and confused for so long it's not true
When did a man ever bargain for you?
Lots of people talking, few of them know
The soul of a woman was created down below . . .

Couples, barely moving, melt into each other's bodies — boyfriends and girlfriends, lovers for now and forever, and it all seems so simple now, how good this night feels. What comes next? Here, in the middle of an ordinary tiled floor, with everyone and no-one watching, we're all feeling that lonely, forbidden fruit jangle of hormonal interest.

So bad, so good. In four minutes it's over and the spell is broken as April Wine pulls us to safety with gentle angel bells, easy guitar, bass and straight up vocals telling us what we all want to hope and believe and *"Tonight Is a Wonderful Time to Fall in Love."* And many do believe that could be true, as we float across the gym floor, singing softly to a tune Myles Goodwin wrote to capture this feeling, this floating-on-forever hope about our futures,

The two of us together
Doing things the way we do
And nothing seems to matter
As long as I can be with you.
And you know she can feel it
Cuz that's the way she likes to fly
Goin' on forever
And knowing that's the reason why.
She says tonight is a wonderful time to fall in love.
Tonight is a wonderful time to fall in love . . .

Down the hall in the cafeteria kids are sitting on tables, leaning on posts, talking and nudging up to get close enough to touch that special One, hoping he'll notice me in the glare of the fully bright lunch hall or wishing she would look at me just once with that dazed and knowing look in her eyes. There is chatter, there is teasing, there is laughter. There is Jack Grayson, a loner, a tough guy with few friends who is rumoured to be selling drugs from his locker outside Mrs. Gibson's English class. He's a handsome guy with white-blond hair and a slightly crooked smile.

And what a crush I had on him then. God how I wanted to feel his arms around me, pulling me to him, urging my face up to his with sweet, gentle words of passion. "I want you, Teale, I want you." Whatever that was supposed to mean to 16-year-old sweetheart me. To be wanted was not sexual, it was bigger than that, spiritual almost, grander than the sky in Texas somehow and otherworldly, and I didn't know then that wasn't the way things worked.

So we talked now and then, shyly and uncomfortably, in the halls of our school in that time long ago, and my heart pounded just a little harder when our paths crossed. By some mad twist of fate I never managed to have even one class with him, though we took the same basic course load and suddenly there was the second last dance of Grade 12 and he was there gently taking my hand, pulling me onto the dance floor, taking me in his arms and holding me, holding me, standing there holding me while words penned by Rick Davies and Roger Hodgson of Supertramp fame begged Teale to

Give a little bit
Give a little bit of your love to me
I'll give a little bit
I'll give a little bit of my love to you
There's so much that we need to share.
So send a smile to show you care ...

When it was over, my body shook and we stood there, burrowed tightly into each other, strangers barely knowing each other, barely aware of each other yet loving, holding, giving, taking, taking pleasure in the miracle of touch. It was all there except the one thing that would make it work: the courage to speak and the reality of compatibility. Jack held me, moved me, whispered some strange words in my willing ears, tender and persistent and then, as the last strains of the song faded away into the night and the others — whoever they were — began drifting off the dance floor, Jack Grayson took my face in his hands, leaned my face up to his and we kissed, a long, secret, yearning kiss, our first, our last words of passion and understanding and desire. It would never come to anything and we both knew that even then. I was the class scholar, the track-and-field star, the volleyball team captain; I did all my homework and held down a part-time job I did it all the right way. Jack Grayson sometimes came to school, sometimes not. His world was one of secret deals and older men, and God alone knows what other trouble he got up to.

What was the hook he had in me? And I in him? Two years after graduation, it was rumoured that he had been sentenced to two years less a day for a minor drug-related charge. And five years ago I heard he had checked into the psych hospital for some schizophrenia-related illness, said to be caused by a long history of drug abuse. I tried to call him once upon a time, got his number from an old phone book but a woman answered and I hung up, like a thirteen-year-old afraid of getting caught making a prank phone call. Was he all right? Did he remember what we'd said in one lonely, tender kiss, wrapped gently in the passion of a warm, winter's hug, that once I could still feel, on cold snowy nights, when I was alone and lonely? Poor Jack. Poor Teale.

There is no time for melancholia now, though because Elton John has just surprised the crowd with the first unconnected chords of a song he wrote with band mate Bernie Taupin that swings easily into lyrics we all know and remember now 'cause he's still saying

> *Hey kids, shake it loose together*
> *The spotlight's hitting something*
> *That's been known to change the weather*
> *We'll kill the fatted calf tonight*
> *So stick around*
> *You're gonna hear electric music*
> *Solid walls of sound.*
> *Say, Candy and Ronnie, have you seen them yet oh*
> *but they're so spaced out, B-B-B-Bennie and the Jetssssss*

The piano is sultry, an easy-bad surprise as we listen to the crowd roar, the kids cheering for Elton, applause, the beat, beat, beat, and B-B-B-Bennie and the Jetsssssss echoes through a crowded auditorium somewhere shiny and enormous, we can see the lights glittering, spotlights shining on Elton's gotta-be way-out costume, clapping handsintime to the wonderful steady, easy beat of that song, that song. There's a whistle from the crowd, but you can hear the darkness, smell the music, moving along just fine, we were almost there, almost everywhere in that year before the bloom faded. But before we can stay for long we're carried into a great big gymnasium somewhere else dark and cavernous and hundreds of people are sitting on the floor clapping the floor twice then clapping their hands together. Countless times throughout the song we hear the Blapp smack clap backdrop to Queen claiming the stage as Freddie Mercury hollers Brian May's immortal words:

> *Buddy you're a boy make a big noise*
> *Playing in the street going to be a big man someday*
> *You got mud on your face, big disgrace,*
> *Kicking your can all over the place singing*
> *We will we will rock you.*
> *We will we will rock you.*

Shades of Teal

Blapp smack clap. Blapp smack clap, monotonous, steady, unyielding, till the electric guitar takes over and leads right into the softer chapter, the one Freddie Mercury wrote and asserted, his appeal for a man's dignity, his proud call to action:

I've paid my dues, time after time,
I've done my sentence but committed no crime,
And bad mistakes, I've made a few
I've had my share of bad kicks in my face but I've come through.
We are the champions my friend . . .

And we were. The harmonies are beautiful, lyrical, echoing down the long chamber of memory that connects us to those days of music — the joy of the beat, the jungle of the drums beating, throbbing, keeping us there, glued to a vast and crowded red and white and beige and black tiled floor and, wondering what was going to come next and suddenly I am back in the here and now and there is no Jody the DJ, no Jack Grayson, no faint tang of cigarette smoke and vodka, mixed in with the stuffy smell of sneakers and sweat. There is no pale-faced Dinah Wilson crying in the parking lot, no mother standing guard at the front door when I get home, no lying awake reviewing the magical events and sensations of the evening in the delicious solitude of my bedroom.

Like princes and princesses, dancing at the ball, hoping for a token of love's warm embrace, hoping he would be the one, the forever-till-I-die one for me. The fairy tale writ large upon the landscape of a high school gym floor. Who closed the book, and when? We were so innocent then. And sweet and gentle and yearning and never so lonely as I am right now. It was all so real, everything was so possible when I was 16, 17, 18 years old and breathlessly seeking my prince.

Just a handful of years later, when I first laid eyes on David Masterson, I knew the search was over. He was the logical end of my fairy tale dreams of love and devotion, romance and commitment. My prince had come, and my prince was intelligent, handsome, educated, polished, sociable and possessed of a terrific sense of humour. My prince said he loved me, he said I completed him and he said he respected me. Swept away on the wings of romance, the romance that maybe existed only inside my own imagination, I gave in to his wooing, gave in to a heart that said "Dance with me." and I danced, and I danced.

We ate well, holidayed well, and entertained with the best of all possible resources. And when David listened, when he really wanted to listen, he looked at me with his full attention and I felt more important than I'd ever felt before. And if he did things I didn't like, I would tell myself that marriage means compromise.

I'd have to remind myself of this more and more often as the years went by. The man I loved, the man I was committed to forever, teased me, annoyed me, ignored and offended me. But you can't abandon a marriage over little things like that, can you?

No, divorce has to have a real cause, like habitual infidelity or physical abuse or criminal behaviour. David wasn't nasty. David wasn't a playboy. David never hit me, really. David wasn't even boring. We would be married forever. But he would never hold me tenderly in his arms for the last dance of the night, never whisper sweet words in my ear, never stroke my face and tell me how much he loved to be with me, never respond to me with passion, never scoop my lips into his in the hungry, passionate embrace of love...

It took me three years of marriage to realize that's all I ever wanted in a prince, but by then, it was too late to look for it.

12

The rain was teeming down on a dark Friday night sometime before our third anniversary and the windshield wipers made a squeaking whine as they struggled to clear water off the cold glass of David's sporty two-year-old BMW. I loved his new car —it had a gorgeous leather interior, power everything, a swanky sunroof, and plenty of legroom. David said it had a big engine, and although I wasn't crazy about the colour —a champagne brown that was supposed to radiate expensive elegance —it was better than the old bucket of bolts I had to drive. As David so reasonably pointed out, I always took public transit to work (like the good citizen I was), and, unlike him, I never had to impress anyone.

"You're a civil servant, for crying out loud," he said. "No one cares what kind of car you drive."

David sincerely wished he didn't have to spend so much money for wheels, but people in the business world were predators and alert for any signs of weakness in an adversary.

"If you don't look successful, Teale, they won't think you're any good at what you do. If they don't think you're any good at what you do, then they won't do business with you. We want them to do business with me, don't we Teale? Geez, a thousand a month isn't so bad when you think of what some of the other guys in the firm spend on a car. Imagine if I drove a top-of-the-line Benz or a fully loaded Audi!!! Whoa! And don't forget the insurance on those babies!!! We're lucky I can get away with a Beamer!"

"One day, the world is going to hand me business on a silver platter," he said, smiling at me.

Silver platters are good.

I thought about what he'd said for a moment, realized he was right, as usual, and felt sullen anyway.

"But a better car would be nice, David," I said.

"Don't worry, I'll get a better car in a year or two. This one's nice enough for now —I'm not complaining or anything, but it isn't all that impressive, you know?"

"Well, um, actually, I meant it would be nice if *I* could drive a better car," I ventured. Nothing ventured, nothing gained.

David just looked at me. It was a surprised look. A slightly annoyed look. This was something he hadn't thought of before.

"Aren't you just glad you've got wheels at all, Teale?" he asked. "Plenty of people don't own a bicycle, let alone a car. And you didn't have any car at all when I met you. Just give me a couple more years —two more good bonuses and I'll get a new one. Maybe you can drive this car then." He smiled that cooperative, loving, smile of his, expecting my compliance, pleased when it appeared. I nodded, absently. He had such beautiful eyes. Maybe one day I would get to drive this car. I should be more patient.

But my 14-year-old black Ford Mustang was a problem *now*. I shuddered to think about the effect advancing senility would have on its already nasty personality. It wasn't fond of exerting itself, particularly when a large construction vehicle was riding its bumper. And it had perfected the art of the mistimed stall.

On outings of more than 20 minutes, it would practically sit down on the curb, wipe its forehead, and whine, "I'm hot and tired. Give me a drink." This was Stang-speak for "Holy Crap I'm overheating – WATER! QUICK!" My Mustang's transmission was unreliable, too, sometimes flatly refusing to slip into gear. Shifting became a power struggle, and backfiring was par for the course. Oil spots on the driveway prompted David to ask why I didn't get my car serviced more regularly. Getting the beast to start involved something akin to tribal ritual. The heater worked sporadically, the air conditioning not at all, and the radio had long since given up the ghost. I could depend on the wiper blades as long as it wasn't actually raining and I'm not sure the shocks had ever been all that good. Although I was certainly grateful to have any car, I had to admit to an enormous fear of driving that vehicle. I was afraid we were destined to meet our Maker together. And I had a hunch that that would have been all right with David's mother. She had been the Mustang's first owner, passing it on to David's sister, who had let her boyfriend drive it for a few years before handing it back to Mumsy, who then generously allowed me to buy it from her for several thousand dollars more than its book value.

David had thought that my buying his mother's car would endear me to her, and the fact that I used my own hard-earned cash to do so really ought to have impressed the rest of the Masterson's, who secretly thought I was out to harness the family fortune. I wondered about that fortune, actually, as David and I didn't see any of it floating into our bank account, and David was extremely reluctant to talk about it. Sure, his parents had given us substantial help in buying our house, and every winter they paid for us to fly to Florida to visit them at their stunning oceanside villa. But otherwise we had surprisingly little to do with them, and David didn't seem to have any Masterson cash. I began to believe they were incredible tightwads —for one thing, the Black Mustang with the black heart did not appear to have ever been well maintained.

"David, are you sure that car is safe?" I had once asked him.

He looked at me, horrified.

"You don't think I would let you drive around in a dangerous vehicle, do you, Teale?" he said. "You're my wife —I would rather die than let anything happen to you." He put his strong arms around me, pulled me into him, and kissed the top of my head. "That old horse has millions more miles in it before it's done."

"Kilometres," I corrected him. It was nice to catch Mr. Metric in a measurement error. He smiled down at me.

"Kilometres."

And so I kept the car. What else could I have done on my salary? And I often smiled to myself at the memory of the tenderness David had shown me.

"Teale, I would love to get you a nice new car —tomorrow," he said that rainy Friday night. The BMW's electronic wiper blades swished softly. It sure was quiet in his car. "We just can't afford it." He shook his head regretfully, looking every inch the humble husband. It was true. I knew. I did the bills. I wrote cheques for thousands of dollars every month to credit card companies. I queried the hundreds of dollars spent on dinners I hadn't shared and the hundreds more spent on clothing. I'd never dare to spend such amounts on myself.

"You don't go anywhere where you need to look good, Teale," David had once replied when I told him I wanted to buy a new outfit. "My job is more important than yours. I'm supporting this family. My appearance is everything to your future." So right, so right. Silver platters.

As for the meals out: "Client entertainment is so important in my business. If I do well, then you and I will be rich some day." Some day. And yet I was puzzled as to why we weren't already rich on his $150,000-a-year salary and my meagre $50,000. How could two people not be incredibly well off earning $200,000 a year?

David was working his way up in the dog-eat-dog world of corporate finance. At 31, he already had a reputation for being a hard worker, a relentless pursuer of the perfect deal, a tough guy, a man who got things done. I never really understood his business. He'd explained it to me when we first started seeing each other, and I had listened with rapt attention as he spoke of leveraged buyouts, stock and share options, hostile takeover bids, poison pills, and corporate strategy. I asked numerous detailed questions, but I was never really sure I understood anything other than the fact that he put people who wanted to buy a company in touch with people who wanted to sell a company (and vice versa), managed the deal to its closing, and took a great big chunk of money out of it for his company, Lewis and Simms. Well aware that the business world is full of nasty people out to cheat widows and orphans of their precious savings, he also took a keen interest in the ethical side of the business and had become something of an expert in ensuring that all Lewis and Simms deals conformed to a modern code of ethics. Lewis and Simms was a very forward-thinking company. That meant causing no harm to the environment and, above all else, it meant ensuring that women had pride of place at board meetings, luncheons, and other high-profile events. He was on his way to becoming a star in the head-spinning world of Canadian finance. And he was *my* husband. Gosh, I was proud of him.

The Toronto office of Lewis and Simms was a subsidiary of a giant New York firm, but it employed upwards of 150 people, and David was, apparently, one of their leading lights. He did, indeed, work very hard —in the office by 8:00 a.m., seldom home before 8:00 p.m. Weekends weren't sacred, although he never missed his golf games on Saturday and Sunday mornings. Spring, summer, and fall; rain or shine. He was frequently invited to dinners and receptions, and sometimes it was mandatory that I go along as "wife of."

"Yup, gotta bring the old girl out and show her off every now and then," he'd say. I would smile at the preposterous notion that I was an old girl.

But old girl or "wife of," it all meant that I was expected to look lovely, listen carefully, and smile a lot. Yes, I was a "wife of." We tend to say "spouse of" nowadays, since the supportive husband has theoretically become almost as prevalent as the supportive wife used to be. Being a supportive spouse is an extremely important job. If you had to hire a stranger to be a supportive spouse, it would cost you an unconscionable amount of money and you would go broke, so it is very helpful to have a committed household contract with someone who can be convinced to do it for free.

The supportive spouse is expected to keep him or her-self happily occupied for countless hours a year while the Important

Spouse goes to work early, comes home late, and disappears for days (sometimes weeks) on end on important business trips to exotic locales. (The important spouse often insists that it's not what it looks like —in fact, it's no fun to visit these places alone, and all you get to do is work anyway. Tell that to your therapist.) Supportive Spouse must look after all the details of running the home, including shopping for groceries and cooking dinner, paying the bills, and picking up Important Spouse's dry-cleaning (which s/he forgot about last week when it actually *wasn't* an emergency.) Supportive Spouse is happy to let Important Spouse sleep in on weekends, nap at will, and golf or lunch or shop for fun. Supportive Spouse spends a lot of evenings home alone or out alone, because unexpected work has suddenly cropped up that Important Spouse must attend to in order to build his/her reputation as the company's star performer and the whole future of the entire world depends on Important Spouse getting that work done. Supportive Spouse must never complain, because that would sound petty and jealous, and even though s/he may feel like s/he works as hard as Important Spouse, s/he doesn't make as much money.

Important Spouse busts his/her butt to buy Supportive Spouse stuff s/he wants, according to some versions of the story. Important Spouse makes all kinds of sacrifices for Supportive Spouse, apparently. A few times a year, Supportive Spouse is trotted out at public functions or company events in order to make Important Spouse look stable and happily connected to someone who is moderately more intelligent than leaf lettuce and substantially more attractive. So, you see, although Supportive Spouse plays this very important role in Important Spouse's work life, s/he doesn't need to drive a decent car. And as long as both parties to the arrangement are reasonably happy working as a team, everything tends to work reasonably well. And if one of them gets to drive a BMW all the time, then the other one gets to drive it every now and then. Right?

The BMW was a dream to drive. And, as we cruised through the rain-washed Toronto streets, humming along in companionable silence, hurtling through time and space like a little planet with pretty hubcaps, I was entranced by the beauty of the night that twinkled at me through streaming glass. I watched, transfixed, as the lights of oncoming cars burned through the sheets of wet air mist. Eerie halos of light encircled the street lamps above us. There is something so holy about the quality of light in a rainstorm, and —

"Why are you so quiet?"

"Hmmm?"

"We've been in this car for nearly twenty minutes, and you haven't said a word to me for the past ten. Everything all right?" David liked attention.

"Well, I was just looking at the sky and thinking how beautiful it was and wondering how I would describe it to someone who had never been out in the rain at night. Don't you just love a rainy night?"

"Yeah, I guess it's OK."

"No, no —not just OK, David! Look at the streetlights shining up there in the fog with that murky amber glow. They're like tent poles holding up an enormous dark canvas. What if we were actually in a huge tent lit by millions of tiny points of light? What could possibly be out there, beyond the safety of the tent? Don't you ever wonder about things like that?"

"No," said David. He looked at me sideways, frowning. He didn't get it. He didn't wonder.

"What's tonight, unofficial poetic license night?" He smirked. He was very witty.

We were on our way to the lovely west-end home of David's dear friends Janey and Robby Johnson for a friendly fondue dinner. We had dedicated ourselves to cultivating a decent social life —the kind my parents never had, but which was, of course, second nature to the Mastersons — so we accepted every dinner invitation that came our way. It meant that we'd have to reciprocate, but I loved to cook. We worked hard and played hard, and every now and then we had an evening like this one that crystallized in my mind as a memorable occasion.

The Johnsons had achieved success at a fairly young age. Robby, an accomplished and respected orthodontist, had a taste for beauty and design, and Janey, a lawyer, loved art. Their house was set back from the road in a secluded neighbourhood, shielded from view by an old-fashioned stone wall ,a row of cedars, and a slight rise, all artistically undulating around the property's perimeter. The grounds were meticulously kept —the lawn manicured and the flower beds filled with spring blooms. Off to one side was a tennis court and there was a huge diamond-shaped swimming pool set in a rock garden behind the house, out of sight, and ivy climbed soothingly up to the eaves. A wrought-iron gate led into a courtyard set with a beautiful little angel-shaped fountain and the front entrance was framed by two fluted concrete columns. We rang the bell, and heard, faintly, from within, the first few bars of Mozart's "Elvira Madigan" symphony. No expense had been spared to perfect this dream home. I was awed and, truth to tell, envious.

I could never have afforded to buy even our three-bedroom brick-and-stone beauty on my own salary. But this was how I really wanted to live —luxuriously. Maybe someday, if we worked really hard and David kept driving expensive cars for the sake of the family...

I felt a little too casual in my dark-blue cotton skirt, but I'd put on a dressy little sweater, and my shoes and earrings matched my purse, so perhaps I'd do for the occasion. There was only so much one could accomplish on a tight budget, and I had to buy all of my clothes secretly, from my own salary. I made monthly retirement and pension fund contributions, and 10 percent of my paycheque went into a joint savings account we kept for emergencies. The amount left after taxes was paltry. I had to run my own car, buy the groceries, pay the phone and hydro bills, pay for my own entertainment, hairdressing, and makeup, and buy birthday and Christmas gifts for family and friends. David paid the mortgage and the heating bill and covered almost all of our shared entertainment. He also paid any expenses related to our holidays, which tended to be stressful visits to his parents in Florida simply because his parents paid for the airfare. There never seemed to be much money available for clothes for me, which David considered frivolous anyway, since I worked with bureaucrats all day.

"Your clothes always look OK to me," he had once said. I was certain that other women could tell that I shopped at clearance centres and second-hand stores. Just about everything I wore was old and unglamorous, of poor quality. These were not the clothes I wanted to wear. They were generally ugly, unflattering, serviceable. I used to love to splurge on myself every now and then —I'd save up and buy an outrageously expensive outfit and stun the crowd with how put-together I was. All that had come to an end a few years back. There was just never enough money. When David received a salary increase, I thought it might be a good time to ask him for a little help with some of my bills, but before I could summon up the courage to ask, I noticed that the stress lines on his face had deepened.

"What's the matter, Davey?" I asked.

He gave an enormous sigh. His shoulders slumped and his head sagged.

"I don't know, Teale. I try and I try and I try, but there just never seems to be enough money for everything. I wanted to buy you a really nice Christmas present this year, but I just can't manage it. I love you so much, and I really want to give you all the things you want, but money's just a little too tight right now."

He looked at me, eyes clouded with concern, face grim.

"But David, I don't need fancy things to make me happy. We have everything we need, and we have so much fun all the time — that's enough of a Christmas present for me. Don't worry about it, we'll get by. We'll work it out together. We're a team, remember?" And I smoothed his furrowed brow and kissed him gently on the cheek. "We're a team!"

And so Christmas that year had been modest —as usual. David gave me a jigsaw puzzle featuring some beautiful hummingbirds, brilliantly red and turquoise and purple. And I, naughty girl that I was, had saved for a year and bought David a set of graphite golf clubs. Expensive? Dreadfully! Outrageously! All that money for some sticks to whack a ball with? But he'd been talking about those clubs non-stop since early spring.

"Next year, I'm going to get some of those new graphite clubs," he'd said as he cleaned his old clubs in the basement at the end of the season. "Then you can have these old ones." And old they were, passed on to him by an uncle when David was just 16 years old. But they were still quite serviceable.

"Gee, thanks, David!"

As he unwrapped the great heavy box that held the fruit of months and months of serious saving, his face lit up like that of a six-year-old who has just received everything on his Christmas list.

"Wow, these are beauties!" he said.

"I know you said you were going to get them in the spring anyway," I replied, "but I thought you might want them ahead of time just to know they're yours."

"Wow, thanks! I bet you even got me a new bag to put them in, too!"

No, I hadn't got him a new bag, I thought dejectedly. I fervently wished I had.

"Oh," said David.

Despite the lack of a bag he was clearly excited and I thought he was going to sleep with his new clubs, he was so happy with them. He fondled them all through the Christmas season and could hardly force himself to put them away when we took the tree down. I was so glad he was pleased with the gift. The joy of Christmas truly is in the giving, and I was thrilled to have made my husband so happy, although the disappointing lack of a bag hung between us. So what if the clubs had cost me more than I could afford? How do you quantify the happiness you give others? What more could I ask for?

Well, a china cabinet, maybe. I really wanted a china cabinet. But that would have to wait a few more years. We had talked about it on and off for ages, and David didn't see the need, but it wasn't really about need for me. It was about desire. My grandmother had bequeathed to me her entire mint-condition set of Royal Crown Derby china, and I couldn't wait to display it in a worthy setting. It was currently packed in boxes in the spare room closet, but I hoped that one day we could place it in a beautiful cabinet and use it every Sunday. I loved my grandmother. Dad's mum was fun and irreverent and energetic and loving. I still missed her chuckling English accent, the way she cocked her head when she was listening to someone, the way she'd perch her glasses on top of her head and then promptly forget where she'd put them. A granny is a precious thing, and my granny's china was a reminder to me of how much I loved her.

But the china cabinet would have to wait and at least David was thrilled with his new golf clubs. When spring came, I knew he'd be out again on Saturdays and practicing at the driving range —unless it was raining too hard. If it was, he'd no doubt hold court in the clubhouse instead.

The night before our dinner with Janey and Robby Johnson — perhaps in a fit of pre-game jitters, since I didn't know our hosts very well —I had asked David what I should wear.

"Oh, it's probably real casual."

"Could you check for me, please?"

"Why?"

"So I don't look like an idiot again. I'm tired of turning up in the wrong clothes, David." I'd stopped swaying long enough to take a stand.

"You worry too much, Teale." David was wearing his "poor Teale" look. "Nobody cares what you look like as long as you're good company. So what if you always wear the wrong thing — people don't care! You do your best to look as good as you can, and that's all that matters." This was his comforting speech. I had heard versions of it before. He hugged me and gave my hair an unwelcome ruffle.

"I guess." Clearly I would have to figure this one out for myself.

"You always look fine, and I'm hardly ever embarrassed by your appearance. Any old thing will do."

Any old thing will do. How many times had I heard that old chestnut? The action shifts to a Thursday night a year or two earlier. The camera zooms in on David and Teale at home. In a few day's time, they will attend a get-together hosted by Lewis and Simms, corporate captains.

"What's the dress code Saturday night, David?" Supportive Spouse should verify which attire will reflect best on Important Spouse. It's in the rule book, I'm sure. Silver platters, you know.

"Wear something casual," Important Spouse instructs.

And so Casual Teale goes to the casual dinner function in her sensible wool skirt with matching sweater and penny loafers, only to be blinded by the sequins, and satin, four-inch heels and arched looks of the wives, girlfriends, and lovers of Lewis and Simms employees. Strike one. A painful night —one to be consigned to the locked closet of embarrassing memories.

Cut. Four months later, the camera again seeks out Teale and David at home on Fairlawn Ave. It's a Tuesday morning, and Teale is doing her makeup while David knots his tie. They are both crammed into the little upstairs bathroom, and both face the mirror. Teale has run out of mascara again and is pumping the wand wildly in and out of the tube in hopes of squeezing out just a little more for the day. . One is not supposed to do this, as one risks contaminating the black goop that will be applied to the tender eyelash bed, but who actually follows all the hygiene rules where mascara is concerned? There might be just enough for one more day. Drat! Teale realizes she should have bought mascara on payday. Now she will have to wait another nine days. She feels so bland without mascara.

"What kind of a function is Thursday's reception going to be, Davey?" she asks, suddenly.

"Fairly formal," he says decisively. But Teale is catching on.

"What are you wearing?"

"I guess I'll go straight from work in my business suit —I think it's one of those snazzy outdoor deals, you know, with one of those big tents and an orchestra of some sort.

"Are you sure, David? I don't want to look stupid *again*." Teale has reached for a spear.

"Teale, I'm only telling you what I know." He's offended now, because she's doubting him.

And Teale arrives in a saucy little black number with a bow at the waist and matching shoes, evening bag, and dangly earrings. She sits on the sidelines while David joins in the square dancing. He's wearing casual slacks, a sweater, Docksiders, and a great big smile. She holds his sweater while he dances, drinks sangria by the boatload, and waits until she gets home to cry in the privacy of the downstairs bathroom. Strike two.

The funny thing was, Cinder-Teala usually thought that she looked pretty good until she arrived at the door of the palace.

"How do I look, David?" I had asked an hour before Mozart began chiming inside the front door of the Johnson's *Architectural Digest* dream home. Pre-game jitters.

"Those clothes look OK. Hey, have you seen my cashmere sweater, Teale?"

"No, no, really, David! How do I look?" I wanted a real answer. Maybe I wanted praise.

"Oh, a little huffy tonight, are we?" he asked. I chose to ignore that.

"No, not at all. I just want you to tell me whether I look all right —I mean, I don't know what the plans for the evening are. How I look is important to me."

"Well, you know something Teale?" he had adopted his fatherly voice now. "I think you spend far too much time worrying about your appearance." He turned to the mirror and began buttoning his shirt. "*Professional* career women don't spend all day cluck-clucking in front of a mirror. They get out there and perform for their corporation, for their country, for their cause. Fussing about how you look is very old-fashioned, and frankly I'm surprised that you would stoop to that level. You're better than that, aren't you?"

I looked at him, the fire gone from my soul and anger hung from my lips like a thin silk of drool. I was confused.

"David, are you questioning my professionalism?"

"No, no, no, of course not. I just wonder why a woman with your intelligence and understanding and personal strength would trivialize herself by obsessing about her appearance, that's all. I admire you, Teale. The woman I married doesn't care about clothes or the way she looks; she's a deep-down real-life thinking person. She's hard-working and interesting and kind-hearted. I didn't marry you for your looks, you know —you're no Barbie doll, you know."

I just stared at his back as he buttoned his handmade French shirt. Something stirred again inside me.

"Now, where did I put that sweater?" The conversation ended there, and I spent the next ten minutes assuring myself that I was indeed professional and intelligent. David was right. One's appearance was only relevant on the most superficial level of social interchange. It really needn't concern "thinking people" like David and me. I so admired his brain! His approach to life was so sensible, so down-to-earth. He was always so calm, so cool, so *right*. It humbled me.

And so tonight at the Johnson's it would be different —a triumph for me. What did it matter what I wore? I was a world-beater, I was strong. My man thought I was intelligent and professional. I stood just a little straighter than usual as Janey Johnson opened the door. Glancing at her black pencil pants and oversized cotton sweater, I realized I was dressed just right. Thank God!

"Oh, Teale, what a beautiful sweater," she gushed. There was hope for this evening yet.

The Johnson's foyer was a decorator's fantasy: coral-coloured walls, overstuffed white chairs, Persian rugs, and a richly patterned mosaic tile floor. The light fixtures were modern and dramatic, and the art that hung on the walls was real: huge oil paintings, dainty watercolours, charcoal drawings, pastel sketches, and sculptures — everywhere. I could have spent the entire evening gazing at each piece in the collection, one by one. David loved art too, but he was really there for a good time with our hosts and the other guests — people he considered "substantial" men and women, just like us. I had met them all at various times over the past few years, and I'd discovered that they had myriad inside jokes that dated back years. I still wasn't getting most of them and whenever I asked, David to explain later, he promised to do it later. He never did and I would forget and I ultimately never felt any closer to these people who were so important to my husband. Janey and Robby and Carole and Tim Larson had been friends since their university days. Tim was an orthodontist and Carole was a writer. Rounding out the party were Eric and Carmela Rinders, who were teachers.

"What are you writing these days, Carole?" I asked, jealously. I thought briefly of my own career as a media flack for the provincial government. To me, writing was a hallowed occupation. To be a writer was to exist on a plane far above the work-a-day world, to be exempt from the banal hardships of everyday existence, to inhabit a realm where the imagination could soar —a realm where what was actually said and done could be magically replaced with what might have been, or should have been, said and done; where stories flowed freely from one's innermost secret places, tripping and rippling like a runaway brook ending who-knew-where but somewhere intense and beautiful and uplifting. To be a writer —a real writer, not a hack journalist or a writer of stuffy speeches —was to be exalted, to be...

"Poetry," said Carole. She looked at me coolly as she took a long drag on a long brown cigarette. "Lots and lots of poetry." She had a raspy voice that did not sound poetic, really.

"I write poetry about dogdirt, poetry about underarm hair, poetry about pools of blood. Real-life poetry." Her lips wrinkled into an imitation of a smile as she spoke, but she sounded bored and terribly self-important. Carole was a little older than I was, perhaps about 34, and she had beautiful volumes of long blonde hair, hair that cascaded down her back like a golden waterfall. She looked and moved like an established writer might: her long, thin fingers, nails painted fire-engine red, punctured the air as she spoke; her hands were strangely at odds with the rest of her body —she was short and curvy. Carole was fond of jewellery. I marvelled that she could afford to spend such an obvious fortune on personal adornment. How I would have loved to go shopping for jewellery —costume pieces, or whatever struck my fancy. But I was too serious about my responsibilities, too worried about the mortgage and the heating bill and David's credit card expenses. Besides, I could just imagine David's reaction if I went on a jewellery-buying spree.

"You paid how much for that thing?" he'd demand. "You do realize that money is tight, don't you? We could have bought some stock options with that cash. We could have brought down the mortgage. I could have put that money toward a new car for you. And you bought *jewellery*? You know, Teale, I try to keep us more or less solvent, but it's very difficult when you insist on behaving so childishly. I guess you and I just have different priorities..."

Naturally, there was no convincing comeback to a statement like that. He was right. He was always right. But sometimes I wanted to be terribly, terribly frivolous. Sometimes I wanted to be wild and exotic and a little predatory, like Carole was. Sometimes I wanted to shed the good-girl gift wrap I always wore and turn tigress —prowl through the world like an untameable seductress. I wanted to wear bold colours and do something dramatic with my hair. I wanted to wear intriguing jewellery and unusual shoes. I wanted to samba until dawn and drink martinis and champagne. I wanted to fly to New York for the weekend and shop at the most exclusive boutiques —just once. Carole could get away with doing everything I secretly yearned to do, but why did I disrespect her for it? David, of course, did not approve of my little urges. But did his opinion really matter? My mother had cared about my father's opinion, even though there was clearly no real romance between them. I could never really understand it. She barely spoke to him, but if the opportunity arose for her to do something out of the ordinary, her stock response was, "Oh, but your father just wouldn't approve." I guess that was a safer way of saying, "I just don't want to." Or, "I've given up trying different things."

David and I were dramatically different people from my parents, so any need I might have for David's approval would have to be based on something other than fear. I truly wanted to please him. I wanted him to see me as the perfect wife he always seemed to think I could be. It never occurred to me to wonder why that was important to me. And it's too late now. But there Carole was that night —a sultry, slightly dangerous, terribly experienced woman of the world wearing a huge chunky necklace that appeared to be little more than a pewter rock on a pewter chain ("No, it's platinum, actually," she said, eyebrow raised. I suppose one ought to know the difference) and matching earrings. The big gold ring on her finger bore the letters "FU." She wore a tight black sweater unbuttoned just a little too far for mixed company and, as many well-endowed women tend to be, she seemed casually proud of her breasts. Her skirt was a black-and-gold sarong that fell open when she sat, fully revealing her shapely thighs and raising the obvious question in the minds of all present: Was she wearing any underwear? One hesitates to judge someone for such a small transgression, but I've never met a married woman who genuinely likes the type of woman who is obviously *sans culottes* in mixed company. And I wondered how it made Carole's husband feel? I always wore underwear myself, and I'm quite certain that David would have been more than a little distressed at the thought of me parading around so seductively in front of his friends. Actually, David probably would not have appreciated such a show in private either.

Tim looked at his wife constantly, touched her, caressed her back, and laughed at her coarse jokes about ingrown toenails and her sex life. He watched her the way a little frog might watch a large and dangerous water snake —a mixture of fear and respect curdling his features. I knew right then that I would never be a writer.

There was little enough to be said about Tim Larson. Tall, quiet, and presumably madly in love with his wife, he spoke mostly when spoken to Tim was an orthodontist, worked with his hands, made a lot of money, and spent little of it. That night, I noticed that he didn't jump into conversations about topical issues. After a while he left Carole's side and disappeared into the kitchen, where he lingered for the rest of the evening, chatting amiably with Janey. Just shy, I thought at the time. And Janey was so gregarious and friendly and anyone could warm up to her instantly. She seemed to sincerely want her guests to enjoy themselves. She radiated approachability, she seemed so down to earth, a quality I have rarely noted in lawyers, male or female. She was, however, a corporate lawyer, not a mainstream, Bay Street, down-in-the-trenches lawyer; her niche was in what many of her colleagues would consider a backwater of the profession. She worked regular hours and made good money, and the legal issues she dealt with were not the kind that would keep her awake at night —the kind of life-and-death, career-threatening conundrums that had many a Bay Street predator tossing and turning. Janey was fun, and with her short dark hair neatly sprayed into place, she even looked like a Janey. I liked her.

Shades of Teal

Alicia and John Clark were at the Johnson's that night too. Like David, John was a director of the Royal Yacht Club and he was an avid and respected sailor. Although David and I rarely sailed together after our first year of courtship (and never since we'd married), John and Alicia took their sleek, thirty-five-foot yacht, "The Goodfellow," out for a spin several times a week. David often called from the office on a Friday night to say he was going out with them, but it was usually too late by then for me to go home and change and get back down to the club in time to join them. David always felt really bad about that. John was a money manager at a big downtown firm, and Alicia was a housewife. She was lovely and calm and always had a sweet smile on her face. We didn't speak much. She was very hard to get to know, and I hadn't a clue what kind of "getting-to-know-you" questions to ask a housewife, particularly one whose children were in school all day, who employed a nanny and a housekeeper, a gardener and a cook (of course, the gardener and the cook were only part-time helpers).

I considered myself a working woman, and I was rather proud of the fact. When I did ask Alicia what was new in her life, she would tell me, earnestly, that she was overseeing the renovation of her kitchen, or deciding on new Persian rugs for John's office, or planning their next Club Med vacation, or trying hard to decide between turquoise or maroon drapes for the family room. How were the kids? Melanie, seven, was doing very well with her Russian lessons, but the little scamp had cut big holes in all her private school uniforms; and David, four, was excited about starting his third season of alpine skiing lessons. The boy's private tutor was trying to talk them all into going to Florence, because it would give young David a tremendous boost in his art appreciation classes.

The kids were so busy she hardly ever got to see them, but, goodness, what's a mother to do these days? Children need every advantage, don't they?

Oh. Of course. We all need a few of those.

Shades of Teal

13

Passing judgement on someone else's parenting style is a lousy thing to do, especially when you don't have any particular or immediate plans to have any children of your own. I was pretty sure, however, that my kids, if and when they finally did arrive, would never have alpine ski lessons at age less-than-eight or the opportunity to play scissor-face with an expensive school uniform. David and I had talked about kids a few times, enough to know that we both wanted them some day and we agreed completely on everything to do with child-rearing. We knew we wanted me to stay home with them for the first few years to give them a great start in life, and that I would then trot back to work to continue my fulfilling career. Hopefully it would be by then.

I hadn't been at my job for very long when I met David, but I'd already realized that I wouldn't keep it much longer. After several years spent struggling to survive on a junior reporter's salary, I'd been seduced into applying for a job with the provincial government —the pay was good, there were no weekend or overnight shifts, and the work was supposed to be fascinating. It wasn't a bad job as jobs go. The nine-to-five hours meant that I could get home in time to make dinner for David and get a few things done around the house before he arrived, and the weekends were my own.

The work was reasonably interesting in the beginning, and the issues kept me learning and talking to intense people, not the cheerfully sarcastic folks I was used to meeting in a newsroom. I wrote press releases, speeches, and briefing notes for the Minister of Justice. I talked to reporters and answered their questions about everything from criminal code regulations and prison conditions to the wheelchair accessibility of provincial court buildings. I attended communications strategy meetings with top bureaucrats. And I collected what seemed to be a nice healthy paycheque. I am not highly educated. I have a bachelor's degree, and I've taken a few French courses. I like to read, and I used to think of myself as quite sociable. I am a dynamite hard worker. And I felt quite pleased to have entered the bureaucracy. I think I would have been quite happy except for the fact that my colleagues were dead lazy.

I'm the kind of person who arrives at work half an hour early, who cheerfully works through lunch, and who cannot leave one minute before quitting time, even if there's absolutely no reason to hang around. I don't make personal calls at work, and I don't like office gossip. I work as hard when the boss is standing beside my desk as I do when he or she is out of the office, and I absolutely hate working with people who don't share my work ethic. Perhaps it was the malaise of the time —jobs were plentiful and money came easily. Sting sang with the Police and a hundred million bottles floated around the oceans. In those days, most established young people I knew planned for second houses on quiet lakes, holidays, new cars and kitchen renovations and maybe a few more CDs to round out their collections. We assumed that our upbringing and education would ensure that we'd never wind up on the wrong side of the tracks, and perhaps some of us felt we were entitled to a free ride on the taxpayer's coattails.

David was a hard worker too, but we disagreed completely about my job. He liked the idea of having a wife who worked in government, and although I had only met the Minister a few times, David liked to tell people that I was a key part of his communications strategy team. This was true only in David's imagination, and for a while I tried to correct him, but I eventually gave up since my opinion on the matter was clearly not wanted.

He embellished descriptions of my colleagues for his listeners as well —according to him, I worked with an elite team of crack publicists who defined the very syllables of professionalism with every stroke of their pens. Six months after our marriage, I was desperate for a new job. David needed me to stay where I was.

Shades of Teal

"Teale, you've got a great job, and I'm so proud of you!"

"David, I work with the cast of a Saturday morning cartoon show. I'm so frustrated here!"

"Come on, Teale, it can't be that bad."

I growled.

How bad was it?

Meet Alana, thirty-six years old, a government worker for the past fifteen years, currently classed as a PRO-5, earning $63,500 to $67,000 a year. Alana is a blatant lesbian, which lends a little cachet to our unit, since our total acceptance of her —in fact, our downright enjoyment of working with her —proves just how open-minded we are. Alana looks great. She always has a terrific haircut (short, honey-blonde locks), gorgeous clothes, and trendy accessories. Her pantyhose cost a fortune, I am certain. Alana cannot write a coherent sentence to save her life, and she has a somewhat relaxed view of work hours. She's usually in by 9:30, except on the mornings she goes to her massage therapist, and her luncheon engagements tend to be a little long —say, in the order of two to two-and-a-half hours. She usually slips out of the office a half hour early because she gets headaches at the end of a long work day —you know how it is —and she often calls in sick.

Because Alana tends to be a little unreliable, she is given very little work to do. There have been altercations between Alana and Derrick, our manager, but Alana usually wins because she goes straight to the union with cries of sexual discrimination, so Derrick ends up spending an inordinate amount of time in meetings with union people (did I mention that Alana is the union rep?) and government lawyers, and there are forms to fill out and hearings to attend and —well, it's just a little bit much for Derrick to handle. One day, while I was tearing around with a list of seven reports to complete in less than three hours, I happened to see Alana, in her office, leaning over, painting her toenails a lovely shade of hibiscus pink. I was starting to hate that woman.

Derrick passed by her office moments later.

"Alana, are you all right?" he asked, panic in his voice. After all, it isn't every day one sees an employee bent double in her chair, especially when there are 11 reports, three speeches and 17 news releases on the work list. Even Alana knows that sometimes she's got to put the pedal to the metal.

"Oh yes, Derrick. I'm just painting my toenails," I heard her call.

"Oh, um, glad you're OK," he said.

"Grrrrrr," I muttered.

I probably would have been able to handle her repeated propositions if it weren't for the fact that she was such a lazy individual. Something just didn't add up in the grand work distribution scheme of things. I had gay friends —people with whom I shared a value system, with whom I could talk and laugh and complain about all manner of things. My gay men friends were especially important to me. They were great company and I knew they would never pressure me to climb into bed with them. Ever. That was nice.

If Alana was annoying, then Lisa was just plain disturbing. Lisa was a very serious person, obviously quite bright, with a Master's degree in psychology and an encyclopaedic memory. She started working for the government a few months after I did and was actually quite likable, once you got to know her. Which was hard to do because on her first day of work she was two hours late, and things didn't get much better from there. Derrick was not impressed, and she apologized like crazy, but the next day she was late again, and the next day and the next and, well, she'd already been hired by then, hadn't she, and you can't fire someone before her probation period is up. The union wouldn't like it. About once a week, Lisa managed to make it into work by 9:00, but the poor girl suffered from terrible migraines, so she quite often had to leave work early. Sometimes, she would show up wearing sunglasses and sit for hours in a foggy daze. I suspected hangovers or a problematic drug addiction, but Derrick quietly spread the word that poor Lisa suffered from a sleep disorder and had a very hard time waking up in the morning. For a while, he decreed that the first person to arrive at the office —uh, that would be me —had to call Lisa to coax her out of bed, which, quite frankly I resented, sleep disorder or no sleep disorder. I had actual work to do as soon as I got in the door, and it could take a solid ten minutes of ringing to get Lisa to answer the phone. Sometimes Lisa was still really late, and Derrick would loom up in my office doorway with a disappointed expression on his face, and in his unhappy boss voice he'd ask, "Teale, weren't you supposed to wake Lisa this morning? Everybody says you were first in. Why didn't you do it?" Eventually I told Derrick I was getting a little tired of playing wake-up service. Could he please ask someone else to do it since I wasn't getting all my work done? Instead, he changed Lisa's hours to 11 a.m. to 7 p.m. Goodness knows what she did half the time, since the switchboard closed at 5:30, and just about everybody except the Minister left the building promptly at day's end. And of course she had to fit lunch in there somewhere. Poor Lisa. She was always still there when I left work, looking conscientious and professional in her blue cashmere sweater or bright-red leather jacket. Dress for success, I guess.

And there was Frank, a 350-pound, 30-year veteran of the government bureaucracy who knew everything there was to know about anything, governmental or not, and what he didn't know he thought he knew, so of course there was no arguing with him. Frank was a good worker, although he couldn't write either, and Derrick always sent Frank's work to me for editing. This did nothing to improve my relationship with Frank, and every editing session deteriorated into a bickering session —I'd be pointing out his misuse of simple words and his confusing run-on sentences, and he'd be irritably defending his stylistic integrity. One day, we were going over a briefing note in Frank's office when the Minister's press assistant appeared at Frank's door.

"Come in, John, come in. Sit down. Teale, I want you to run along and get those corrections done immediately," Frank said. It wasn't the patronizing dismissal that astounded me so much as the greasy squeeze he gave my left buttock as he uttered it. I stared. The Minister's press assistant stared. Frank beamed.

"Hurry up now, Teale. I don't want to be kept waiting on this. Now, John, what can I do for you?" Frank the big shot.

As soon as I was certain John had left, I marched back into Frank's office, shut the door, leaned across his desk, and jabbed my index finger at his face.

"DON'T. YOU. DARE. EVER. TALK. TO. ME. LIKE. THAT. AGAIN. AND IF YOU EVER TOUCH ANY PART OF MY BODY AGAIN I WILL CHOKE THE LIVING BREATH OUT OF YOU BEFORE TEARING YOUR LUNGS OUT WITH A BROKEN WRENCH. AM I UNDERSTOOD?!"

Frank just looked at me.

"Whew. We're a little testy today. What's the matter — got your period?"

I slammed his door hard on my way out. A few minutes later, Derrick marched into my office, sunk into my spare chair, and sighed.

"Teale," he said. "I don't want to have to write a note to your file about your behaviour with Frank today, but you realize that slamming doors is highly inappropriate in a work environment, and you're going to make our department look bad if you can't control your temper."

"Derrick," I sputtered, "that enormous windbag down the hall sexually molested me in front of the Minister's press assistant! How can you complain about *me*!"

"Now, Teale," Derrick replied in his most managerial voice. "If Frank had actually done such a horrible thing, I am quite certain you, of all people, would have marched right into my office to complain and file an official investigation form." He stood up. "I'm on your side," he said. "You could have a great future here."

I'm sure I could have had a great future there; however, I would likely have had to have been lobotomized first, which was not, really, how I wanted to spend the remaining days of my life. David just couldn't fathom how debilitating it was to spend one's days in a poorly managed work environment with parasitical companions all day. He wouldn't hear of me quitting.

"Teale, the decision is entirely up to you. It's your life, it's your career, and I can understand perfectly if you want to do something else for a while. But are you sure you would be happy going back to reporting, assuming you could even get a job now? Remember how much you hated the night shift? And the pay was pretty lousy. We have to save money, don't forget, because when I go back to school on my post-graduate fellowship in the fall we aren't going to have my salary anymore. Maybe when I'm done with school you can get a job you really like."

His words made sense. But as the months passed, I began to use more and more of my sick days. I began spending lunch hour out of the office. And I started sneaking out a few minutes early every day. Work wasn't much fun anymore. By the time David and I were happily ensconced in Janey and Robby Johnson's living room munching mini quiches, mussels on the half shell, phyllo-wrapped brie, and something that involved seaweed, I was actively considering a career move. I was thoughtful that night, not participating much in any of the conversations playing out around me, but I was listening to every word —or so I thought.

I haven't said too much about Eric and Carmela Rinders. They were old family friends of the Mastersons Senior, although to this day I don't understand why. Both were teachers, and both had specific ideas about how the education system should be changed to accommodate children.

"The system should be funded on a user-pay system," said Carmela. "And if your child doesn't want to go to school, then he shouldn't have to go. He's not going to learn anything in that frame of mind, and his teachers aren't going to want him around, either. So you should only have to pay for the time your child is in school. Very simple, really."

Eric nodded solemnly and said, "Thank God we don't have kids!"

And so the evening unfolded in a series of interconnected and fascinating conversations. These people were young, like us, well off, well educated, well travelled, and highly polished. They all had nicknames for each other like "Cricket" (Eric), "Luscious" (Alicia), and "Spitty" (Tim). They all ate out most nights of the week, and the women spent many a happy hour trading names of cleaning ladies, caterers, and decorators.

The evening passed in a carnival of food, drink, and wickedly entertaining conversation. Except for Carole, who held court from her throne in front of the crab cakes, the women helped in the kitchen, the men talked sports, and everyone caught up on families and friends and traded tidbits about business and leisure activities. I was finally starting to feel a little more comfortable around these people. Now that I was getting to know them better, I thought they were all very nice. Perhaps I would fit in after all.

By midnight, the plates had been cleared away and many empty wine bottles had been consigned to the sideboard. Eight liqueur glasses were held aloft for yet another toast to humanity. We were all the best of friends. What a wonderful night. David, of course, was the life of the party. He could always be counted on to tell a funny story or an off-colour joke. There was a lull in the conversation, and this gave him the opening he needed. We had been talking about wives. The men had all related charming stories to illustrate the ditziness of their spouses, who tittered appreciatively and struggled desperately to come up with a witty return.

"*My* wife is charming, accomplished, intelligent, and perfect in every way," David began, tilting his glass in my direction. I smiled and nodded my coy thanks. "But you'll never guess what she told me tonight." He rolled his eyes.

Shades of Teal

Six pairs of eyes turned toward my charming husband, and six sets of lips curved into expectant smiles. I couldn't imagine what it was I had said, but everyone was feeling warm and giddy, happy and congenial, ready to share a laugh.

"She said she thinks the streetlights are tent poles holding up the sky and that the universe is going to collapse. Ha ha ha ha ha."

Polite tittering all around.

"Oh, Teale —how unique," Janey squealed. "Well, David, it could be true!"

I just smiled a confused little smile. "I don't think that's *quite* what I said, David."

"Not only that, but she's decided to start a worm farm in our backyard. Jeez, we'll never have another picnic out there!!! Ha ha ha ha ha.

"Guess what else —she said she wants to teach inner city kids how to write poetry. Ha ha ha ha ha." He was on a roll now.

"I bet none of *your* wives had a stuffed toy named Mickie Dickie. Ha ha ha ha ha. What's more, she was nearly raped once —saved herself by pouring glue on the jerk's willy, giving him —wait for it, folks —a sticky dickie. Ha ha ha ha ha. She's afraid of the dark now, of course. Gee, Teale, where was Mickie Dickie when you needed him? Not a very tricky Dickie —just too picky I guess, eh? Didja at least give him a hickey? Oh, God, I guess I'm a sicky. Ha ha ha ha ha."

The stories came thick and fast —some were true, some were twisted versions of a reality that was supposed to have been a private dream, a flight of fancy, a quiet experiment, a deep-dark secret never intended to reach the light of glittering night. This night had been heavy with expectation, filled with beautiful illusions — we were happy, relaxed, well-fed people in the prime of our lives, enjoying ourselves among friends, sharing stories in a spirit of generosity. But the stifling blackness of the night was now seeping in through the windows of the Johnsons' dream home. Beautiful illusions are possible at night, but illusions are so easily smashed.

Voices, voices, voices, laughter circling around me oh God why did this have to happen to me? Why won't he stop? WHY CAN'T I MAKE HIM STOP? *Try harder, Teale!*

Or don't try at all.

The nightmare evening at the Johnson's finally ended. David and Tim remembered that they had an early golf game the next morning and they were going to feel like dirt by then.

Everybody dried their tears of laughter, patted me on the back, and told me what a wonderfully good sport I was. I smiled politely. Yes, I was a wonderfully good sport, saying my goodnights and sliding gracefully and gratefully down the front path and into the relative safety of David's BMW.

We drove home through the mist of a cloudy April night, silent and separate.

"What a great party!" Oh jeez, what are you thinking, *now* Teale," he wanted to know. He chuckled at the memory of his storytelling triumph. Maybe I would let loose and give him some material for his next monologue.

I was thinking that I was utterly humiliated. He had taken my private moments of wonder and vulnerability, twisted them into something banal and stupid, and held them up to ridicule before a group of people who were not quite my friends but no longer strangers. I was thinking how shocked I had been to hear him proudly use secrets I had entrusted him with as fodder for a series of cruel jokes.

I was thinking how disgusted I was that no one had tried to stop him, that they had all just lapped it up and enjoyed a good laugh at my expense. I was thinking that my husband was a traitor, not the classy, charismatic, debonair citizen of the world I thought he was. I was thinking I couldn't share anything with this man without getting hurt. These thoughts were hurtling through my brain like leaves in a hurricane.

"Nothing," I said.

We got home that night to find two life-altering pieces of news awaiting us. The Paris-Sorbonne University had written to say that David had been accepted into the Advanced Studies Program in International Business, and they were also offering him a course to teach. And Bright's Pharmacy had called to say that the urine specimen I had dropped off at noon had come back positive. I was pregnant.

"Well *that's* a problem," was all David said before stomping up the stairs to bed. "You'll obviously have to get rid of it." He had his spear at the ready.

I stared after him. "Get rid of our baby?!"

"I'm going back to school, and you're going to have to get a job. There's no room for a baby in that plan, Teale." It was all so clear-cut for him.

"I'm not getting rid of a baby because it's inconvenient, David."

"Oh come on, Teale, be reasonable. Call the doctor tomorrow, and she'll arrange for an abortion. It's easy. Especially since we've caught it early."

We had caught it early, like a learning problem or a snag in your pantyhose. Catch it early and you can fix it. You can fix anything these days.

"No, David," I said. Although the room spun and my knees felt weak and I couldn't breathe and I was scared to death, I did not sway. "This baby is mine."

"Crap. We'll have to discuss this in the morning. I'm too tired to argue with you right now. But this just can't be."

The thing I had secretly hoped for, longed for, wanted with all my heart, though never spoke about, was short months from fruition. My heart rang with the joy of becoming a mother. I wanted the whole world to know that I was carrying precious life inside me, that pure love for my little one was already coursing through my soul, that I would never be the same again, that nothing mattered but this.

I didn't care what car I drove. I would forgive my drunken husband for the stupid things he had said. I would quit my job to nurture this life. The tears streamed down my face and I thanked God for this wonderful gift. I was so lucky!

I turned to my husband and shook my head.

"No, David," I said. "We have nothing to discuss. We are not going to argue. I am having this baby. And you are going to have to wrap your head around the idea of being a father nine months from now, whether you want to be or not."

"But Teale..."

"Piss off and go to bed, David."

And he did.

I crawled into bed beside my man. He was, when all was said and done, still my man. And the baby was mine, too.

14

But it turned out that the baby wasn't so decisively mine after all. David wanted it gone, wrenched from our lives like a thistle from a garden. The discussions were loud and bitter.

"I don't *want* to be a father yet, Teale! I'm not emotionally ready to do a good job as a dad. One day, yeah, I'll be the world's best. But now I need to focus on my academic work. That'll be the icing on the cake for me. It'll give me the edge I need to really take off at work. I can't do that with a screaming brat around all the time. And, let's face it, things are tight enough already. We need more money."

"But David…"

"But nothing, Teale. We agreed I was going to go back to school again, and you said you were totally behind the idea. You're supposed to support us now. You can't just go and change the rules like that. You can't do that to me, Teale. You lied to me!"

"I didn't lie, David! You had a hand in this pregnancy too, you know."

"No, you decided to skip the birth control. How do I know this child is even mine?"

"That's just stupid, David! When would I ever have time to mess around with anybody else? There's no such thing as a milkman anymore — and, by the way, Mr. Self-righteous, the pill is not 100 percent effective." I was screaming now. "And it's your fault I missed taking it for four days last month."

"What do you mean *my* fault? What am I supposed to do? Hold you down and force it down your throat?"

"Ha ha — very funny. You don't even remember, do you?! You called me at work to say your mother had invited us down for a long

— *very* long — weekend in Florida, and you gave me exactly three hours to pack and get out to the airport. I was rattled, David!"

"Oh, don't give me that! You're always rattled."

"That's not true! I raced home to pack for both of us, and you couldn't leave me alone. You kept calling with lists of stuff I had to track down and pack for you! By the time I got all your stuff into a suitcase, you were on the phone yelling at me to hurry up or we'd miss our flight. A little help would have been nice, you know. I shouldn't have to do everything all the time!"

"I do a helluva lot more for this family than you do, Teale. And I don't see why it took you so long to get a few things together, and what's all this got to do with you screwing up and getting pregnant anyway?"

"For pity's sake, David, with you threatening to get us on an even earlier flight, I barely had time to pack my own bag, and what with all the panic you were causing, and having to find your stupid cufflinks, I just didn't think of birth control pills." I was on the verge of tears.

"Sounds like an excuse to me. If you had really been serious about our future, you would have kept those pills in your purse and had them with you all the time. The truth is, you just aren't a team player. Now you've ruined our future. Nice work. And on top of it all, you're right on track to be fat and ugly before you even hit thirty. You know how much you worry about your weight to begin with. Great."

I am not a beautiful woman, though, God knows, I sure want to be. In high school, I was an average-looking girl with mouse-brown hair, bad skin, and no chest. Not the worst-looking teenager in town, but the boys didn't exactly beat a path to my locker, either. They all ran *panting* after Lidia Fussbaum, and girls like her, though. Lidia had gorgeous, thick hair that was always curled just right, and her mother sent her to a salon to get it professionally streaked. Lidia wore far too much mascara, and her sweaters were always about two sizes too small, so nobody could miss the fact that she had enormous boobs. Her skirts were too short, and her pants were too tight, and I hated her because she always spoke like a coy little girl when there were boys around, but when she was with girls, she sounded just like the rest of us. Rumour has it that after high school she set herself up in a little apartment with the help of a married man who bought her nice things like a car and Hawaiian vacations and a full length mink so she wouldn't pester him to leave his wife. But that's just a rumour.

I still feel a little like the awkward teenager I was. At one point, I actually thought it was kind of David to help me focus on losing weight. But having a baby wasn't about gaining a little weight.

"You have such a problem with your weight already, Teale," he said, gently now. "Do you really want to regain all the weight you lost? They say you never get your figure back once you've had kids, and all I hear from you now is how fat you are. Why make it harder for yourself?"

Good question.

I often bemoaned the fact that I was a little plump, and I'd struggled with my weight ever since I met David. Although I had managed to bring myself down to a size 2, I still felt huge when we attended one of the charity dinners organized by David's mother. It's tough to out-skinny the beautiful people, and while I would have been thrilled to be among the gorgeous scrawny women smiling out from a photo on the society pages, I guess I was either too chubby or too irrelevant to make the cut. Such photos of David's mother appeared with regularity, which made sense because of all the charity work she undertook. David's sister, the tax lawyer, was photographed fairly often, too —I guess keeping a high social profile was good for her business. (I happened to know, however, that she was a size 8.)

Being a size 2 was extremely important to me, but achieving that number never really felt like enough. Each morning, I stood on the bathroom scale, fingers crossed, hoping it would tell me that I'd lost another pound. I was determined to keep shedding until I reached a weight that would signify, in my mind at least, perfect womanhood. Every month I came up with a new target —125, 120, 118, down it crept, all the way to 115, which melted into 112, which was far too big when 109 beckoned. And that lasted only as long as it took to catch sight of 107, which felt disgraceful compared to 105, 104, 102, and, finally 100. But then 100 pounds started to seem too much for a woman of my height, and every morning I'd step back onto the scale —five feet, seven inches of obesity perched on two chubby feet framing the little window in the scale. That window held me captive. One more pound, just one more. Dear God, scrape these ugly rolls of lard from this grotesque and disgusting stomach, these flabby hips, these wobbly thighs! How can I live in a body so huge, so heavy? There, see how my belly bulges? It looks like I swallowed a basketball! My God, how can I get rid of it? Just one more pound and I can break 100, the barrier to happiness. I can do this, I can weigh less, I will get rid of this hideous fat and finally feel pretty and light. Forgotten now is the secret thrill of the pound I lost yesterday. All that matters is the fresh pain of being too big to be beautiful and the new goal that will ease it.

Keep going. You can do it, Teale —you can win this war on obesity. And I did. The needle on the dial inside the little window kept arriving at its quivering balance lower and lower; it fell past 100, past 99, and on down into a world below reality. Shhhh, Teale.

People congratulated me on my impressive weight loss, but no one understood what was driving it, least of all me. Although I never consciously thought about what I was doing or why I was doing it, deep down I felt proud of my strength, proud of the power I had over my body. Here was something no one could take away from me. Here was something I could do alone, and well.

"Are you eating properly, Teale?" asked my suspicious mother, who had worried her whole life about her weight, who had spent decades thumbing through women's magazines for low-calorie recipes for meatloaf and chicken stew. My mother, who would never touch dessert, who had tried every diet ever published, who had warned me constantly as I grew up to watch my weight, to limit my calories, to take care that I didn't lose my figure too early. "Men don't like women who are chubby dear," she would say. No, of course they don't. All the poor, vulnerable heroines of my childhood had married well precisely because they were pretty —and *skinny*. Snow White, Cinderella, Sleeping Beauty, and every other female protagonist in children's movies were Barbie-doll thin. And they had big eyes, big breasts, and slim legs; they had little-girl voices; they sighed soft, gentle sighs; and they sat and waited for a handsome prince to come along and rescue them from singledom. Fairy tales were never about chubby girls. Even if they were, you can bet those chubby heroines would never manage to bag the handsome prince. Oh, sure —there were probably a few lonely and unhappy skinny women out there somewhere. But it was mainly plump women who were the losers, and I sure wasn't going to be one of them!

I can't blame David, really, for my obsession with weight loss, and it's not fair to blame the Brothers Grimm, either. But I do think we're all a little responsible for buying into the concept that a woman's beauty is inversely proportional to her size. We've all heard a man evaluate a woman's physique as though he were judging a cow at a cattle auction. He might be fat and bald, nearsighted and endowed with a set of teeth that could drop a tree, but he's got an opinion on the little cow down in the ring.

"Whoa! Look at the size of those haunches, Frank."

"Oooo-eeee! Geez, Bill, she's a real heifer!"

Sadly, in the larger arena that is life, this is not a compliment, and although no harm is likely intended, such talk makes women terrified of weight gain. And it doesn't stop there.

"Yeah, Dolly's got a nice personality, but gawd, what a big butt!"

"No kiddin' —she's got so much belly fat she looks like the Michelin Man."

"Yeah. Maybe she *is* the Michelin Man."

Yuk, yuk, yuk.

And then these experts in female anatomy, these connoisseurs of the flesh, proceed to comment on the physical flaws of every woman they have ever met.

"I dated a woman once who worked part-time as a zombie in a haunted mansion in Baltimore, and she didn't need makeup! She was one ugly doggy."

"Why did you go out with her then?"

"I felt sorry for her, you creep. I'm not a heartless jerk, you know."

These goodhearted gentlemen then take a few more sips of beer in silence and watch another touchdown on the big-screen TV at Earl's Sports Bar.

"Then why did you dump her?"

"She got all clingy on me, man —started talking about where the 'relationship was going,' and all that stuff. Who needs it? I can get another woman to look after business, no sweat!"

Yuk. Yuk. Yuk.

Rolls of fat hang over the belts of the men indulging in this little conversation. Both badly need a shampoo and a haircut. They have pimples and acne scars. One of them covers his face as best he can with a beard and moustache. The one who doesn't bother to take the facial-hair route says, "Hey, man —I know my skin isn't perfect, but a chick has gotta love me with all my faults or not love me at all, right? I've got a lot to offer, and she should feel damned lucky to get me —know what I'm saying?"

"Yeah, bro. Gimme five."

And their teeth! If I had a set of choppers like that, I'd have them pulled out and replaced. Can you imagine kissing such a mouth? How would you ever explain it to your best friend? "You *kissed* that guy? Are you out of your mind? Good Lord, Dolly, he looks like the weasel that swallowed the chainsaw."

And Dolly hangs her head and shakes it so that her long hair covers her shame.

"I know, I know, I know... but he was so nice to me, and we were having such a nice time, and I, well... I just felt we were really *getting* somewhere, you know?"

Dolly hasn't yet witnessed a graphic demonstration —like this imaginary conversation in Earl's Sports Bar —of the fact that men who stridently demand female perfection are rarely prize specimens of manhood. How do these men get away with it? Have their parents taught them nothing? Or is this just the way the game has always been played?

Maybe it's our own fault. Maybe we women expect too much of ourselves. Despite what we have learned in the past few decades about our rights, our choices, our new and ever-expanding place in the world, we are still buying into the skinny aesthetic and driving ourselves crazy. Now, don't get me wrong. As much as any woman, I'd love to walk into a room and see heads turn and jaws drop at the sight of me. But would it have mattered? At that point, I was probably too busy starving myself to notice.

David was an attractive man, to be sure, but he insisted that he would never judge me based on my looks alone. He had married me, he said, for my sparkling personality, my common sense, my good humour, my honest soul. I would remember years later the many premarital hours we'd spent engaged in stimulating discussions; we'd gone to the theatre and the symphony, and we'd enjoyed our intellectual connection. And so what if he'd point out a little roll of flab from time to time and asked if I'd gained weight? He was helping me be beautiful. Wasn't he?

I thought of going to a weight-loss clinic, the kind that advertises on TV with promises like "Lose 30 pounds in 30 days!" Now that was an offer no woman could refuse. But I couldn't spare the time. I couldn't spend every Wednesday night learning how to count calories and cut carbs, but it would have been nice to meet other women with weight problems. It wasn't that it was so hard to lose weight —you just had to stop eating —but it was a lonely pursuit.

I did have some friends. Dinah Westcott, for one —big-hearted, fun, and lovable Dinah. She came for dinner one night wearing a turquoise cape, a gauzy pink-and-green tunic, hot-pink stirrup pants, and gold stilettos. What a sight!

"Wine for him, and flowers for her," she smiled. "My goodness, Teale, why haven't you had me over before this? What a gorgeous spot! Hello, David. Nice to see you again. How are you doing these days?"

"Hi, Dinah," David said.

David was not at all pleased to be entertaining Dinah that particular evening, so I had worked hard to put together a wonderful meal.

"What can't you just go out with her somewhere?" he'd grumbled when I told him that I wanted to invite Dinah over.

"We should have my friends over sometimes too, David," I'd replied. "We just entertain your friends, and it's only fair that I get a turn to connect with my friends as well."

"But there's a game on."

"David, please be nice to her. It would mean so much to me."

He promised he would be charming.

To dull his misery and perhaps buy his bonhomie, I had prepared some of his favourite dishes. We began with jumbo shrimp and a spicy dip, a platter of oysters, and caviar-topped cucumber slices. I served shot glasses of vodka to chase the oysters. I knew Dinah didn't like seafood, but I also knew she would politely refrain from saying so. I set out a creamy liver paté for her and me to enjoy as we sipped our Riesling.

"Dinah, we've been waiting all day to see you! Have you heard the latest about City Hall's plan for the parks system?"

David sat uncomfortably in his favourite chair. The conversation was at least as interesting as any we'd ever had with David's friends. Dinah was no slouch on the intellectual front. Over the appetizers, we discussed what she'd been reading lately, a stock tip she wanted to pass on, and her youngest sister's new boyfriend.

We moved to the dining room and had roasted red pepper soup with homemade crackers and a tangy Japanese salad while conversing about Amnesty International initiatives in South Africa, a cruise Dinah was planning for September, and a new finding about the DNA of pigs. The main course was a beef bourguignon I'd braised for hours, accompanied by noodles for David and roasted potatoes for Dinah and me. We chatted about Dinah's gay cousin's wedding, Dinah's plans to go back to school, and my new hairdresser.

We were having a great time —at least Dinah and I were. But by the time we hit dessert, it was clear that David had opted out of the conversation. In fact, he picked at his food and said nothing at all. He repeatedly rose from the table and went roaming upstairs, where he could be heard flushing the toilet and washing his hands, then he'd return to the table with an expression on his face similar to that of a dead fish.

"Is David OK?" Dinah asked after his third abrupt departure from the table.

"He's been having a tough time at work," I said in a low voice. "He's usually much friendlier, but he's had a few deals go sour. Next time you come he'll be in a better mood." I was anxious to show off my husband, and I wanted my friend and my mate to like each other. Dinah was willing to make allowances for a bad day. She carried on gaily as though she didn't notice that anything was wrong.

"I'm sure he's a real pet," she said to me later.

The evening never really perked up. David left the two of us alone over coffee and cheesecake, and an hour later, when Dinah was at the front door preparing to leave, I had to call him up from the basement to say goodbye.

As soon as the door closed on my dear friend, he sprang back to life.

"Wow, she's got a big butt," he said.

"She does?" I asked.

"Huge," he said.

"I never noticed her butt," I said.

"Well it's big," he said. "I'm glad yours isn't that big. She's loud, too."

"Gee, I don't think she's loud. She loves a good time, that's all. She has a great sense of humour and we have a great time together. You weren't exactly Mr. Personality tonight yourself, you know." I was teasing, sort of, intending to jolly him out of criticizing my buddy, a solid size 12 but a lovely person nonetheless. David was usually the life of the party when we entertained, but tonight, when I had finally managed to fit one of *my* friends into our hectic social calendar, that side of him had been missing in action. And it had been so important to me that everything go well.

"Well, I didn't have a good time." He wasn't angry, of course, just cold and honest. "The meat was tough. Your friend seems like a nice, average kind of person, but thank God you're not as fat as she is yet."

15

It was the word "yet" that stuck in my mind. Was my rear end growing? Was David worried about my weight? David had liked Darien's rear —small and neat, tiny twin melons, firm and ripe. But this wasn't just about Darien. I was competing for David's affection with the dozens of women who appeared in the pages of the porn magazines he hid in his sock drawer, magazines that I, in my liberal-hearted way, accepted as an inevitable "male thing." And there were the porn flicks in a box in the basement —dozens of them —that David swore were left over from a stag party he'd thrown at university. "The guys made me keep them," he had said apologetically, humbly. The women on the covers were skinny, always, with huge boobs, moist lips, and a bad-girl look on their faces.

An awesome amount of flesh can be bought in this world for the price of lunch at a roadhouse. Flesh comes with blonde hair and blue eyes on page 12, brown hair and green eyes on page 26. You can get breasts with enormous nipples, breasts with small nipples, breasts with rings and chains. But all these forms of flesh come with a tiny waist. By page 29, flesh has red hair and hungry lips. It wants you, Mr. Magazine Purchaser, and just for today you can call her Debbie. Or Janna. Or Tasha. She is French, she is Greek, she is the all-American girl next door. See her crouching there on the floor, see her naked body lunge forward to bring you into her world of unending delight? She is almost smiling, and she is a perfect woman. How can you resist? You deserve her.

She — they —were perfection, and they were simply not me. Were they what David really wanted? Were they the reason he only wanted to have sex with me once every few months? Although they say that men need an outlet, that men read skin magazines like women read fashion magazines, I cringed every time I found the latest edition tucked safely away among David's socks and underwear. They reminded me of my failure to please my man, my failure to be the woman he wanted me to be. I would never be an airbrushed dream, but I was the best I could be. Every time I tried to nudge us towards intimacy, no matter how I raised the issue, David turned me down. Sex had to be his idea.

"Hey, Teale," he would leer. "Want to screw?"

"Sure!" I would always answer, relieved that after two months of waiting, yearning, asking for a little night magic, he was finally interested in *me*. But it wasn't really me he was after, it was a hard, mechanical release with the image of Deirdre or Lara or page 29 stuck in his head and driving his libido. He would get on top and dive deep into me, pumping fast and furious, building toward his release. When he was done, he'd roll back over to his side of the bed and fall asleep.

"David you're hurting me," I would sometimes venture.

"I'll be finished in a minute," he would pant. And he would lunge on while I held my breath, eyes shut tight against the moment of passion I had stubbornly believed would be better when we were happily-ever-after married. When he was finished, I would curl up on my own sliver of the mattress, hold myself together, and wonder how I could make it different —more gentle, more interesting, more satisfying. I had tried to talk to him about it, but he hated talking about sex.

"I can't talk dirty with my own wife, Teale," he patiently explained.

"But David, this isn't about talking dirty, it's about improving our sex life."

"We have a wonderful sex life, Teale. Aren't I good for you enough in bed?" He was hurt now, offended at this perceived insult to his prowess.

"David, you are a magnificent lover, I ache to have sex with you, I want to do it more often —every night, if possible. But sometimes I would like it to be, well, you know, just, maybe...different."

"What for?"

"Because, well, sometimes it hurts, and I just thought it might be nice to, you know, take it a little slower, maybe try other ways, and, you know..."

"Oh come on, Teale, it can't be as bad as all that. You've never complained before. Why am I suddenly not good enough for you?"

"It's not that, David, n-n-not that at all..." I stammered.

"You're having an affair, aren't you?"

"Good *God*—of course not!"

"I don't understand you, Teale. I give you everything—a big house, lots of new friends, holidays, a car, clothes. Everything you have is because of me, and now you turn on me and say I'm no good in bed!"

"David, that's not what I said at all, it's just that..."

"Just *what*?"

"I don't know..."

"Then if you don't know you shouldn't complain. I'm going out."

And with that, David huffed out of the house. He was gone for hours, returning at 3:30 in the morning, relatively sober and totally uncommunicative. Meanwhile, I lay awake berating myself for being so insensitive, so cruel, so inept at handling the most important relationship I would ever have. Where was he? Was he all right? Sometimes he would drink and drive. How could I possibly make it up to him? I had driven him into the arms of another woman, that's what I had done. How could I have been so stupid? This was all my fault!

Not knowing how to improve the situation, I became resigned to it. I counted my other blessings so I wouldn't feel sad. My husband was a hard worker, a good-natured companion, a supportive mate, a loving spouse. Sure, he was imperfect, just as I was, and sex was only a very small part of a happy marriage. If we were compatible in every other way, we didn't really need it. True pleasure in life comes from satisfying conversation, intellectual compatibility, shared interests, fulfilling work. So what if I had a lousy body my husband hated? I would just have to work on it.

I never took a vow of anorexia or consciously decided to make myself disappear. It just turned out that way. It was a secret, of course, one I couldn't even reveal to myself. How could I have faced such a harsh truth when I was still locked up in my lonely mental tower, still fervently believing that my marriage was a fairy tale, a dream come true? I —Teale? Me? —had boarded a plane for happily ever after and ended up in a living hell. The problem was, I couldn't tell the difference.

And so I threw myself into our life. We were booked every Thursday, Friday, Saturday, and Sunday night for months in advance: business dinners and receptions at expensive hotels, dinner dates with friends, and parties to celebrate just about everything. We went to plays and concerts. He golfed. I cleaned the house, cut the grass, and shopped for groceries. He worked; I worked. Now and then, we would watch TV together on the old couch in the family room. Now and then, I would go out with Dinah or another friend, Sarah, to a movie or dinner, but leisure hours were scarce, and David didn't like it when I wasn't there with him. He wanted me all to himself, he said. He missed me when I wasn't there. Didn't I want to be with him too? We stopped going together to visit my parents. David was awfully busy, and he'd never felt very comfortable with my folks anyway; besides, they never did anything interesting, so they had nothing interesting to talk about. I was too busy to make a big deal of it —there was the next event to plan and the next dinner to attend, and every night when we got home, starry-eyed and giggling from too much brandy and so much witty conversation, I would lock myself in the little bathroom off the front stairs, slide my finger down the back of my tongue, and vomit.

Life was good.

My pregnancy meant that things had to change, of course. I had to eat. I had to stop rejecting food. I had to slow down. Most of all, I had to fight to keep my baby. Whenever David mentioned abortion, I said "No."

"You're being stubborn, Teale," he said.

"Yes, I am."

"Don't you realize that this is going to ruin our lives?"

"No."

"If you're pregnant, you won't be able to get a good job in France when we go. I know how much you hate the job you have now. Don't you want to do better?"

"No."

"Liar. Look, Teale, an abortion is not that big a deal. Everybody's getting them nowadays. It doesn't mean you're an awful person anymore. The stigma is gone."

I just looked at him.

"This is my baby, David, and I am going to give birth to it, whether you're beside me or not. You might as well stop complaining, stop coaxing, stop bullying, stop demanding, and stop talking about it because that's just the way it is. Get it?"

"You never do anything to make me happy, Teale. Very sad, very sad." He looked up at the ceiling and sighed. Then his face took on a black look, and for a split second I thought he was going to hit me.

"I used to think we had a great thing going," he said as he left the house.

David started working a little harder, being away from home a little more often. He stopped telling me funny stories about things that happened at the office. That was fine with me, because for the first three months of my pregnancy I was sick and very tired. I threw up three or four times a day for weeks on end and fell asleep at 6:00 every night. This was going to be my first and last pregnancy. How could women go through this more than once? But by the end of my first trimester, I had managed to pull myself together and was ready to move to France for David's two-year study plan. Somehow I did the packing, rented our house, and organized our documents. We were ready for a grand adventure.

David didn't mention abortion anymore. He had gradually gotten used to the idea of becoming a father, and he started to take a mild interest in the progress of the pregnancy. Perhaps he would come around. Perhaps not. He also became pickier about certain domestic things. The house was never quite clean enough for him. I should really try to change the vacuum-cleaner bag a little more often. Could I please, for crying out loud, use a different brand of detergent to wash the kitchen floor? It was never very clean anymore. His shirts weren't satisfactory; maybe I could find a better dry cleaner? My cooking wasn't quite up to scratch; I should spend more time in the kitchen. I was spending too much money, and I wasn't very interesting company —all I did was sleep and throw up. John Clark's wife, Alicia, had apparently been wonderful company throughout both of her pregnancies; I should call her and find out what I was doing wrong.

Fortunately, I was too tired to care about his litany of complaints. All I knew was that I was in love with the child growing inside me, and that this love would carry me through any disaster. This kind of love would never die. This kind of love was beyond forever.

"Hush little baby, don't you cry..."

16

My brother, Joey, had a new job in the car business, and one of our last obligations before moving to France for David's triumphant return to academia was to head off to London — Ontario, my home town — to celebrate. My mother had planned the celebration perfectly, hunting down car-shaped place cards and Hot Wheels serviettes, and ordering a race car cake from the local grocery store. . There were balloons and streamers and baskets of chocolate-covered nuts. Mom was enormously pleased in an I-always-knew-he-could-do-it kind of way. She was the only person on the planet who hadn't given up on him, and here he was, Joseph Covey, being named *manager* of Auto-rrrific, London's largest, sleekest, most successful car maintenance establishment. His photo crowned an announcement of his appointment in the business section of the local paper. He would now be attending Chamber of Commerce meetings as Auto-rrrific's official representative. Wow!

It had been a long road. My brother has a kind heart. He's very bright. He likes people. He works hard once he gets his butt in gear. But he's way too trusting. He sailed through elementary school with flying colours, but something went horribly wrong as soon as he hit the well-trod corridors of Parkside High. I had the high school scene figured out a good two years before Joey got there, and I wanted nothing to do with my irritating little brother when he finally showed up. I guess I might be partly to blame for his failure to thrive. I could have helped him out. But I was too wrapped up in my own concerns which, at the time, centred around apple-splash eau de cologne, Cutex nail polish, weekend sleepovers with my friends and learning how to apply eyeliner with a perfect touch. I played cards with my girlfriends at lunchtime, completed all my homework at school, gossiped constantly, and trained incessantly for volleyball. A little brother was an embarrassment. My mother had instructed me to look out for him, and when I failed to do so he found other protectors.

Boys are beasts. They create their own brutal pecking order. If you aren't a real tough cookie, then you're going to get the stuffing beaten out of you unless you have friends who can watch your back. Joey was not athletic, so that avenue to peer respect was closed to him. He was short and pimply until he was 17, so he didn't score with the girls, either. He was smarter than anybody I knew, but he didn't dare show it because it's not cool to get great marks. Joey just didn't fit in anywhere, but he eventually fell in with some guys who accepted him as long as he was willing to steal beer and bring it out to the parking lot at lunchtime. Joey thought they were nice people once you got past how rough and scary-looking they were. They smoked cigarettes, which at first he hated but gradually came to like. If he pretended to be tougher and meaner than he really was, then the parking lot boys would talk to him sometimes. They didn't treat Joey very well, but he kept trying to win their respect, and that seemed to involve stealing more beer.

Joey told me years later that he didn't think stealing beer was a big deal. It ended up in his locker one stalwart brown bottle at a time. At first it came from the colourful cases of Pilsener Dad had stashed in the basement. If Dad noticed that his beer was disappearing then he never mentioned it. After all, he might be wrong, and it would be embarrassing to accuse your children of stealing the stuff and then find out you'd been too inebriated to remember that you'd consumed it yourself. My friends were all sweet and silly, girlish and naive – just like me – so why would I have taken the beer? (He knew I thought it smelled disgusting anyway.) And how could he suspect Joey, with his pimply face and lopsided grin, who, at 14, still slept with Paulie, a tattered snuggle-teddy? And although it was never discussed at the family dinner table, Joey still slept with the light on. This was not the kind of kid who'd steal beer to buy the favour of the rough punks at school. Anyway, I doubt my parents suspected that kids our age drank alcohol anywhere, let alone in the parking lot of Parkside High.

My parents knew many of these parking-lot toughs. They had watched them grow up alongside Joey and me. Such nice children; such nice parents. Mom and Dad would remember Bev and Ernie Taylor's little boy, Jonathon, who had been as cute as a button in his T-ball uniform and tousled brown hair. Wasn't he the one who used to tell all those silly jokes about cows? Suddenly, he is 16 years old and stands five-feet, ten inches in a size 11 shoe. One hundred and fifty pounds of teenage boy are buckled under his belt and he's not so cute anymore, especially with half a dozen beers in him. And there was Doris and Ted Bishop's kid, Tommy – he had been a really great little soccer player and *so* polite. All the moms hoped their little boys would be as nicely behaved in public as Tommy – and as sweet. But Tommy had swerved off course somewhere along the line, and even though he'd turned into a 17-year-old Adonis, his charm disappeared like magic when a girlfriend made him angry. He had a dangerous allure. We all knew he could get a little mean and rough, but, my gawd, was he ever dreamy looking! His breath stank of cigarettes and beer on a Saturday night, but that *smile*!

Of course, the parents never knew anything the kids didn't want them to know, and so the parents never worried. Parkside High was a great school full of the nice children of neighbourhood friends. It was known for its contributions to the Remembrance Day Parade and its food drives for the needy. Beer? Oh gracious, no!

And so it was easy for Joey to slide a beer or two into his backpack each morning and pop the empties back into the case when he got home from school later on in the day. He wrapped the bottles in his gym clothes or extra sweater so they wouldn't clank as he walked. The boys at school made him feel good about it, after a while. They even started to let him have a slug or two himself, and so he joined the fellowship of guys who knew how to take the edge off a tough day with a few brew before lunch. Joey started to feel pretty good about all of this, and he wanted the guys to like him even more. This meant procuring more beer, and the only way a 15-year-old who looked like a 12-year-old could do this was to steal it from the neighbours. This was actually easier than it sounded, if you could keep the pounding of your heart from bursting your ear drums

– the slightest sound is important when you're sneaking into people unlocked garages at night.

A garage is a great place to store beer. It's cool, and it's usually convenient to the kitchen or the basement stairs; if the beer is in the garage, then the wife can't complain that she's always tripping over the blasted cases. And if she can't see the cases stacked up like colourful promises of a good time with friends, then she isn't going to notice how fast the supply is depleted and how much money hubby spends on beer and why can't she have a new vacuum anyway? And God forbid they should go out for dinner once in a while. And looking at all those cases reminds her that Cliff doesn't do anything anymore but sit around and drink beer. He's a crashing bore — but he does pay the mortgage. Yes, many men find that a garage has its advantages. A garage isn't a great place to store beer in a city like Ottawa or Montreal or Lethbridge because those places are too frigging cold. But in London, Ontario, where winters aren't really all that bad, it works just fine.

It worked for Joey, too, for a very long time. Our folks thought it strange that he wanted to go out walking at night sometimes, so Joey started writing letters. What a nice boy he was turning out to be! He wrote to Grandma Lamoureux in Toronto and our cousin Tony in Barrie. He wrote to the Raisin Bran people to complain that there were not enough raisins in their cereal and he wrote a letter to the Olivia Newton John fan club. He wrote to the newspaper asking for a free copy of a photo of a winning soccer goal. And he wrote, heck, he wrote to everyone and no one (some of his envelopes contained blank paper). At the time I thought it a bit strange that he was such a nerd but he'd always been a bit quirky and I was usually busy talking to my friends on the phone, so it was good to have him out of my hair.

The logical time to mail all those letters was at night, of course, after Joey's homework was done (yeah, right). Off Joey would trot at 8:30 or 9:00 p.m., letter in hand, and half an hour later he would reappear with tiny beads of sweat collecting along his hairline. I'm not exactly sure where *I* would have stashed stolen beers. Years later, Joey told me he'd hidden them in the furnace room, lowering them carefully through a back window. It struck me as a stupid place to choose since Dad was always checking our wheezy old furnace, but Joey never got caught, so obviously he knew more about the intricacies of the project than I did.

When he got a little older Joey developed some mysterious leg cramps. The doctor thought this condition might improve if he got more exercise. Joey took this advice very seriously and started going for long walks at night. His buddies were liking him better and better all the time.

Jocy got really good at stealing beer. Then he started helping his friends steal other things, too. Some would say it was all pretty innocent, but in fact it was the start of a life of minor crime. Joey, 17 years old, was behind the bleachers at the opening game of the Parkside football season when he hatched the idea. He was sitting with Mark Johnson, a real creep if ever there was one, in the tall peaceful grass. They shared a joint and quaffed beer while the cheerleaders chanted and pranced and the September sun beamed down on a world that was prettier than it deserved to be. Joey was happy to be there, in the moment (he had no particular plan for the future anyway), coolly ignoring the football team hunks who were charging up and down the field in what always seemed —to Joey — to be an exercise in futility. People in the bleachers stood and sang, hollered, and cheered while Joey and Mark lolled and listened to the sound of the wind in the grass. Years later Joey told me that's when Mark invited Joey to join him one night when he went out hunting for stuff to steal. It would mean some good cash, he said. He knew a guy who would buy the stuff from them and they'd split the take 50-50; it was a two-man job, and Mark couldn't think of anybody he'd rather have watch his back than Joey. Joey was flattered.

The cash sounded good to Joey, since he wasn't big on working. My parents had been after him for years to get a part-time job, but he maintained that it would get in the way of his school work. Every mark Joey the "anti-Einstein" got was precious to our folks in those days. After a while they just gave up. Although my parents gave him money for lunches and the odd movie out with his friends, that just wasn't enough. Now Mark was offering him something exciting, daring —manly, even. So every Friday night the two of them would creep in and out of dark houses wearing dark clothes. I have no idea how much money Joey actually "earned" at his "job." In fact, if I had known anything about the business it I would have blown the whistle. Joey later said that it was a lot more interesting than stealing beer. In fact, it was a great little business until the night he jumped from the side window of a house and landed in the arms of an officer of the law. That changed a lot of things for Joey, but he got a suspended sentence, thanks to the expensive arguments of the best lawyer our folks could find.

Joey was barely making it through school, and our parents had no idea what to do with him. After a couple of years of attempting to coax, cajole, lecture, manipulate, and befriend my brother, I disowned him. He wouldn't listen to anybody. He didn't care about anything. He had turned into a nasty, creepy jerk. My mother cried a lot and my father yelled a lot. They took Joey to a psychiatrist, but nothing seemed to work. They wanted him to stay in school; he didn't even bother to talk to them.

He showed up or not, depending on his whim. He drifted through another couple of years doing Lord knows what with his time. He'd occasionally chat with me, usually when he needed a loan he had no intention of paying off. I didn't really care what he was doing, and I didn't really like him anymore, but he was my little brother, and I felt some obligation towards him. It seemed as though the future held nothing for Joey, no promising highlights of a great life waiting to be led. He was headed nowhere, and that was just fine with him — if he even bothered to think about it.

By the time Joey was 21, the pattern was established that our parents would kick him out of the house and after a while he'd move back in. I thought his expulsion should be permanent —what was the point of all that back and forth? He figured he'd become an auto mechanic. Drug dealing was looking like a dead end since his buddy Pascal was found with his throat slit in a downtown alley. I remember when Joey found out about it. It was a beautiful summer day — the kind when the sky is bluer than a robin's egg and there's a nice gentle breeze playing with the leaves on the trees and the sun is glittering on everything and you just can't wait for 5 o'clock to roll around so you can rush out into all that fine golden light. At about 2:30 in the afternoon Joey called me collect at work. He was crying and keening.

"Calm down, Joey! What on Earth happened?"

"Pascal...Oh my God, Teale — he's dead! They cut my buddy's throat! He was doing a deal with some dude from Toronto and we were supposed to meet for a few beers at lunchtime and he never showed up...I went looking for him and there he was, in the alley beside the drop-off, and there was cops all around and an ambulance but I asked a guy and he said the poor bastard had been dead for hours and — Jeeeesus, Teale — this isn't supposed to happen — not to Pascal...his girlfriend just had a baby...what am I going to do without Pascal?"

"Oh, Joey..." How could I be of any help at all? How could I even come close to understanding his world, his pain, his loss, his desperation? He hated me for my sincerity, my work ethic, my success in creating a life that allowed me to skim well above the surface of disaster while he swam through the dark spaces of the world, avoiding detection, always hoping for the big break that would propel him into the light. We had nothing in common, aside from genetics and a shared beginning in life.

"I'm at a dead end, man, a real dead end. What am I going to do? What if I'm next? They just cut my boy's throat and left him there to rot! There was flies all over him, man!"

I had nothing new to offer, nothing he could grab onto and use to turn his life around. I had tried before. He always ignored his prissy big sister because I just didn't get it. And he was right. I couldn't figure out why he didn't apply that great big brain of his to something worthwhile. He was proud of his "work" in a covert kind of way, but he couldn't walk into a bank and get a mortgage or finance a car. He was a nothing. Just like his friend Pascal. And I loved him anyway, in that frustrated, tired way women love drug addicts and alcoholics and unfaithful husbands who promise to do better and don't.

"Get out, Joey. Get out and get clean and find something to do with your life."

"Yeah, yeah, that's what I'll do this time. This is it, Teale — I gotta get out."

Naturally he didn't. Ever notice how hard it is to start something new and scary even though you're really driven to do it? Sometimes all you have to do is take one little step outside your comfort zone to get started on a whole new adventure, but it's so fraught with terror. Your head spins with "What ifs?"

"What if it's too hard?"

"What if the pay is lousy?"

"What if it doesn't work?"

"What if it's no fun?"

"What if I'm not good enough?"

"What if I change my mind?"

And that little step becomes harder and harder to take.

"I'd better think about it some more."

"I'll have to figure out how to do it."

"Maybe things will work out where I am now."

"I'll just keep things the way they are until the spring. Or maybe the summer. Or until I'm 25. Or 40."

"What's stopping you from changing, Joey?" I asked.

"I don't know," he said.

And he didn't know. He enrolled in Fanshawe College's auto mechanics school and was giving that a half-hearted try. But he wasn't making a whole lot of money at the part-time job at the lube shop he was working in and I knew he was doing a little "work" on the side just to make ends meet. This interfered with his coursework and it was looking as though Fanshawe was another dead end for the boy with no plans anyway.

Until he met Divane.

Joey told me the whole story of his romance with Divane one night when we were driving home from a Glass Tiger concert we'd gone to one weekend in Buffalo. We weren't exactly close as brothers and sisters go – I disapproved of him at almost every turn. But he was my brother and he was really great company – he was charming and curious, courteous and kind. If he could ever get himself straightened out he was going to do fabulous things with his life. If.

Divane was blonde, very blonde, and she had dark, bushy eyebrows that contrasted starkly with the platinum softness of her shoulder-length hair. She was a little shorter than me, which meant that she was quite a bit shorter than Joey, who measured in at 6-foot-2" by the time all that milk he drank got finished with him. Joey had met Divane in a bar, one of those nice ones women tend to like because they're clean and sleek and full of plants and great music. Or rather, Joey *didn't* meet her there, since she steadfastly refused to give him the time of day, even though he spent a whole evening trying to make small talk with her. He tried to impress her, and, let's face it, even pick her up, but he struck out. As she prepared to leave with her friends, he touched her lightly on the shoulder and said,

"What's the matter, do you have a boyfriend already or something?"

And she smiled an oh-so-Divane smile, looked up at him, her dark eyes dancing, and replied,

"No. But honestly, honey, there's more to life than a little flirting in a dark bar and I don't go out with boys I don't know. I've got things to do in my life and for all I know you could be a drug dealer or something."

"Do I look like a drug dealer?" Joey asked in astonishment.

"Well, no," she said.

"Thanks," he said, cringing quietly inside.

"Look," she went on. "You could be the sweetest guy on the planet but I need a lot more information about you before I even think about finding that out. A gal can't be too careful you know."

She poked him in the chest with a long red fingernail.

"But thanks for the interest," she added shyly.

She smiled sweetly, and turned away.

Joey was confused. He was dressed okay and he was clean. He was probably the most charming male in the bar that night — he'd often been told that he was an attractive guy. He had nice manners and a great sense of humour. What more could a chick want?

"Do you want to see my resume or something?" he asked. He didn't have one but it didn't hurt to call her bluff.

"It's not about what you put on paper, it's about what you put in your life," she said.

Joey just stared at her. He wanted to hand her a great line, one that would stop her in her tracks and make her melt into his arms. But he had no idea what it would be.

Divane left leaving Joey without so much as her name.

That got Joey thinking, I guess. Here was a woman unmoved by his charm, his lopsided boyish grin, his size and strength, his courtesy, his generosity. She was looking for something he didn't have. She wasn't interested in drifting in and out of relationships, which, Joey had found, most women were quite happy to do. This babe even had criteria for engaging in conversation! Who did she think she was? How could *she* ignore *him*? Boy, the next time he saw her, he was going to give her a piece of his mind. Or maybe he would just drive her crazy by ignoring her. That would teach the uppity little thing a lesson. He smiled at the thought. In the meantime, he might just work a little harder at that auto mechanics program, maybe start going to classes a little more regularly, even do the homework for a change. Some women just think they know everything about a guy.

Joey haunted the bar where they'd met. By the time he saw Divane again, he had finished his second semester at Fanshawe and was looking forward to the next term. He was living at home again, still making a little money on the side, and acing every test he took. Joey could take apart just about anything; one day he would be really good at putting things back together again, just the way Lord Chevrolet had intended. When he saw Divane, his palms got all sweaty. He was just about to walk coolly by her table to demonstrate how much he was ignoring her when he realized she was there with a guy — a very handsome guy, as other guys go. He also saw that she was smiling a lot. He spent the rest of the evening discreetly asking around to find out if anybody knew that blonde chick with the tall guy. No one did. She looked like she was having fun, and, more to the point, her well-dressed date looked like he was having fun too. Joey most definitely was not. He felt like an outsider. He went home that night and opened up his textbooks and studied until the sun came up. He felt awfully lonely.

Joey finished his first full year at Fanshawe, enrolled for the second year, and got a job in a mechanic shop that specialized in shocks and lubes. He had pretty much left the street side of his life behind, although money was tight. He saw Divane at the bar twice more but didn't stop to say hello. The second time, she caught his eye as she was leaving and smiled. Joey's heart lunged and he had a smile on his face for days afterward. By the time Christmas break came around, he was ready to swallow his pride and talk to Divane, no matter who she was with – if he ever ran into her again.

As luck would have it, Joey had agreed to run a few Christmas errands with our mother that year. She had sprained her ankle and needed someone to drive her around and help her hobble in and out of a few important places in town, one of which was Elke's Salon on Richmond Street. Joey had never been into a hair salon, let alone one that offered massages and aromatherapy, but Mom's appointment was for 11:00 sharp and she simply couldn't manage without him. My father would have rather eaten a dead rat than walk into a salon. So Mom leaned on Joey as she limped slowly into Elke's, and although Joey was happy enough to help, he felt like a baby seal in a fur boutique.

"Hello, Mrs. Covey," said the receptionist sweetly.

"Oh, hello, Lindsay," Mom smiled. "This is my son, Joey." Joey looked at Lindsay and then looked quickly away as though seeking an escape route. He'd become "Joe" to most people — in fact, he hadn't been called "Joey" by anyone outside our immediate family for about eight years now so this was awfully embarrassing. He just wanted to hand Mom over to Lindsay and get out of there. Mothers could be such hard work. Glancing around, he found himself gazing into the merry dark eyes of a familiar young lady with very blonde hair. She stuck her hand out and with a great big smile said,

"Hi, my name is Divane. Like Divine, only with an A."

Joey was speechless.

"This is my son, Joey, Divane," said my mother cheerfully.

If Joey had been another kind of man he might have grabbed this chance and parlayed the encounter into a dinner invitation, or at least a coffee date, but he was Joey — er, Joe — and this was the mysterious Divane, and he could barely manage to close his mouth and keep from looking like a 12-year-old confronted with his first Playboy centrefold.

"Nice to meet you, Divane," he sputtered. She smiled. He smiled. My mother ignored them both.

"Now, Joey — here's the list of errands you promised to do for me while I'm here. Margot is picking me up at 2:00, and I'll need that wrapping paper, and..."

And on she went.

I'm sure Joey heard nothing of what she said. He would have been quite happy to sit in the reception area for three hours so he could keep an eye on Divane, who was, he had now discovered, a hairdresser. Quite a good one.

Their courtship was a painful one. Joey took to dropping off little presents for Divane at Elke's reception desk, but of course no-one in the family ever suspected he had a crush on someone. He was secretive about the whole thing so I felt pretty flattered when he told me the whole story.

He'd slink in through the salon's smoked-glass doors and quickly deposit a red rose, a small box of chocolates, a package of herbal tea, a tiny teddy bear, a book of silly poems, a pottery mug. Then he'd slip away again before he had to talk to anyone. Joey rented a little apartment for himself downtown and graduated at the top of his class. He was hired by Auto-rrrific and felt proud to have a permanent, full-time position. He was falling into the routines of adult life with the determination of a bull. His little presents for Divane were becoming more infrequent since even the most ardent flame needs to be fanned once in a while, and because he rarely got a glimpse of Divane, he began to let go. He was far too proud to march up to her at work and ask for a date with all of the salon's female clientele and staff looking on, and he had no phone number for her. Then one night he was sitting in the bar — their bar — lost in other thoughts, when she slid onto the stool next to him, ordered a rum and coke, and said,

"So, wanna go out with me sometime, Joey?"

Joey looked at her, speechless as usual, and thought about it.

"Yeah, I'd like that," he said.

"What about tonight?" she said.

"It is tonight," he said.

"Well, you could take me for pizza or something. I just got off work and I'm starving!"

Joey was surprised to sense something akin to a great and majestic bird beating its wings inside his chest. He felt wonderful. As he looked at Divane, beautiful Divane, he felt at once humbled and invincible.

"Whatever you like, Miss Divane."

"There are rules, however, Joey," she said.

"Shoot," he said.

"Pizza means pizza, and that's it."

"Check."

"If we have a nice time, it can be pizza next week too."

"Check."

"Treat me right every time I see you or we're history."

"Check."

"You have to keep that job and work hard or we're history."

"Check."

"I don't date liars, cheaters, or lazy boneheads."

After a couple of months of pizza, coffee, walks in the park, and beers at the bar, Divane started feeling like Joey was maybe a pretty decent guy after all. She liked him. No, she was starting to realize she was crazy about him. Joey had never experienced such a slow start to a relationship before, and it was driving him nuts, but he recognized that he cared more about Divane —and her opinion of him —than he'd ever cared about anything.

And so there were more rules.

"My friends don't have to be your friends. If you don't like them, then keep your opinions to yourself, and I'll go out with them on my own."

"Check."

"Stay clean."

"Check."

"Date no other women."

"Check."

"Don't try to borrow money from me."

"Check."

"Hurt me and we're history."

"Check."

Making love with Divane was the most exciting experience Joey had ever enjoyed.

When David and I blew into town on our way to France, Joey and Divane were standing in our parents' kitchen discussing the future and ignoring the past, so caught up in love with each other that it almost hurt to look at them. David smirked and snorted. He thought that Divane was common trash and Joey was a loser. He didn't use those words. He didn't need to. It was written all over him — the superior arch to his eyebrows, the way his lip curled as he sipped his scotch (the hundred-dollar bottle he'd brought my father to ensure there was something drinkable in the house.)

As soon as he ingested his last mouthful of cake and let his fork clank down onto one of my mother's best china dessert plates, David announced that it was time to go.

"Sure, David, as soon as we're finished cleaning up," I said.

"Oh come on, Teale. I'm sure your mother and Divane can look after all that. We've got a long drive ahead of us, and we don't want you out too late."

Divane looked into David's frowning face as he spoke, her natural effervescence muted. She glanced at me with pity in her eyes and waited to hear what I'd say.

"David, I would really rather stay and help," I said.

David let out a big sigh.

"Well, Teale, I'm just trying to look out for your best interests."

"Go ahead, Teale," said Divane kindly, her small hand nestled inside Joey's large one. The room was quiet now. There was a small smile playing on Joey's lips — he had the look of a guy who's happy just to feel his woman's touch, who only wants to think about her and how she looks when she gets up in the morning…and goes to bed at night. My father had pushed his chair back from the table and was toying with his coffee cup. My mother was standing in the doorway to the kitchen, a fresh pot of coffee in her hand. David's eyebrows were raised. The whole room was waiting to hear what I'd say. I felt trapped.

"Let's just stay until the dishwasher's loaded," I said smoothly. Everyone started breathing again. Except me.

17

The sound of a lullaby sometimes makes me want to cry. It makes my heart ache to be reminded of the beloved, protected babies we all once were. Or long to have been. All the lullabies are there, buried deep inside me. Sometimes they surface for a moment, wafting like a trio of harmonies unbidden into my inner ear and echoing through the chambers of the musical instrument of me. I grasp at those magical sounds, repeat them, roll them around my mind, my memory, my heart. They well up in the back of my throat, making my soul quiver and my vocal chords reverberate. It is not so much the music that soothes me as the sense of being safe and comforted, of feeling that I have been rocked gently in mothering arms. I know that my forehead has been tenderly stroked and I have heard the crooning voice of a mother's endless love.

Maybe others have felt it, too, in a quiet moment, resurrecting their infant self; possibly regaining that early sense of being blessed and protected. Perhaps a part of them is like a part of me, still locked in their mother's embrace, supported by that quenching, drenching, wrenching swirl of arm-nestle that held them safe until they could crawl, as do I now, to the safety of a distant shore. Surely she sang to them, their mothers, and maybe somehow they remember, even childless, even today, snatches of the songs she laid down in their hearts before they struggled to this state of independence we so soggily embrace as adults. Independence.

Now run.

Run home to the place inside you that's locked away, that innocent place where you used to live when you loved the world and all its creatures, when Time had not yet grabbed you by the throat and choked the breath of hope out of you. God knows I wish I could go back to that time and place when all things were possible, that time when I believed that I would glide out of my mother's world and into the embrace of the prince who would care for me and protect me. If I had been able to do that, then I would have been saved. But instead I found myself on the cold and crumbling steps of a vacant English church, my heart strangled, deeply frightened and confused about who I had finally become.

The not-me.

The windows of that church were broken. Glinting shards of glass pointed up and pointed down, pointed crazily in all directions. Inside, battered pews, stained floors, strewn garbage. Desecration. Here I sensed, for perhaps the first but not the last time, that my prince was my opponent. I wish I had known long before that day that the future he offered me was a toxic brew, not a sweet succession of delights culminating in a happy ending.

Ah, Prince. You cheated me. With you by my side, there were to be no long years of marital bliss, of loving my man, of holding his hand on the street, of brushing a stray lock of hair from his eyes, of warming his body with mine. You killed my dream of eagerly awaiting the sound of his key in the lock, his foot on the stair, his voice whispering tenderly in my ear "I love you." The years were supposed to be filled with love, with the happy voices of children in the yard, on the stairs. On her wedding day, Teale had been so convinced it would all come to pass exactly as she had always imagined. The years would pour slow and fulfilling into her future, a steady stream of goodness and warmth and – wait a minute – who said that this is the way it's supposed to be? And why *isn't* it true? Why can't an innocent girl, a sweet, gentle, kind-hearted, generous girl, grow up and marry a wonderful man and live happily ever after? Where did Teale, my dear, gentle, vulnerable Teale go?

There is no answer to that question.

She's gone.

Just gone.

Shades of Teal

To the "not-me":

It didn't matter at first that I had drawn down my retirement savings funds to pay for David's education — our years abroad. He came first right now, and besides, being pregnant, I wasn't exactly an equal partner, as David, my prince, had made, gently, clear. I had thought I was equal, or at least as equal as I could hope to be, but you are only equal if the other party accepts you as such. As soon as he or she has doubts – and as soon as you *realize* that he, or she, has doubts – the game's up and your whole world starts spinning off its axis. The house of cards tumbles.

"Teale, Teale, Teale," David said softly. He was standing on the step above me.

Graceful old trees stood on either side of the church entrance, and a plump hedgerow patrolled the edges of the cemetery directly in front of us. The church was built on a hill, and I turned to look down the short lane that led to a country road. Off in the distance some cows grazed peacefully. David, now silent, followed my gaze. Acres and acres of green spread before us and they were dotted with stone farmhouses, broken fences, and trees, their leaves dancing in the cool breeze. It was a breathtaking sight. It would have made a magnificent painting. I felt very, very cold.

David took me in his arms and held me tenderly against his chest. "You aren't earning any money right now, and you aren't doing anything that'll help the family's future. I'm sweating my buns off over books and lectures and weekend study sessions so I can make more money for *us*. You spend your time cooking and shopping and moping about how miserable you're feeling or how tired you are. You can't expect to be able to veto our spending decisions. You're a weak link right now – mind you a very nice one – and you'll just have to trust that I'll do the best thing for us. And I will — I promise, old darling."

He pinched my cheek, a little too hard.

"But David, I don't think we can afford a holiday in Eastern Europe right now. Money's tight and the food budget is stretched as far as it will possibly go as it is. Touring Czechoslovakia and all that doesn't seem logical at this point."

"Just cash more of your retirement bonds. You still have some left, don't you?" His voice was soothing. I rested my head against his chest. I hated arguing with him. It was such a lot of work.

"Yes, but I think we should save them for a rainy day. And anyway, didn't you say you had RRSPs to cash in case we needed them?"

"Of course I do, plenty of them, but they're for emergencies only. We discussed that already, Teale. I am in a much higher tax bracket than you are, so it costs us more money to cash mine, and, like I've said many times, I think we should be very careful about how and when we use them." That was so logical. His arms tightened around me and he inhaled deeply.

"It smells so good out here in the country, doesn't it?" he said.

"All I'm saying is that I think a big holiday is an extravagance we can't really afford, David. We still need an awful lot of things for the baby, and..."

David dropped his arms abruptly and stood back from me.

"Good Lord, Teale, that baby has more stuff than I do. Just stop spending money like we're millionaires and we'll be fine. As far as this holiday goes, we'll just borrow a little more money from my parents. On second thought, scratch that. Dad already thinks you're an expensive wife, and we wouldn't want him to think worse of you because we asked him for more money. Would we?" He looked at me thoughtfully.

No, I thought. That's for sure. I still hadn't recovered from the humiliation of the stamp collection incident. I probably never would. The Mastersons would probably never accept me as a social equal, but I was far too proud to let anyone accuse me of chasing their money. I had even signed a pre-nuptial agreement stating that if David and I should ever split, I would not seek a penny more than I was legally due. Naturally, I would never leave David. It was unthinkable. And I was loath to have David's parents think I was soaking them for a grand lifestyle.

We had borrowed $40,000 from the Mastersons to help cover our expenses for our two years in France. We also had all of my RRSP money, my government pension, and my savings — which amounted to about $25,000. David was drawing a small salary from Lewis and Simms for some consulting work, but he had no savings to contribute and felt it was critically important that he not cash in his RRSPs unless it was a matter of life or death. What a guy! Always thinking about the future.

We should have been able to manage on the money we had, but for some reason our calculations were always off and we kept coming up short. Our credit card debt was mounting steadily. I bought all the baby things at church rummage sales and second-hand stores and our apartment was certainly a long way from the Ritz. I watched my pennies carefully and never bought anything for myself. After all, as David so rightly pointed out, what's the point of buying clothes that wouldn't fit in a few months?

Of course, David needed things, but that was different. And I was prepared to be conciliatory, since the money in question wasn't technically my own.

"OK, but aside from the money thing, I'm not sure I really want to be away from my doctor right now," I said. "What if something goes wrong with the pregnancy?" Tears were forming in my eyes. I was starting to sound like a whiny worrywart, even to myself. Time was, I didn't worry about anything, I just knew everything was going to be all right, somehow, and the main thing was to kick back and enjoy the day. Time was, I felt strong and confident and free. Time was, I didn't cry — well, hardly ever. Time was, I couldn't be manipulated into doing anything I didn't want to do. Time was, I didn't have this wretched knot in my stomach all the time, as though I were always doing something wrong and was going to get caught. I was never really sure about anything anymore. Except my love for David.

Rewind to Teale, age 21, sitting — no dancing, actually — on the porch roof of a house on Brock Street in Kingston, Ontario, drinking beer with four very cheerful friends and feeling as though she has just found a cure for all the evils in the world. She's just completed her fourth year at Queen's University, this very afternoon writing a final exam on Shakespeare and submitting her thesis, "Images of Homosexuality and Promiscuity in the Romantic Poetry of William Wordsworth" — to the great relief of her professor, John Taylor Weekes. Her favourite professor. Her lover. Wordsworth raises some intriguing issues related to the subject of homosexuality. Perhaps he never intended his words to be understood in such a context, but isn't that the marvel of literature, that it sends us off on intellectual tangents that allow us to see life in fresh new ways? That it makes us grow *intellectually*? After thinking intensely about the issue and engaging in numerous debates in the Quiet Pub with friends both straight and gay, Teale has concluded that the heterosexual lifestyle is loads more fun than the homosexual one, at least for her. She has fully and ruthlessly examined her sexual identity and determined that she's a raving heterosexual.

The late-April sunshine beams down on the somewhat inebriated gang on the Brock Street roof. They're singing "Moon River" for the twenty-seventh time and waving at passing friends. Their fellow students are cheerfully packing their belongings and heading home to take on jobs, buy cars, rent apartments, and generally beat the world into submission. The trees are just in leaf, and the world is indeed a perfect place.

Dinah Westcott is with Teale on the roof. She wears a pair of dirty old jeans and a ripped red, blue, and gold rugby shirt. She is a political studies major, president of the student council, and a world-beater. Tomorrow, she's going to Montreal to become a marketing trainee at Bell Canada. One day she will start her own marketing consulting company and make a lot of money. She will have numerous affairs but ultimately decide she's not the marrying type. Finally, at age 45, she will meet the man of her dreams and have a baby with him. They will marry and, after many years of not believing in marriage, Dinah will be unbelievably happy.

Simon Curlew is definitely the most unsteady member of the porch roof gang, having popped open his first beer six hours earlier. He is going to take his engineering degree and put it to good use building bridges in Nigeria on behalf of an international aid organization. Tomorrow, Sheila Johnson, an arts grad, will kiss him goodbye at the train station and trudge back to her apartment, where she will cry for two days. Simon, however, will feel a little relieved that their two-year relationship is ending. He has begun to feel constricted by it — it just doesn't feel good anymore.

Not wanting to hurt Sheila's feelings, he has hung on until graduation so he can make a graceful exit. He will encourage Sheila to go out and meet new men who might be, um, better for her. Twenty years later, Simon will be grateful to Sheila for believing in him so passionately, since the woman he does end up marrying is about as emotional as a dry cork. Although she will be an attentive mother to their two sons and an asset to his career, she is brittle and undemonstrative. He will wonder whatever became of Sheila.

Sheila loves Simon deeply. When they weren't getting along, she had a couple of brief affairs with guys she met in her classes, but Simon's the man for her. The thought of him leaving for Nigeria makes her feel desperately lonely. He will be leaving her. After her two-day cry, she will go to the student pub and drink too much. She will leave with some guy named Eric (or is it Donald?). They will have fantastic sex that night and Sheila will start to believe she might get over Simon some day.

After numerous other visits to the pub followed by wildly enjoyable romps with guys she doesn't even remember afterward, Sheila gets a "reputation" and she has some surprising liaisons. One morning she wakes up with her cousin, who is visiting from Jersey City. One morning it's her roommate's father. She finds a job selling advertising for a radio station in Winnipeg, figuring the change will do her good. A couple of decades later she's no longer a perky redhead with a winning smile; she's a bleached blonde with a cynical grin and many wrinkles. She smokes too much. She's been through two marriages — both unmitigated disasters — and has learned that she can't have children. Too bad. She is still angry with Simon for leaving her. Life would have been so different if she'd had faith in something.

The other guy on the porch roof on this beautiful April day is Joshua Elders. The others consider him a likable geek, but he has a thigh-slapping sense of humour and gets along with everybody, everywhere. He makes everybody feel good. Nobody expects him to amount to much. His marks are good but not great; he's managed to stay in the commerce program for four years although he has far more interest in anything with the word "beer" attached to it. Because he's so damned nervous around girls, he has a hard time getting a date. He's not bad-looking, but he's no head-turner. There's no indication that 20 years on he'll be earning over half a million a year (plus bonuses) as a bond trader, that he'll be vice president of a major North American investment organization, or that he'll own properties in Toronto, Muskoka, Florida, and Wales.

Along the way, he'll also acquire a wife — an extremely vivacious, supportive, good-natured lady with the unlikely name of Violet. Together they will build a remarkably solid marriage, have three nice kids (who are also destined for great success), and plan a wonderful retirement for when Josh finally decides to cash in and retire. Josh won't be able to believe his luck.

And there is Teale. Her smile is wider than a Moon River mile, her floppy, mouse-brown hair is pulled back in an unruly ponytail and her Queen's rugby shirt looks like it's had some unfortunate experiences in the off-campus laundromat. Housework will never be Teale's strength: she will always be irritated at the thought of cleaning things that don't stay clean. Teale is going to have a magnificent future. She's a helluva hard worker — she's managed to complete her degree while waitressing at a diner on Princess Street. Teale is looking forward to a career in journalism. She wants to go to places like Lebanon and Beirut, Cyprus and Brazil. She passionately wants to write about world events as they unfold. She has served as a stalwart reporter for the *Queen's Journal*, pumped

Shades of Teal

on coffee and donuts and churning out copy until 3:00 or 4:00 a.m. twice a week in the journal's newsroom, with Bruce Springsteen rocking her on as he boomed out of the paper's not-so-state-of-the-art cassette player. She feels alive and on-target and powerful when she's reporting. She's going to make it all happen, and no one can stop her. Everything she decides to do she gets done with enormous verve. She is dedicated. She is focused. She even borders on brilliant at times. Everybody knows she'll succeed in life. Straight to the top.

So why is she in France now, not working, not writing, and not choosing to do much of anything except clean the house and cook for David and all of his shiny new friends? She doesn't own a typewriter, let alone a computer, and she's worried all the time about everything. Money. The baby. What David's family thinks of her, since she's not from a financially comfortable family, as David tends to point out. Frequently. She and David will never be able to borrow money from her parents if they want to go on a last-minute vacation. David has pointed that out numerous times, too.

She worries about whether she's bought the right kind of orange juice (there is one that David simply cannot stand —he threw a whole carton of it against the kitchen wall the other day, and it took her ages to clean that mess up). She worries about the weather (she badly needs a new winter coat but David has made it clear that they can't afford it). If only spring were near.

Teale worries about having enough money for groceries to feed the friends David invites over, and she worries about getting to the public Laundromat often enough to make sure David has clean clothes. She worries about ironing his shirts properly, because if they aren't perfect, he'll crumple them up and put them under the dirty clothes in the laundry hamper and she'll have to do them all over again. It would be nice if he could just leave them on a hanger. She knows she has to work to perfect her ironing; he says she should be able to get it right by now. Why is ironing so hard?

Teale also worries about where David goes when he leaves the apartment at 10 or 11 at night and doesn't come home until 3 or 4 in the morning. He creeps into the flat and lies down on the couch so he won't wake her. She is not asleep —in fact, she hasn't slept since she heard the door close behind him when he left. Teale worries about her looks and whether she is gaining too much weight. She worries that David never makes love to her anymore. Ever. She worries that she has become boring. She worries that David won't love his baby, that he won't hold it and snuggle it and talk to it and smile at it. Teale worries that giving birth is going to hurt. Teale is sick with worry, and she is always pale and cold and tired. She has become a shadow of her former self. She feels like the shadow of a shadow.

That old picture proves it. Teale still has it somewhere, the shot of the porch roof gang —five young people frozen in a photo on the cusp of an adulthood they can almost feel, almost picture, but not yet understand...soundless, their mouths form the words of a song that old guy Johnny Mercer wrote, a song that was timeless even then, timeless and touching...

Moon River, wider than a mile
I'm crossing you in style, some day
Old dream maker, you heart breaker
Wherever you're going I'm going some day.

Two drifters, off to see the world
There's such a lot of world to see.
We're after the same rainbow's end, waitin' round the bend
My huckleberry friend, Moon River and me.

Huckleberry Teale would never have been able to understand why Pregnant Teale is so damned fuzzy-headed about everything. If you have a problem, create a solution. It's easy! Did Teale mention equality? What's that about? There is equal and not equal. Teale will always be equal, with all the rights, privileges, responsibilities, and pleasures that it entails. End of sentence. Next? Huckleberry Teale never doubted herself —the future was waiting. Pregnant Teale's future extends only as far as the end of today.

"Man, you worry a lot," David was saying. "The baby isn't due for another five or six weeks. Surely you can take two or three weeks so your husband can have a vacation. I'm tired, Teale. I've been studying really hard lately and I teach continuously, in case you hadn't noticed. I finally get a break, and you won't let me take a rest. This marriage isn't just about you, you know. I have needs, too, but what do I keep hearing? Teale needs maternity clothes, Teale needs fresh milk, Teale needs to buy clothes for the baby — a baby, by the way, that already has four sets of those pyjama things and two track suits. When I married you, I didn't take you for a greedy spendthrift, you know. I thought you were different from other women, that you would be happy with the way I looked after things, that you would show some appreciation for how hard I work. But no. All I hear about is how you need this and how you need that. Need or *want*, Teale? I thought this money was *our* money, not *your* money, and that we would decide together about the things we were going to spend it on. But no, every time I make a suggestion you're always there, shooting it down, spoiling my fun, ruining my day with your negative attitude. Every goddam penny I have ever made has gone into the house or your lifestyle when I really should have been investing in my education. But, oh no, your bloody house costs a fricking fortune to maintain, and you decided to go ahead and have a baby. I don't have the luxury of a fat savings account to fall back on right now, Teale. If I don't get this designation, then you can kiss your future as a rich housewife goodbye, babe, cuz I won't be able to make enough money to support us anymore. If you don't choose to support me like I've always supported you, then I think you have to ask yourself what this marriage is all about and why I bother hanging around."

The historic ruins of the old church we were visiting were located a few miles from a village whose name escapes me now; all such details have swirled away like dead leaves from a tree in a fierce fall storm. It all happened so long ago. Time, the bastard, grabs at my life and tears it to pieces, scattering the remains of the woman that had been me, sending them ever farther from my reality. A real woman in a real world. Away the moment flies, twirling and burning higher and weaker, leaving nothing but a pathetic little puddle of tears at my feet, feet that were so much like the ones that stood, so long ago, on the steps of a quiet old rundown church. Burgundy it was, maybe. Provence. The church was old, anyway, with broken windows, and graffiti carved into the backs of the solid oak pews. There was a central aisle down which so many young couples had travelled over the centuries on their way to the altar, to a commitment before God, to their future. Had they argued over family finances? Of course not, in those days. Women left the decision-making to their husbands and didn't dare meddle.

Chattel.

It all seemed so wrong to me now, standing on the steps from which so many wedding parties had tossed rose petals, delighted in the match that had just been made, husband and wife, mated for life. A match just like ours.

In those far-off, long ago days, a woman's place truly was in the home —or the fields, perhaps. Her hands were always full, what with cooking, cleaning, sewing, bearing and caring for children, and generally doing everything she could to enhance her husband's position in the community. She had a job —she didn't need another one. There, standing on the steps of this very church she waited with her husband for the crowd to thin out, the night to turn dark and the start of the long trip back to their solitary cottage for a celebratory meal and the consummation of the marriage. She would stand beside her husband through everything, patiently forgiving his transgressions — his selfishness, even his infidelity. Whether he was kind or harsh, soft-spoken or domineering, she knew her duty; she'd been raised for it and so embraced it as inevitable and she awaited a new life after death; she bore it all and died. Perhaps she lies in this churchyard, the tattered remains of her Sunday dress shrouding her spare white bones. She sleeps the centuries away, patiently waiting for another chance at a happy life with a loving man. There are times when she pines for something more —the something more I once promised myself as I devoured teen magazines filled with lipstick promises and mascara fulfillment. She'd be embarrassed to know that sometimes I wanted my man to want me for my flesh alone, not my even temperament or my positive outlook or my inquiring mind. Sometimes I wanted to render him powerless and vulnerable. There was nothing holy or redeeming about my desire to couple with my man, but there it was, all the time. Covered, hidden, shameful, somehow.

The church is empty now.

I had handpicked David from the line-up of love. I went over it all again in my mind. He was handsome and intelligent, hard-working and educated. He liked to travel, he loved the theatre and the symphony, and he was sociable. He was able to spend time alone without pouting, usually, and he respected me greatly, he always said so, anyway. Of course I should love such a man! I had tried, with no luck, to get a job in France. I spoke fluent French, thanks to Granny Lamoureux who had been a bona fide Quebecer and who had insisted on communicating with her grandchildren in French. Although I didn't see her all that often, she had lit the fire of ancestral pride in me and with a little French blood running in my veins I had mastered the language.

But realistically, although I had a great attitude about the project, who wants to hire a pregnant foreigner? So what if my man spent a lot of money going out to bars and brasseries without me? So what if he bought cases of expensive wine to enjoy, without me? So what if he had told me that I mustn't buy more than a couple of maternity outfits because I wouldn't need them for long? So what if he got upset when I asked for another twenty francs for food ("It's not like *I'm* eating a lot of this extra stuff, Teale. Can't you get along with fewer groceries?") So what, so what, so what? He loved me, that's what. When I was sick with the flu he called a doctor and asked what he should do for me. When I missed my family he suggested I call them. When I worried about the baby he told me everything was probably going to be all right. He loved me. He even *told* me he loved me! What right did I have to complain about anything? Here I was in France, for crying out loud!

Most women would give their eye teeth to be standing here on the steps of a crumbling church in a lovely English village with a man so bent on building a future with me that he was willing to put his career aside for two years to improve his skills *and* his marketability. He was doing it for me and our children. It was my duty to contribute every penny I had and devote all of my energy toward our common future. David was so selfless!

Giving everything you have —that's what marriage is about, isn't it, Huckleberry Teale? Just as it had been four hundred years ago, and four hundred years before that. I had an important duty to my husband, a duty I'd been incapable of understanding when I was only 22 years old.

The thought of Huckleberry Teale smouldered in the back of my brain. I didn't feel strong anymore. After three-and-a-half years of knowing and loving my man, I was feeling a little abandoned, wounded, outcast, even. Would there ever be a time when I didn't have to back down to maintain marital peace? Would there ever be a time when I felt free and easy and unguarded with my husband? When I could laugh at something I thought was funny without worrying that he would mock me for it? How could I be married to such a perfect guy and feel so uncomfortable about it? There must be something wrong with *me*! Maybe I wasn't trying hard enough.

Well, then, I would try harder. It just wasn't my turn right now, and that was okay. Perhaps one day it would be my turn to wear beautiful clothes and enjoy bistro meals all the time. One day it would be up to me to decide where we would take our holidays and when. One day it would be me who went out and made friends and invited them home for dinner parties, regardless of the cost. David could do the cooking. One day...in the meantime, I stood on the church steps and thought about my dear departed sister asleep in the churchyard beside me. I thought about how hard she had worked and how meekly she must have accepted her status in the world. Times had changed. I still believed that —or at least I thought that I should believe it. David was, as usual, right. He did need a holiday. Maybe that's why he had been so grouchy lately. If it entailed sacrifice on my part, so be it. There was plenty of time for me to have the things I wanted to have, to do the things I wanted to do. It was David's turn now. But I would take my turn, believe you me!

Shades of Teal

The few moments we spent on the church steps seemed like a lifetime. A lifetime of looking into each other's souls and waiting for the other to blink.

"Of course, David." I said. "You're right. You do need a holiday. I'll cash more RRSPs and we'll go have a good time. The only thing that matters is that we're together."

David flashed his million-dollar smile and gave me a quick hug. I fought back tears.

"That's the spirit! Let's go celebrate with a nice bottle of red and an apple juice for the young lady!"

I lumbered off to the car, seven and a half months pregnant, happy at having made the right decision – but, no, not happy at all. The pain of compromise, of humiliation, was searing —it took my breath away. Nothing made sense anymore. My prince was happy now. I knew that if I voiced what I thought, what I felt, it would make him miserable, and he'd bounce that misery right back on me. How were couples supposed to resolve their difficulties if one person didn't give in? But did it always have to be me? These questions whirled furiously in my head as I opened the car door and eased myself into the front seat. David already had the engine running.

"Hurry up, Teale. It's cold out there."

I watched the old, old church recede in the distance and thought of the centuries rolling by. Some day my bones would lie in a lonely graveyard, my dreams unachieved, forgotten. But I was young and strong now, a blooming bud in the prime of life. Still, it would have been awfully nice if someone had wanted to hold me gently and sing to me every now and then, to tell me he loved me, that I was worth holding.

Hush little darling don't you cry,
Momma's going to sing you a lullabye...

18

Travelling is one of my greatest joys and I love collecting experiences I can hold forever as memories in the dusty museum of my mind. I grew up in a town whose art gallery was located on the third floor of the public library; it did not contain a single Picasso. My town had been founded in 1797, which was impressive by Canadian standards but no big deal when measured by European expectations; I suppose it shouldn't surprise anyone that cultural institutions were gestating quietly in the background of people's daily lives.

That being said, I felt a little deprived growing up because nothing all that interesting had ever happened in our neck of the woods. In London, Ontario, there were no cave paintings, no Gothic cathedrals — no monumental events like the signing of the Treaty of Versailles or the founding of the United Nations. No Napoleonic army had ever tramped across our farmlands and no crusaders had ever knocked on the door and asked for a glass of water on their way to kill the infidel. There had never been a guillotine set up in the town square. No fine ladies of the court had fanned themselves while the king danced with the queen in the local castle, and no chateau had been built across the river to accommodate the king's mistress. Women had never been burned as witches. There had been no violent religious conflicts. The only plagues we knew of were those inadvertently inflicted upon Native peoples by the European explorers and traders. It seemed to me, growing up as quickly as I possibly could, that London didn't have a history at all. If you wanted to immerse yourself in the grandeur and glamour of the past, then you had to look further afield — to Eastern Europe, say.

Names like Belgrade and Budapest, Prague and Kiev, felt dramatic tripping off my tongue. The thought of walking streets once trod by exotic historic figures caused me to shiver with the excitement of learning. I could wrap the achievements and the sufferings of humanity around me and see how they felt. Our impending visit to Eastern Europe would be a fabulous opportunity for me to immerse myself in the tastes of hearty slavic food and the sights of glorious historic city with architecture I had not yet glimpsed. It would be a chance to hear languages I would be unable to understand as they tripped off the tongues of strangers standing in the shops and on the streets of cities I could not yet even imagine. But, although I had agreed to go, I was approaching this two-week trip with lead feet. And I was frustrated with myself for being so damned gloomy.

"Teale, do you know how many women would kill for the chance to go to Eastern Europe for two weeks?" David had said the night before we left. No, actually, I did not know, nor did I care. I was worried sick about being away from home (whatever home was anymore) just a few weeks before my baby was due. And what was going to happen now that I had drained a few thousand more dollars out of my precious RRSP? I had practically killed myself at a job I hated to tuck that money away; it was supposed to be used for our retirement, not boondoggles to Budapest.

No, this trip was not a good idea, and it bothered me that I was dreading it; it bothered me that I felt confused. I had clearly chosen to go. So why did I feel as though there hadn't really been a choice? Of course there had been a choice. There is always a choice. Did I have a choice now?

Think, Teale, think!

What had the options been? David had been determined to take some of my RRSP money and have a holiday because he felt he needed a break. I could have flat-out refused to go along. It would make me feel better about myself, probably, and Huckleberry Teale would be mollified — at least for the time being. But David might have gone on this blasted holiday anyway, just to prove a point. And, if I had decided to be really bloody-minded and refused him my RRSP money, he would have found it under a different rock and I would end up owing somebody else for the pleasure of David's vacation. Taking such a strong stand against him would have created a huge schism in my marriage and left me stranded in Paris on the verge of having a baby my husband didn't want to begin with. Would he leave me for good? Was this little trip to Eastern Europe worth a divorce? No. It was risky to go away, I figured, but much riskier, from a long-term perspective, to stay home alone. So, like millions of women the world over since the beginning of time, I made my choice: I would do what he wanted to get something I needed. It was all pretty clear-cut.

While my logic was sound, it was revolting to have to make such a choice. Marriage means compromise, but shouldn't both partners be compromising? I was clearly supposed to love and support my husband, as he was supposed to love and support me. But why did I feel as though I did all the loving and all the supporting? There was a fundamental inequality here that troubled me, and I was having a hard time putting my finger on it. I didn't really want to examine the gut-wrenching question of whether David and I were contributing equally to each other's happiness. The answer had to be yes, or what did my life amount to? Why was I even inspired to ask such a question?

I knew my husband pretty well. David often said that men and women were equal. He believed that men made a big mistake when they refused to hire women to do promotion-track jobs, because women had a lot to offer. In his experience, there was no real difference between male and female employees, and denying women the chance to make their mark in business was simply wrong. David was a terrific supporter of women's rights —- he often said so himself. I had heard him tell his boss at Lewis and Simms that it was high time the firm looked at its hiring policies and its training opportunities for women, that women had a crucial role to play in the future of the firm. If something was troubling me, it certainly wasn't David's attitude to women.

But maybe David had a hard time transferring the concept of equality from workplace to home life. Maybe he thought I couldn't contribute babies to the household and be equal because motherhood wasn't a real job. As a stay-at-home mother, you don't get paid, you don't get holidays, and you aren't eligible for sick leave or workers' compensation. You aren't given a company car. You can't change jobs and become a mother to a different family if the working conditions are awful or you don't like your colleagues. You can never be fired. You can't be promoted. There are no training courses you can take and no opportunities for advancement. At the end of 18 years or so, you finish the contract with no compensation or severance pay.

So anyone who takes on the job is not only disposable after 18 years, but also completely useless. Mothering is not recognized as such, but it's such an important job that the world would descend into chaos and despair if hundreds of millions of women were suddenly unwilling to take it on. That had to count for something! But what counted at the moment was David's opinion on the matter.

I began to wonder if I had fallen under an evil spell, one that was causing the disintegration of the love magic that had brought me and David together. I was starting to notice things I had missed, things that were a poor fit for the fairytale I had been living. David wasn't compromising the way I was compromising. Or was I so muddled by pregnancy hormones that I couldn't tell anymore?

I loved my husband, and he was wonderful. I had a lovely house on a nice street waiting for me in Canada. A beautiful baby would soon be nestled in my arms. We were travelling. Life was perfect. Those were the facts; that was reality. The prince cannot be both charming hero and evil master. That does not make sense. That is illogical. Therefore it isn't possible.

Isn't it?

I was confused again. I couldn't think. It was as though a mist had seeped into my brain, obscuring the facts, clouding linkages that should have been obvious. I didn't really want to see, didn't want to think. I knew I had married a prince of a guy. I repeated that to myself and felt better. I was ashamed that I'd ever suspected otherwise. The man with the mean spirit, the selfish snarl, the self-righteous determination to get his own way at any cost, he was an illusion, a figment of my ridiculous imagination. I thought I had caught a glimpse of him, but I must have been mistaken. The life I was living was exactly the one I had always dreamed about. Maybe I should have asked myself if it was the life I still wanted or the default life I got when I decided not to make a fuss. But I did not ask those questions. Not then, at least.

And so we travelled East, David trotting on ahead with a great big smile and me dawdling resentfully behind, looking for a place to sit down or, just as important, a washroom. A proper one.

We saw the Czech Castle and the Charles Bridge before taking in an opera in Prague. Much against my better judgement, we went to the Chernobyl Museum in Kiev. What if there were still some stray radiation floating around in the etheric neighbourhood? We visited Heroes Square, the City Park and yet another opera house in Budapest. We trooped through the Belgrade Fortress, the House of Flowers and the National Assembly in Belgrade. It was all far too much sightseeing for my liking. I was exhausted.

David drank lots of beer; I swilled plenty of milk. The weather was fine and David was happy. I had no reason to complain.

In the end, the baby bundled up inside me was none the worse for a little vacation, although I slept hardly at all and worried constantly that something bad might happen while we were away. I was such a worrywart! David always said I worried too much and he was probably right. But a first pregnancy is fraught with the unknown, the unexpected, the unlikely. How do you recognize what's normal when you don't in any way resemble your non-pregnant self and you have no friends or family available to ask? Every strained muscle, every sharp kick, sent me scurrying to my pregnancy manual for instructions, directions, or comfort. David was right: travelling pregnant was easy, and I had the added bonus of never having to cook a meal, although I stared longingly at the bottles of wine David ordered with his dinner. My baby lay curled in the nurturing comfort of my belly, growing stronger, more human, more loved every day. Soon he would be born. I knew I was carrying a boy, knew it as certainly as I knew my own birth date, my favourite colour, my parent's address.

I ached to hold my baby in my arms, though, to feel the soft curl of his fingers around my own, to nestle his little head under my chin, to put his hungry mouth to my breast, to croon lullabies to him as he fell asleep in my arms. I ached to look solemnly into his eyes and tell him about the stars and the Earth, to drink in his milky little baby smell, to kiss his naked tummy as I changed his diaper or dried him after his bath. How I would love this baby. How I yearned to meet him. David did not understand. Throughout the long days of the first trimester, I had slept and eaten well — despite my morning sickness. I had learned to eat normally again and dedicated myself to building a healthy baby. I was relentless. Calories be damned — this child needed nourishing. The second trimester was easier. Life resumed its busy staccato; I typed David's papers, made dinner, travelled on weekend excursions with David to Alsace and Luxembourg, entertained David's school friends, went to plays, purchased cases of wine for David to enjoy with his dinner. And I ate heartily, taking pride in my role as builder of a healthy baby.

"Man are you ever eating a lot these days," said David. "How are you ever going to lose all that weight?"

Time began to pass slowly. Each endless week carried me closer and closer to my baby, to the magical 40-week threshold after which my baby could arrive any day, any hour, any minute. How I wanted it to be *now*, how I wanted to hold our child in my arms and tell him how loved he was, how cherished. David would feel the joy then, I knew, for how could any father resist his newborn child, sighing and gurgling in his arms?

David's humour had improved after our vacation. He had seemed pleased that I'd almost kept pace with him during our long walking tours of the cities we visited. He even went out and bought the baby a little receiving blanket, which he thrust into my arms with a gruff comment and a small smile.

"This is for the baby," he said. He was coming around, and I was overjoyed!

19

We couldn't afford a change table or a rocking chair. We purchased a crib from a church sale, which was better than nothing but I worried that it wasn't safely constructed. I asked a neighbour to look at it, and he made some adjustments for me. All the baby's clothes were second-hand, and while it would have been nice to have beautiful new outfits for my darling to wear, everything was so horribly expensive. We couldn't have it all.

David had recently set out his rules for parenting, and it seemed pointless to argue. He wouldn't look after the baby alone until it was weaned, the baby was not to sleep in our room, and I could buy nothing new for the baby unless he approved, since I tended to be extravagant in my spending habits. In addition, I was not to expect him to change diapers, and if I was truly intent on staying home with this child, then he expected me to become pregnant again within a year.

"Within a year, David?"

"Well there's no point in dragging it out, is there? Once the next one's here you can either have more or go back to work. It'll be up to you." He smiled at me — one of his big, winning, loving smiles. He kissed my cheek and stroked my hair.

"Thanks, David," I said, tears of frustration filling my eyes.

David was really into the swing of things now, and I didn't want to argue with him, since he had been so against becoming a father when I first became pregnant.

"Suits me," I said. I pulled my lips into a replica of a smile and positioned my face in front of his so he could see how happy I was.

I hadn't always been so compliant. I remembered long discussions with boyfriends past about incompatibilities that had ultimately derailed the relationship, and I hadn't been afraid to say what I felt then. Daniel wanted the option of being unemployed every few years, because he "shouldn't be expected to work *all* the time." Eddie felt that affairs were perfectly acceptable because "they actually strengthen a couple's relationship." Norris was strictly against personal possessions of any sort, and Allan believed that a woman's place was in the home. No, no, no, and no. Huckleberry Teale had not been afraid to disagree with these otherwise lovely men, and relationships that had endured anywhere from two months to two years evaporated with no harm done. Was it because we weren't married that I felt no obligation to work things out, to compromise, or to back down in order to keep the train on the right track?

And, of course, I had not been pregnant.

Jason was born on a cloudy day when the temperature was falling and pressure changes were making my joints creak like an old house. We were back in Paris, recuperating from our holiday and enjoying our temporary home. It was a typical Paris row house, a little bit grubby with its brown brick with white trim, and we occupied the middle apartment, which meant I had to haul the groceries up the stairs. We were reasonably close to the Eiffel Tower, however, which was some compensation, and there was a wonderful boulangerie just around the corner where I was able to purchase our daily ration of crusty French bread. The charcuterie around the corner carried a lovely selection of cold cuts and patés and there was a charming little bistro a couple of blocks further on that made an unbelievably tasty soupe au pistou.

But David had started complaining about how expensive our holiday had been. I was wondering whether I should offer to cash more of my RRSPs and trying to decide what to cook for dinner on Saturday, when some of David's bistro friends would be coming over. The last few weeks of pregnancy are trying for most women, and I was no exception. Everything hurt. I was enormous and clumsy. I was always hungry yet suffering constantly from acid indigestion. It hurt to stand up and it hurt to lie down. I couldn't sleep. I wanted my mother. I wanted to go home and I didn't want to go anywhere. When was this blessed baby ever going to arrive? And as I sat at my dressing table, looking at the lines on the face of the tired old woman in the mirror, propping my tired head on my hand, dreading the day to come, wishing David would get out of bed so I could wash the sheets, feeling deeply irritable and unfriendly, I felt a rush of water between my legs: the long-awaited signal that my baby was finally on his way.

"Whoa," I said. David rolled over and groaned.

"David," I said, "come on, it's time to get to the hospital — quick!"

He opened an eye and looked at me.

"How do you know?" he croaked.

"My water broke! Come on — we have to get ready and go!" I stood and made my way to the bathroom, scooping up the clothes I had carefully laid out the night before. Panicked butterflies fluttered in my stomach. More gushes. This was surely it! My God, he's coming *today*! I could barely contain my excitement — and my fear — as I washed and dressed as quickly as I could.

"Any contractions yet?" David called from the bedroom.

"Nope!" I hollered back.

"Do we have to go right away, then?"

"I think so."

"I could use more sleep, Teale. Can't you call your doctor and find out if we have to get going right away?"

"But the doctor said to come in if my water broke — besides, I *want* to go in right away."

"I don't. There's going to be nothing to do there."

"Please, David, this is really important to me. I've never done this before. I need to get to the hospital."

"Just call the doctor — maybe you don't have to go in until tomorrow or something."

By now I was getting what I thought was a real-live birth pain, although in hindsight it was just a little baby pain. I sat on the edge of the bed trying desperately to remember how to breathe through a contraction. I couldn't remember. We had gone to prenatal classes together — maybe David would know.

"David," I gasped. "How do I breathe during labour?"

He opened one eye.

"Beats me," he said.

The pain was now a strong cramp.

"Shoot!" I said.

"Don't swear, Teale."

"I didn't."

When the pain had passed, I looked around for my pregnancy book and started collecting things I wanted to take to the hospital. I had already packed a bag, so I felt reasonably well prepared, but I felt panicky and slightly sick when, five minutes later, I was hit by another contraction. Where was that book? My hands were shaking. The pain subsided.

"David," I called from the living room. No answer.

"DAVID!" I needed to yell.

"What?"

"I'm in labour. Get up. We have to go to the hospital."

"Teale, you can't be in labour already — you're not due yet." Through my distress, I was actually impressed that he'd remembered the due date.

"Well, I'm pretty sure..." Before I could finish my sentence, I was gripped by another contraction.

"David, I don't like how this feels. Please take me to the hospital."

"Sure, Teale, I'll get up in a minute. I'll want a coffee, though."

"I can't make coffee right now, David," I yelled from the living room. I was now bending over and gripping the arm of a chair, struggling to hang on through the pain. "Take me to the hospital."

"I'll take you to the hospital if you get me a coffee," he said sweetly. This was not a great time to tease me. Still he did not get up from the bed. I thumped into the kitchen and started setting up the coffee-maker.

There was no sound from the bedroom. I knew I didn't have to call the doctor. I knew we should probably hurry. I started timing the contractions as the rich aroma of fresh brewed coffee bloomed through the apartment. Seven minutes apart. The coffee finished dripping and I seized the pot and filled a cup — not the chipped one, David didn't like chipped dishes. I splashed a little milk into it, carried it, steaming, into the bedroom, and put it down on David's bedside table.

"You are an absolute angel," he said as he hoisted himself up to lean against the headboard. He pulled me to him and gave me a lovely little kiss on the cheek. The pain started growing and I was panting. I bent over the bed, clutching the headboard. This was going to be a long day. David picked up his cup and took a sip. He leaned over and gave me another kiss, this time on the top of my head, and threw his feet into the sheepskin slippers I had bought him for Christmas.

"All right, Teal-i-o," he said. "Let's find you a doctor." He headed off to the bathroom.

Five minutes apart now. That was close enough to risk the necessity of a home birth, wasn't it? I struggled over to the bathroom just in time to hear the shower start. I pounded on the door. No answer. I turned the knob. He had locked the door. I screamed through the keyhole: "David get out of there and get me to the hospital or you will have to deliver this child yourself!"

No answer.

Nine minutes and two contractions later, he wandered out of the bathroom. He was all nonchalance, his hair freshly washed and combed, aftershave applied.

"I don't think you need to be quite so worried Teale," he said. I ignored him and concentrated on the contraction. "It's very important to relax while all this is going on. You're far too stressed out. Come on now, let's just calm down. How about a glass of water? Would you like a glass of water while we get ready?"

"Call 911," I said through gritted teeth. "The contractions are four minutes apart."

He slipped on his jacket, took me by the elbow, and steered me towards the front door. David was always very good at taking control. I had the presence of mind to grab my overnight bag on the way out the door. It was misery getting down the steps and into the car, but the car was parked, miraculously, right outside our townhouse. By the time we were racing down the street towards the hospital, seven minutes away, tears were running down my face and I was screaming in pain.

"For pity's sake, Teale," said David, "you don't have to make that much noise."

I was terrified.

David let me out at the emergency room door and drove off to park the car. I hobbled inside and looked for the triage nurse.

"Hello, and how can we help you today?" she asked politely in French.

I doubled over, tears streaming down my face.

"Ah je vois!" she said. "Come, everything will be just fine. We'll find you a wheelchair and speed you off to maternity. You'll be meeting your new baby soon, and you're going to want a cozy place to sit. Martin come to emerge, please." Moments later, Martin rolled up with a wheelchair.

"We're going to make everything all right now," said the nurse. "You just sit there and let us take care of you. Sh, sh, sh — now what's your name?

"Teale Covey," I said. "No, wait, it's Masterson, Teale Masterson.

"All right now, Teale, we'll look after you. Take her to maternity, Martin, please. I'll let them know she's coming."

I was swiftly transported to maternity, stripped of my clothes, and wrestled into a hospital gown. David took forever to show up, which earned him a scowl from Marie-Claire, the midwife assigned to my care. The monitors were all plugged in and everything was happening far too fast.

Pregnancy specialists avoid the term "labour pain." They prefer euphemisms like "contractions" and "cervical dilation." The books I read talked about finding comfortable positions for each contraction and rocking back and forth on all fours to help ease backache. They talked about the importance of staying calm and patient and noted that breathing properly makes the whole process much easier. All of this pretty chatter had led me to the expectation that if I did laboured and birthed my baby the *right* way, it would all seem like an afternoon at the playground. Nobody talked about the wrenching pain of childbirth or the disorientation that accompanies that pain, because "every labour is different." There is no mention made of the conviction that a woman in the throes of childbirth might have that she cannot withstand that much pain without dying from it – at least that's how I felt — and there is no warning given that bringing a baby into this world can hurt as much as having a critical body part amputated without anaesthetic.

But, brave, naive little woman that I was, I chose to proceed without painkillers. How bad could it possibly be, anyway? This was a choice David supported. "After all, it won't last for days or anything," he said.

But the agony just gets worse, and even the most noble of intentions are likely to be abandoned. Half an hour after I got to the hospital I realized I wasn't going to make it —the pain was far too intense. It is not uncommon for a birth to last 15 to 20 hours, and I figured there was no prize for pain endurance. The important thing is for both baby and mother to survive the process.

"I need an epidural, David," I blurted between contractions.

"Come on, Teale — pain is simply a question of mind over matter. You can do this. Keep at it, old girl." He sounded calm, but his forehead was wrinkled and his shirt was damp with sweat.

"No, it's too much," I groaned. And screamed and cried. Tears streamed down my face. I was hysterical.

"You're going to scare the other mothers, Teale," David said sternly.

I didn't much care who I scared.

"Teale, you've got to stop making all that juvenile noise," he said. A little later he added, "For heaven's sake! Get control of yourself. This is ridiculous — it can't be *that* bad."

"I. WANT. AN. EPIDURAL. GET. IT. FOR. ME. NOW. OR. I. WILL. KILL. YOU. LATER."

Every contraction seemed to surge into the next with no regard for time or tide, nature or relief; I felt my body edging closer to death, my insides flowing with blood that was the pain within me and around me, pain that jolted me then possessed and controlled me. Time ceased to have meaning. There was just the flooding pain, the cutting and cleaving, dividing and joining, surrounding and defining. Just pain.

The labour lasted only seven hours. Not bad for a first-timer, I later learned. The epidural I craved could not be administered because the anaesthetist could not be found. David left several times for coffee breaks. He was disgusted with my lack of willpower. The midwife and nurses did a magnificent job keeping me going — coaching my breathing, easing me into a warm whirlpool bath, rubbing my back, walking with me, giving me ice chips to moisten my mouth, smoothing back my hair. They calmed me and they nurtured me as I performed the miraculous job of bringing a new life into this world.

In the end, David was present for the birth of his son, his beautiful son: Jason Edward Masterson, seven pounds, nine ounces of lustily screaming boy. Nothing else mattered anymore. I held my little wonder in my arms and cried. He had been worth the wait. David might want to send me off to work in 12 months' time or rush me into another round of motherhood, but I didn't care. Huckleberry Teale might chide me for giving up on my dreams, for compromising myself into oblivion, for letting a stranger crawl inside the shell of me and live my life on my behalf. But I didn't care. All that counted now was the perfect wonder of mothering, of creating life, of holding this life in my arms. Mine to love and to protect, to guide and to cherish. This was reality. The only one I needed.

20

If pregnancy and birth aren't tiring enough for a woman just add in the care and feeding of a newborn: the adrenaline rush of the project quickly dwindles into a debilitating fatigue. At least that's what happened to me.

About the only coherent thought I could etch onto the pages of my fresh book of motherhood was that my arms must have been terribly empty without Jason to hold. He was perfect and precious, the lovelight of my heart, my first born child. I am sure my dying thoughts will recall the rapture of seeing him look at me with those dark wondering eyes, barely focusing on the features of my face and watching my lips change shape as they formed the words that spoke of my unending love for him. I told him about the fun we would have, the books we would read, the games we would play and the joy of living we would discover as I helped him grow up to be the remarkable man I knew he was meant to be. We lay there for quite a while after his arrival, he and I; his father, exhausted from participating in the miracle of birth, had gone home to sleep. Jason had already had his first sucks at the breast, hungry, greedy efforts to extract from me the milk that would start the chain of growth so vital for survival. I unwrapped his little body and looked at every tiny little part —his precious, fragile fingers, his fat, rolling neck, the pink, still-bloody smoothness of his chest, his scrawny haunches and his soft doughy knees. I counted every narrow little toe and every sweet little finger and kissed the soft spot on the top of his beautiful head. He was perfect.

Hospital staff took Jason from me to conduct the normal testing all newborns undergo and while he was gone the nurses allowed me the luxury of a warm bath during which the blood and sweat of the previous hours swirled off and away from me with the last remnants of the woman I no longer was.

Shades of Teal

I marvelled at how changed I was. No longer just Teale Masterson, wife, anymore, I was much more important than that. I was mother of Jason, giver of life, sustainer of humanity, tired goddess in my own right.

Later I told David of my transformation and he chuckled.

"Yeah, you're important for your boobs right now," he said.

Obviously, David didn't get it and I just wanted to take my little baby home.

Home, when we got there, was exactly as I'd left it a few days earlier: David's dirty coffee cup sat where he'd put it down on his way to take me to the hospital and it didn't look as though dishes had been done or anything tidied in my absence. I guessed David had been busy coming to the hospital except that I hadn't remembered seeing very much of him while we'd been there.

Checking out the stroller in the main floor hallway of our row house I began to fuss a little about safety issues. Neighbours had said ours wasn't a very safe district and I worried that going out for walks with Jason might be dangerous. David said I was being silly.

"I wouldn't worry about it, Teale – who's going to attack *you*? It's not like you're a beauty queen or anything and you don't exactly look well-to-do."

He was right again, of course – David was so logical! My clothes were all second-hand and well-worn. I hadn't had a haircut in months and there were holes in my shoes. Our stroller was something David had found in someone's curbside garbage and he'd brought it proudly home so I could patch it up with string, wires and more than a little good luck. I was sure it was safe but it looked odd. Who would ever attack me hoping for money? We had agreed that our money should be spent on experiences, not things, and that meant our resources mostly went towards travelling. There had been lovely trips to Versailles and Dijon, to Brittany and the Pas de Calais. We had been to Monaco and Provence, Angers, Reims and Marseilles — anywhere, in fact, that sounded interesting on a Tuesday evening as we looked ahead to our weekends.

"As soon as the baby comes we'll go to Belgium," David had said, with a cheerful grin.

"OK," I had answered, having absolutely no concept of how I would feel after giving birth. It couldn't be that bad. Millions of women went back to work mere weeks after having children. Surely I could travel. It sounded fun.

And so, with little Jason Edward only three weeks old we packed the car and headed north for an endurance test. My baby cried from 6:30 every evening until 11:00 every night, took a break until around 1:00 and then cried for another couple of hours before falling into a fitful sleep that lasted until around seven in the morning. At that point he woke up for another hour and then slept until noon. David, of course, was too tired to stay awake with the baby and finally hit upon the cheerful idea of separate rooms.

"No point in both of us staying up all night," he said. "It costs a little more but it's worth it. At least if I'm rested I can be more help to you and I'll drive more safely too."

That was logical but I'm not sure I liked it and endless nights were followed by endless days spent trying desperately to grab a quiet nap in the back seat of the car.

"Why did you bother bringing me along, David?" I asked on the fifth day of our excruciating holiday. His excited descriptions of the sights he wanted to see left me cold. The baby did not like lunches in cute little bistros. The baby did not like bracing walks on the battlefields of Waterloo. The baby did not like touring castles or being jostled in and out of the car seat. The baby only wanted to eat, sleep and cry. All I wanted to do was to lie down on a soft mattress and pass out. David, on the other hand, was in his element. He slept soundly every night, ate hearty breakfasts every morning and he strode the historic sites of Belgium as though he owned them. His energy was highly distasteful to me, although I was so tired I couldn't muster much more than a cursory sneer which he always seemed to miss.

"You're a great sport, Teale," he said. "And a great map reader." He kissed me lightly on the forehead. "How's the baby today?" We were in a Bed and Breakfast in the middle of what appeared to be nowhere. The baby was just the same as the baby always was. Tired, cranky, and hungry. Or hungry, tired and cranky. Maybe he might be cranky, hungry and tired. My nipples hurt from constant sucking and the stitches that held together the enormous rip my son had made bursting out of my body were enormously painful. I had hemorrhoids the size of golf balls. And I needed sleep.

"The usual," I said. "I want to go home now — haven't you seen enough?"

"Teale, you can't see all of Belgium in just five days. We still haven't been to Brugges yet. I was thinking that since my break lasts another week we should just nip up there tomorrow for a few days."

"I want to go home now, David. I'm sick of dragging my butt —

"Watch your language, Teale!"

"I'm tired, David and I'm not having any fun. I want to sleep in my own bed and sit in my own chair and look after my baby within the walls of my own home. I can't make a cup of tea when I want one and the coffee in this country stinks. I can't eat when I'm hungry. I can't spend half an hour in the bathroom because other people might want to use it. I miss my parents and I don't have any friends and I hate being here now. You won't even sleep with me anymore."

I was weeping uncontrollably by this time. It was all so horrible and I had reached my limit; my husband seemed oblivious to my misery. David stared at me for a moment but Jason woke up and started screaming before he could speak. David walked out of my room, presumably to get his breakfast, and I stumbled to the bassinet we had brought with us, picked Jason up and began to nurse. The soothing comfort of milk filling his belly quickly calmed my little tiger and he settled in for a long leisurely morning feed while I continued my cry. I just wanted to go home, wherever home was. I just wanted some peace, whatever peace was. I just wanted someone to put their arms around me and kiss my forehead and tell me everything was going to be OK. This whole trip had been an expensive mistake. There were the nightly B and B fees (two separate rooms), the meals, the gas, the entry fees to the great museums and art galleries of Belgium. David had bought a new sweater and a case of brandy. He had also bought his secretary back in Toronto a new woolen skirt. It was two shades of blue with a cream stripe in it. Size 8.

"I think she's about this big," he had said. "There's no point in buying you one, Teale, although I sure wish we could, but we don't know what's going to fit you now that you've had the baby."

"I would really like a souvenir of Belgium, though, David," I said and at the very next town we stopped in he hopped out of the car and bought me a T-towel with a clock tower on it.

"Here's your souvenir," he said brightly. I was touched in a hurt kind of way.

But now I just wanted to go home. By the time Jason's feeding was over and I had changed his diaper and dressed him smartly in his best blue sleeper, David was back at the door, suitcase in hand, new sweater proudly displayed over his right arm.

"Not ready yet?" he called from the doorway. I just shook my head. He hurried off down to the car, to return a few minutes later as I finished packing up Jason's things.

"Just my stuff to put away now," I said miserably, holding the baby with one hand and struggling to fold yesterday's shirt with the other.

"Here, I'll take the baby," he said and I looked at him, stunned. It was an offer he almost never made.

"Can I go to the bathroom, too?" I asked.

"You won't be too long, will you?" he asked. I shook my head.

"OK then," he said, smiling. "Way you go!" The baby immediately started to cry again. I scurried off down the hall with my makeup bag, quickly brushed my teeth and washed my face, luxuriating in knowing someone else was holding my baby for the moment but stressed because I knew they were both unhappy. By the time I returned to my room David was frantic.

"He's hungry," he stated.

I obediently unbuttoned myself and reached for Jason who immediately upon feeling mommy's hands around him, vomited copiously and stopped crying. I felt lucky there was a clean shirt still tucked in to the bottom of my suitcase so I put Jason in his bassinette and quickly changed while he wailed. David didn't raise his eyes from the guidebook he was reading across the room until after I had suckled Jason back to sleep.

"Ready to go?" he chirped.

I lay on the bed for an answer and closed my eyes. If only I could have an hour in bed!

"Come on Teale we have to go," David said. "They're going to want to make up the room for the next guests."

Of course. I threw my things into my suitcase.

"I've paid already," David said helpfully. I nodded dumbly. David picked up my bags and headed off down the hallway, whistling, while I followed with Jason and my purse. I was too tired to care where we were going, or read another damned map or even to ask David what his plans were. I stowed the baby in his car seat in the back seat of the car and climbed in beside him. I leaned my head back and closed my eyes as David wheeled the car out onto the road.

"Here's the map, Teale," he said as he handed it back to me. "Take us home."

"Oh, David, thank-you!" I gushed. I couldn't believe it — my husband was so wonderful, so considerate, so sensitive...all I wanted was to get home and get to bed. And he was willing to drop all his plans just so I could be happy. I started to cry again.

David smiled and looked at me in the rearview mirror.

"I love you, Teale," he said quietly. "We're in this together, you know."

Although he said not a word the whole drive back to Paris, I could tell he was relieved to be going home too. As time went on, and the disastrous trip to Belgium faded into history, I sometimes heard David regretfully tell the story of how he had always wanted to see Brugges but that I hadn't been interested so he had never gone. Sometimes the story went that he had wanted to take me to Brugges but that I was so depressed after giving birth that I couldn't cope and he had decided he should just get me home. Both stories were true. But they left out some critical details.

"What a great guy your husband is," his friends would tell me. I would always nod. Yes, yes, he was wonderfully caring.

My little baby grew. He discovered his hands and his feet, his fingers and his toes. He learned to roll over and sit up and crawl. He got his first taste of baby cereal and then graduated to mushy cookies. He learned to walk. Every day was a miracle and watching my son discover his potential, test his strength, create an ever-expanding world of competence, humbled me. One day I turned around from my task at the stove and realized that almost 12 months had escaped my grasp since my little boy's birth. How could that have happened so quickly!

"Time for another one," David said.

"Yeah, right," I said. But David raised his spear of logic.

"Teale, you don't do anything all day anyway, you might as well have another kid running around here."

"What?"

I didn't do anything all day? I did laundry, made meals, shopped for groceries, cleaned the apartment, changed the sheets, mopped up at least a thousand spills a day, gave a reluctant child a bath, cleaned up after the bath, read stories, played with blocks, entertained David's family when they came to visit, fed David's friends, travelled with David and never had a minute to myself. My weight was finally dropping and I was starting to feel human again.

"Let's wait until we get back to Canada." I said. "I'm finally starting to feel I've got my act together, David...another baby will just mean I can't have fun anymore because I'll be pregnant and sick and tired all the time. These are precious years for Jason and I don't want to miss out on them because I'm pregnant and exhausted all the time."

"Oh, come on, Teale, a work-horse like you? You'll be fine, you don't give yourself enough credit. Pregnancy wasn't that bad for you — and we decided that we were going to have the kids all close together," he said.

"I don't remember even discussing it," I said.

"Yeah, we decided we were going to have them really close together or you were going to get a job."

"I'm not allowed to work here, David."

"Then I guess you'll have to have another baby. We'll be going home in the spring anyway. Or you could work illegally here. Look at you, you're just wasting away here when you could be doing something useful with your life."

"I think I am doing something useful, David. I'm looking after our son."

"You don't want to get lazy, though, do you Teale?" he asked.

"What?"

"You aren't getting any younger you know — we're going to have to get on it as soon as possible so we'll be able to spend more time together when we're older and the children have left home."

Of course, what he said made perfect sense. I wasn't getting any younger. I did want lots of kids. I didn't want to go back to work. There wasn't a moment to lose. Trapped by biology.

Plus, this was a man who hadn't even wanted a child when the first one started to plan its arrival – if he wanted more already, maybe I should just run with that idea before he changed his mind.

David smiled.

"OK," I said.

And so we conceived again. David seemed happy, to my great relief. Jason was only just over a year old — still a baby himself in many ways — and I was tired. The effort of creating life from nothing but a single microscopic pair of cells is enormous and the raw materials come wholly from within a woman's own internal eco-system. Everything she eats, drinks and breathes is magically transformed into the lovely little baby she eventually creates. It is a vast time of "no's". No coffee, no alcohol, no food colouring. No smoking. No energy, no sleep, no comfort. Feet hurt, bones hurt, pelvic muscles hurt. There is an enormous array of other inconveniences that go with pregnancy but ultimately a woman just quietly goes about her business, trying to focus with patience on the new baby set to arrive in seven months, five months, only one more trimester, 10 weeks, 35 days, 12 days, any time now. She endures. She waits. She shops. She rests. She keeps busy. She looks for signs that the pregnancy is progressing well, that the baby is healthy and thriving, even now, as it prepares itself for life outside of Mother. She compares every pregnancy's progress with every other pregnancy she's ever had and with every pregnancy anyone else has ever had. She becomes an encyclopedia of symptoms. If she has religious inclinations she prays more than at any other time in her life; if she does not, she just hopes a lot. I happened to fall into the praying category and I felt thankful that God hadn't given up on the human race yet, that each birth we gave was somehow His way of giving us another chance to finally figure out how to keep ourselves from annihilating each other.

"OK," He is telling us. You can have one more generation, one more chance to keep your line alive. You, the daughter of Eve and Rachel, Sarah, Rebecca and Mary, you the mother of hope, the giver of life, I have chosen *you* to take part in the holy effort to keep your species alive so don't let me down. And for pity's sake teach this generation to play nicely."

Well, sometimes I think He's saying that. But other times I think He's given us the short stick, put us in charge of something we can't control. While we women dedicate the really knock-your-socks-off prime years of our lives to creating life and helping it grow, nurturing and protecting, encouraging and teaching, there is an entire phalanx of men, in the prime 20 years of *their* lives, who are every bit as dedicated to ending life or causing it to suffer. They are the soldiers, the generals and bureaucrats, the businessmen and the politicians, the spear-chuckers, actually, who are completely focused on organizing for war. Look anywhere in the world at almost any time in history and you will find men involved in the intricately messy business of killing people —masses of people — because they are in the way. Every single bullet those people order and ignore exists for the express purpose of killing some poor mother's son. Some poor mother who spent nine long months of her life growing her sweet little boy in the nutrient soil of her belly.

She ached for his birth, longed to hold him in her arms, sang to him tenderly as she held him for the first time after he crushed her bones fighting to be born. And then this magnificent boy grew up, strong and brave, held a gun and died and his mother cradles his sightless form in her arms as she wails for the life she built from nothing but the air she breathed, the food she ate, the milk with which she washed down the bitter fear of another war. We birth them and we bury them. This is the tragedy of motherhood.

My second pregnancy was different from the start. I was to birth a little girl this time, a beautiful curly-haired laughing-eyed little girl who made it only as far as her 23rd week inside me. There she died, I never knew why, but her death was a death as surely as it would have been had I felt the privilege of holding her after 20 hours of painful labour. The doctors said that sometimes there are no explanations for the death of an unborn baby. Mostly, when things are not the way God's Nature intended, the unborn children are quietly sloughed away before anyone knows they've started to grow. That period that was a whole week late was actually a little Nathalie who would have been born with no brain. The period that was three days overdue could have been a Timothy who was missing a liver and a heart. They are better off not, we say. But for my little angel, the one who sits on my shoulder from time to time, singing or whispering or playing with my hair, there was no explanation for her death. She simply just died.

When I went for my monthly checkup the doctor couldn't find a heartbeat and further tests confirmed she was gone — gone from my life and my future, gone from the family photos that were to sit on the mantelpiece over the hearth of my heart. I will never know what colour her eyes were to be or what her favorite cartoon was or even if she liked strawberries or red apples or butter pecan ice cream. I will never hold her or lie next to her in bed, cradling her in my arms, her soft hair tickling my nose when she moves in her sleep.

She didn't even have a name yet but in the shadows of the dreamworld that is the unspoken well of my soul, I call her Lara. Not "Laura" with a "u" in it. She was and is and evermore shall be, "Lara", with the "you" missing but hinted at, almost there. I had to give birth to her anyway, because her lifeless body was too large and developed for other options and when it was over, I cried until the tears wouldn't come anymore. And then, like all woman everywhere, when the tears were over, and I'd had a little sleep, I got up and made myself a cup of tea.

David, for once, said nothing, did nothing. He put his arms around me and held me for a few minutes as I shook with sorrow. Eventually, he just went out. His kindness soothed me even so.

21

Remember that woman you knew – that friend or colleague, the relative, maybe even you yourself – who fell blindly in love with a man nobody liked? How could she have missed seeing how selfish, manipulative, arrogant and lazy he was? He was reasonably attractive with smile lines around his eyes and beautifully proportioned lips. She loved the sound of his laugh and the crooning purr of his voice when he turned his gaze upon her and spoke. The touch of his hand on hers melted her heart and made the tiny hairs at the nape of her neck tingle.

Over time, and it really didn't take all that long, she became his protector and defender, devoted to his every wish, lost in the bubble of his love for her; she became surrounded by the walls of delusion, safe in the tower of his strength, drugged by her need for his approval; she thought he was misunderstood.

And she would never let him go.

Not when he chose to go fishing with his friends on her birthday.

Not when he denied she'd ever lent him all that money.

Not when he went to her mother's house for dinner, drunk.

No, she forgave him his sins, his transgressions, his shortcomings, forgave and forgot, while the chorus of her friends, humming in the background of her life became more distressed, more insistent:

"You deserve better, sweetie, leave him."

And still she hung on.

She hung on through the abortion.

She hung on through his job losses.

She hung on through raging anger and unexplained absences.

She hung on even when her heart no longer raced at the thought of seeing him again.

"You'll never leave me," he boasted. "You'd be lost without me."

One day she arrived home early from work, a headache raging between her ears, her heart quiet with the deadness of the disillusioned. There was a naked woman in her bed astride the equally naked man she had hoped was her hero. At first they didn't see her standing in shocked silence at the bedroom door.

"Oh crap," he said when he finally noticed her. The woman in her bed said nothing.

And then your friend lost her dead calmness and started screaming, throwing things, kicking him out, them out, everyone out, raging against her stupidity, naiveté, idiocy, how *dare* he do this to her?

"I can explain," he hollered above her tirade, and it was a surprising thing for your friend to hear. It stopped her for a moment and she wondered how the situation could ever have an explanation beyond the obvious?

"Get out," she screamed. "Get out of my room, get out of my apartment, get out of my life. *Both* of you."

And they did.

That afternoon she changed the locks, closed her bank account, took his name off her VISA account and booked a last-minute discount trip to Cuba, a tropical paradise where she could safely drown alone in the darkness of rum. He called 15 times before she left and begged her to listen, to forgive. He showed up at her door but she called the police and they escorted him away.

"You'll pay for this," he hollered as he left.

She already had paid. And she cried because she missed him.

It's a story we've all seen, heard, read about and mourned. Sometimes these friends of ours do end up dead. Sometimes they end up penniless. Sometimes they spend the entire rest of their lives looking over their shoulder worried that he's following them, watching, waiting for his chance to finally get them, make them pay for the damage they did to his life, his reputation, his ego. Why didn't our friends notice what everyone else saw? Or were they just too trusting?

Damned fairy tales tell it all wrong.

Sleeping Beauty danced to her castle in the clouds at the end of her story having spent a whole half hour with her charming Prince Phillip. Cinderella danced with her handsome prince exactly once. Snow White had never even actually met the guy who kissed her and woke her from a charmed sleep. And off they all charged, each one crazy in love, ready to give up their friends, their families and their sweet little habits in favour of the man who they crowned, on the spur of the moment, "The One" with whom they should spend the rest of their lives.

For the first month or even two, everything was probably an awful lot of fun. There was plenty of money, a nice castle to live in, servants and a fine stable of horses for going off on romantic little picnics in the country. The food was all prepared and served beautifully and I'm sure they must have had a seamstress or three on staff to ensure a steady stream of great new clothes with which to impress the peasantry and various visiting dignitaries.

Sounds like a fairy tale to me, too.

But what happened when the first blush of excited romance wore off and there wasn't a present or sweet new delight waiting for the princess next month or next season or even, maybe, next year? What happened when Cinderella or Snow White or Sleeping Beauty *disagreed* with their mate? Didn't anybody ever get bored in these stories, or irritable? And what happens to a Princess who has ditched her whole life for a guy she barely knows and then ends up married to him before she realizes he is, unfortunately, a first class creep? (And yes, it happens to men, too, poor bastards.)

I suspect Cinderella had a pack of kids and her prince was awfully busy when he got that promotion to king. She became more independent as time went on, started a few little charities to keep herself busy, looked after the children's education, supervised her staff...and tried not to think of how unhappy she was with her husband. He turned out to be a bit dull, if you can believe it. Nice enough guy — but he worked all the time. He'd tolerate the occasional ball but wasn't interested in too much entertainment. After 15 years together she had ensured the succession and was surprised to realize she was bored silly. They never fought. But they never laughed together either. Cindy felt more distant from her man with every passing year. For his part, the king admired his pretty wife and was truly pleased with himself for marrying her. She was a bit giddy at times but generally let him get on with his real mission in life, which was to govern wisely and expand his kingdom.

Snow White had a different problem on her hands. Far from being bored, she was continually struggling to help her husband make ends meet. He swept her off her feet all right and they did marry, of course. But as it turned out, Snow White's prince was the family ne'er do well and had racked up stacks of gambling debts. They left that part out of the Disney version. He was a charming fellow and a terrific lover, all of which kept Snow happily distracted for a very long time. Eventually she tired of his endless promises, however. There was never enough money for the little things a woman likes to have in life — like a new brush when the handle breaks off the old one or a new face cloth when the old ones wear into tattered squares of shredded fabric.

Snow became keeper of the family's financial conscience and eventually her prince came to despise her tight hold on the purse strings. They fought. She cried. He hit her only on occasion and always apologized the very next day. It was good for her to know that he was still the boss, after all. And after all that struggling, one day she died, worn out by a life of struggle and wishing her Prince was, well, a prince.

Sleeping Beauty fared better. She and Prince Phillip were rather similar in temperament and they both enjoyed a good party. The kingdom was relatively well off and they were truly happy for a very long time. There were children and nannies and holidays and after a number of euphoric years together there developed a spark of mutual respect between Sleeping Beauty and her Prince that eventually grew into a love of a deeper sort, a more reverent love, one that carried them into and through the years of difficulty and loss that plague all adults, eventually. They were devoted to one another and they actually *did* live happily ever after.

Which makes me believe that it is *possible,* but perhaps not actually very *likely,* to find everlasting love on the spur of the moment. Maybe it takes months, maybe years, of intense talking, listening, watching, feeling, understanding, querying, testing, challenging, disagreeing and investigating to know if someone else is worth our forever.

I think we've been foolishly blinded by love, lust, or longing for centuries.

At the beginning of her affair with Henry the Eighth I bet Anne Boleyn never imagined she'd finish her life with her neck stretched over a chopping block. Murdering a wife is common enough today to merit national emergency status but everybody shakes their head over *King Henry's* viciousness. He wasn't the first and he wasn't the last to kill his mate and for every guy who's succeeded in putting a woman out of his misery there are probably another 1,000 who've thought of it. At some point Anne Boleyn was probably thrilled to bits at the thought of becoming Queen of Henry's castle. At what point did she start making excuses for his behaviour? How many excuses did she make for the guy before he took the final advantage of her endless understanding and sent her to her death?

"If he didn't care about me he wouldn't be checking up on me all the time," she likely sighed, proud to generate so much attention.

"Sure he has a temper but it is hard to be King!"

"He notices my appearance," she cooed after a harsh criticism. "If he didn't care about me he wouldn't have said a thing."

So much myth, so many excuses for what simply boils down to brutal behaviour, whether it's coming from Henry the Eighth or Hank Tudor. If the chemistry is there, we reason, the rest of it must be too. That first rush of passion floods our veins and clouds our vision, and we become lost in a meadowland of sensation, lost in an overwhelming desire to bond with a guy we are sure sees us as we really are. We barely know him, although we swear we must have known each other in another life.

"I can't believe he exists," we crow. He is exciting, fun, sensitive, caring, honest, responsible, dependable, sexy, warm, gracious... etc. But when he meets our friends and doesn't show the warmth we swear is there, we begin the endless parade of excuses to win at the court of public opinion.

"He's tired."

"He's worried about his job."

"He's run into some bad luck financially."

"His friends have deserted him."

"His parents didn't understand him."

"His new boss isn't fair."

When the first blush of passion fades and we remain committed to this man — who doesn't seem to be *quite* so much fun anymore, our friends start to worry.

"He loves me like crazy."

"This is just a bad patch."

"Things will be better next month/next year/sometime soon."

"If I only try harder, things will come around again."

"We're in this together."

Eventually, when the panties are found between the cushions of the living room couch, or the hotel bill indicates there were two people in that room, we have to face the writing, in our hearts. We are humiliated, humbled and shocked. Our friends, however, aren't surprised. Somehow they knew this moment would come.

22

Preparations for our return to Canada have all been lost in a jumble of details that crashed onto the shore of my life like a tidal wave, leaving me sputtering and gasping for air. Everything seemed to need doing at once and I always seemed on the verge of a nervous breakdown, whatever that was. I could barely keep a civil tongue in my head and I was always too tired to stay up past Jason's 8:00 bedtime. I jumped at every little noise and I never actually felt cheerful or hopeful any more. Everything was hard and I felt lonely.

I'm actually impressed that I accomplished as much as I did with a young boy glued to my leg all day. Packing for home after two years away was a huge job. There were the linens and house wares, books and trinkets accumulated almost thoughtlessly as we made our steady way through our daily lives. There were the special pillows I had bought in hopes of easing David's emerging back problems and the two beautiful desk lamps I had surprised him with on his birthday. There were several hundred books David had bought to help extend his library and stacks of academic and office paperwork. There were sweet little watercolour paintings we had bought at a flea market and two bronze sculptures of warriors David had found in an antique store He just couldn't resist them. There were flights to book and passports to update. There was the good-bye party we threw for ourselves and the countless invitations we tendered to friends to come and see us in Canada. There were bank accounts to close and bank accounts to check.

It was all overwhelming for me. While it wasn't monotonous, it wasn't all that interesting, either. What saved me was the comforting anticipation of returning to our home in Toronto where we had been so wonderfully happy in those first few years of marriage; the prospect of seeing my family again made me feel lighter. There were sleepless nights going over details of what had to be done and what could be ignored. It was almost more exciting to be going home than it had been to leave. I took to crying a lot.

My parents had come to see us in France for a two-week visit when Jason was about five months old. Seeing them again had been like a breath of fresh air for me and a lengthy jail term for David. It was wonderful to see my mother cradle her grandson and chat away to him like a playful mother hen. And she was a terrific help, busily preparing meals, folding the laundry I brought home from the Laundromat, vacuuming, dusting, cleaning and humming all the while. She was in her element. We talked about babies and children, clipping coupons to save money on the food bills, inexpensive recipes for delicious meals and the merits of English versus Canadian tea. We went out for lunch, just the two of us, and left my father and David in charge of Jason for a few hours, which felt like a holiday. David rarely looked after Jason but with his in-laws watching he wanted to put on a good show.

My dad cuddled Jason and dandled him on his knee, changed a few diapers and made David seem completely out of step with fatherhood. The strange thing was I had never pegged my father as a "Daddy" kind of a daddy and yet, there he was, chortling away with baby slobber on his whiskers and the smell of sour milk on his shirt.

David, on the other hand, who had promised to be a hands-on dad before any children arrived, just never seemed to jump in there. He had said he thought fathers should be completely immersed in parenting their children but when no help materialized within the first three months of sleep deprivation, I questioned whether he actually meant it. By the time Jason was six months old and I began pressing David to become more involved with his son, David swore he was useless at fathering a little baby but that as soon as Jason was a year old, he'd be in there like Flynn. At a year...well, I'm sure I don't even need to finish that sentence. Sometimes that's just the way it goes – we hear the words, face the disappointment, scrape up a little more hope and start again. David was a reluctant father.

When my parents ended their two-week stay with us and left again for home David breathed freely again but asked me several

Shades of Teal

times to please stop crying. For the first time in my adult life, I missed my parents. I began writing to them and calling them every few weeks to see how they were doing. I had long chats with my mother about diaper rash and cradle cap and weight gain in infants. I finally felt we had something in common. I was determined to see my parents more often as soon as we returned to Canada and to bring into my home the people I wanted to connect with – not just David's friends, much as I liked them all. When we got back to Toronto, I would be able to dig into a real routine, not dabble with the fantasy of a life abroad.

Eventually we boarded an airplane, ordered two glasses of champagne and headed for home. Any thought of settling down to a cheerful domestic routine went right out of my mind, however, as soon as I saw the mess our tenants had made of our home.

David had rented the house to a couple who were related to Carole Larson, wife of David's friend Tim. Because his friend had made the connection, David had nobly refused to take a damage deposit.

"These people are Carole Larson's family, Teale," he had patiently explained. "I'm sure they're just as nice as Carole." I never once said "Carole Larson is a jackass," although I felt like it. She had managed to publish a couple of books of poetry that had become critical hits in their own dreadful way but I thought they were hideously depressing, packed with dirty language and intellectually vacant. David would have said I was just jealous.

From France it had seemed that everything was going well. David had assured me that Tim and Carole were checking in every now and then but two years is a long time and when we reached our front hallway with our suitcases, diaper bag and excited relief at being home again we were met with a shocking sight. The floors were filthy and the walls were spattered with food flecks, paint and other materials of unknown origin. Almost all of the furniture had been stained, ripped or broken and pieces of the remote control for David's TV were scattered all over the main floor. This wasn't a serious problem because there was an enormous crack across the front glass of the TV and some bare wires stuck out from the place a plug should have been.

In the living room, the pretty plaster dado in the ceiling had been smashed in several places and some of the crown moldings over the window had been taken down. There were cigarette burns on the marble mantelpiece over the fireplace and there was a huge crack in the mirror that hung above it. Water stained the ceiling. In the kitchen, I discovered that one of the burners on my stove didn't work and the barriers keeping the food on the fridge door were all broken so salad dressings and ketchup and olive jars could no longer park there. Dark orange marks that looked suspiciously like fire damage strafed the linoleum in the corner near the back door. Elsewhere, I discovered that some of our curtains were missing and taps were dripping. The upstairs toilet overflowed and hardwood flooring on the upstairs level had been gouged. One of the cupboard doors of the lovely old-fashioned cupboard built-in to the upstairs hallway was gone. Bathroom cupboards were broken, drawers didn't draw and half the tiling in the tub surround had been cracked, as though someone had been in the habit of showering with a hammer. Furniture had been smashed and carpeting had been miserably stained. I was dismayed at the amount of work it was going to take to make our home livable again.

"What happened here?" I asked, rhetorically, of my husband.

"What's the matter, Teale" David responded smoothly, coming up behind me in the bedroom with a bland look on his face. Our bed frame had been broken and the curtain rod was pulled halfway out of the wall.

"David, this place is a dump! Everything is broken, damaged or missing – what on Earth are we going to do about it all?"

"Well, Teale, you have to expect some damage when you rent out a house – it's a well-known fact that tenants don't take care of a property as well as homeowners do."

"David, they trashed the place!"

"Relax, it's not all that bad. You'll have it back up to snuff in no time."

"David, I can't fix this disaster myself. I don't have the tools to rip out linoleum, or repair bathroom tiling! We're going to have to hire someone to do it." I was on the verge of tears again. Dammit!

David sat down on the bed and looked at his feet. He put his elbows on his thighs, looked up at me and sighed. I didn't answer. He didn't move. Finally he said,

"We can't, Teale."

"What do you mean we can't? Of course we can, you just pick up the phone and dial a number and the next day some guy comes over and starts fixing things. It's very easy, David," I said icily.

"No, I mean, we can't afford it, Teale. There's no money left to hire anybody to fix anything."

"This is no time to tease me, David. We've got at least $5,000 in RSP money we swore we'd keep aside to get us on our feet when we got back. This is an emergency. Or call your friend Carole Larson and ask her to dun the money out of her cheesy relatives!"

David was quiet for a few moments. I was bursting to talk.

"It's not that simple, Teale," he finally said.

"What's not simple, David?" I asked archly.

"The money's gone."

"Gone."

"Yeah, it's gone."

"Gone."

"Gone."

"IT CAN'T BE GONE," I said, disbelief ringing throughout the four walls of my withered home. "It was there three months ago. You promised me there was $5,000 sitting there to cushion us while you caught up with your pay schedule in Toronto. We are in Toronto now, David, and we need some cash. We have to buy food and diapers and gas for the car. We have to pay our hydro bill and our phone bill. We can't wait a month for your pay to kick in because we've already maxed out all our credit cards. We have that $5,000 sitting there so your son can eat. And we need some of that $5,000 to hire a repair man to come and start fixing up the damage your friends' relatives did to our home."

"They're your friends too, Teale," David said reproachfully.

He cupped his head in his hands and looked at the floor.

"We spent it."

"*We* spent it? Oh yeah, exactly how did 'we' spend $5,000 in savings in three months?"

"Oh, cut it out, Teale, you're always hyper when we disagree – it's like you're out to get me or something."

"I'm not out to get you David," I said calmly but bitterly. "I'm out to get an answer to where all that money went." Truth to tell, I was starting to panic and I was barely able to hold back the waves of tears that so desperately wanted to flow. We had borrowed money from David's parents to help us buy our house. We had borrowed money from David's parents to start up a household in France – first and last month's rent, the down payment on a second-hand car to drive while we were there, our airfare over there. It had added up pretty quickly. And although David had been paid a reasonable amount of money to study and teach and do some consulting work for Lewis and Simms in Paris, we had burned through about $30,000 in RSP money for entertaining – things like cases of wine and trips to Florence, Paris, Geneva and Heidelberg. We'd burned through another $10,000 in pension money that I'd amassed while working and we had spent the $5,000 I had sitting in my savings account before we left Canada. David had no savings and had not collapsed his pension plan. There had to be some money left now. This was impossible! I did not have a penny to my name – but he should.

David groaned. Was he feeling badly or thinking hard?

My head was spinning, trying frantically to figure it all out. I hadn't spent frivolously on clothes or baby gear. I didn't drink much or eat out with friends – in fact, I hadn't made any friends while I had been in France because I'd been so busy with the business of life. Naturally I had done a lot of sightseeing, as cheaply as I could. Where had all that money gone?

"Just spit it out, David, you'll feel a lot better if you do."

I don't know where it went, Teale," he said.

"You can surely do better than that, David," I said, something approaching a backbone starting to snake up my spine towards my cerebral cortex.

"All right. I crashed the last $5,000 six weeks ago and lent some to my sister and some to my brother. They're both buying their own homes now and they're feeling the pinch so I volunteered our assistance. It was the brotherly thing to do."

"You lent the entire amount out to your brother and sister."

"Yeah."

"Didn't you think you should even talk to me about it?"

"Well, Teale, it's not like it's *your* money."

"I know David, but we are a family and in a family you talk about things like that before just roaring out and doing it. I would never even consider handing Joey and Divane $5,000 without discussing it with you first, no matter how badly they needed the money."

"Well it wasn't $5,000 each, Teale," said David.

"The end result is the same, David," I said sadly. "Now how are we supposed to manage?"

The situation didn't make sense and I felt the mist of confusion swirling down around my shoulders again, obscuring my vision, distorting reality. My husband, my prince, was an honest guy. He worked hard and looked after his family. He always put us first. He said we were a team. This must be a mistake, a slip. He got confused. He forgot. Maybe I was in bed so early he didn't want to wake me to talk about it. Maybe Jason had been having a few bad days of teething and had been screaming so much that conversation had been impossible. Maybe it had happened when I had had that bad cold. Maybe…oh, the maybes were endless. David had messed up and we were in trouble. At least he was owning up to it and he appeared contrite, sitting there on the edge of the bed like a dog that has just accidentally peed all over the living room. But what a jerk.

He never apologized. But eventually, David picked up the phone and borrowed $5,000 from his father. He refused to get a workman in, although a new TV set mysteriously appeared in his den one Saturday afternoon.

"Don't you think it's about time we became a little more careful with our money, Teale?" he had asked solemnly. I felt terrible that I didn't know how to go about doing that and angry that he had the nerve to say that to me. I knew that eventually David would start making more money and we would start hiring experts to fix the things I could not fix myself. I was home with my beautiful son, my husband was at last back at work he loved and I could busy myself with the business of running a home. Maybe it wasn't a nervous breakdown I was having; maybe it was exhaustion. Maybe it was stress. I felt like smashing my fist into a wall at times but I thought if we could just get through the next few weeks leading to the next few months, everything would improve. Screaming at David wasn't going to fix the problem.

David started going out to social events by himself more and more since I was just too tired to make it past 9:00, and I was always reluctant to leave my sweet little man with a baby-sitter. Amid sarcastic comments about how boring I'd become David would leave, sometimes he wouldn't come home at all and for months I didn't care.

I tried to mother well and the loss of one baby made the act of caring for Jason even more important to me. Although I grieved often for the little girl I did not get to tuck in to bed at night, I grieved alone. Occasionally David and I would eat together after Jason was in bed but usually he would take his meal into his den and sit alone while he watched TV. I longed for his company and waited all day to talk to him, to ask him about his day and tell him about ours but there didn't seem to be an easy way to start a conversation any more.

We played roles from a 1950s sitcom, but the "com" part was missing, since there was no laughter, no joy, no cute jokes or witty repartee. Just the desperate fatigue of motherhood and the bone-headed determination to make it through just one more day.

Where had all the romance gone? Would it ever come back? I supposed we still loved each other but it was a different love now. David would roll over in the middle of the night and insert himself into me for some conjugal relief and while that had to count for something, it actually didn't count for much. I tolerated his sexual advances like I tolerated everything else in the marriage.

There was a distance between us that I hadn't been aware of before, a sense of another reality emerging that we carefully avoided discussing. Was this what had happened to my parents' marriage?

Was I living somebody else's life? The clothes in my closet belonged to a woman with no flair or style, no elegance or whimsy. I used to pride myself on looking well put together. Now I was happy if I was wearing two matched socks with no holes. This was not *my* dream, *my* joy, *my* enchanting reality. But if it wasn't mine, whose was it? And more to the point, why was I living someone else's life?

We eventually found a baby-sitter, a teenager who had moved in down the street while we had been away, and I reluctantly started accompanying David to his steady stream of dinners, receptions, parties and concerts. We had begun to entertain regularly — four or five course meals that took me all week to prepare. It would have been nice to have my husband all to myself on a real date from time to time, to see if we could work our way back to enjoying each other again, but every time I suggested we have an evening together alone he accused me of being anti-social. I certainly did not want to be antisocial. And I suppose I was lucky – I could stay home with my son, look after my family and enjoy a good life.

One Thursday night in June, I was busy cleaning up the dinner dishes, trying to ignore the marks on the linoleum and the broken fridge door. One day we would buy a new fridge and a new stove and put new flooring in the kitchen. One day we would also buy tea towels that had no holes in them. One day I would splurge and buy myself some yogurt. One day I would get a pair of new shoes. One day I would get a smart haircut.

David walked into the kitchen and leaned against the counter, arms folded, chin up slightly, like a bull sizing up its prey.

"I guess it's time for another baby, eh Teale?" said David.

I stared at him.

"What?!"

"Time to make another baby."

"Right now, David?" I asked.

"Yup. Jason's two, you're over the last disaster of a pregnancy and you've got plenty of time on your hands. We want more kids, don't we?" He softened slightly. "I mean, at least, I do." He looked at me, earnestly, gently, lovingly for a change. He put his arms around me and kissed the top of my head. I was stunned and did not respond.

"But I'm already busy, David, and I don't think I'm ready to try again, I still miss her," I protested, tears welling in my eyes.

"Oh, come on Teale, you're not that busy — you're at home with one kid, how hard can that be?! Plenty of women do what you do *and* work full time. And you're complaining about being busy! Jeez, you'd think you were running a country or something!" It was his way of teasing me.

David, of course, had never spent an afternoon, let alone an entire day, with his son. He couldn't know how draining it was.

"David I'm not sure I want another baby right now — Jason is still *really* little and he needs a lot of attention...if I get pregnant again I'll have no energy to do *anything* and I'll be even more tired than I am now. Let's wait a couple of more years before we try for another one."

"Well, that's fine, Teale, but if you don't have another baby then you'll just have to go back to work," said David. "We already agreed on that and time is slipping by."

"I still don't get that, David. Why do I have to either have a baby now or go get a job?"

"Because you're a housewife, and it's embarrassing for me."

I felt I'd been sucker-punched.

"Anybody can look after a kid," he added. "Day cares are full of caring people who make a living watching little kids. You're a smart lady — you should be contributing to your community."

"But David, looking after my son to make sure he grows up to be a good person *is* going to benefit my community."

"Sure, Teale, you can believe that if you want to but the fact is it's not real work and you can pay somebody to do the same job. You should be working."

I was in shock but in control.

"I invest my whole heart into looking after our son David, and it is exhausting work. We're up at 5 am every weekday morning and he doesn't stop until 8:00 at night. You're not around on weekends much so you don't have a clue how much work parenting is and I don't think anybody else in the world could do half as good a job as I do. I don't get a break, David and you've never even spent an afternoon with your son so you don't know what you're talking about!

The tears had started welling up in my eyes again. GRrrrr! Why was I always so weak?!

"Teale," cautioned David. "I am very involved in my son's life."

I looked at him and wondered how he came to that conclusion. But before I could gather myself up and come up with some sensitively logical way to refute the statement, he was chatting away again.

"And you don't know what it's like to be out there in the work world. I bust my butt for my family and you don't have to lift a finger around here. The mortgage is paid and the hydro is paid and you just got back from a two-year holiday in France, for crying out loud. Who pays for all your new clothes? Who pays for all your fancy haircuts? Who pays for the expensive clothes for your son? I do, Teale, that's who, and I think it's time you showed a little appreciation for how hard I work."

"I do appreciate how hard you work, David," I said.

"Well?"

I never had enough money to take my son to McDonalds but David went out for dinner with friends and put $400 meals on his credit card. He swore up and down he was expensing it all and we got every penny back. But I never checked. And did he really *want* to be out entertaining people at expensive restaurants all the time?

Of course not! Who could enjoy that! He was doing it for the future of his family, that's what it was all about. He was sacrificing everything for his, ungrateful little Supportive Spouse, me.

David drew himself up to his full height and put his hands on his hips. He stretched his neck up in a belligerent fashion and looked down at me.

"I don't want to go back to work or have another baby right now David," I said quietly.

"That's just great," he said. "Do you have any idea how humiliating it is to have to tell people my wife is a housewife? I'm the only guy I know with a decent downtown job whose wife isn't a *professional*. I hear it all the time 'My wife's a doctor.' 'My wife's a lawyer.' 'My wife's a teacher.' 'My wife's an interior decorator.' And then I have to step up to the plate and say 'My wife's a housewife.' I'm the laughing stock of Bay Street, Teale, because you're too lazy to get off your big fat fanny and get a job. Thank you, Teale, Thank you very much for nothing."

David huffed off to his den and slammed the door. We never fought – it was shocking to see him slam a door.

Jason was in bed, the house was silent and I was in tears. Embarrassed him, did I? My chest felt heavy as I thought it all over. This had the markings of a make-or-break the marriage issue. Either I had another child or went back to work. If I didn't do either, I could be looking down the barrel of Divorce. Divorce with an adorable little boy and no job. I loved my husband, I supposed, and he paid the mortgage. But if he left me because I wouldn't have a baby or get a job I was toast. My son might starve. I felt stupid and inept. Everything seemed so confusing, for some reason.

There was only one decision I could make: I had to get a job. We had to try to keep this marriage going for the sake of our son.

And maybe, some day, we would soar again together...

23

The next day I parked Jason in front of his favourite cartoon and set about revising my résumé so I could start my job search. I was amazed that I had never realized how important it was to David that I work. I had thought I knew everything about him. The superficial things like his favourite colour (orange), his favourite meal (deep fried squid with caviar), and his favourite city (Amsterdam) were easy.

But I knew crazy, intimate things too, like his earliest memory (smearing ice cream in his sister's hair), his biggest fear (dying young) and his third happiest moment (the day he got the job at Lewis & Simms). I knew his handicap in golf, his mother's middle name, his exact weight and his shirt size. I knew that he refused to use a toothpaste tube that was more than three-quarters empty and I knew his stand on women's rights, his opinion on capital punishment and his views on immigration.

I could read my husband's moods better than any thermometer and I knew when to cook an expensive dinner, when to make sure the house was spotless and when to change the subject. On this issue of me working, however, I had to admit that I had been blindsided by my own ignorance. How can you live with someone for five years and not know the one thing about them that is destined to have the biggest impact on your own life? How could I have possibly missed the importance of my career to my husband?

Times have changed since our mother's day. Now that we women have the right to work there is a vast expectation that we *should* work – whether we want to or not. Think of the women who marched in protests, burned their bras and chained themselves to government buildings. Their goal was to give their daughters and grand-daughters a world where they could speak out with authority from the board room table and the conference podium. No-one was giving them the corner offices or private limos to the airport and they were sick to death of being called, "honey." They were fighting unfair attitudes and oppressive workplace policies.

They knocked themselves out so women like me could slip seamlessly from kitchen sink to corporate head office.

Refusing to take up a salary was like failing to take up arms during a barbarian invasion. In the battle of the sexes, both sides have to be on the battlefield in order to figure out who's winning. If one entire gender were to throw down their briefcases and stomp away in search of a spatula, well, now, that would mean there was no battle, wouldn't it? How could a woman possibly leave the battlefield to the enemy?

David wanted me out there with all those other tough-minded career women, helping my sisters pave the way for another new generation of working women, a generation that would be even less oppressed and unhappy than the ones that came before. He wanted me in that battle, fighting for promotions and benefits and nicer washrooms. He wanted me fighting for equality and a bigger paycheck. He wanted me in that bloody war so he could be proud of my fight for my gender. So he could wink at his friends over a few beers one evening and say

"My wife's a *professional!*"

But if I were out there relentlessly fighting for the opportunity to display my equality, who was going to be sitting at home, relentlessly fighting for my little boy's future? If I were working my thrilling 9-to-5 shift on the front line of the economy, who was going to be running my demanding 24/7 shift on the frontline of humanity? Who was going to teach my little boy how to tie his shoes, spell his name, remember to say please and thank you and put the toilet seat down when he was finished in the bathroom? Who was going to be there to catch the countless opportunities every day that must be harnessed to teach a child to be joyful or considerate or determined or honest? Who was going to be my son's emotional safety net, his external conscience, his translator, his reliable interpreter for the work of an inconsistent world?

And finally, if I were busy fighting for recognition of my skills, my talents, my rights and my value in society, who would be there to fight for his? Isn't that what a mother's for? To plant her feet stubbornly and firmly in the murky soil of an unclean world and be the unmovable support against which her children can safely fall when they fail? Or when the world fails them? Was daycare going to do everything for my child that I had made a sacred oath to do for him first? Not bloody likely.

But what I did for my son, for my family, counted for a big fat ZERO, on any scale, anywhere. Everybody knows that working is Important. Having a Job means having a measurable identity.

How can you possibly measure or characterize a career that might involve running non-stop around the house all day cleaning toilets, saving a toddler from certain death at least eight times in a three-hour period and getting gum out of the wall-to-wall?

The next day's requirements might include 12 minutes of colouring, 4 minutes of play dough, seven minutes of sitting on the living room floor with a stuffed dog on your head and an hour of reading the story of Barney the Backhoe over and over. And over. And, by the way, don't even think about skipping a word here and there because little Einstein, who is only two feet tall, has memorized the entire book and doesn't actually need you to read it to him but it makes him feel good to sit all snuggled up on your lap and listen to your voice give sudden life to what appear to be meaningless little squiggles on a colourful page. What value can anyone assign to *that* experience?

By nine o'clock in the morning you might have to spend half an hour collecting up all the dirt from the living-room floor because the phone rang and the toddler was quietly trying to take the houseplants for a walk. Next it's on to another half an hour of cleaning the flour paste off the kitchen floor because it took half an hour to clean the dirt off the carpeting in the living room and the doorbell rang and the phone rang again and by then you were just too rattled to notice that the toddler wanted to surprise mommy with a nice home-made cake.

It's impossible to think of a label to describe a trip to the grocery store with a child who doesn't want to be there or perhaps missed his nap that day. The myriad tasks and activities of a mother with little children add up to a virtually nonsensical and indescribable experience and so the rest of us tend to think that being home with one's children isn't really a valid "job" per se.

It doesn't fit in to any job description anywhere in the work world – and not even working in a daycare can measure up to the stress of being home with your kids because in a daycare you are entitled to vacation days and sick days and at the end of your shift you can shut the door behind you and go sit by yourself in a shopping mall if you feel like it.

And, too, those of us who have never survived the insanity of a year or two as an at-home mother find it all too easy to romanticize the experience – note, not the "job" – as a delicious game of adult hooky characterized by being able to spend all day in your sweat pants, calling all your friends and relations for chummy conversations at 11 in the morning, catching "Oprah" on TV at least once a day and being able to slide into a hot bath with a steamy novel at 3:00 in the afternoon if you darn well feel like it. Sounds like a great gig! But it isn't really "work".

Those of us who *really* work have our buns out the door by 7:39 every morning to start the race to day care. By then we've showered, prepared the lunches and snacks, put fresh diapers in the diaper bag, and managed to throw the dirty shirts in the car so we can run them over to the drycleaner's at lunch time.

All day long we are grinding our way through other people's priorities, desperate to get a raise, a promotion, a day off or a free lunch at that new restaurant that just opened up down the street. We know we work hard and we have a job title to prove it.

In fact, that title proves something about us, it gives us some elusive moral quality that relates to our worthiness in the eyes of humankind. There is a nobility in the very fact of being "Complaints Supervisor" or "Customer Service Agent" or "Receptionist" or "Vice-President of Sales." Women have fought long and hard for the right to join the mad scramble up the ladder of success. That's what equality is about, right? A woman's right to earn enough money to stop being a drag on our men's salaries.

If we want to be *considered* equal, then we have to behave as though we are, for crying out loud. That means we need to have a job, just like all the men have had back down through eternity. The benefit is that we get paid the same. (Maybe.). And we just might get a little pension benefit at the end of the line as a reward for mentally designating the children we made "somebody else's problem" and pulling our weight in society's dog-eat-dog work world. What kind of a woman doesn't want to work? I'll tell you: a lazy one.

In the eyes of a society made better by woman's right to work, I was lazy. I certainly didn't feel lazy — I never seemed to have five minutes to myself, in fact even going to the bathroom was an event attended by an audience of one. Sometimes more, if you included the various action figures and trucks that accompanied our journey around the house. We had a retinue, my little Jason and I, and we talked non-stop all day long to them and each other. My days were full of making meals and cleaning up after them, playing with stickers and sparkles and paint boxes — and cleaning up afterwards. We hardly ever put the TV on but we did sing a lot of songs and danced and had make-believe tea parties and car races. We were always going out for walks or playing in the park or getting groceries. We made cakes that spattered the kitchen walls and floors and, for some very odd reason, even the inside of Jason's sock drawer. We spent hours looking for things, like missing car keys.

"Jason, do you know where my car keys are?" I asked upon discovering they were not sitting in their customary place on the table beside the front door.

A truly angelic face gleamed up at me and a perfect little mouth sighed, "No, mommy. No keys."

And we set off looking: in drawers and in pockets, on cupboards, had I left them in the car? After an hour and a half I gave up and bemoaned my forgetfulness, cursed the fact that I had been so careless, shuddered to think of what David was going to say when he got home.

"Keys, Mommy," said a little voice as I took my jacket off and hung it up in the front closet. I looked down at Jason who was triumphantly holding my keys and grinning from ear to ear. "Find it," he said.

"Jason, where were they," I marveled. What a great finder!!

"In smimmener," he crowed proudly. Smimmener was Jason's toy cement mixer.

Our days were unpredictable that way, sometimes. Bath-time hardly ever started before 7:30 and bedtime was usually somewhere around 8:00, after the toys were picked up and put away and the last story read. Even after 8:00, there was always more cleanup to do. David's dinner, if he was eating, had to be prepared, and if not I could finally eat myself — and clean up the dishes.

Then there was the laundry to finish up or the ironing to do, the kitchen floor was in chronic need of sweeping and washing and any little extras like painting a room or wallpapering or sewing myself a new pair of slacks had to wait until my darling's little head had nestled itself on its downy pillow for the night. Forget shopping or lunching with friends...there was simply no time. Hobbies? I had heard some women had hobbies, and I suppose that sewing the odd desperately needed little item of clothing was a hobby, although to me it was simply a way of saving money. Asking David for money to buy something I thought one of us needed was generally a humiliating experience since it highlighted the exact type of inequality that a woman's right to work had been meant to redress.

"David, could I please have another $30 for a new jacket for Jason?"

"Thirty dollars!!?! What — is it going to be gold-plated or something?"

"Well, no, of course not, $30 is hardly even enough, for a new winter jacket, David. Fifty would be even better."

"What's wrong with the old one?"

"It's the one I bought at the Goodwill and it has holes in it and the sleeves are way too short – Jason's arms get cold."

"Jeez, Teale, I feel like I'm always handing money over to you for something."

"I'm sorry, David, but I really think Jason should have a new jacket."

"Look, Teale, it's only another few months until the end of the winter. He'll probably need another new jacket next year because he'll have grown. If you were really planning ahead, you would be waiting until next winter to get him a new jacket."

"Don't you think we can we afford a $30 jacket, David?"

David sighed, wearily.

"No, Teale, I don't think we can. You might think I'm made of money but believe it or not I do without things I want all the time. I would like new skis this year but can I afford them? No! I would like to take my sister to Colorado skiing again this year but can I afford it? No! I would like to go to that International Financing Conference in Switzerland this spring but can I afford it? No! We all have to make concessions and compromises, Teale, and I don't see you getting the picture yet."

Of course, I hadn't told him about the fact that I wanted to buy a new purse (my eight-year-old bag had finally bit the dust), or that there were holes in my winter boots or that my gloves were worn out. That stuff would just have to come quietly out of my grocery money. He was right, I guess. I was probably being a selfish spendthrift, an odd kind of selfish, since I just wanted my little boy to be warm and dry all winter.

"But David, please...."

"All right, all right, God you're a demanding woman. Take the freaking money then." And he pulled his wallet out of his back pants pocket and extracted two twenty-dollar bills and flung them at me.

"I want the change back though," he said.

Change back. How on Earth was I going to find a $30 winter jacket? It certainly couldn't be a new one. I had hoped David would realize $30 wouldn't be nearly enough and hand me $50 at least. But no. Back to the Goodwill I guess. The next morning, as he was leaving for work he had instructions for me.

"Are you staying home all day today, Teale?"

"Well, no, I was planning on getting Jason's new jacket and we're out of apple juice again, so I've got to run to Priceright and…"

"Crap. Look, can you do all that stuff tomorrow?"

"Well I guess…why?"

"I've got a courier coming," he said. "Anita made a mistake and had them send it to my home rather than the office."

"Oh, what's coming?" I was curious, of course.

David hesitated.

"Baseball tickets," he said shortly.

"Ahh. Same seats?"

"Yeah — right behind home plate. God I love that game." David was smiling gingerly. He could hardly wait to get his hands on his tickets.

I wondered how much they cost but to ask would create a rift between us just as he was leaving. I knew he had a really important meeting that day and I didn't want to throw him off stride on his way out the door. So I called the stadium and asked. The lady who answered the phone was very nice and said it was impossible to get tickets behind home plate at this late date.

"But if I could, what would they cost?" I wanted to know.

"They're up only slightly over last year," she explained "It's only $2,250 this year."

"Each?!" I asked.

"No, no, for the whole season," she said.

"How many seats does that get me at each game," I asked.

"Only one of course."

David always bought two sets of tickets, so he could take a friend.

The problem with any information you suck in about anything, anywhere, is the logical next question which is, inevitably, "So what?" What meaning can it possibly have for you, your life, your decisions, your actions? I knew David took clients to baseball games. I knew it made him look more successful. That meant people trusted him with their business and it translated into a higher income for him, eventually. Silver platter, you know. I also knew I felt poor.

There have been times in my life when I have actually been poor. These are the times we all remember, when we find ourselves dumping the contents of our purses onto the kitchen table in the hope that some reluctant quarters have taken refuge amongst the shredded Kleenexes, blotty pens and furry candies that bounce along under our elbows all day.

These are the times when we take all the cushions off the chairs and sofas in the living room in the hopes of finding long-forgotten coins that are needed to buy a box of Kraft dinner or a loaf of bread we urgently need. These are the times we search through the pockets of all our off-season clothing just in case we inadvertently left a $5 bill behind by some magnificent mistake of memory. These are the times we gracefully put off creditors with the sad and frustrated and terribly creative explanation that we ran out of cheques and the bank sent misprints so we had to re-order – it may take a few weeks. Or perhaps we explain that we have mislaid the bill. Or can't I *please* just have a few more weeks to pay? These are the times we feel the great and sickening dread of desperation creeping into our hearts.

We can't breathe well. We can't sleep well. We can't imagine how we are going to manage. And we do. Perhaps we *are* poor. But we are so caught up in the struggle to find just another four dollars – or forty – that we don't have time or energy to dwell on our financial status in the world.

We might feel plenty sorry for ourselves. We might curse the fates that have brought us to this impossible stage of life with no resources left to soothe the wounds of doing without. But we manage.

Yes, I have felt poor. But with David's income, it was impossible to say that I actually *was* poor.

I had always taken great pride in doing things right, doing what was expected of me — I did all my homework on time, I always had part-time jobs after school and I stayed busy with sports and other extra-curricular activities. I always did my best and my best was always good enough. I got great marks and I got glowing letters of reference from all my employers. I was a hard worker and a good sport and as far as I knew I had never embarrassed anybody before. What had changed?

I didn't have a clue. But I would fix it. I was no quitter.

24

I was looking for a job as a writer since that's what I knew best and I thought probably David would be proud of me then because almost everybody is impressed when you tell them you're a writer. Everybody *is* a writer. Or wants to be. Or is going to be, someday.

At the point in this story where we are currently pausing, where I'm just about to get back to work after living with a marital charade for God knows how long, I had written everything there was to write. Obituaries. Social news. Movie reviews. Crime reports. Business updates. Biographies. Speeches. Lies. Spending allocation reports Excuses for government screw-ups. News releases. City hall meeting reports, feature stories about home invasions, foam insulation and lingerie. As I sat alone in front of my father's old typewriter at the kitchen table at 9:30 on a Friday morning, I thought about the work I'd done over the years...and became quietly impressed. It was an odd feeling. I had become unused to thinking about myself at all. I thought about the next meal, the next bath, the next party, the next sleep, the next hands-on "Omigod I'm late" detail of my life of wife. But not about me.

I began to type.

One year spot news reporter for the Weekly Eagle, Jensen Ontario. All regular news, CP rewrites, obituaries, social. Some sports coverage. Excellent photography skills. (Yeah, I forgot I could take a damned fine picture, too).

Six months apprentice reporter leading to two years full-time news coverage for the London Gazette, London, Ontario. News, rewrites, night editing, some layout.

Two years reporting for the Toronto Star. God I loved that job, why had I ever left?

And I thought back to the glory of a newsroom, with its rows of industrial steel desks, computer screens akimbo, messy piles of paper everywhere, notepads, books, hats, half-empty cups of cold coffee balanced precariously on top of piles of steno pads, feet up on desks while reporters leaned back in their chairs, talking and listening breezily on the phone, getting the real dirt on someone or something or maybe just talking to their wife or best buddy. Keyboards clacked furiously in the newsroom in my mind as I sat remembering two dozen reporters racing to meet their deadlines, fingers flying over the keys, oblivious to typographical errors — crap I'll fix it later — fluorescent lights humming starkly above bowed heads, people shouting, laughing, screaming for rewrites or that photo, "where the hell is it," "what's the name of the guy in this one, Harry?" "How do you spell that?"

Phones rang, people talked, paper airplanes skimmed over unwary heads, foul language flew, people smiled or scowled or complained or yelled and in the stew of competitive congeniality, insatiably curious people all did their best to get the news out there, every day, every night, round the clock.

A newsroom is a holy, serious and stressful, a place where facts, words, details, sequence, motivation and credibility are merged, piece by murderously important piece, under the skillful, neglectful, time-deprived and often narrow-minded craftsmanship of the reporter at his work. Reporters are arrogant, focused on virtue and professionalism, determined to get the scoop, desperate for another coffee, decent coffee, not the crap that comes out of that damned machine in the corner. They are insensitive jerks, too, daring to ask a grieving parent for a photo of their dead child so they can run it on Page One for all the world to stare in naked curiosity at someone else's wretched pain.

I have heard people call the news-blood of our society cynical and my response is always "Thank God!" They should be cynical! Governments and corporations spend millions of dollars hiring the sharpest, most creative minds they can find whose only job is to manufacture an image and convince people it's real.

Sure some of it's probably factual. But some of it might not be and how is anybody going to know which part is which without the cynical probing of an underpaid guy in an ill-fitting suit who hates his ex-wife and has been up all night drinking? This guy — or gal — has seen lawyers convicted of child pornography, doctors convicted of drug peddling, teachers convicted of armed robbery and twelve-year-olds convicted of murder. Our reporter has it *off the record* that the minister at the Lutheran church near Davisville Ave. did time 20 years ago for assault with a weapon and that the housewife who is running for city council was a call girl with a very bad habit 12 years ago in another town.

Our reporter knows which judges are in the pockets of which criminal organizations, with apologies to the criminals of our community, and s/he knows about the chemical spill that was quietly covered up in a north-western neighbourhood that will remain nameless until she can actually prove it in print. Our reporter is resourceful, imaginative and endowed with a relentless curiosity about the entire universe.

Our reporter skips breakfast, doesn't always get lunch, snacks erratically all day and chokes down a warm chicken salad sandwich while madly typing up the details of tomorrow's page three feature in time for an impossible deadline of 11:00 p.m.

Press conferences that involve free snacks are an enormous relief and although there is always that little hesitation of having one's objectivity compromised by the act of swallowing food provided by the enemy — and everyone is an enemy — the reality is we all did it. Our reporter is always at work, always listening to the unspoken assumptions hiding behind the words of the people around her, always assessing, doubting, wondering and questioning.

And our reporter has stories. Stories about the unbelievably strange things that happened during the last election campaign

"Old Jim Watson, remember him, he used to work at the Sun, I was on the campaign bus with him in '94. God, he was a character. Mooned Chretien eight times on the campaign bus that year..."

Stories about the strange creatures she works with.

"Hey, remember that guy, Thomas or Thompson or something, he had City Hall back 10-15 years ago I think. When he passed out at Jonesy's stag we dressed him in some woman's clothes we found and dumped him on the front steps of the Carmelite convent at Jarvis and King with a note saying 'Forgive me sisters for I have sinned. Please take me in and teach me to pray.' He was so pissed when he woke up!'

Stories about tragedies.

"I can still remember that mother whose three children died in that house fire over on Willoughby – she'd left them sleeping for half an hour while she ran out to the Seven-Eleven for milk at midnight. When she got back, the whole house was up in flames. *Half an hour!!!* Man that was sad…"

God I missed that environment, that noisy, messy, competitive environment where everybody went out for a beer after work or went bowling or grabbed a burger together and talked about everything you can ever imagine in the whole wide world. They were interesting, interested people, connected to the throbbing heartbeat of the world in some vital, intangible way.

Love 'em or hate 'em they were a breed apart, a steadfast, hardworking, determined bunch of tenacious individuals. Of course, some of them were flaming jerks – they are, after all, everywhere among us. But how quiet, how small my little world seemed now.

Would I trade it all in for another day, another chance, cheerfully show up for work at 6:00 p.m. and drink coffee all night while the wire stories came in and reporters filed in and out? There was always someone there, someone to talk to, commiserate with. And there had been Stewey Grant, photog, handSOME and so sweet. ALL the women in the news room had their eyes on him. Some thought he was gay because he never dated women from the Star. When a crew of worn out reporters went for beer after our shift — and stayed hours on end after — Stu and I always managed to sit beside each other, taking part in the regular game of argumentative discussions but giggling and teasing and arguing and chattering continuously, together. There was an attraction there but we never dated, never even talked, really, about how nice it was to touch, to look into each other's eyes and understand, just simply understand what the other was thinking.

Sometimes we lurched back to my apartment after everyone said their goodnights and crawled into bed together, all curled up and cozy in each other's arms, quietly and simply. Usually we made quiet love together, too, but that wasn't the real point. The point was being happy and comfortable and friends, great friends. We talked vaguely once about a relationship, about making ourselves available only to each other but somehow that didn't seem right. Somehow it worked just knowing that every few weeks or months we would have each other to ourselves. Where was he now?

I sighed and turned back to writing my résumé.

The government of course was no news room. Everybody had a nice little office with a nice little computer, a tidy desk, a bulletin board. We each had a door to close out the noise of our colleagues when we were on deadline. Days were busy, research was key, of course, in this job too, but it was somehow safer, less effervescent a job than my work in a newsroom. I would never get a job in a newsroom now, of course. I'd been out of the business far too long. I sure as hell didn't want to work in the government either, though. Whatever was I fit for anymore?

I clacked away on my typewriter, filling in the blanks for name and address, where I'd worked and what I'd done. Education, yes that nice little arts degree was good to have. No awards to speak of, of course but I was known as a hard worker and an easy-going colleague. And, of course, my whole life long I had been told what a good writer I was. I believed it, too. After a little more than an hour I had the bare bones down on paper but there was something a little vacant about this résumé. It needed something. Fancy fonts? A few nice lines? We didn't own a computer, David believing it was an exorbitant expense we could not afford. But there was a little shop down on Avenue Road that rented out computer time by the hour and if I was lucky I could scrounge a few hours together to get a more professional look going for me. I would need a babysitter, though. I didn't really have any friends I could count on to watch Jason for me while I ran out.

Most of our neighbours worked and I really didn't feel comfortable calling on the wives of any of David's friends. They would ask questions.

After wracking my brains for half an hour I called my back-door neighbour, old Rosie Jones, on the off-chance she might come and spend a few hours watching my son while I ran out to re-type my resume.

"Yes, of course, dear," she said. If David had known I was leaving Jason in the care of a 70-year-old woman he would have been furious but I didn't care. I wouldn't tell him.

Rosie was an interesting person, an artist who had converted an upstairs bedroom in her house into a little studio. She was a widow and she fascinated me. We had nice chats about flowers and children, art and cooking. I liked her and I tripped off to the computer store, confident my son would be entertained and safe.

The computer store unnerved me: I felt awkward and out-of-step after years at home but the man who helped me was very kind and after an hour of effort my résumé looked reasonably professional.

"Our printers aren't great," the man behind the counter said, "But take this diskette down the street to 'Grafix' — they're a graphic design company and they'll fix you up."

Shades of Teal

David was going to be so proud of me!

"Grafix," it turned out, was a spotless little shop full of big machines and the smell of toner and cleanliness. It had been around for years and the man in charge — Ed Jones — was fond of his impressive equipment. He was chatty and about 10 years older than me, and I suddenly felt very young.

I knew nothing about graphic design or advertising or brochures or anything that seemed to matter in this world of quietly humming machines and bright lights. Eventually, however, and just out of curiosity, he stopped his monologue about memory, speed and resolution and glanced at my resume.

"You a writer?" he asked.

It was very cold outside and I wanted to get home to my boy.

"Yeah," I said.

Ed Jones scribbled something on a piece of paper and handed it to me.

"Call this guy," he said. "He owns a marketing company I do a lot of design work for. They're looking for writers right now."

I looked down at the piece of paper and read the words he had scrawled. "Conrad Glastonbury, President, Cornerstone Marketing 887-2222" it said.

"Is he in town?" I asked.

"Yeah, they're just about eight blocks south of here," said Ed Jones. "Great bunch of people. You'll like them a lot."

"Thanks!" I said. I had thought finding work would take me weeks, months even, but maybe I would be lucky! I grabbed 10 copies of my tidy resume and headed home. After a relaxing tea with Rosie I fed Jason and put him down for a late nap so I could screw up my courage and call Conrad Glastonbury. His voice was

227

gentle but unfriendly and I doubted my optimistic personality was going to help me get this job. He sounded weary beyond redemption and yet he was rushed, anxious to get things out of the way.

"Look," he said. "I'm swamped, far too busy to talk to you right now. Call my partner, Dev Braxton and tell him I said you're to come in and talk to him first. If he thinks you have any talent I'll interview you too. But don't get your hopes up, kid." And he hung up. It had been a long time since anybody had called me kid. I wasn't sure I liked it.

"No points for courtesy," I thought, dialing the number again. I set up an appointment to meet with Mr. Braxton – who sounded much nicer than his partner — and got Rosie lined up to spend another hectic morning with my firefighter-in-training so I could go in for my interview. This was going to be the most important interview of my life. This was possibly going to save my marriage.

I thrilled at the thought of working with words again but the idea of going back to work scared me half to death. My baby was still so young. I was going to want another one in the not-so-far-off future, too, wasn't I? Maybe this was a bad idea.

What if I wasn't any good at this marketing stuff? What if David still wasn't happy with me? Maybe I should try something different, like retail? What if this didn't work out?

25

Six days later I was sitting in Devlin Braxton's office clutching my portfolio, proudly showing all the articles I'd ever written, along with the speeches, press releases, public service announcements and other works of literary art I could find that might be relevant.

He seemed impressed, although nothing actually screamed "marketing genius" at him. How hard could marketing be, though? It seemed pretty straightforward — brochures, ads, news releases, speeches, newsletters...If you could write a sentence you can write a brochure. Couldn't you?

Mr. Braxton seemed was younger than me by a year or two perhaps and was dressed very conservatively in a pair of brown woolen trousers and a matching brown shirt. He wore a beautiful brown, black and cream-coloured sweater and on his feet were a pair of expensive-looking tasseled loafers. He spoke very kindly to me but I felt grossly underdressed in the stained blue skirt I had had since my days at the government and the not-quite-a-match blazer that I had retrieved from the bottom of my closet. My blouse was, at least, clean. Maybe a job might mean new clothes!

"We're looking for someone to take the heat off Conrad," he said. "Our company is going through a major expansion and up to this point Connie's done all the writing. He just can't keep up anymore and clients are starting to get ticked off.

"What we're really after is someone who's prepared to rent office space from us and work freelance. Some months there will be a lot of work, others there may not be quite so much — so you might need to find other clients. But we want first call on your time. You can work whatever hours you want as long as the work gets done on deadline.

"You'll just have to let us know when we can expect you in."

Sounded perfect to me at that point, except for the rent part.

"How much is the rent?" I asked.

"Three hundred dollars a month," Mr. Braxton said.

"Oh," I said. David would never agree to that.

"You'd make it back from us every month, no problem."

"Hmmmm," I said. "I'll have to think about it."

"Look," Braxton said. "I'm impressed with what you've shown me but you'll have to pass muster with Conrad. I'll set up an interview for you with him and call you back this afternoon. If he likes what he sees then you can decide if you want in or not. Deal?"

"Sure," I said, carefully.

Just then Mr. Braxton's telephone rang.

"Hello," he said. "Hi there beautiful, how's my little girl today? (pause)... Yeah? Way to go, sweetheart, Daddy's so proud of you! What else did you do today? (pause)...That sounds like fun. (pause) ....Well he's just a little boy, he doesn't know any better. (pause) ... What did Mommy say? (pause) ... Well I think it will be OK. Don't you worry about a thing. Can I speak to Mommy for a minute?"

There was a longer pause.

"Hi," he said. "Did you know you're the best mother in the whole world? I can't believe how well you handled that." He was laughing. "I'll be home a little late tonight — can you feed the kids and wait for me for dinner?" (pause) ... I love you too, honey."

Mr. Braxton was smiling throughout his whole conversation. When he got off the phone he blushed slightly.

"My daughter learned to tie her shoes today," he said. "And she and her brother had a huge fight over the goldfish."

"How old are your kids? I asked."

"Four and two," he said. "Have you got kids?"

"One wonderful little boy," I said.

"His Dad must love having a son!" said Mr. Braxton. "'Course daughters are perfect, too. I spend every weekend with my kids. I get up with them early on Saturday and Sunday so my wife can sleep in and I take them out for donuts and juice. Usually we play hockey or ride our bikes but if it's crummy out we'll just hang out in the basement."

"All day?' I asked. That just didn't seem possible.

"Of course," he said. "It's the best time of the whole week."

We chatted a little longer and then he stood up, signaling the end of our visit. Later that afternoon he called to tell me I was to meet with Conrad Glastonbury the following Tuesday at 10:30 a.m. SHARP. I was well on my way to a career, it seemed. Things were going a little too smoothly and a little too quickly. At least David seemed mollified.

Poor Rosie came yet again to watch Jason for a few hours while I went out in search of work. I had told her a little of my anxiety over this whole concept of going out to work and she kindly offered no advice. She found her hours with Jason to be a perfect enchantment but her arthritis flared up from time to time making it difficult to keep up with him. As for me, I was a little scared about everything but I really wanted David to be proud of me. The day of my interview with Mr. Glastonbury was cold but sunny and I made sure I arrived five minutes early for my appointment.

"Teale Covey-Masterson for Mr. Glastonbury," I said to the receptionist upon entering. The offices of Cornerstone Marketing were beautiful — plenty of light-coloured oak moldings, lots of windows, overstuffed chairs in the reception area, some very modern looking lighting fixtures...what a joy it would be to work here!

"What time was your appointment for?" the pretty blonde lady behind the desk asked.

"Ten-thirty," I said.

"Please have a seat," she said. "He's not in yet but I'm sure he'll be here any minute."

I sat and waited. Ten-twenty-five turned eventually into 10:45 and after a while 10:55 and still no sign of Mr. Glastonbury. There were magazines on the coffee table in front of me which I eventually picked up and mindlessly scanned. I had no interest in magazines. I was scared to death. Promptly at 11:13 the front door of the office blew open and a large man in a cowboy hat, cowboy boots and a fringed and studded black leather jacket swept into the offices of Cornerstone Marketing. With an enormous coffee in one hand and a pile of files in the other he grabbed a stack of telephone messages from the front desk and stampeded down the corridor, trailing clumps of snow and whiffs of fresh air mixed with a scent that reminded me of Old Spice cologne behind him.

I looked at the receptionist and she smiled.

"He's here now," she said.

Ten minutes later a buzz at the front desk directed the blond to show me to Mr. Glastonbury's office and I followed her down the hallway, admiring framed examples of the firm's work and wishing I could have a suit like the one the smiling receptionist was wearing. Very tasteful, very beautiful, very expensive. Her shoes were a perfect match and her jewellery was incredibly dainty. She stopped at the very back of the brightly lit office space and showed me the door, beside which was an oak-framed plaque that read "Conrad Glastonbury, President",

"Ms Covey-Masterson, Conrad," she said.

Conrad Glastonbury looked up from a pile of papers sprawled over the entire expanse of his desktop and nodded absent-mindedly at me to come in. There were sketches of an automobile on a road going up a hill in front of him. I held out my hand to shake his and he gripped mine loosely, a cold but gentle touch. I sat down. He took a sip of his coffee. He was, as I have said, a rather large man, quite natty in his appearance and handsome in a rather disorganized way. His features weren't perfect but somehow they all met on his face as if in an agreement to make the best of the situation, despite the odds. He didn't smile as he looked at me and I had rather the impression that I was nothing but a huge inconvenience to him.

I waited. He stopped writing and looked at me. I was sure he was taking in my old clothes, scuffed boots, straggly hair and desperation. Then he sat back and looked some more. A gold clock on the wall beside his desk ticked. I waited for him to speak. He said nothing. He stared at me expectantly. I wasn't going to flinch.

"So?" he finally said.

"So?" I asked.

The man was clearly annoyed.

"You think you're a writer?"

"That's what they tell me," I said.

"All right, what have you got to prove it?"

I opened my portfolio and began displaying the results of seven years of post-university efforts at proving I was, indeed, a writer. The best samples I pushed across the desk at him, and I omitted no details of my best work.

"You've never had a decent editor, have you?" he asked. It was, rather more of a statement, than a question.

"They all seemed fine to me," I said.

"That's because you know jack about writing," he said. "There's not a lot of creativity here and most of this is downright boring." He looked at me.

"I've always been told I was a good writer," I said.

"Yeah?" he said, glancing through my samples. "Is this the best you've got?"

"Yes," I said crisply, beginning to get angry.

"All right, well take it away and if I'm interested I'll call you."

"That's it?" I said.

"What do you mean, 'it'?"

"Don't you want to know what a hard worker I am, or that I always do my absolute best or that I'm very easy to work with or that I'm totally dependable or that you can't scare me away with rude bluster about how unsuitable I am for the job?"

Mr. Glastonbury looked at me with the merest ghost of a smile playing in his eyes.

"No," he said, and the corners of his mouth tipped up slightly in a puckered little grin before he dropped his head to his work again.

I left, convinced I had just been through the absolute worst job interview of my life. That night I told David about my hideous interview and although he was annoyed at first that I had let this large windbag of a man get the better of me he was pleased that I had, at least, taken the first step.

"Look, Teale," he said. "Forget this idea about working and just settle down and have another baby. You can go back to work next year. These guys don't know how to appreciate anybody. You're a great writer."

"No, David, I'm going to keep trying. I'll wait a week or two to hear from Cornerstone and if I don't get any news I'll start sending out my resume. I don't feel up to getting pregnant again right now, you know? I think you're right about me working — it's time to go back and get some more experience."

David looked at me and frowned.

"Well, I disagree, Teale, but, of course, it's your life, you can do what you want with it, I guess."

A week went by, then two weeks and finally three weeks passed with no phone call from Cornerstone. I had pretty well decided to give in to biology. In fact, I was ovulating when Conrad Glastonbury called and very gruffly informed me that he thought I would do adequately well for what he had in mind.

"Be in here Monday morning," he said. The computer I bought that weekend with a cheque from our joint line of credit cost more than $2,000.

"It's instead of another baby," I said to the sales clerk as I walked out of the store with my purchase on a cart. David was furious, of course, that I had spent money so frivolously —"I thought you already had a typewriter," he said in a huff. I didn't care. I looked that night in the newspaper and started calling around for baby-sitters for Jason. I was going to have an exciting career!

I was going to get out of the house! There was nothing that could have spoiled my reluctant joy at finally proving to my husband what a worthy wife I was. David would come around. He was, after all, the one who had wanted me to work in the first place. He would never be embarrassed again!

26

Glastonbury gave me three assignments on my first day of work — a newsletter for a non-profit organization, a news release for a large corporation and a simple ad for a car dealership. This meant there would be a new haircut in my future and decent snowsuits for my son, new clothes for me, lunches out! David and I decided I would work three days a week to make it easier for Jason but it was a tough transition all the same and it was hard to fit all the responsibilities of the life I used to have into the time now available.

"David do you think you could vacuum before the Larson's come for dinner tomorrow night?" I asked late one Friday evening.

"Why?" he asked.

"Oh. Well, now that I'm working I have less time to get everything ready and I really need some help with the housework."

"The Larson's won't care if the house is messy, Teale."

"But I do, David — please, won't you just this once help me out a little?"

He laughed dryly. "You're the one who wanted the big career Teale. I guess you need to learn how to budget your time like I do."

"You benefit from a clean house too, though, David."

"Yeah but you care more," he said.

I somehow found the time to vacuum but I did not enjoy our dinner party that night, or the three that followed.

I took my computer in to my new office and proudly set it up. I had a key to the front door, a lovely oak desk and matching credenza and my own telephone line. I worked steadily on my assignments and at the end of my second week of work I had drafts ready to drop off on Conrad Glastonbury's desk. I no longer called him Mr. Glastonbury but I still could not bring myself to call him Conrad — it seemed like an imposition to use his name at all. With the nervous glimmer of hope and dread that all writers feel when they meet a new editor I knocked at his door late Friday afternoon.

Conrad looked up from his messy pile of files and papers and squinted at his doorway.

"Yeah?"

"I've got my rough drafts ready for you," I said. He raised an eyebrow.

"Fine. Just put 'em down somewhere."

I had laboured long and hard over these drafts and although I had never written any newsletter material, much less an advertisement for anything, I had done my best. Conrad Glastonbury dropped the material he was working on and took my precious copy, scanned it quickly and then went back to re-read it all again. He pulled at his left eyebrow as he read and as I sat across from him my palms, wrapped nervously around my knees, began to sweat. Sometimes Conrad frowned. Sometimes he took the big black pen he held in his left hand and scribbled in the margins. Sometimes he struck out whole sections of my work. Occasionally he grumbled. Eventually he threw down his pen and leaned back in his chair in disgust.

He picked up the sheaf of papers I had given him and threw them across the desk at me.

"What is this garbage, anyway?" he demanded.

I looked at him.

"Wh-wh-what do you mean?" I asked.

"You call this writing? This is nonsense. I can't take any of this to a client! Look, I gave you a job to do – this is crap."

I stared at him.

"What's wrong with it?" I asked, bewildered. I honestly didn't know.

"I don't have time for this," he said. "I thought you said you were a writer?"

"I am — I am a writer," I said. "Well then take this junk back and write it properly," he said and picked up an unopened package of printer paper and flung it at the wall beside my head. I stood up, grabbed the scribbled-up sheets of paper that hadn't proved I was a writer and escaped from his presence, shaking.

"Well what are you doing taking on ads for assignments anyway?" David asked later that night when I told him what had happened. "You shouldn't be doing that kind of work, you should be doing what you're good at like news releases and speeches and stuff."

"But David, they didn't have speeches for me to do and I did do a news release but he said it was no good."

"Well I sure hope you billed him for all that time."

"Not yet," I said. "And David I can't bill for every hour I spent on these projects."

"Sure you can."

No, no, I can't charge Cornerstone for my learning curve — I'm supposed to know how to do this stuff already!"

"You worry too much Teale."

Perhaps I didn't worry enough. The following week I redrafted my material based on Conrad Glastonbury's scribbled comments and tried again. This was the rerun. The knock on his door. The suspicious look on his face. The grumpy perusal of my handiwork. The scribbled comments in the margins. Without a word he handed me my work back and, without even actually looking at me, dismissed me from his office. I was shattered. But I tried again. His comments made some sort of sense to me but I really didn't understand what Conrad Glastonbury was getting at. Eventually I stumbled onto something that he found remotely acceptable and received another three assignments: an article for a banking institution to submit to a professional magazine, a brochure for a men's clothing store and another ad, this time for a well-known local golf course. Meanwhile I submitted my invoice for the month.

"David, this is really hard, this work I'm doing now," I said one evening.

"Oh, nonsense, Teale, you can do anything. Just try harder."

"But I don't really know what I'm doing," I said.

"Writing is writing — surely an intelligent woman like you can figure out how to do it."

"Well yeah, but I don't know the first thing about marketing."

"Marketing's easy, Teale, not complicated like the financial stuff I have to do."

"No of course not, but I'm struggling." Some days I found myself staring at a blank computer screen in a frightened panic, wondering what the first word was going to be and paralyzed by the fear that I wouldn't be able to find it. That first word is crucial since it's essentially the leader of the pack and all the other words are just waiting for the first one to show up so they can take their place on the lines of type that follow it. If there is no first word, there can be no final product and at that time of my life I had no clue how to summon that first word from the drunken depths of misery in which it mulishly lurked. A first word is a stubborn, suspicious creature and it is not easily conned into making an appearance. It particularly preys upon young and inexperienced writers who haven't yet learned that writing is a competition between the writer and the words and that if you can capture that first word —better yet, the first 15 —then you are well on your way to winning the round. I was staring autistically at my computer screen, convinced that I was an utter and abject failure, when Conrad Glastonbury loomed in my office doorway, face as black as tar and eyes spitting streaks of white-hot lead.

"What is this?" he screamed at me, shaking two pieces of beautiful white paper with black squiggly printing on them. I looked at what he was holding.

"My invoice for the month," I said.

"Your invoice for the month," he said. He measured each word out carefully, angrily. "Your. Invoice. For. The. Month." It was a statement.

"Yeah, my invoice for the month. Is there a problem?" I asked in as innocent a voice as I could muster. I opened my eyes a little wider and I could feel my eyebrows were ready to climb off the top of my forehead and onto my skull. I was hoping I looked gently surprised.

Conrad Glastonbury threw the papers down on my desk in a gesture I might take for a challenge to a duel in any other century and screamed in my face.

"Yeah there's a problem! I am not going to pay $680 for work I basically had to do for you" he shrieked. You don't have a clue what you're doing here and you can't write. You're wasting my time, woman, and you're costing me money. You're a fraud."

I waited to be fired but he seemed to have too much trouble breathing to get that last little detail out of his mouth so I jumped to my feet, put my hands on my hips and blustered back at Conrad Glastonbury.

"No-one has EVER called me a fraud before and if you're going to start the trend I suggest you have a darned good reason for doing so. I gave that work my best shot but you gave me absolutely no clues about what you wanted so I ended up having to figure out the tone, the atmosphere and the purpose of these assignments ALL BY MYSELF. If you had taken the time to give me even just a little background on all this stuff maybe I could have delivered a better product and we wouldn't be having a screaming match here in my office now." I was angry and shaking but he backed down immediately.

Shades of Teal

Conrad Glastonbury sat down in the beautifully upholstered chair beside my desk and put his face in his hands.

"Look, kid," he said. "I'm sorry. But your work sucks. I need a REAL writer, one who can make this shit really *cook*. You're not there." His voice was gentle now, regretful.

"Sure you can handle your words and you can spell fine but you don't get beyond the technical stuff. The facts are all there but the heart and soul are missing. You've got to learn to unleash yourself, to make your words leap off the page and grab the reader by the nuts and bring him to his knees. That's the difference between a good writer and a truly *great* writer. I get no boost from what you write. There's no passion here, no sizzle. You don't belong in this business."

I was stunned, and had to fight back the nasty grit of tears in my eyes. This man was telling me I was no good.

"You need someone to teach you how to write," he said.

I looked at him with the pieces of my poor broken heart flooding out the corners of my eyes. I desperately needed a success.

"Will you teach me?" I asked.

"No, kid, I don't have time. I need someone who's already up and running, someone to whom I can pass anything at a moment's notice and know they'll get it perfect first time, every time."

"But I really want to learn," I whispered. "All I want to do is write. Won't you *please*, teach me?"

He looked at me for a few soft moments and then slumped back in his chair — my chair, now — and sighed. He rubbed his hands over his face and stretched his legs out until they were almost touching my chair. He was wearing a pair of black brogues today, polished until they shone brightly against the purple and green flecked carpeting. Conrad always dressed well, even on a casual day in the office. He looked great in jeans, I had noticed. He rarely wore a suit unless he had to, but everything he owned had an expensive look to it. Conrad looked up at the ceiling. It was almost time for me to leave for the day, pick up my son, make dinner and drown my sorrow. Or whatever else I needed to do to feel better about this hideous moment in my life.

Conrad stared at the ceiling while I silently prayed to be released from the horrible shame of being a lousy writer. He looked at his fingernails. He rolled his eyes and tapped his fingers on the arm of the chair. I looked at the floor. Finally, the Great Glastonbury spoke.

"I'll make you a deal," he said. "I'll give you $300 for last month's work. But for the next six months you're on probation during which time you will do everything you can to prove you actually are a writer. I'll try and teach you the craft of writing, although God knows I don't want to. It's all going to be up to you. For those six months I am going to pay you $1,000 a month for full time hours, out of which we will deduct your rent. If you don't like the deal you can walk away from it at any time but if I don't like your work in six months you're gone. Got it?"

It was not a very friendly proposition, especially given that I had been writing for a living years before I had ever even heard of Conrad Glastonbury. David was going to be furious when he found out about this plan. If he found out about it. If I really was as bad as this guy seemed to think then I was unlikely to get another job anywhere else. On the other hand, if I accepted his offer, I might get better, and I secretly thought Conrad was the best writer I had ever read. His work was smooth and creative, fresh and disciplined. The words he wrote samba'd off the pages – they had power. I wanted to write just like him. But he was essentially talking about slave labour here. If I accepted his deal I would be making less than five dollars an hour – a pittance. But I would be working, David would be happy and my marriage would be saved.

"I'll do it," I said.

Conrad nodded, stood up and shook my hand. Without another word, he left my office, and headed back to his lair. It was hard to like this reluctant saviour. But I did.

27

Had I known what a disastrous chain of events I was to unleash by agreeing to become primary slave for Cornerstone Marketing I might not have jumped at the chance to "learn" quite so readily. Obviously I couldn't tell David about my deal with the devil — it struck me that this arrangement was either unethical or illegal or both, and David would never go for that. He thought I was already a good writer – that's what I had told him. Training endeavour? David was unlikely to see it that way. I was a competent writer in the fields in which I had already been tested...but marketing was turning out to be a whole different ball game and I was grossly uneducated about it. I wanted to learn

"Go back to school, then," he would no doubt command and it would be hard to remind him that he had vetoed the idea when I first mentioned it while planning our sojourn in Paris in pursuit of *his* higher education. I had wanted a Masters degree but David kindly pointed out that we couldn't afford it.

"But David, I want to take courses too," I had bravely countered him. Thoughts of Shakespeare thrummed through my heart even then, and I was desperate to understand the layers of meaning that exploded through his words, the subtleties woven through his writing. He was a brilliant man, an emotional genius, a remarkable expert in human behaviour who never knew the impact he had had on me and millions of others. My favorite sonnet (number 116) was a beautiful tribute to love, a glorious, luxurious elaboration of a simple truth that nudged gently against the muddy riverbank of my soul:

*Let me not to the marriage of true minds
Admit impediments. Love is not love
Which alters when it alteration finds,
Or bends with the remover to remove:
Oh, no! it is an ever-fixed mark,
That looks on tempests and is never shaken;
It is the star to every wandering bark,
Whose worth's unknown, although his height be taken.
Love's not Time's fool, although rosy lips and cheeks
Within his bending sickle's compass come;
Love alters not with his brief hours and weeks,
But bears it out even to the edge of doom.
If this be error and upon me proved,
I never writ, nor no man ever loved.*

"Teale, Teale," David had murmured, as he drew me sweetly into his arms. He held me for a moment and sighed, the warm scent of Armani aftershave clouding my thinking for a moment. Then he put two strong, gentle hands around my head and looked deeply into my face, regret flowing soothingly from the very retinas of his eyes.

"You know we need every penny to get through," he had said. I'm a modern guy – I would *gladly* give up the Breadwinner's job if you could earn enough to support us – but English courses aren't going to help you make more money later on. We can't afford it."

And there it was: we *could* afford to spend thousands of dollars on airfare, rent and transportation, as well as holidays just about anywhere in Great Britain and continental Europe. We *could* afford my husband's course fees, books and membership at a private club. We *could* afford clothes for the male of the species, entertainment for him, weekend trips, golf fees and anything, really, that the muddle of testosterone I had married could convince himself was important for the Family. There was always money for entertaining friends, and certainly money for cases of the remarkably fine wine that disappeared from our cold storage room with such astonishing speed.

What a crime to be unable to afford the return trip to the edge of my own intellect that education could provide.

Shades of Teal

I had tried again.

"But David this is really important to me."

"Come on, Teale, let's face it – we don't need you to get more education. You're an intelligent woman – if you want to go fuss with a little Shakespeare just go and read a few of his plays or something."

"But..."

David had given me the exasperated look that signaled the end of the discussion. It hit me then, a teetering, dangerous thought: for all his talk about the *equality* of the womenfolk David did not seem to believe in the importance of *educating* them. At least, not *his* womanfolk.

And now, years later, I was looking for an education of a different sort. How was I ever going to become improve if I didn't take Cornerstone up on their apprenticeship proposition? Now that Conrad Glastonbury had opened the door in my head marked "Improvement Needed" I was tyrannically focused on marching directly through the room that lay behind it. But I was never going to get there —I was never going to get anywhere —if I didn't get off my rear end and make it happen. If I mentioned the situation to David he would undoubtedly talk me around to ditching Cornerstone, getting pregnant and signing up for a poetry workshop that he would ultimately find a way to prevent me from attending. For the first time in my life a tiny little analytical corner of my brain assessed the impact of the gathering impulse to sway towards my husband's compromise. First the head and shoulders would lean a little to the right and then the torso and pretty soon I knew my hips would follow the curve and eventually my knees and ultimately my feet and there I would be, 34 years old, quivering and hopeful and standing easily within range of my husband's spear. It wouldn't take much to finish me off, would it? It was a startling thought.

And then what? The question was a ghostly whisper reminiscent of the Huckleberry Teale I had left behind so long ago.

She had been so strong, so willing to take a chance, try something new, fail if necessary but move forward, somehow. She would have jumped on a leaky old boat in the middle of Moon River if she thought it would take her where she wanted to go. She knew, in fact, *exactly* where she wanted to go. And of course she would get there, even if the river *was* wider than a mile.

If I swayed within range of David's spear this time, she noted, I was going to end up drunk every night dreaming of writing second-rate poems about dogdirt and body hair. Is that what I wanted? Is that what *I* wanted? The question shocked me.

What did I want?

I had wanted a wonderful marriage to a devoted man and a handful of happy children playing in the fenced backyard of our lovely house. I had wanted pretty tablecloths, sociable meals with friends, season's tickets to the symphony and, of course, flowers sitting in a cut glass bowl on my shiny dining room table. Most of all, of course, I had wanted to stay home and look after my children.

I didn't like that dream anymore, it seemed superficial now, and limited. And in the great compromise that my marriage involved, it wasn't possible anyway.

It was time to want different things that I actually had a chance of getting and what I wanted right now was to become the kind of writer even Conrad Glastonbury would admire. I wanted to become disciplined, targeted, creative and effective. I wanted to explode with ability. Glastonbury could teach me those things if I could just get past his thorny personality.

David didn't even have to know what I wanted – in fact, it was probably better that he didn't, since every time I shared a dream, a goal, a hope or a plan he found a way to cleverly neutralize it. If I didn't tell him about my new deal with Cornerstone there would be no arguments, no swaying, no disappointments, no harm done. David had already told me I could keep all the money I made and spend it on whatever I wanted.

Shades of Teal

I would buy a new briefcase maybe. A jacket for Jason. Some new shoes. A pretty lamp for the living room. It would be my own money. Shhhh, Teale.

What I wanted required me to quietly throw myself into my work and say very little to David about my experiences on the job. There were many experiences, of course. I knew less than nothing about marketing, the little ins and outs of graphic design, printing, editing, and least of all, writing for a specific audience. Most of the time I felt scared and inept. Like, for example, the day The Boss handed me a beautiful mock-up of a client newsletter and said,

"Edit this, will ya? I don't have time."

What did he mean, "Edit it?" Hadn't he already edited it? If it had already made it to the design stage, didn't that mean he had approved the copy? Why edit the writing when it was already typeset, with lots of graphic elements swirling around the words? How could I edit copy penned by the Great Glastonbury? Was I supposed to edit the graphics maybe? Pick different colours? Holy Mother of God what had I signed up for? I stared at the mock-up for a full half hour before my heart stopped its thunderous – and exceedingly erratic — pounding. In the internal quiet that followed it became obvious that my brain had simply stopped working altogether. Great. A heart attack and an aneurysm, both on the same day. I expected kidney failure next and perhaps some nice little liver disorder to follow. How was I supposed to get anything done when I had to deal with the distraction of sequential organ failure? Maybe I needed a coffee.

Maybe I needed a reality check.

After a few more moments of neurotic panic I finally put my head down on my desk and turned, in abject desperation to God. Now, the Lord had not featured greatly in my life up to this point. Sure, I was a Believer of sorts, and had had a few panicked but fervently religious moments in the distant past, like when my period was late and I prayed it would arrive before the Stork. But those kinds of prayers, personal as they were, and as nicely answered as they had been, had not turned me into the kind of religious fanatic I was accustomed to seeing on TV. Those people really believed He was out there. I sort of did. I needed Him to pull off another miracle again. Or did he only answer people who were far more fervently opposed to abortion than sex?

"Okay, God," I said to myself. "I have no idea what I'm supposed to do here. No idea at all. Take me by the hand and show me, oh Lord.

"Please.

"*Please!!!*" I waited for the bright light and the voice of the Lord or at least some sign he had been listening. When neither appeared I asked again.

"Okay, God, I'm sure I'm guilty of sin and I never go to church and I drink too much I'm sure, but please, please, *pléase* tell me what to do."

Still no answer. How did this prayer thing work, anyway? I tried again.

"You win, God. I'm in over my head. I should have listened to David's voice in my conscience and turned Cornerstone down and had another baby. Is that what I was supposed to do? Is that why I'm locked in my office on the verge of a coronary and not even remotely wondering what to make for dinner? Sure wish you could talk, God. Sure wish I knew if you were listening. God?"

I drummed my fingers on the desktop and waited while another half-hour went by. God must have more important problems to solve, I decided.

Damn.

I read the articles in the newsletter. A few typos sprouted here and there, and there were some bad hyphenation breaks. Other than that I had no clue what to do with this thing. The newsletter was aimed at the employees of Rectobin, a big-name industrial waste management company that wanted to friendly-up its reputation with staff and encourage them to feel good about their employer. The first article was all about how Rectobin had revamped its entire management structure and was refocusing on the human aspect of work. The second article talked about how psychologists today are urging all of us to look on adversity as an opportunity to learn. Other articles dealt with the company volleyball team, the Rectobin recycling initiative, a recent speech given by company President John Drbovnic and a cute little piece on efforts to upgrade the company's computer systems.

After reading the whole thing, God had still not answered my pleas so I put my ego in my back pocket, grabbed a humiliating white flag from my imaginary briefcase and walked the terrifying 30 steps to Conrad Glastonbury's office. He was on the phone. Should I stay? Should I leave? He motioned at me to sit in the plushy burgundy swivel chair across from his enormous messy desk. Although I thought I was being quite quiet, I was sure he could hear the chatter of my teeth and the knocking of my knees.

I was wearing the same outfit I had worn to my fateful job interview nearly two months earlier – gotta get some new clothes, I thought. I wondered if I was ever going to get paid. Conrad Glastonbury was still listening intently to the person on the other end of his phone line so I busied myself with looking at the posters on the walls of his office and reading the spines of the books on his bookshelves. I cursed the wait. Better to have the guillotine slice quickly and cleanly through your neck than have to wait in line for the experience.

"Why don't you take it easy this afternoon?" he was saying gently.

"Well, look, I'll look after the kids tonight so you can get out for a few hours..."

He was talking to his wife.

"How much money do you need?"

He gave her money?

"Sure, if you want to go out tomorrow night too, I'll make sure I'm home early."

Had David ever offered to watch Jason so I could go out? Fat chance.

"Okay."

"I love you too."

He actually told her he loved her! The conversation I had just overheard blew all panic over my missing editing skills into outer space. I tried to imagine such a conversation between David and I while he was at the office. Whoa! David hated to be bothered at work. The odd time I dared call, like, say, when Jason stuck a kidney bean up his nose and had to go to Emerge or when a pipe burst in the basement or when American Express had called with an angry demand for money, David always sounded as though he were busy doing something else that was so much more important he was stunned that I expected him to actually listen. I had, in fact, in a moment of soft affection, called David the week before just to say hello and our conversation had gone something like this:

"Hi David, it's me."

"Hi. You're not going to give me another one of those boring 'guess what Jason's doing now' stories, are you Teale?"

"Of course, not, David, give me a little credit." Well, actually, that had been the plan but clearly this was not a good time.

"What is it then?"

"Um, I just missed you." I said quietly.

"Yeah me too, anything else?"

"No, uh, that was it I guess."

Shades of Teal

"I'll be late tonight."

"'Kay."

Click.

"Bye."

Glastonbury didn't seem the type to welcome interruptions at work either but somehow he seemed to have all the time in the world for his wife. How come a total jerk like Glastonbury was so nice to his wife on the phone when a great guy like my husband was harder to talk to than peanut shells? Come to think of it, Devlin Braxton always dropped everything to have a quiet conversation with his wife on the phone, even asking me, on occasion, to leave his office so he could talk to her privately. What on Earth did they talk about? And what was with the presents? These guys always seemed to be buying their wives nice little knick knacks — for no apparent reason. I had seen Dev come in from his lunch hour with boxes of pretty soaps or specialty chocolates he had bought for his wife and I had recently caught Glastonbury gift-wrapping a sizable gift certificate to a beautiful woman's clothing store.

"Whoa —is it your wife's birthday?" I asked.

He looked up slowly from his careful task and shook his head. He was trying to wrap the certificate around a package of expensive gourmet coffee, just so she wouldn't guess what it was. It was an awkward job.

"Anniversary?" I asked.

"Nope," he said.

"A get-out-of-the-doghouse-free card?"

He cracked half a smile and looked up sheepishly at me.

"No it's just a none-of-your-business-but-I-love-my-wife kind of a thing."

I stared at him.

"Some men do that you know," he continued. In his oh-so-superior way. "We buy our wives presents for no good reason other than that we want to make them happy."

I thought about that comment for days afterward. I didn't know men did that. David certainly never did that. But he tried to make me happy in other ways. Like...forcing me to choose between getting a job or having another baby so I wouldn't be an embarrassment to him? Like...giving me tickets to a play he wanted to see for my birthday? Like.......well...keeping the mortgage going on the house we lived in. And for that matter, what did *I* do to make *him* happy? The answers came thick and fast. Well, I always brought him a fresh coffee while he was showering in the morning.

I never nagged him to watch Jason if I wanted to go out. I just never went out. If I made myself a snack or a drink I always offered to bring him something as well. In fact, even if I wasn't snacky I'd often offered to get him something. If I borrowed his car I always put gas in it (although I rarely got up the nerve to borrow his car!). I ran his errands. I took out the garbage so he wouldn't have to do it. I did all the housework. I took the cars in for repair. I bought him beer every weekend. I made sure there was always wine in the house. I cut the grass. I called his family on their birthdays. I cooked special meals for him. I entertained his friends and colleagues, even when I was too tired to think about cooking or cleaning.

I never argued with him about how he spent money, knowing that it was, after all, his money and, as he had pointed out countless times before, it was not my business to censor his spending habits: he was the main breadwinner. If there was a TV show on that he wanted to watch that conflicted with something I wanted to see I always skipped my show. There was always a little birthday celebration with homemade cake waiting on his birthday every year, even on the years he went out on client dinners. Why did I do it? Because I loved him.

And what else did he do for me? A dangerous question.

Even Celia, the pretty blond receptionist whose clothes I so admired when I first met her had opened my mind to a different brand of husband when she booked off for a week not long after I first started with Cornerstone. Celia was very blond, very stylish and very size 8 but she was very friendly and kind-hearted.

"Going somewhere fun?" I asked.

She blushed a little.

"John surprised me last week with a seven-day Caribbean cruise," she said.

"Whoa" I said. "Are you ever lucky!" I said. "Is it your anniversary or something?" I had heard people sometimes went on cruises to mark a special anniversary.

"Oh no," said lucky Celia. "He just knows how hard I work and how much I appreciate a little break now and then, so he saves his money very quietly until he has enough for something really special and then he springs it on me!" She was smiling.

"Is that ever nice!" I said, thinking longingly of how wonderful it would be to go on a Caribbean cruise with David.

"Oh yeah, my husband is a sweet-heart!" said Celia. My sweet-heart of a husband had no idea how tired I was! Working full time under the stress-inducing fear of failure, running around after one irresistible little kid when I got home, cooking, cleaning, entertaining, doing the bills, keeping everybody happy.

The stress of being on probation was starting to show, although I was doing my level best. I would show this Glastonbury devil what kind of a writer I was! He would be impressed with me yet. His bookshelves held all manner of interesting books on language and writing. There were books of famous quotes, books on grammar, books on writing fluidly, books on psychology. There were large books on behavioral analysis, books on cognitive therapy and one very pretty looking book on Harley Davidson motorcycles. There was a commemorative edition on "Woodstock" (he claimed to have been there) and a little tiny book on mixing perfect cocktails. There was a first edition copy of the collected works of Charles Dickens and a book on the history of the guitar. Glastonbury seemed to have fairly eclectic tastes. My husband still hadn't coughed up all the antique books he had once boasted that he owned.

As I sat there patiently — or rather, cowering quietly — I felt nervously lucky Glastonbury was tolerating my apprenticeship.

He hung up the phone and I spread the newsletter mockup out on the desk between us and looked at him.

"You said you want me to edit this."

He glanced at me as though I were an extra "d" at the end of the word "stupid" and then looked back down at the piece he was working on.

"Yeah."

"Edit this." I repeated.

"Yeah. You got a problem with that?"

Tears were welling up in my eyes and I cursed myself for being so weak. What was I doing here???

"I-I-um-ah don't know what you want me to do with it," I stammered.

Glastonbury looked up from his work, exasperated.

"Edit it," he said. "*Edit* it. EDIT IT." He was almost screaming at me.

I took a deep breath. A very edgy, shaky deep breath. I would not lose control.

"I know that but what am I trying to do with it? Make it shorter? Make it look prettier? Change the graphics? Make it longer? Revise the headlines? Change the copy?" There were tears streaming down my face now and I could barely speak. But I was not crying. I would not give him the satisfaction. No nightmare could ever come close to the terror I felt as I looked in Glastonbury's face and saw the utter disgust with which he regarded me. I thought he might hit me but instead he picked up a book, flung it against a wall, grabbed his cigarettes and stormed out of his office.

I sat there for a few moments grateful for the ability to breathe and then slowly packed up my stuff and made my dismal way back to my office and shut the door. I put my head down on my desk and fought the tears that were clamoring to find an outlet. They would have to be very quiet tears, if they won, because this was a place of business. Professional women do not cry. But my shoulders heaved and my eyes welled up in spite of my determination. My nose clogged and my head ached. Everything was lining up to make it a record-setting cry.

I was done for.

I had never disappointed anybody in my career before, or so I believed, and here I was blowing my one chance to improve myself professionally. I was no good at anything and I had no idea how to improve. What was David going to say when I told him I'd been fired? How could I ever hold my head up again? After what seemed an eternity a soft knock came at the door. My heart sank. Before I had time to clean myself up Glastonbury had opened the door and stood before me.

"Are you going to sit there playing house all day or are you going to get some work done?" he asked. I just stared at him. "Come with me, he said gently picking up my mockup and leading me down the hall into the boardroom. He turned on the lights and shut the door.

"Sit down," he said, and pulled up a chair beside me.

"Okay," he said and drew in a big breath. "Okay. I'm not good at teaching people stuff and I don't want to do this. But when I say edit something, I mean clean it up in any way shape or form necessary to make the communication smooth and economical, attractive and to the point," he began. "Our designer took raw copy I gave him and threaded it into a design he came up with before I had a chance to really think about what I had written. This newsletter is supposed to be going out in four days and it's nowhere near ready. I want you to look at each article and turn it into something that makes perfect sense. Clean it up. See this widow?"

He pointed to the word "claim" sitting alone on a line at the end of a paragraph.

"Where there are widows at the end of a paragraph I want you to revise the sentence so the line ends cleanly on or near the right hand side of the column. A widow might be a small word — but it takes up valuable space and will make a piece look choppy. Where the headlines look too aggressive, I want you to whittle them down to a more manageable size. But they still have to make sense. If a picture looks stupid, get the designer to take it out and put something else in. This is the client's main tool of communication with employees and it has to make the client look really good — professional, intelligent, approachable. Anything you have to do to this piece to meet that goal, you have my permission to do.

"Take this pen," he said, "and begin."

For the next 15 minutes we sat there discussing things I thought might improve the newsletter. My head was pounding and I was grateful Conrad wasn't yelling. The piece we were examining was top heavy, I thought, with one great big block of copy dominating three-quarters of the front page.

"Can't we put breakers in the middle of this article and turn part of it to the second page?" I asked. I was proud that my career in newspapers had taught me the word "breakers".

"Sure," said Glastonbury.

"Then we could maybe make this picture larger and beef up this second article and add a small picture to give the page a little more interest."

"Go for it" said Glastonbury.

"This headline sucks," I said. And then I was off in my own little world of 'what can we do to make this work better. Finally Glastonbury left me to my devices and I immersed myself in the joys of both re-writing his copy and changing the look of the page.

After an hour or so I took the whole package down to Henry Chasen's office. Henry was about 45 years old and worked as Cornerstone's chief graphic designer. He looked rumpled, as though he slept in his clothes, and his hair was long and flecked with gray. I guessed that he had actually been at Woodstock and that he had dragged some of that historic event forward with him as he grooved ahead into new decades.

His studio was messy, with capless marker pens strewn everywhere and computers stacked up on the floor by his feet. Paper littered the floor and the remnants of several sandwiches lay rotting on various work surfaces. A little CD player, perched dangerously on the corner of a filing cabinet, spewed out classical jazz music and a stack of CDs, some in their cases, some not, represented a tortured tower of 20th century longing staggering up to the ceiling. A cigarette, unlit, dangled from Henry's lips and a dirty red bandanna kept most of his long gray hair out of his face.

"Hi Henry," I said.

"You look like you've been hit by a bus," he said.

"Just the wrath of Glastonbury," I said as I sat down on the swivel chair at his drafting table.

He nodded, knowingly and chuckled. Few people in the Cornerstone fold had avoided Glastonbury's anxiety attacks and although most people could be seduced by his charm when it served his purpose, everyone knew there were times when you barely got out with your skin intact.

Henry was no exception. Having worked closely on all manner of printed projects with Glastonbury he knew there were times when Glastonbury was likely to throw something, and times when the something was actually a really kind word. Henry coped very nicely by simply pretending the man was not even there, turning up the volume on his CD player, and sticking another cigarette in his mouth. He might even light it. Or he might play with it until Glastonbury stopped hollering at him. Sometimes he got up and went to the bathroom. Henry was cool.

"This is the Rectobin piece," I said, spreading a scribbled and somewhat tear-stained collection of paper on the drafting table. Henry wheeled himself over and looked at my scratchings. He whistled. He picked it up and squinted at it.

"I can see why he lost it," he said. And then winked at me. "Okay, girlie, take me through it." For the next 45 minutes I explained what I wanted him to do and what all my arrows and squiggles meant. Henry went over to a filing cabinet, pulled out a piece of paper and handed it to me.

"These are standard editing marks," he explained. "If you learn them and use them then it'll make my job go a little faster next time."

I took the piece of paper and beamed at him.

"Thanks, Henry!!!" I said. He just smiled at me and turned back to the board.

"I can get this done tonight and it'll be on your desk tomorrow morning," he said.

"Okay," I said quietly. "I guess I'll see you tomorrow." I was finally onto something.

28

That night David and I met for dinner at a little Chinese food restaurant he liked and although he begrudged the money spent on dinner with me, we had to meet our lawyer about our wills and the appointment was set late enough in the day that it made sense to catch a quick bite before heading home.

It is an undeniable fact of life that we are all going to die and it had taken me months to convince David to get our wills drawn up so that we were each other's sole beneficiaries; my next challenge would be to somehow convince him to rework his insurance policy so the funds would go to me rather than his 10-year-old niece. That was going to be a tough job.

David had taken on the policy before Jason was born and although I felt I should be the beneficiary he had insisted that his niece would need the money more than me because I was working.

The old "greedy Teale" label was bound to crop up again and although I no longer bought into it I needed to make sure Jason would be looked after. The huge relief of having our wills organized cheered me after my stressful day at work.

"I had the most interesting day at work today, David," I said.

"Oh yeah?" he said.

"Yeah, I learned how to edit a newsletter! It's really neat.

"Why would you ever take a lousy job like that?" he asked with an incredulous sneer.

"Pardon?"

"Well it seems to me that's not the kind of work you should be taking on for these people, Teale. You should be doing longer articles more in line with your seriousness as a professional journalist."

"Well this is new for me, Davey," I said. "It's really cool how it works and what's involved – I had a ball once I finally got the hang of it."

"Well, I still don't think you should be doing that kind of work. And you're working an awful lot of hours for these guys. I bet they don't appreciate you at all."

"Well, appreciation is all in the paycheck, isn't it?" I fibbed.

"Which reminds me," he went on "I looked through your accounting book the other day. You're doing it all wrong." I froze.

"What do you mean, David?" He had me there, for sure. David knew everything about keeping track of money and I was not much good at it. He had shown me the basics and I had listened as carefully as I could. It was hard to believe I had blown it already!

"Well, Teale, you need a larger accounting book. And your columns are very crooked. It's important to be neat and tidy when you're keeping track of money."

Well, there wasn't much I could say about it. A larger accounting book I could get. Neat and tidy I could certainly improve on. But these did not sound like radical issues.

"Am I doing the rest of it right?" I wanted to know.

"Well, more or less."

"Great!" I was relieved. I smiled. A few minutes of silence ensued while the waiter set our wonton soup down in front of us. I took enormous pleasure out of going out for a meal and even though Wong Lee's House of Chinese and Canadian Cuisine was not an exotic restaurant, it was very nice to have someone cooking for me and cleaning up afterward. The waiter wished us a pleasant meal, bowed and walked away. We were the only diners in the restaurant which was not surprising as it was still only 5:30 on a Tuesday afternoon. I picked up my porcelain spoon and dragged it across the top of the yellow broth.

"And, too, Teale, you're weight's creeping up again. If you really want to be taken seriously in the business world you're going to have to trim down a little."

I just stared at him. It was true — that very morning David had passed behind me as I stood naked on the scale and said:

"Wow, you've got a huge butt!"

At the time I was willing the needle of my scale to find the number 92, down from the horrifically enormous 93 pounds I currently weighed and somehow the combination of standing on the scale, looking at the numbers, and listening to my husband's voice had hit home with me. In that very second I wondered how a 93-pound woman could possibly have a fat bum. Something was wrong with the numbers. Something was wrong with something, although I didn't know exactly what that was.

The mist felt like it was lifting a little and as I sat across from my husband and listened to him list my failings I wondered how it was possible for me to be so wrong all the time. There was something wrong with this picture, perhaps, but I was starting to think that maybe it wasn't me. I tucked the idea away for later consideration and changed the subject.

"Hey David, don't you just love the shape of this bowl? It's simple but so artistic." It was a plain Chinese food bowl, round and wide at the top with gracefully sloping sides that led down to a narrow pedestal at the bottom. On the sides, painted in light blue, were dragons and bushes, all dancing, it seemed, around the bowl in a celebration of life and motion. It was beautiful, I thought, and so simple. It held my wonton soup now but it could also hold potpourri or chocolates, candies or coins...and it would look equally lovely no matter what was inside.

"Teale that's got to be the stupidest thing you've ever said in your whole life," said David, his eyes wide in surprised concern. "That's just a stupid ordinary little bowl. It will never be anything *but* a stupid, ordinary bowl and the fact that you think it is something *other than* a stupid ordinary bowl means...well..." He paused for effect. "Anybody with half a brain can see you're overreacting Teale. I hate it when you get all soggy over stupid things – it's so embarrassing. Who do you think you are to talk about a bowl as if it's real art or something? Do you have any idea how embarrassing it is for me to have a wife with such moronic ideas about things? This bowl is not art, Teale, this bowl costs ninety-five cents at the local Chinese gift emporium."

"But David things don't have to be expensive to be beautiful," I said weakly.

He looked at me darkly.

"Since when do *you* know anything about beauty?" he asked and I started to cry.

I couldn't breathe. There was something desperately wrong here but I didn't know what it was. Please God tell me what is wrong, tell me why I can't breathe, can't think, can't talk, can't answer this man who I am supposed to love for all eternity. OH GOD WHAT IS WRONG WITH THIS PICTURE??? I stood up from the table, grabbed my purse and scurried off to the Ladies room to cry.

I crouched on the floor, braced my back against the wall, put my head on my knees, and cried. I cried until there were no tears left, until my body, wracked by grief, and pain and misery ran dry.

"What's wrong with me, God? I pleaded. "What did I do? Why is everybody so impossible to please?" Why was I crying all the time? Had I finally lost it? What had happened to me? I cried some more.

Eventually, of course, I stopped crying and tried to breathe, tried to ignore the hiccoughing sobs that still wracked my body, tried to pull myself together enough so I could walk out of the Ladies Room and go home, whatever home meant.

I stood up and stared at the crumpled face of the woman in the mirror and told her to smarten up and think bigger. I looked at the lines forming at the corners of her eyes, her blotchy skin and the mousy brown hair straggling along the side of her face. I looked her in the eyes and asked her what her problem was and in a flash clarity she gave me the answer:

"*That* man is not my friend," she whispered. "If that man were my friend, he would treat me with respect, he'd encourage and support me and he'd throw a little kindness my way from time to time. He wouldn't treat me so disdainfully and he wouldn't find fault with the things I do or say. He wouldn't throw sarcasm at me like the weapon it is and he wouldn't criticize me for a simple opinion."

A friend might disagree and might argue with me but they wouldn't call me stupid. A friend doesn't behave as though every interruption is an inconvenience or an intrusion. They don't put their hand up a person's skirt and call it a game. They certainly don't pretend to unlock the front door to make someone else feel unsafe. They don't make other friends feel guilty for wanting to clothe their children. A friend shares. A friend mirrors back to another friend the best qualities they see, not the hopeless piece of garbage David seemed to think I was.

It was an extraordinary revelation.

My husband was not my friend.

As I sat there waiting for calm to take over again, all the pieces started to fall into place: David was never happy with my body. He rarely wanted to make love to me. If our quarterly effort at sex hurt me, he would keep going anyway. He spent money on everything he wanted but accused me of greed when I wanted something for our son. He never wanted to spend quiet, peaceful time with just me and he never wanted to spend time with my friends. If I used my imagination in some manner I was accused of being weird. If I complained about his rudeness I was accused of having no sense of humour. Maybe I didn't have a sense of humour any more.

I had thought I was supposed to simply accept and love my man exactly the way he was. But did he reciprocate? No! This man was always tinkering with something — how I looked, how I acted, how I felt, how I thought, even my perception of beauty was under attack now, and that wasn't how friends treated each other. David didn't love me just the way I was. Maybe David didn't love me at all.

I stayed locked in the bathroom for more than an hour, dazed by the revelations that flowed into my heart that night. When I came out, David was gone.

I took a cab home, relieved the baby-sitter and kissed my son, asleep in his bed. And then I crawled up to bed myself and slept soundly until I heard David come in sometime after 2 a.m. I feigned sleep while he undressed and came to bed. I hoped he wouldn't touch me tonight. In fact, I hoped he would never touch me again for the rest of my life. The honeymoon was over now. Perhaps the happily ever after part was too.

29

There are times in our lives when we blithely, even stubbornly, ignore reality and sashay through the hours and days of our existence as though everything is fine. And if we are very lucky or very wise, or very miserable, there are also times when we get on with the ugly job of examining the dog dirt that's stuck to the bottom of our stilettos so we can go do something about it.

It's not a pretty job.

And because it is not a pretty job, and because we have become experts in the fine art of ignoring our unhappiness, and, oh yes, because we have no idea what we're supposed to do now that we're aware of the problem, we may be guilty of prevaricating for a while. Such was my situation as I drove my dilapidated old Mustang down Avenue Road to work every morning.

I was unhappily married. It had been a stunning revelation that froze me into a state of breathless panic. Up until that dreadful scene in Wong Lee's grubby little restaurant, I had believed I loved my husband. Oh, sure, there had been moments of unhappiness along the way, but Marriage is Compromise and so I had manfully dusted my selfish little quibbles under the carpet of wedded bliss and carried on with the business of marriage. I couldn't do that anymore.

I was wounded to the quick.

I had always liked the drama of that expression whenever it jumped out at me from the pages of a hysterical women's novel and I never heard the phrase without visualizing a tall woman in a long gown swooning onto a damask sofa with the back of one hand compressed to her forehead.

"Dorothea was wounded to the quick," the book might say.

I knew *exactly* what that looked like. But in those overcast days of confusion and worry I suddenly dropped the coddled and sarcastic view of pain I had carried around with me for so long and truly *felt* its meaning — and the fragile sense of nobility it conferred. Wounded to the quick means your internal organs are in danger of shutting down because the pain in your heart is radiating so intensely throughout your body that you just cannot fathom how you are still standing. It means you have barely enough strength to hold your head up off your shoulders because the substance of your whole life has just been shredded into hamburger meat by the realization that everything you'd believed up until now was a complete and utter lie. Wounded to the quick means you feel infinitesimally small and insignificant and almost entirely absent from the present tense of your life because you are senseless with anguish. It may sound like a wonderfully dramatic expression, but as an emotion it really sucks and it is impossible to live that way and still make forward motion into the next hour of your life.

And so, as I trundled off to work every morning thereafter, hoping my vehicle would make it through just one more winter, I instinctively kept my mind busy with other things – well, with the only other thing I actually had to think about at that time, specifically, my work. This probably would have helped my marriage somehow glue itself back into something resembling a sham if I hadn't finally fixed the car radio in a fit of pique generated by the lack of nice sounds with which to mask the groans and complaints of an unsafe vehicle, not to mention the need to distract myself from a desperate need to cry.

Some people think it's a bit of a stretch to connect fixing a car radio with divorce and, also, many others wonder how any woman – or man – can simply trot out to the driveway with a screwdriver and a pair of pliers and magically repair an instrument that hasn't made a sound for five years or more. Truth to tell, repairing my car radio was an intensely frustrating experience that entailed visits to the library, a mechanic, a sound shop and, finally, a really good audio centre. After countless hours and $135 which I had to hunt, lie and beg for, I had music again. David never even knew. Frankly, he probably didn't realize the radio had long ago given up the ghost but I didn't care. This was a secret success and I hugged it quietly to my soul and grinned, randomly, for days afterwards. I had made something good happen, something that loosened David's hold on my opinion of myself, like a small wind lifting the corner of a dead leaf just a little off its bed in the cloying mud. I was still enjoying the sweet murmur of autonomy the radio had given me several weeks later There it was, a dreary Monday morning, and it was suddenly lightened by the song that blew me out of the mud and brought me crashing against the shore of a cold wet beach with only fairy tales for fishing line and tears for cold company. It was a haunting song about me and every woman out there like me who knew about sadness, despair and the vagaries of hope. It crawled into my head and wouldn't crawl out again. It prowled around inside me, a caged tiger waiting to pounce. It insisted I listen. It insisted I act. And so, first I listened:

> *Every time that I look in the mirror*
> *All these lines in my face getting clearer*
> *The past is gone*
> *It went by like dust to dawn*
> *Isn't that the way*
> *Everybody's got their dues in life to pay*
>
> *I know what nobody knows*
> *Where it comes and where it goes*
> *I know it's everybody's sin*
> *You got to lose to know how to win*
>
> *Half my life is in books' written pages*
> *Live and learn from fools and from sages*
> *You know it's true*
> *All the things come back to you*
>
> *Sing with me, sing for the years*
> *Sing for the laughter, sing for the tears*

Sing with me just for today
Maybe tomorrow the good Lord'll take you away

Sing with me, sing for the year
Sing for the laughter sing for the tears
Sing with me, just for today
Maybe tomorrow the good Lord will take you away

Dream on Dream on Dream on
Dream yourself a dream come true
Dream on Dream on Dream On
Dream until your dream comes true
Dream on Dream on Dream on Dream on
Dream on Dream on Dream on

Sing with me, sing for the year
Sing for the laughter sing for the tears
Sing with me, just for today
Maybe tomorrow the good Lord'll take you away.

"That was "Dream On" written by Steven Tyler and performed by Aerosmith, of course," said the deep but cheerful voice of the morning drive announcer, unkindly breaking in on the spell the music had woven around my heart. How could this magnificent song have been written by a trashy seventies rock band? How could they have created such an incredibly beautiful song?

Every time that I look in the mirror
All these lines in my face getting clearer...

Aerosmith. Not the band that came to mind when one thought of inspirational tunes or thought-provoking melodies. I had always dismissed Aerosmith as a heavy metal band with nothing to its credit but a lot of noisy guitar and painful screaming. This song was pure genius. I had to hear it again. What was it they had said?

The past is gone.
It went by like dust to dawn
Isn't that the way
Everybody's got their dues in life to pay.
Ahhhh!

So many pasts – they *were* gone! There was the past with the cocky dancing Teale smiling, grinning and challenging her way through her days, the one where Teale stayed at a job she hated because her husband needed the money for more education, and even the past where Teale tiptoed around her husband's sleeping anger, worried about what he would think or what he would say or how her feelings might be crushed if she made a wrong move – all of it was over. Today would be over one day as well, gone, swish, in an avalanche of new days and experiences, people and hopes. I had paid my dues.

I know what nobody knows
Where it comes and where it goes
I know it's everybody's sin
You got to lose to know how to win.

Had I lost enough yet to get on with the winning part? I had lost my way, my spirit, my determination. I had lost my voice, my balance, my passion, my overarching sense of wonder at the world and all things in it. I had become small Teale, now, trying to take up as little space as possible in the life that was no longer big enough for both me and my man. There was barely even enough room for David in my life, he loomed so large in the spaces surrounding my vision. There was only enough room in my life – and certainly only enough energy – for tiny little things that didn't hurt when I looked at them or thought about them, the automatic things like making the coffee, cleaning the bathroom, stirring a sauce, folding some laundry. I could cope with only the tasks that required me to be nothing more than a shadow at the edge of my own life. I never read a book anymore because it meant too much thinking, too many opportunities to compare the imaginary world, the world of What Might Be, with my own life, the Life That Was. Shhhh Teale. Who was she, this quiet Teale? I had become the kind of woman whose main concern was to try to vanish as softly as possible into thin air, the kind of woman who irons sheets in the fading twilight of a lonely Saturday night.

Half my life is in books' written pages
Live and learn from fools and from sages
You know it's true

All the things come back to you.

Half my life. No, not quite half my life, perhaps one-third was over, if I were very lucky. How had I made it count? By causing a radio to come back to life? Aerosmith band members had made their lives count by writing and performing wildly popular music that resonated with millions of people. David made his life count by excelling in the field of complicated financial transactions that I never really understood. I had thought that by looking after my man and his home, no, our home, I would create a bounty of goodness that the world could draw on and grow through. I had thought that by looking after my little boy, helping him to grow and flourish and exceed himself, I would make the world a better place for future generations. What I had succeeded in creating instead, was a shell, a fraudulent excuse for a reality that did not even exist in my own imagination any longer. A fairy tale. How could I have been so blind and so stupid?

Sing with me, sing for the years,
Sing for the laughter, sing for the tears
Sing with me, just for today
Maybe tomorrow the good Lord'll take you away.

What if the Lord did take me away tomorrow? What would my life have meant? Would I be proud to go, proud that I had stood tall and made an honest stand for or against anything?

No, not yet.

My death would pass unnoticed, just one more quiet breath of wind over a barren landscape. If I died, the song of the life I left behind would be silent and unsung — primarily because I did not sing anymore. And I did not laugh, did not rejoice, did not feel, did not dream. Perhaps I was already dead. How would I ever know? This song, this Dream, called for courage and it was calling for changes.

"Get with it, lady!" the song shouted to me. "You're supposed to celebrate the sweetness of living *inside the bitterness* of that very same life. *Get it?*"

"You need to live and feel and hold on and suffer and sing until the crazy traumatic joy of it all bursts from your breast like the explosion of birth — messy and painful and miraculous."

Mind you, the song said it so much more succinctly than that. But, if that was the message, that meant new lesions, new pain. In spite of the agony of life, you still had to have a dream.

A tall order.

I doubted that David had wilfully set out to crush me; he had simply chosen to be his own inevitable self one careful, thoughtless gesture at a time. I had been the accidental victim of the cleverly chosen and cheerfully scathing comments that robbed me of dignity or shamed my intelligence. So, too, had the curl of a lip or the sarcastic lift of an eyebrow sent an admirable, brilliant and piercing arrow straight to my self-image. He had never mocked me in order to hurt me; in fact he would deny he had ever mocked me at all. None of that was *supposed* to hurt. Where was my sense of humour? What was the matter with *me* that I took offence to harmless words, deeds, thoughts uttered in jest? Oh sure, there had been the odd cuff on the cheek or back hand to the right breast. The damage done was collateral. He would never do anything to *really* hurt or demean me – he just wasn't that kind of guy.

None of the hurtful things he had said or done to me had been focused on my sense of self-worth or my self-respect; they were not about destroying me. In fact they had had nothing to do with me at all. Everything was all about him. At the same time, I had chosen to accommodate his ego, had chosen to make no fuss when a large one was forgivable, for the simple reason that to take offence over a sarcastic, if amusing, comment or a lifted eyebrow is petty. To complain about an "honest mistake" is unforgiving and therefore bad-tempered. To make a big deal over a small thing is to be guilty of being a "small person" and not the "thinking person" David expected me to be.

In essence, I had chosen to tolerate the intolerable.

And David had rejoiced in his power over me, my willingness to please, my determination to be a good little girl. He had abused my trust. Spear-chucker 100: Swayer 0.

Dream on, dream on
Dream yourself a dream come true

David couldn't have taken my dreams away without my permission. It was time to revoke my permission.

I left work a little early that day and on the way home I made a dramatic and uncharacteristic expenditure at a music store, picking up three Aerosmith CDs. It took me a long time to find what I was looking for. My tastes ran mostly to blues and folk music – with a little Oscar Peterson and perhaps some Spanish Guitar thrown in for good measure — and although I was familiar with Aerosmith in general I couldn't name a single one of their albums. I ended up picking the band's 1973 debut album, 1975's "Toys in the Attic" and their Greatest Hits from 1980. Who knew? Maybe I would one day develop an affection for Aerosmith. Maybe I was a closet rocker!

David's comment, when he saw the covers stacked neatly beside the stereo was

"Oh, I see you're into drug music now."

"It's not drug music David," I said with no smile.

"Of course it is, Teale. That marketing company is obviously full of bad influences."

I didn't answer. What was the point? We passed the rest of the evening in a cool silence that was broken only when I accidentally dropped a plate of cookies on the floor, shattering the plate and spilling pieces of sweet chocolaty crumbs all over the kitchen.

"What did you do that for?" asked David, with the stern reprimand of a disappointed, blaming parent in his tone. I had no answer available. What a stupid question.

Shades of Teal

Sing with me, sing for the years,
Sing for the laughter and sing for the tears
Sing with me, if it's just for today,
Maybe tomorrow the good Lord'll take you away.

I played that song every morning, after David left for work. Jason started learning the words.

Dream until your dreams come true.

I dreamed about writing. I dreamed about respect. I dreamed about making more money, about buying a new car. I dreamed about traveling and singing and being cheerful and happy. I dreamed about freedom and love. I dreamed about new clothes. I dreamed about a holiday where I could do whatever I wanted and buy something because it pleased me.

As the weeks went on I became more and more excited about my work for Cornerstone. There was no doubt about my stature as low man on the totem pole: I answered the phones when Celia took her lunch; I operated the fax machine when we wanted to send press releases out to the media for PR campaigns; I made routine calls. I went to the post office when required. Periodically I was asked to bring coffee to the boardroom for clients. And in my spare time I drafted copy for newsletters, news releases, brochures, advertisements, guest columns and anything else Conrad Glastonbury shoved my way. Sometimes he would buzz me on my intercom and snarl a request for my presence in his office. Other times he would wander by my door and politely ask if I could join him for a few minutes. He would go over the material he needed produced in more or less detail, depending on his mood and I would be dismissed back to the refuge of my office to do my work.

I loved having an office. The silence of my four walls greeted me every morning when I walked in and calmed the jangled nerves left by the jarring notes of a disintegrating marriage march. I took to taking my wedding ring off and storing it in the ashtray I kept on my desk for the odd wayward cigar I smoked defiantly when no-one else was in the office. David thought smokers were losers. I was starting to think David was an asshole.

Dream until your dreams come true.

David and I became more distant than ever. He was never home for meals and he made more plans than ever to be away from me on weekends. Jason and I were just as happy to have the house to ourselves. We liked our own company and Jason was not always comfortable in his father's presence. David was a Daddy who unerringly found fault in something Jason did or said. Was that the kind of father I wanted for my children?

"You let him eat bacon with his fingers? Jason, cut that out."

"Jason, put your pyjama top on, it's wrong to run around in only your pyjama bottoms. Teale, why do you let him do that?"

"His manners are hideous. Aren't you teaching him *anything?*"

Much as I loved my working life, I loved being with my son even more. I scooped Jason up from daycare and the two of us lurched home in the car singing songs and looking for cars — red ones, blue ones or green ones were Jason's favourites and I favoured fast ones, no matter what the colour. Once home I would throw on some old clothes, start dinner and cuddle up on the couch to read books to my son. Sometimes we would play games sprawled on the living room floor together, two heads bent over a set of marbles or a container of modeling clay. Always there was laughter. Never was there the wondering question of when Daddy was going to be home.

Although I always prepared enough dinner that David could have some whenever he decided to show up there was, more often than not, an empty box of pizza on the kitchen counter when I got up the next morning or some empty Chinese food containers in the garbage. Who knew what else he was ordering in while I was asleep in my bed? David rarely came home before 11 p.m. in those days and, because I was getting up so early, I was usually in bed by 9:30 or 10:00. Although neither of us mentioned the hideous scene at Wong Lee's the estrangement between us clearly stemmed from that night. We communicated solely through notes scribbled and left taped to the fridge. I didn't even care.

30

I tried a few times to talk to David about our marriage but he huffed and puffed and told me there was nothing to discuss. I wanted to tell him how much he had hurt me, how devastated I had been by what I saw as his selfishness. I thought if I opened the door to discussion we would be able to find our way back to a new model of marriage, one based on friendship and respect. I didn't know how to get there and I needed his help.

But David didn't want to talk. He acted as though I had somehow mistreated him, as though I were a negligent, abusive wife and he was the injured party. Did I have it all wrong? Was I really as innocent as I thought in all of this? How had I failed him? When I asked him as humbly as I could to tell me what grievances he had against me, he harrumphed away and said.

"Well if you haven't figured that out by now I am certainly not going to tell you."

What good was that? He pointedly moved his belongings into the spare room down the hall and while I felt relieved, I also felt sad. The disintegration of a marriage is a painful process and although it may start with the cold hard shock of a massive fight, it will often linger for months — even years – before either dying entirely or exploding in a spectacular parade of passionate crimes.

I have heard it said that we marry for high-minded concepts like "Love" or "Romance," "Loyalty" or "Integrity" but that we divorce over small details like lousy manners, sloppy housekeeping or disagreements over money. When we meet the love of our life, we ignore the fact that he doesn't tidy up after himself or drinks too much or tends to interrupt us in mid-sentence. We see what we think is his finer, truer, self – his appreciation of beauty or his wonderful mind or his kindness to animals. Maybe we are charmed by his terrific sense of humour or his beautiful brown eyes. We melt into our lover's best qualities, admiring them, applauding them, building them up into the sum total of that wonderful human being's existence on Earth. What we slowly realize, however, is that the man who loves beautiful things is selfish and unkind, the one with the wonderful mind is narrowly focused on his achievements. The sense of humour we loved at first is really full of cruel and sarcastic criticisms. Those eyes? Perhaps they stray. We deny the existence of a bad side for so long that we are slow to figure out that there is one.

I saw David as imperfect now and maybe that's why he self-righteously began sleeping in another bedroom, refusing to discuss the situation, refusing to justify his actions.

"David," I said that fateful night. "We can sort this out, don't you think?"

He looked at me and sneered. "*We*, Teale? I believe it is you who are having a problem, not me."

"Well, don't you want to be part of the solution?" I asked.

He just looked at me and guffawed.

"Yeah, right," he said. "With *you?*"

"David, I am having all kinds of conflicting emotions about our marriage right now and I want to move back to being happy with you again. I'm not sure why this is all happening but it's tearing me apart and I want to turn things around." I was, once again, on the verge of tears.

"I have only one thing to say to you, Teale," he answered. "Either you get your emotions in line or I will make sure you lose everything. You will lose your house, your car, your son, and every single thing you own. If you don't solve this little slump you're in and PRONTO, you are going to be the big loser in *this* marriage. You will be an ugly, lonely, hungry old woman and I will remarry and have many *well-behaved* children and unimaginable wealth." And he stomped off. Hardly the words of a suitor anxious to woo his bride back onto the path of holy matrimonial bliss. And they scared me. I didn't doubt that he could take everything away from me. But I didn't understand why he would want to. The next day I slunk into work, tired, upset, depressed. What was I going to do now?

"Cheer down," Glastonbury called airily as I passed his office door. I stopped, backed up and looked in the door.

"You talking to me?" I asked.

"Yeah. You look like you've lost your best friend or something."

"Not yet," I said

"Trouble in paradise?" he asked. I just nodded. "Well it's bound to get better," he said. "Every marriage goes through some bad patches sooner or later —you just have to be committed to working things out, you know? Talk it over with him and he'll come around."

"Yeah, sure," I said. "He refuses to talk and he declines to listen." I sat down in one of Glastonbury's two cushy guest chairs and sighed. "You know, it wouldn't be so bad if we could just start working on things but it's like we've reached this huge roadblock and I have no idea how to breech it."

"You say he won't talk and he won't listen?" he asked.

"Yeah and it's my birthday today and he's going out of town for two weeks. He didn't even wish me Happy Birthday this morning."

Glastonbury looked sad.

"A birthday's a big deal, Covey," he said, ignoring my married name and making me feel like an equal. He took a drag on the cigarette he had been cradling in his left hand. I had heard it said that Glastonbury had tried to quit at least a dozen times in the past 20 years but he obviously had not succeeded. Although I didn't like the smell of cigarettes, I did admit to a secret affection for baby cigars, which I would buy, hide and secretly puff at every now and then. Their soft gray ashes accumulated in the pretty blue ash tray I dropped my wedding ring into every morning and every now and then I would clean the ash tray and start collecting more. Nobody knew, not even my very best friends, and although it was 8:30 in the morning and I had not even been drinking, I felt an overwhelming urge to smoke my brains out. David would kill me if he found out I smoked cigars. He considered all vices, except his own, to be signs of a weak personality but they allowed him to adopt a "holier than thou" attitude when the occasion suited him.

"I used to think so," I said, standing up. "Well, I got work to do. See ya."

"Wait, wait," said Glastonbury. I turned to look at him from the doorway. "Why don't you write him a letter and tell him how you're feeling? That's what I do when my wife and I have a fight, in fact I know a lot of people who do that. It really works!"

I nodded. "Yeah, maybe I'll do that."

The day dragged on in the usual flurry of activity, the offices of Cornerstone Marketing humming with work for three new clients and although I was working hard on two newsletters and a press release, all in various stages of production I found it hard to concentrate on work, for once. A letter was a great idea, I thought. Why hadn't I thought of that earlier? Glastonbury might be a total dirtbag a lot of the time but he was obviously reasonably bright and he seemed to know a thing or two about relationships. Perhaps not enough —Celia had mentioned once that he was currently sailing through his third marriage and, appearances to the contrary, there were some rough seas involved. How anyone could live with the man was beyond me. But a letter was a great idea. At lunch time I went out and bought a fresh pack of cigarillos and when I returned I was a little annoyed when Celia said Dev needed to talk to me in the boardroom. It sounded serious but I had work to do and a letter to compose. Surely Dev knew I was up to my eyeballs already. I sure hoped I wasn't in trouble again.

I opened the door and there, assembled and smiling, were the dozen or so employees and affiliates of Cornerstone Marketing itself —all singing Happy Birthday in front of an enormous round cake, beautifully decorated and flaming with an indeterminate number of candles (it was, in fact, my 35th birthday). I was touched that people I had known for so little time would go to so much trouble for me. David didn't call.

After the cake and a few laughs we all went back to work and by 2:30 my brain was practically on fire with ideas for my letter to David. I jotted them down in the little notebook I kept in the briefcase I had secretly purchased with my previous paycheque.

When David called the next evening we had a little non-conversation during which he did not even mention my birthday. He didn't ask to speak with Jason, which struck me as petty so I put Jason on the phone so he could talk to his father. When I got back on the line he was angry. Would this man ever stop being angry?

"Teale, I don't have time to listen to a little kid yammer on about TV shows, why do you do that to me?" he said.

"Yes, of course, David. I'll talk to you when you get back then," I said and promptly hung up the phone. What a jerk. This was his own child, for crying out loud. I never wanted to talk to David again. I never wanted to see him again. I hoped his plane crashed in flames on the way back to Toronto. That was a pretty harsh thought. Maybe he just wouldn't come home.

Dream on indeed.

When David returned, I had his letter sitting on the pillow on the bed in his room.

"Dear David," it began. And for 10 pages the letter detailed how unhappy his behaviour made me. In my letter I told him all the things that had hurt me over our years together, all the painful little prods he had given me, the bruises and slights, unkindness and criticisms; I ended with a plea to go with me to counselling, to save our marriage.

Dream on, dream until your dreams come true.

I was still hoping we could stitch things back together and recapture some of the magic that had reigned over our wedding day. I was terrified of David's response and was sitting down at the kitchen table, fingers curled around a soothing cup of tea, when he came downstairs, face as black as thunder, mouth working like an oversize bass trying hard to get a fisherman's lucky hook out of his mouth.

While he'd been gone I had found a respected marriage counsellor and although she was expensive, I figured she would be well worth the cost, if it meant we could find some happiness together again. At least I was motivated. Jason was in bed, sleeping, I hoped, as I thought our conversation might well be loud and unpleasant and I didn't want to scare him. I took some deep breaths. David was reasonable, he would do the right thing. And surely he wanted this marriage to work. Surely he wanted to be happy too. I was terrified.

David gripped both sides of the table with his hands, knuckles turning white with the effort and the anger that was churning within him.

"Don't you ever. Ever. EVER INSULT ME LIKE THAT AGAIN!!!" he screamed.

"But David," I said, screwing up all my courage. "Don't you want to fix this marriage, make it better for both of us? We can make it work I know we can, we just ..."

Before I could finish my sentence his right hand flew up and took aim at my face. I raised my hands in shock, trying to protect myself from the blow that knocked me to the ground.

Shades of Teal

"I want to kick you, you stupid little, self-centred bitch," he yelled, from his stance above me. "I want to hurt you and leave you senseless but you don't deserve my attention. You are worthless, Teale, worthless! And I can make you pay any way I want. You're a stupid, worthless piece of crap. You never do anything right and I'm sick of your snivelling!" he yelled, punctuating every fifth or sixth syllable with a kick at a table leg. The last one scored a direct hit at my kidneys and it hurt like hell.

I lay on the floor whimpering.

"Screw you, Teale. If you think you're going to get out of this marriage with anything you can just forget about it. I will make you pay. I will make you poor. I will make your life a living hell and I will enjoy your agony." With that he began throwing and breaking everything he could touch. I had never seen David lose control before. After four or five minutes of frozen terror, I realized the telephone was ringing. David stopped, gathered himself up and took a deep breath. He walked purposefully to the phone. I crawled away and up the stairs to my bedroom

"Hello?" he said.

"Well, Johnson, how's it going?"

"Yeah New York was great, just great."

"Yeah, can we talk about it tomorrow, I've just come home and I want to see my family...."

His conversation continued for several minutes more but by then I was lying on my bed crying and listening to make sure David didn't approach Jason's room, or mine. I heard the front door open and close. David had gone out.

"Tomorrow I'll find a lawyer," I promised myself. "Tomorrow I will have him thrown out of my house. Tomorrow my son and I will start our new life without him. Tomorrow I will start to dream."

I felt numb.

31

The past is gone.

Although I felt suddenly and calmly finished with David, it took me another two months to force him out of the house. I was reluctant to get a court order forcing him out of his own home because I was afraid of what he would do.

I was afraid we would be homeless. I hoped he would just decide to leave eventually, and during that hideous time of waiting I lived in constant, choking fear. Sometimes he would stay out until three a.m. and then burst into my bedroom, fully clothed and yelling his hatred. I didn't deserve his generosity, his money, his name, my own life. I hid the kitchen knives but his rage scared me and I took to bringing Jason into my bed to keep him as safe as I could.

Sometimes David didn't come home at all. I had hoped he would leave me first so I wouldn't feel guilty about ruining his life...But, of course, that's what I wanted him to do and he had made a career out of denying me the things I wanted. Why would that change now? When my fear became too much to live with, and my hands shook as soon as I got out of bed after nights of not sleeping,

I finally got a court order barring him from the house. That's when the nightmare really began. Fortunately, I am not now a statistic, stretched out on a cold metal slab in some morgue somewhere, or languishing in pieces on a forest floor, covered in leaves. I guess I have to thank him for that much. But I am part of the living dead.

Naturally David was stunned to be turfed out of his own house. I was in shock myself. It wasn't really his fault, was it? And how had it come to this? That beautiful romance that had seemed so thrilling and timeless in the beginning, those stars in my eyes that had made the whole world shine...How was it that I didn't see my husband for what he really was: self-centred, self-absorbed, self-righteous. How was it I had betrayed myself so thoroughly?

Nothing he did after his departure made me regret the decision to leave him, in fact, the brutality of his legal attacks confirmed my determination to separate my life from this poisonous man.

There have been the legal affidavits that claimed I was mentally unstable, complete with reports from psychiatrists I had never heard of, let alone met. There have been the legal papers claiming I was unfaithful, that my son might not be David's own flesh and blood, that I spent money wildly. Apparently all was well until I decided I wanted a career instead of a family. Then I began neglecting my family and becoming "unresponsive in bed." I refused to go to counselling with my husband because I claimed everything was his fault; all he'd ever wanted was to fix the relationship.

The legal papers have said I was repeatedly rude to my husband's family. My own family never contacted me because they didn't like me. I had no friends because I was unfriendly. I refused to entertain David's friends. I was an uncaring mother. I refused to accompany my husband on work-related social events. I never entertained with him because I was selfishly involved in my career.

The point of it all was: Custody. There is a good guy and a bad guy in every divorce and all the marbles go to the one who stakes out the good guy high ground. David had tried so hard to be a good husband, a loving partner. He said.

The car has been tampered with, the health insurance cut off with no warning, the house insurance removed. It turns out that David had put a second mortgage on the house without telling me and there is no trace of the $50,000 I didn't know I had signed for. No property tax has been remitted to the City for the past two years and the credit cards — which are in both our names, although I was never allowed to carry one in case I was too extravagant —are completely maxed out. I owe an awful lot of money. There are bank loans and lines of credit I never knew about. And somehow I am expected to pay it all back — or at least the half that is legally my responsibility — out of my $20,000 a year salary. Dream on.

The aftermath of my marriage is gruesome but I am relieved to be out of the misery of commitment that took me out of myself and into the not-me.

I'm worried, though.

How many others — just like me — started their marriages with white satin and seed pearls and are now treading warily through the nuclear disaster of a marital misfire? How many others are cowering bravely through the collapse of the dream they thought was blissful, the reality they thought was sustainable? How many wanted a dream but are living a nightmare?

Divorce is devastation but it is also a relief. These wounds will heal.

I'm grateful for Conrad, the surprising and majestic demon who leant me his house on this gray but soft old beach. I need the rest, the beer, the gulls and the antics of the soggy dog who has been chasing the sticks I throw for hours now, it seems. How did I ever end up here? And what now, what next?

David was true to his word. I lost almost everything: the house, the car, the holidays, the lifestyle — gone. The numbers reflecting the money I owe are so big they are laughable but I don't find it very funny.

I ache.

I have managed to keep custody of my perfect, wonderful, wounded little boy. He still visits his father, for now he wants to, at least. I swear I'll never read another fairy tale. Or believe in one.

Reality is here on this beach with the stupid gulls circling to drown me with their pathetic calls for more of me, the cold wind, the pounding waves wearing down my strength. And the silly dog making me smile in spite of myself. I may not believe in fairy tales any more. But I do, finally believe in me.

I won. I triumphed over one man's mean spirit and my own desperate need to please. I walked innocently down the black tunnel of wedded humiliation and resolutely out the other end. Alive but not unscathed. Wise but not yet renewed. Determined but not yet confident. So much of me I shed in that tunnel. So much of me is still cocooned inside my dreams, the ones that now drive me out of bed every morning and keep me hopeful all day long. That much I won, at least, and that is a celebration.

"I WON!" I scream at Trooper and the gulls, the tears salting the furrows of my face, ensuring nothing sleek will spring from the soil of my soul. I won because I did not give up. I won because I have new dreams to follow — hopeful, tearful, vast and elegant dreams that are mine and mine alone.

I won because I am reborn into a new life, one full of the lessons I learned in the old one that didn't work.

And cursed being that I am, I won because I still carry a black nugget of hope around in my raw, flesh-eaten heart. I hope that one day I will feel calm again. I hope one day I will finally get it right.

Damned birds, they're still reeling around out there, up there, free, like me, to wheel through their lives regardless of the rain, the cold, the dark and the thunder of life. They can show me how to fly, perhaps. As Trooper today has shown me how to throw the stick anyway, in spite of my despair.

The truth is, there are no endings – happy or otherwise. It is all beginning. Every single miserable day of our lives, no matter how entrenched we are in the blindly comfortable routines we have created, we get the precious gift of choice, of being able to choose our life, our actions; our friends, our partners. We get to start over if we want to, the very next minute, the next hour, the next day. It takes courage, maybe, but starting over can happen with the speed of a light turning on in your head, showing you with sudden clarity and shock, that the reality you live is not the reality you want. And the only one stopping you from creating the reality you actually want, is you.

So those are the choices I've made. And despite the pain, the grief, the wrenching anguish of single motherhood, there is maybe some solace out there for me, for all of us who thought we had the answers, only to find they were just questions phrased backwards.

And the solace is this: in every life there is one small silken thread of hope dangling in front of us, a thread we can sew into the fabric of our future, and carry like a good luck charm that will never let us down, no matter how bleak the world seems at the time. What that thread, that goodness, that truth, says to us in our worst moments and hardest choices, is that there are no tragic, tearful endings, just a whole web of tragic, tearful beginnings and every one of them nudge us towards the strength to dream until our dreams come true.

You have to lose to know how to win. You have to suffer to know how to be joyful. And you have to keep putting one leaden foot in front of the other and carry on long enough to walk through your pain and into the brighter future that comes, inevitably, whether you believe it's there or not.

It's overwhelming and it hurts and sometimes all you get is one miniscule grain of hope in a whole beach of despair. Sometimes that's all you need. It's a tiny start. But it *is* a start.

Once upon a time....

About the Author

Susan Crossman is a freelance writer with several decades of experience in the fields of journalism, government communications, PR and marketing and her focus these days lies in the creation of business documents that build reputations and inspire commitment. Although the work is intriguing and satisfying, she's found that inside the heart of her professional approach to words beats the jungle drum of a creative writer.

What's a gal to do?

Widowed three years ago, Susan currently juggles her freelance writing work with the care and harassment of two young children and in the rare moments when she is sure no-one is looking, she sneaks off to wrestle with the untidy task of writing for fun. The result has been the publication in 2011 of several essays in the Globe and Mail.

The fall of 2011 marked the release of **Shades of Teale**, her novel about a woman's journey through marriage to divorce.

Skating along the theory that what she doesn't know might hurt, Susan has worked hard to become a Master Practitioner of Neurolinguistic Programming (NLP), an expert in social media marketing and search engine optimization, and an awfully strong supporter of the value of chocolate as a medicinal agent.

She is fluent in French and Spanish, completely comfortable with possibility and imperfection and absolutely useless with a vacuum.

Shades of Teale is her first novel.

You can find out more about Susan's business writing and creative writing at www.crossmancommunications.com

Manor House